A Cloak of Fe

**Book Three of the
and the De
Story of Anna of Cleves**

By G. Lawrence

Dedicated to Tony and Joan,
For friendship, laughs... and mending arrows.

Chapter One

Hampton Court Palace
January 1541

Tick... Tick... Tick...

One of the King's many clocks from his immense collection was sounding behind me, every strike of the hand moving encroaching upon my spirit like an axe about to fall. If I listened close, I could have sworn I could hear sand pouring, an hourglass emptying, a skeletal hand holding that glass of time up as my life drained away, wasted before my eyes. *Cease being so dramatic,* scolded my mind, the sensible part of it at least. *We have not been here so long that you should start mourning the loss of your life and youth.*

That was true enough. We had not been here as long as my mind and the pains in my back caused from standing upright, shoulders back and head straight, were suggesting, but it was also true that we had been waiting some time. I was not the only one thinking it.

All about me people were shifting on their feet, muttering, glancing about. The careful poses of controlled courtiers, people trained through experience and repetition to stand still a long while, were breaking down. Some voices muttered muted, cautious, some were angry, all sounded confused. I tried not to look impatient, but I was beginning to wonder if I would be turned away at this, the last obstacle as I stood before the last door between the new Queen and me.

The Earl of Sussex and Lord Audley, the Lord Chamberlain, had been hurried inside to consult with Queen Catherine more than an hour ago. I was unsure what topic they were speaking of which was taking so long when I was due – overdue now – to be presented to this woman who once had been my servant, and hardly the highest of them. Catherine

Howard now was my Queen, sitting in the very place, and in possession of the very husband, I myself had held until most recently.

She was welcome to them, the chair, the man, the titles. I relinquished all with relief.

It occurred to me, however, that perhaps Catherine did not know this, and that was why there was such a delay. Perhaps she was deep in fright, suspecting I would be mean, cruel, snub her or attempt to demonstrate how inferior her previous station had been to mine, before she became Queen of course. My natural titles and station were far higher than hers, this was true, but I hoped she knew me well enough to know I was not of a temper to be vindictive over this difference between us. Was she trying to find out how to address me? There had been a few who had been confused about that, mixing 'highness' and 'majesty' in the first days when I had become sister to the King, so I was occasionally named *Maj..ighness* by stumbling tongues trying to swiftly adjust to the new order of things. Some of the combinations of titles blurted out at me I had found I rather liked. I was in a unique position, perhaps I should be awarded a unique title.

Mayhap it was none of this and in actual fact the new Queen was unwilling to meet me, and this whole plan to invite me to some of the Christmastide events at court had been the King's. Perhaps she did not want to see me, to cast eyes on a woman whose place she had stolen through wiles and sexual crafts, which is what simple minds might believe if one listened to whispered conversation floating about court and beyond. Perhaps Catherine felt guilt, uncomfortable and abrasive as a hair shirt rubbing against her soft, youthful skin at the thought of seeing me again. Perhaps she was trying to shame me, exert her authority and position over me by making me wait to see her.

Perhaps it was nothing, none of these dark suspicions, and the delay was due to something mundane.

Though I doubted it.

I glanced at the door. It still showed no sign of opening.

My eyes passed over this outer chamber in which I stood. Although plainer than the one I was waiting to enter would be, it was still magnificent, bright tapestry on the walls, a roaring fire in the hearth, gilt paint on the swirling, elegant decorations of the ceiling. Inside the Queen's chamber there would be chairs of velvet, cushions of the same material, tapestry, gilt paint wherever the wall or ceiling could be seen and the richest ornaments of all, the Queen's finely dressed ladies, resplendent in silks and velvet, damask and lace, diamonds and pearls would grace the chamber. I breathed in. Were I to take any of this as an insult, this long pause in this outer chamber, I might think it was to remind me all this had been mine and was not anymore.

These chambers had been decorated and renovated for me when I was Queen, yet I had never used them when I held that post. I had not really had a chance to dwell in each palace of the King in the short time we were wed. Six months a Queen, that was the tale of Anna of Cleves. People might say that with pity, think me shamed. I thought myself lucky, in more ways than one.

I did not mind losing these rooms, my chambers at Richmond were just as fine to my eyes. When I moved there and the King had annulled our marriage, I had been given eight thousand nobles – an English coin of gold - as well as plate, jewels, tapestry, hangings and furniture, and in addition Richmond itself and other houses. I was rich, and I was free, a well-kept *pitiable* cast-off woman of the King. The thought of anyone feeling sorry for me made me want to laugh. How little they knew. There was even a lead platter in my kitchen which once had belonged to Arthur Tudor. It now had the black lion of Julich stamped on it, the house of Von Mark taking precedence over the old prince of the Tudors. It had a pleasing symbolism to it.

Of course, when I say all that was here at Hampton might have been mine, that was not true. The concept of a queen owning anything is an illusion. What of this would have been mine in truth? It all belonged to the King, just as I had. Catherine was his property now, the woman plumped down amid all this glory, yet owning none of it. I suppose the same could be said of me, that I owned nothing in truth for it would revert to King and Crown upon my death, but I had more which felt like my own than ever I had in my life, and I could do with my days what I liked. Catherine could not say that, so whilst she was Queen, I believed myself better off.

I even had started new streams of revenue. My household had been somewhat shocked and not a little pleased when they heard I had ordered 800 tuns of beer, which was around 201,600 gallons, from my cupbearer. Probably they thought they were in for a finer time than normal, and my house was ever a merry place. Sir Wymond Carew, my Receiver-General, and a spy set by the King into my household, had made it his business to know what I was up to with all that beer. "I see it not as any of your business, Carew," I had said briskly, for I disliked the man. "It is not your office to question my purchases."

"The King would want to know why his sister has such a taste for beer, Highness."

I narrowed my eyes at the scurrying serpent. The man was already reporting on all my doings to someone at court. I was not sure whom. He had been set to watch me and to read and translate my letters. His brother, Denny, was a great favourite of the King's, which was probably why Carew had this post. It certainly was not because of his personal charms, for he was as spare of those as I was of malice.

"The King knows," I said. "I have applied to my good brother for a licence to export beer. You did not think I was to drink two hundred thousand gallons of beer myself, did you?"

I had sent him away then. I had no time for the man, for he was rude and surly and spent all his time trying to find something I was doing wrong, so he could run to the King or whatever master was his at court and tell them of it. But still, the licence had been granted and the trade was profitable. I was fond of English beer and ale, and thought others would be too if they tasted it, and I had been proved right. I was now making a pretty penny on exporting beer, which lasted longer than ale before spoiling, due to the hops.

A voice drew me back to the present. "Highness, do you think this delay is intended as an insult?" Olisleger whispered to me, right in my ear so no one else in the waiting chamber could hear him. I shook my head.

"I am sure the Queen is merely delayed by matters of state," I whispered back.

My translator and advisor, who was also the Vice-Chancellor of Cleves, fell back, though the offended look on his face did not fall from his features. Olisleger was protective of me, all my people were, indeed all the common people of England had become intensely more affectionate and protective of me ever since I lost my crown and gained a brother. It is odd how the minds and hearts of people work. As long as someone is above them, they have not a shred of sympathy for them, unless the one above them be the *very* highest, then he can do no wrong. But fall from grace, and sympathy becomes yours. It was said that the moment another Queen Anne fell from power the people felt for her, and when I tumbled gracefully from my throne all the people of England suddenly discovered they loved me. Yet plenty who swore I had long and deep been in their hearts were the very ones who had derided and slandered me when I had first stepped upon these shores.

Was that love? Contempt and derision when I had great power, affection offered only when I slipped a rung or two lower on the ladder that was court? The ways of the world and the truth of people's hearts ever were a mystery to me. That was not love as I knew it.

I wonder why it is that we find it easier to love those who fall beneath us, why it is harder to love one above us. Is it because love prefers equality, or because we fear to lose hearts to one above, so seek to drag them below? Do they threaten us less, if lessened? Is love so scared of what it loves that it must render it powerless before affection is shown? Dark are the days when this becomes so, yet perhaps I was in that darkness already and knew it not, my eyes blinded.

I glanced sideways at Katherine, Duchess of Suffolk, who was starting to look rather odd, a cross between anxiety and anger dancing on her face, which she was also attempting to conceal. I took it as a mark of her affection for me that she struggled so to control her expression. A consummate courtier was Katherine, accustomed to disguising her true emotions.

One had to wear a mask at court, it was too dangerous to be seen in truth.

My friend had greeted me when I arrived and taken me to my rooms two hours ago – or perhaps it was three now? – so I could freshen from the ride through snow and ice my household and I had taken from Richmond to get here. Some of the way by boat we had come, the barge pushing floating islands of blue-silver ice from our path, then by horse when the river became too frozen for the boats to sail further. I had insisted we come mostly by road, though men told me it was safe to ride the horses at a walk upon the Thames where it was frozen solid. They might be sure of the solidity of the ice, but I was not, and I had no wish to risk my horses. Precious beasts they were, their hearts and souls more honest than most men.

I could see my good friend Katherine's mind ticking away as regular and solid as the clock on the wall, wondering, as Olisleger had, if the Queen was attempting to exert some kind of feeble power over me, if this was a public demonstration to keep me in my place. People in the chamber were all suspecting the worst too, all except me. Although thoughts of ill wishes had flittered through my mind too, I was not willing to latch on to them. There were many I thought badly of at court; Catherine Howard was not one of them.

The Queen certainly had been interested in me when I arrived. I knew this because Lord William Howard, Catherine's uncle, had come to meet me. It was made to appear as if it was an accident that he happened upon me just as I dismounted and was embracing Katherine of Suffolk, but it was not. The man probably thought he was highly subtle, but it was as obvious as the sun in the skies that he had been sent to intercept me.

"Highness," he had exclaimed, eyes wide as he swept to a bow, looking astonished by his own good fortune in encountering me just at the moment of my arrival.

"Lord William Howard." I inclined my head, hoping he would take my smile as one given in pleasure at seeing him, and not one tickled with mirth at his poor acting abilities. "A pleasure to see you, and God's blessings on you and your house this Christmastide."

"Thank you, Your Highness and if I may be so bold as to wish the same to you? Did you have a good ride here?"

"Tolerably so, my lord. The King's roads are well kept and the ground hard with the cold, so the horses found them easy to navigate." I smiled wider, watching his eyes narrow, checking my temper, my mood, my face. Really, were I assessed any closer he might ask to look in my mouth to check my teeth were hale, as one did when buying a horse. "Tell me, did the Queen and my royal brother the King welcome the present I sent to mark the New Year?"

I had dispatched two large horses, in size clearly more suited to my former husband than the Queen, with violet trappings and saddles. It was a handsome gift and although the second horse might have been a touch large for Catherine, who was in form as slight as she was in years, I had not wanted to send an unmatched pair. It might be thought a comment on the unsuitability of the royal couple. Catherine was as the first flower of spring blooming, as the King was the last screech-owl of winter crying into the frozen night.

It would hardly do to point this out to the King, of course, so the horses had to match. No doubt Catherine herself was already well aware of the differences in more than just age between her and her husband.

Lord William beamed at me. "The King was touched, Highness, greatly so. He could not stop talking about the magnificence of the horses, saying how you, his glorious sister, understood him so well."

"And the Queen?"

"She was merry with them too, happier still that the King was happy, for as you know, as any good wife is bound to be, the Queen is always merry when her lord is."

I wonder how many men abuse their minds with hollow fictions such as this? I asked myself.

More than any woman can count, said the sardonic voice of my predecessor. I smiled. She did not appear often these days, since I became safe she had drifted from my mind, but every now and then another Queen Anne was back with something to say. I suppose the habits we form in life must also follow us to the grave. She had never been one to leave men or women in any doubt of her mind.

I had excused myself to William Howard swiftly since it was cold, and the bottom of my gown was wet, which was making me colder still as it swayed against my stockings. Inside I had gone with my friend. "The Queen is well?" I had asked as Katherine of Suffolk led me to the chambers I was to occupy.

Finding a cheery blaze roaring in the fire I sighed with some relief and stripped my damp gloves from my hands, passing them to Madge, one of my maids, with a smile. As Madge reached the door, heading off to put the gloves out to dry in another chamber, Katherine Bassett, my chief maid, who was that moment entering the chamber, plucked them deftly from her hands as if it should be an insult that a lesser maid had carried them a few feet. I smiled to see it. Kitty Bassett, who had actually almost ended up in the household of my friend of Suffolk but due to delay and accident of fate had come to mine instead, was a little possessive over her duties to me, but she could not be everywhere at once; she had been bringing warmed wine for us. I indicated to Madge to carry on as she glanced at me, unsure if I would rebuke Kitty. "See to the book chests," I said to Madge, and received a smile. The book chests were an important job, just as important as seeing to my gloves. There were, everywhere, hierarchies of power and influence. Kitty went to set down the jug of steaming, spiced wine on a table and pour it into the goblets waiting there, placing my gloves reverently beside her.

"So," I said, looking to my friend. "The Queen? How does she?"

"She has been in a fractious tither all day," groaned the Duchess, throwing herself down onto a cushion by the hearth as my servants hastened about the chamber, opening chests to find fresh clothing for me. There was water heating on the fire, dried rose petals and sprigs of rosemary floating in it, releasing a sweet smell. The rosemary reminded me of my wedding day, and I shivered a little. "Her temper has become short, her brows anxious and her tongue wild and flapping." The Duchess offered me a weary expression. "My friend, the Queen is quite terrified of you."

"She has no call to be, I mean only to be her friend." I took a cup of wine from Kitty and smiled gently at her, and the girl beamed back as if I had given her all the wealth of the world.

Katherine took a cup too and gulped some down with obvious relief. It clearly had been a trying day already. "I would advise, Highness, that you make that friendship as obvious as possible, as soon as possible. The girl is flying apart at the seams at the thought of seeing you, and of everyone at court seeing the two of you meeting. It is not just her, either. Every ambassador in England is here, panting to have you do something which demonstrates contempt of the Queen. Rumours of you being mistreated by the King and of Catherine casting you from your throne are as rife on the Continent, so I hear, as they are here in England. Everyone wants to see if you are happy with your lot, as the King tells them, or if you are being kept a prisoner, as many suspect."

I smiled. "Both, in truth, are accurate descriptions of my state."

Katherine laughed a little, but her warning tone resumed in her next words. "Our ambassadors to Cleves and other lands are being ignored by ambassadors of your homeland when at foreign courts they meet. Some of your relatives are crying out for your return and are saying you are a prisoner here. Men of Cleves do not speak to those of England when they see them at markets or other courts. I hear at recent meetings of men of the Holy Roman Empire that lords of Guelders were confused for they thought you still Queen, as your brother had made no announcement you had become the King's sister rather than wife. Kings of other lands speak scathingly of our King, saying how badly he has treated you, a high-born, virtuous and worthy woman." She finished her wine. "There is a lot riding on this meeting, my friend. Be prepared."

"Prepared for what?"

"The lion's den."

Apparently, my entrance to the lion's den was to begin when those doors before me finally opened and I was allowed in to see the Queen. But the lion was shy of the swan, it seemed. I continued to stand still and upright, my shoulders and ankles starting to ache, as the minutes ticked by, the many clocks of the King noting each second which passed with their golden hands. I kept my own hands folded before me and my face passive. I would not be forced by boredom into an expression of indignation, nor would the delay cause me to sigh. If the Queen needed more time, time she would have.

Then the door opened.

"The Queen would have her good sister enter," brayed the page on the door. He sounded relieved.

The doors opened wider.

I kept my chin up and eyes steady as I stepped into the chamber. People lined the walls, all watching me. Flanked by attendants, I promenaded in, my hands crossed before me, eyes demurely on the floor. With gentle grace I glanced up to nod at the Queen's ladies as I passed. I saw a few eyes open wide with astonishment and I knew why. I looked quite pretty these days, I needed no one else to tell me, though they did often, for I could see it in my own mirror. Dressed in a becoming gown of crimson velvet with gold tassels, with my light brown-gold hair loose and streaming down my back, covered in black silk and topped with a French hood rimmed with pearls, I looked as well as any of the great beauties of court. My calm face was serene and confident at the same time, a winning combination and one achieved through practice. My skin was bright, not worn and browned as it had been when first I came to England. I looked plumper, my cheeks not so pinched. The weight suited me, making my curves more generous, my skin younger. It was the beauty of being no more in fear of my life, and of living in freedom. I had never been pretty before, because I had never known liberty before.

As I walked with poise and elegance towards the Queen on her dais, musk and lavender wafted from my skin like the gentlest breeze. I bathed every week now, even in winter. It was far more frequently than anyone else in England did. I would never have another rumour spread about me that I knew not what cleanliness was. The King, in truth, had started the last one, but I would end the chatter he began in an effort to slander me.

I looked up at the Queen. Her gown shone bright with diamonds and her arms were heavy with bracelets, her fingers too looked weighted down with gold. The King, so I had heard and as I could now see, had given her more presents than he had offered to any other wife, even the one we never were allowed to name. People laughed about his generosity, jesting the new Queen was weighted down with jewels on purpose, so young maid could not run away from old goat. It might not have been far from the truth. There was an obligation, was there not, in the giving of so many presents? Did the King know that he had to buy the affections of his young wife, because she would not have married him had her family not pushed her to? Perhaps somewhere deep down he was only too painfully aware of the indifference of her heart and wanted to buy her affection, make her beholden to him. Or perhaps he felt indebted to her, for accepting his aged hand in her young one? Clearly he was aware that even the title of Queen was not enough to compensate for the Persephone of our age being matched to Hades?

But as I looked up at the bejewelled Queen, I noted the items causing the brightest sparkle in the room were Catherine's hazel eyes. Shimmering with terror, they were, vivid as a fire lit on an exposed hillside on the darkest night of winter. Katherine of Suffolk was right. The Queen was terrified of me.

I wore jewels, but not as many as the Queen. I looked more tasteful, refined, I knew that. I had taken an interest in my dress of late and was talented at the art now. Pearls shimmered from my hood, gold glinted on my fingers, my neck and waist, but I was not dripping with riches, as the Queen was. There was a light powder on my face, glistening like alabaster, a careful application of kohl on my lashes and brows, and a thin layer of cochineal on my lips. Catherine was clear of cosmetics. With her fresh face she looked like a child, which was what she was. The King had married a woman who could be his daughter, or granddaughter, in age. Under all her finery and jewels and gold she looked like a child playing dress-up, and I realised that was probably how she felt, an imposter playacting as Queen, a role she never had desired and now feared.

Poor child.

I could feel every eye of every woman and man in the chamber on us, burning into my skin. The Queen evidently felt the same for her cheeks began to flush with shame. Catherine could feel people comparing us. I looked regal, calm, contained. She was squirming in her gown, her skin hot against the many jewels of the King. As I reached the dais, I thought in one moment more she might bunch her skirts in her hands and fly away, running out of the palace. Her jaw set as I came before her, her eyes afire with fright. She thought I had come to pass judgement upon her, as the rest of the room already was doing.

It was time to teach the court of the King another lesson.

As I reached the space before Catherine's throne, I swept into the most graceful, and deepest, curtsey I could perform. It was a public mark of high, unquestionable respect for the woman before me.

"Most Gracious Majesty." Without trembling or shaking, I held my deep curtsey, my eyes reverentially upon the floor as my voice throbbed with sincerity, warmth and humility. "I am honoured beyond measure to be brought into your presence."

Chapter Two

Hampton Court Palace
January 1541

"I will leave my gentle ladies alone." The King's face betrayed intense weariness, shadows deep under his eyes in the mellow candlelight. "I desire my bed most keenly, but I wish you all the happiness of the night to spend in each other's company."

Drummers sounded a beat low and deep as an ancient heart pulsing in the shadows, a lute continued to strum, light as the breeze of summer. Chatter of people far away joined the music, drifting as the heavy incense did through the air. There was a scent of wine and witty conversation on the air. To my mind, the night was young yet, but the King was of course twice my age and had yet more years still on his wife. Hades needed his sleep.

"You are sure you will not stay, my love?" the Queen asked, although in truth I think she did not care if he was there or not. This day had not been about the King for once, it had been about the Queens of this land, one past and one present. Perhaps he could feel that gentle yet insistent exclusion and did not welcome it. Men accustomed to everyone acting as if they are the most important entity in any room often resent it when, even for a spare moment, eyes glance elsewhere.

"I am." Bowing to me, then taking his wife's hand to kiss, he smiled. "My good sister and wife will pass a merry time in each other's company, talking of womanly things."

And with that he was away. Catherine turned to me, her bright, young face flushed with happiness.

"He adores you, Majesty," I said, watching the King depart. He was limping a little, the fetid leg giving him trouble again, rotting under him as he stood. Was it a constant reminder of death, I wondered? The scent of putrid meat, as such we all will become one day, ever floating about him as he lived. Did death whisper in the King's ear that one day all of him would smell the same?

I smiled at Catherine. "It warms my heart to see my good brother so content." In truth it was not his contentment I cared about. It was the Queen's.

The day had been a victorious one. After my entrance and deep curtsey, I had remained on the floor, knees bent on the ground as I held my position of respectful supplication. For a moment I believed the Queen had forgotten how to speak she was so astonished, but eventually, in a stutter, she asked me to rise. I refused.

"Your Majesty honours me by asking," I had said, easily loud enough for everyone in the room to hear. "But *I* will honour my Queen by remaining upon my knees."

It had been taxing to keep my countenance, in truth. It looked as if I had fallen in a pond full of gaping guppies. Everyone was staring at me. Even Sussex and Audley had been so shocked by my overt respect for the Queen that they had for a while resembled gargoyles gawping from a church wall. The women in the room could barely believe it. As I addressed my Queen, I spoke in a voice rich with tenderness and friendship, but never abandoned the timbre of deep respect I had used upon entering. Determined to set the Queen at ease and to demonstrate to everyone else that I was her good friend, happy servant and contented sister, I strove with every moment I appeared in public to make this obvious. I had shocked everyone. No one had expected me to act thus.

It should not be that respect and friendship are such revolutionary, unusual qualities that they stagger a court, and one not lacking in the outrageous and scandalous, to see them, but there you are, that is how the court of the King was. Had I walked in and slapped Catherine, impolitic though it would have been, I think they would have been less amazed.

And it continued. I was not done amazing the nobles of the land. When I looked up at the Queen it was with affection in my eyes. When I answered a question, it was with respect. In between those times I kept my eyes on my hands. With everything I had, I demonstrated regard and esteem for

Catherine. To all outward appearances, that meeting passed as if the new Queen was meeting a woman who had admired her from afar all her life.

Stupefied as she was by surprise, gratitude and not a little bafflement, I thought Catherine might fall off her throne as the conversation continued, and yet there came a light shining in her eyes of hope. Still there was mistrust, a little, but she hoped, and how desperately she hoped, that I was honest in my actions.

The King had arrived after the Queen and I had spoken for a while on the state of the roads and praised each other's gowns. I was still on my knees until he raised me up, his face flushed, those icy blue eyes warm for once as he beamed, looking vastly pleased with me. He had bowed to Catherine, embraced her, then escorted both of us to a supper held before ambassadors and notables of court.

As we entered, I noted that I had been placed near the bottom of the table as the King and Queen sat at its head, a clear indication of my new status, and something that could potentially offend, yet I betrayed not a whit of annoyance. I allowed myself to be seated, thanking the King and his wife for inviting me to their table. Eating carefully, and with delicate refinement, I proclaimed each dish a triumph and told my new brother and sister all about my own household – "provided of course through the generosity of my dear, sweet brother, the King," I mentioned – where I was insisting all food set upon my table be English. "I set myself a task, Your Majesties," I said, lifting my goblet of wine, "to sample every dish that ever has been presented at court." I laughed gaily.

"You prefer English food, then, Your Highness?" Catherine dipped roasted venison into a spicy sauce, rich with pepper. Although I evidently had calmed the Queen's fears, I still heard a spike of quivering uncertainty in her tone.

"I prefer *all* that is English to anything any other country may offer, Your Majesty," I smiled brightly, as though being asked anything by the Queen was the highest compliment a soul could hope for. "England is the greatest of all countries in the world, as all men know... Englishmen to their joy and comfort, and all other men to the sorrow of abiding envy."

The King and his men had chuckled at my quip, glancing at me with admiration. I had learned how to charm Englishmen by that time. It was not hard, simply compliment them and insult another nation, or all other nations, and they would be merry.

I glanced up to see foreign ambassadors looking not nearly as pleased by my comment. Although lips smiled, I could see displeasure glimmering in eyes. Those of Chapuys especially. Katherine of Suffolk had told me the Spanish ambassador was keen to keep an eye on our shared supper that night, and most especially on the King's treatment of me.

"Why?" I had asked my friend before this dance of family began before the court.

"He wants to ensure there is no indication that you could be accepted back as Queen," Katherine had informed me. "Your brother is enemy to Chapuys' master, and Cleves' sympathy for Lutheran teachings makes you a heretic in his, and his master's, eyes. Catherine is much more to the liking of the Emperor. Bishop Gardiner has been telling the King of Spain how *very* Catholic the new Queen and her family are."

I had rolled my eyes a little. I loathed how people of the court here used faith as a weapon against one another.

"There have been false rumours," Katherine had gone on, "that this invitation to court is part of the King's plan to restore you as Queen. All over England people are saying this to one another, my friend. These rumours go hand in hand with that gossip which emerged not long ago that you were with child, and all the rumours are untrue, of course, but still people repeat them. The King wishes this to stop. This meeting is a little pageant, set up to demonstrate to the people that the King is happy with his wife and that you, now popular in England and respected in Europe, are too, as his sister. The King does not like the whispers bounding about Europe naming him dissolute and cruel, accusing him of behaviour toward a high-born lady which is unbecoming of a knight. If he can make it obvious you are happy, that you accept Catherine as Queen, rumours of his brutal behaviour will cease and he will be shown as good and just."

I pondered this. "But Imperial ambassadors are here for they want to make sure I will not be restored?"

"Indeed. And that you truly accept Catherine as Queen. You will be watched every moment you are here."

Her prediction, made that morning, had come true. All through supper I felt eyes on my back, a prickly sensation as if I were in a forest with a bear watching me from the shadowed undergrowth. I was thankful when the meal ended and we retired to another room to watch dancing. I had been brought my favourite English ale, a light brew flavoured with herbs, and the Queen and I had talked. Not to appease the ambassadors about the room or the King, but for the sake of the Queen herself, each word that tripped from my lips was intended to reassure Catherine's obviously unsteady spirit. The King had been talking to his men, women's conversation of gowns and embroidery not being of particular interest to him, but he had glanced at us from time to time with a benevolent smile on his lips. He saw chatter, lightness, not noting the depth and meaning passing between the Queen and me.

It mattered not what we spoke of, that was not the point. It often is not in the conversation of women. More subtle than men ever will believe are we creatures set at their sides. Our conversation must be more careful, since we are property of husbands, fathers, sons or brothers who want us not to share aught with each other; prisoners should not be allowed, after all, to converse. It might grant them notions of freedom.

Through silent signals Catherine and I had been expressing support and fellowship. I could feel genuine, if desperate, friendship reaching out from her, solid as a hand of flesh, clasping one which stretched out from my heart. Solidarity and friendship I offered, and she lapped it up as a man in the desert drinks water. She was so alone, I could feel it on her, a cloak of sadness. This slight offering I gave of my friendship should not have meant so much, but to a child unsure and afraid, surrounded by enemies and people who would love to see her fall, her safety reliant on one man who was ever unstable and unpredictable... yes, to such a person my friendship meant a great deal, perhaps more than I ever would know.

When the King announced he was to go to bed I had been surprised to see how late it was. I had barely noticed the hours passing.

I watched the bejewelled back of my former husband as he left the chamber and turned to gaze into Catherine's eyes. "The King is kind to me," Catherine said, her bright eyes looking haunted a moment. "And patient. I am not... I am not suited to the role he has offered me."

A bare few hours ago she would never have thought of expressing such an honest, potentially damaging thought to me. Now, she trusted me.

"I see nothing amiss in your deportment, Your Majesty," I said. "You are kind and gracious, warm and affectionate. You carry yourself with dignity, yet are approachable. That is all a queen should be." I smiled, my eyes dancing. "The King sees that, as will all others, in time, and they will be grateful for you."

"I am so glad you came to court," Catherine said in a rush.

Poor child, I thought, not for the first time that day. Surrounded by wolves all waiting to bite her ankle and lame her so she could tumble to the ground and the feast on her flesh could begin. People thought her haughty and shrill, when she was simply anxious and isolated. This was no all-powerful Queen before me, but a scared girl desperate for fellowship. The moment I offered my affection she had opened like a flower sensing the warmth of the sun. She was so scared, of everything, I could feel it.

"You thought I would resent you," I murmured, my voice low. "I would have you know, Majesty, nothing could be further from the truth."

"I did think that," my former servant admitted. "I want you to know how greatly I admire you. When I served in your chambers, I was happy to be with a good mistress, to serve a good Queen. When the King made clear his feelings for me, I was afraid."

"As was I," I whispered. "But sometimes we fear too greatly, do we not? Sometimes fate is kinder than we expect. The King did not love me, and although I respect him greatly, I was not the wife for him. Now, I am a woman of independence and wealth. I can remain in the England I adore and enjoy it. The King has a wife he loves, and you are Queen. And you are a kind heart, Majesty. I saw that long ago, and it has only become truer as time has gone on." My smile grew. "Had you been, as I suspected once, the mistress of the King I doubt we could have been friends, but now all things are changed, so we can. Fate has been kind, so we should be thankful for its generosity, and repay it by knowing joy."

"You are a woman of great wisdom," the Queen said, looking about. "I fear people of court will see us and think I compare ill to you."

I allowed my eyes a little roll. "If I could offer one piece of advice, and meant in the most sisterly way, it would be to ignore what others think, Majesty." I glanced about the chamber. "All these people, all these eyes, you can control neither what they see nor what the minds behind them think. Spend all your time fretting about what other people think or feel, and you ignore the one thing you can master, your own heart and mind. All you can control is yourself. Once you know that, you are free. Others may think and do what they wish; you will be master of your mind and soul, happy within yourself, controlling your actions and your thoughts. That is all you can control in this world, and it is enough. When you feel sad, think of all you have and how fortunate you are, think how you may make yourself cheerful that day, and do that. When people see you are happy within yourself, they cease to try to bring you down, and they cannot do so in any case because you control your emotions, not them. Rely on no other but yourself, and you will be happier."

"But what of the King?"

"He will be happy to see you happy. If you are merry, he will look upon you and think, 'my wife is full of joy, so she is content with her life and with me'. If you are sad, the King will think you are discontented with your lot. Make yourself happy, and you will make him happy."

Catherine looked flabbergasted by my advice. Probably she, like most of us women, had been instructed all her life to please others. My advice was the opposite of that teaching. But I had learned that my mother's lessons were true. In a world where a woman has no power but through others, the only thing a woman may master is herself.

"You think it strange a woman like me, raised in isolation rather than a worldly court, should think thoughts no woman should, Majesty?" I asked.

The Queen nodded.

"My mother took me and my sisters aside when we were young, and told us this," I said. "When I heard her words, it was as though I had seen the night sky for the first time, and there found the brightest star. I have tried to follow her counsel since. I cannot control the world or other people, but I can master myself. I can linger on thoughts that will make me happy rather than dwell in misery. I can ask myself, what can I do today that would bring me satisfaction? It does not mean to become selfish; my mother was clear about that. Sometimes what makes us most content is making someone else happy. The lesson is to command yourself. Let others think what they may. They are not your responsibility. You are."

"Your mother is wise, as you are," the Queen said.

"Perhaps the greatest wisdom is the simplest thought." I took a pull on my wine. "There is so much noise in the world; sometimes we miss whispers. So much colour that we may not see the slight light. I am not perfect in following my own teachings. We must watch and adjust ourselves all the time. If I find myself starting to walk into darkness, I try to stop myself. I try not to think in extremes. I say to myself, yes, bad things happen, but so do good. I think of the things I am grateful for, and often find there are many more than I thought, which makes me humble. Armed with the knowledge that I have much and am fortunate, that I have faced bad times and have prevailed, there is much I can do. When you face darkness, lingering on all that has gone wrong or might go wrong does nothing to aid you. It only drives you deeper into the darkness. That is not the way to escape. To find a way out of darkness you must have light. That can only be ignited by you. When danger or sadness come, strike a flame. You are the source of your own light and darkness. Know that, and peace is easier to find."

We sat in silence for a moment. Catherine seemed to be absorbing my words. "You are happy, in your new life?" she asked eventually.

"I am become a woman of pleasure," I said roguishly, my eyes sparkling as they glanced upon men and women dancing. "And why should I not? All my life I did as I was bid. I obeyed, I submitted, surrendered and cast down my eyes. Now, I am the sister of the King of England, unmarried and without a father or natural brother to command me to do things I want not. The King is a good brother. He does not want me to marry or leave

England, so we are in perfect alignment. I, too, have no desire to wed again. I shall do as I want. I thought I was trapped by submission, although I knew it was a woman's lot. But I found the trick. Submit to the right man, at the right time, and a woman gains liberty."

I laughed. "I jest, of course. I know this is not the rule for all. I know I am lucky. Most women gain nothing by playing the faithful dog, but somehow dice were thrown across my table and they came up with an outcome that favoured me. I was fortunate. My freedom is one of the blessings I count each day. I am well aware how remarkable it is."

The Queen laughed with me and gazed on me with an admiring expression, but her eyes were sad. I knew why. I had become what Catherine had once been when she was a maid of court; pleasure-seeking and free, my one master turning his eyes from my private life, so I could do as I wished. Catherine was now as I had been; captive and commanded.

But she could become what I was, if she had patience, if she was careful, if she trusted the dice as I had. The King was old, he did not look well. Catherine was young. If she could outlast him, she would be as free and rich as I was, a royal widow with a grand jointure to call her own. If she could endure this time of darkness, particularly if she could make another son for the King, she would know power and influence beyond her time as his wife, and if no child? She might still outlive him and marry again, and I could guess where she would want to marry, were she free.

"Would you dance with me?" Catherine suddenly asked. I beamed. As my almost-equal in status, the Queen was my perfect partner.

"I would be honoured, Majesty." I smoothed my crimson skirts, the gold tassels sparkling in the light of the little lanterns hanging on the walls. "I have learned many English dances now and adore all of them."

We walked to the floor, and before the eyes of court the Queen and I stood opposite each other. Musicians struck up a *branle gay*, a dance best suited to the young and nimble. The King's trumpeters sounded a blast, calling attention to us, then began to play, as drumslades and sackbuts joined the voices of the Queen's minstrels, Thomas Evans and William More.

I stared at Catherine and she at me. The rest of the world vanished into a haze as we locked eyes and began to dance. People about the room blurred into the background. I kept my eyes on hers, and the Queen kept hers on me.

We twisted about each other, hands clapping as thunder in the air as we twirled. Our feet stamped in time, beating with the sound of the drum. As if we moved to the same ancient heartbeat of the world so we curled about one another, two snakes dancing in the desert, two minds at one with one another, in union most perfect.

When we came to the end, Catherine jumped to hear the applause which erupted from all around us. She had forgotten we were watched, just for a moment. I smiled at my new sister, her cheeks pink and her eyes bright. I knew she had taken my advice, concentrating on herself as she danced and not on what other people were thinking. In doing that, Catherine had enjoyed the dance and had impressed court. For a while, she had lost her troubles and I was glad of it.

We turned to the crowd, hand in hand, then to each other, curtseying low. "Now, Majesty," I said. "Let us choose young gallants to grace the floor with."

The Queen was clearly delighted. She did not often have the opportunity to dance now, but I was the King's guest of honour, so if I wanted to dance with men of court it was only proper that the Queen join in as well. To refuse would be an insult. The Queen could not have suggested this, it would have been improper, but since I had it was only polite for her to join me.

In keeping with decorum, each of us took hands with nobles of high station. Catherine danced first with Sussex and I with the Queen's cousin, Henry Howard, Earl of Surrey. Surrey pranced after my dignified feet like a mad ram. Sussex was a more sedate partner for the Queen, but his stamina was unmatched. As Catherine twisted and bent about him, steps careful, poised and elegant, he bounded well, not as high as Surrey, but demonstrating strength all the same.

At my insistence, we changed partners with each dance. Neither of us tired. On the fourth, Catherine took hands with Thomas Culpepper. Not afraid to be seen dancing together, since the Queen had danced with many that night, they lined up opposite each other.

Poor girl, I thought again. *Does she think no one sees?*

Perhaps the court did not see what I did. He was, after all, one of many men she had danced with that night. Her cheeks could have been flushed with the enjoyment and exertion of the dance, her eyes might have been bright with wine, her smile wide for happiness in her marriage, but I knew they were not. Her eyes shone when they saw Culpepper, her breathing quickened, those dark eyes of hers became black, the pupils bulged wide. When Catherine looked at Culpepper, her heart was in her hands, ready to be handed over to his keeping.

"You look beautiful this evening, Majesty," I heard him say as the music started and he stepped close to her. With a smile, Catherine twisted sideways, her gown flowing alongside mine as I turned at the same time. After us the men pranced. We lifted shoulders, shifting to look away from them with a careless shrug as they raced to catch us. In perfect time, ringing like cannon fire, the Queen and I clapped hands, our feet merrily tripping away as our hips swayed in time with the beat of the drum.

I glanced at Catherine. She looked beautiful, powerful, elegant and merry. This, I reminded myself, was the power of kindness, that with a simple offer of friendship a person terrified and brittle might be made content and stable.

We so often believe there is power only in destruction, that to pull something down has more meaning than any other act, but the first power, the greatest, was that of creation.

God saw a void, a darkness, and to it He brought light and life. That is the most honest power of the world, and I swore I would uphold it, always, even if no one else here thought to.

Chapter Three

Hampton Court Palace
January 1541

I woke early the next morning and before I had opened my eyes I felt contentment steal upon me. Those are the best of times, when before waking joy rises with the dawn itself, infesting the spirit. It happened frequently these days, when I remembered my freedom, my friends.

I rose from my bed, trying not to wake Madge, my bedfellow of the night just passed, there to keep me warm as I slumbered. My women were still asleep but although I had little rested, I felt fresh. Catherine and I had danced through the night and into the early hours of the morning, grey light coming to seep through the huge windows of the Great Hall, mingling with ochre candle and lamp light before we retired. My feet could not be worn out, it seemed, and neither could the Queen's. Others had sat down or gone to bed, their muted conversation dissipating along the stone and brick corridors, but we had danced on, content in each other's company, stopping only to talk and drink wine. It had only made me merrier to hear the ripple of conversation about us as we danced. Words rose and fell, alighting on the notes of musicians as they played, tumbling at our feet as we pranced. People had marvelled at our happiness in each other's company. Seeing us together was like witnessing two old friends reunited after years apart. Had anyone come to court that night and not known our history, they would have been astonished to find the situation was actually a woman meeting the rival who had supplanted her.

"Highness, I am sorry," the bemused voice of one of my women, Jane Rattsey, came from somewhere on the floor as I stepped about her pallet bed, shared with Dorothy Wingfield, who still was asleep. "We should be up to attend you." She yawned so hard I thought her jaw might lock. Tears glistened in her bleary eyes as she rubbed them and looked up at me. I smiled gently; not everyone had my tolerance for slight sleep. It had only come upon me of late, as if now my life was mine indeed, to be lived as I wished, I could little afford to waste a moment in slumber.

I put a finger to my lips. "Shush," I whispered, "sleep on a while. I will sit at the window. I want to have time alone to command my thoughts."

She was already asleep upon the word *shush*, I thought. I chuckled in silence and went to the window in the outer chamber. The chamberers were already busy, clearing cards, dice and plates from late night games – or rather early morning ones – I had insisted on when the dancing was done and we had returned to my chambers. The chamberers fumbled in their tasks as I emerged, surprised to see me alone, creeping out of my own chamber, but I told them to continue, I just wanted to sit alone for a while, to look upon the view and to collect my thoughts. One, unable to restrain the urge to serve even when told not to, brought me a cup of light ale, flavoured with herbs, refreshing to a tongue which had drunk wine for most of the previous night. They opened the ornate shutters, and I sat at the window sipping my ale, feeling the cool, dark air of a winter's morning creep through the glass as a fire lit in the room kept my body and toes warm. Outside the grounds were beautiful, a creation of silver and diamond. There was frost on the ground everywhere there was not ice, sparkling as Catherine's eyes had been last night, alive with friendship.

Later, when my ladies had woken and come to rush about me, combing my hair and helping me to wash and all the time apologising for having slept later than me though I said it was not required, Katherine of Suffolk turned up at my door.

"I thought to find you still abed, Highness," she said, curtseying to me. "The Queen sends me to enquire if you passed a good night, as she hopes with all of her heart that you did," Katherine grinned. "You have won a friend, it seems."

"A friend was easily won, Your Grace, for she was starved of affection and when I offered but a little she leapt to take it," I said, feeling as sad as I was happy.

"You sound as if you pity the Queen, the highest of this land." Katherine's voice was teasing, for she understood the realities of the Queen's position as I did.

"You, who understand my heart well, my friend, you know my feelings for the Queen. The terror in her when she saw me yesterday! I can barely contain the pity I felt for her then. Even thinking of it now I feel it may overwhelm me. Only once have I felt like that in my life, yet she feels it all the time, every day. I can see it. I understand her well, for when I was in her position I felt much the same, yet I think she feels it more keenly even than I did. That girl is insecure, my friend. She expects an enemy about every corner, and now she has found a friend, well... look at how sweet and kind she turns rather than shrill and commanding."

"You have brought out the best in her."

I shook my head. "The best was there, already in her. Other people were merely nurturing the worst. No dog is sweet and merry when backed into a corner by others snapping sharp teeth in his face."

Katherine Willoughby rose. "What should I tell our mistress, then?"

"Of my night?" I pondered as my maids lifted my arms and tied my sleeves to my gown. Sleeves were always a separate part of the gown, for then winter sleeves with fur could be added when needed, or lighter ones for summer, and different colours of sleeve could be added to different gowns. Have enough sleeves, and with just two gowns a woman could look as if she had a thousand dresses, all different. Of course, I had many gowns and sleeves now, but I still remembered the tricks of dressmaking my mother had taught me.

I abruptly turned to Katherine, which caused my women to dash in a little half circle about me, trying to hold on to the part of the garment they were securing. I giggled and apologised as they smiled at me. "Tell the Queen I passed a wonderful night, replete with sweet dreams of the Queen and me dancing together, and tell my royal sister that I send her compliments, and send too my hopes that she will have time to walk in the gardens with me this day."

Soon enough Katherine was back. "The Queen fair bounced out of her bed at the mention of a walk," she said, smiling and shaking her head. "She would like nothing more than to walk with you and is scrambling to get her clothes on so she will be ready any time you wish." Katherine of Suffolk smirked. "You know, I think if you decided you wanted to become Lord High Admiral or command the King's armies in Ireland, if you asked it this morning the Queen would rush to have you appointed."

I frowned a little, though my eyes were as mischievous as my friend's. "Fitzwilliam might be a little put out, to find me on his ship commanding his men, and I have always rather enjoyed his friendship."

Katherine laughed. "I simply mean you could ask for almost anything, and it would be yours today."

"The price of friendship is friendship returned, and that is all. I want nothing more from the Queen. In truth, I am rewarded enough with the thought that I amongst so few have offered her kindness. I feel special, though I wish I were not. I sometimes wonder if there are good acts, in truth, for there is always a little happiness to be found in the doing of them, so they never are unselfish."

"Why does an act have to be unselfish to truly be good?" asked my friend. "If you derive pleasure from it, surely that only makes it doubly good, for it has brought joy to one, then to another."

I acquiesced, cocking my head in thought. "Perhaps you are right, perhaps it is the causing of pleasure we have trouble with. Too often we are told any pleasure is sin, so it is wrong. But I think there are exceptions."

"So do I."

We met in the gardens, Catherine and me, and walked together on crisp paths crackling with silver frost. Diamond buttons on the Queen's sleeves glinted in pale sunlight, sending light sprawling into dark corners. Her eyes glittered upon me with friendship and affection, and mine reciprocated.

Catherine almost scampered at my side, and I was reminded of a hound who has been treated badly by all, then found a kind master and, not knowing how to express happiness, shows gratitude for being treated well with every leap and lick. This was what I loathed about the King's court, why I stayed away. That kindness should be so rare that when someone starved of it experiences it they are rendered frenziedly grateful, that is a foul thing. A person should not have to be grateful to have been treated with respect, should not have ever been made so desperate that they feel beholden to any expression of love.

I would not be long at court. The King did not want me there, I was too embarrassing, too much a reminder of past mistakes, and I did not want to stay for I abhorred this pit of vipers, but whilst I was there I was determined to do some good. So, as we walked, I talked to Catherine, asked of her likes and dislikes. It was small conversation, never fated to change the world, but to a lonely girl it meant everything. I knew the King's conversation from my time as his wife. He cared nothing for what Catherine thought, just as he had not cared for my thoughts. It is astounding how isolating it can be to be in company with a person who cares not a whit what is inside your head. I remembered all too well how his eyes had drifted when I expressed an opinion, how a slight curl had come to his lips when I expressed a reflection he obviously thought contemptible. What truly is contemptuous is to treat another person, one who you have sworn to uphold, protect and respect, in such a way as he had treated me.

I suspected that, although whilst he shouted loud and long he loved the Queen, he treated her the same.

Catherine and I talked of dresses and food, of hunting, riding and playing cards. All little things, but it is astonishing how enriching conversation, offered by one who truly wishes to know you, can be. I was twenty-five, she sixteen. Less than ten years there were between us, yet the gap felt wider. I felt as a mother to her, protective.

"I do so admire your cap," she said to me as we wandered the frosty gardens. I put a hand to the decorative hat, almost to remember which one it was, I had so many by then, and a smile lit my face.

It was one of blue velvet, with pearls sewn into its rim, a dark veil hanging from its back to cover my hair and a swan's feather stuck into the fabric. Such caps as these had been quite popular in France and I had ordered some when in Calais, liking the look of them. The hat was new, but the feather had been with me a long time; Sybylla had found it one day in the marshes as we hunted and had given it to me. It was fresh and clean as the day she had found it, unusual really, since most feathers found thus are despoiled at least a little with mud. Sybylla had said it was a sign the hidden people had left it for us, that she was meant to find it, "and to pass it on, to a friend," she had said, handing it to me.

I had kept it since, using it to decorate items like this cap. "I am pleased you like it, Majesty," I said. "My sister gave to me the feather. It is a sigel of our house, the swan, and so I have ever worn it since."

"You are close to your sisters? You have two, do you not?"

"I am blessed to have two, indeed, and one brother. We women grew up together, so we are close."

"I was sent to my grandmother's house when I was a small child." Catherine sounded sad but there was an edge of something else I could not quite place... fear, perhaps. "I did not meet my sisters again until I came to court and we were grown. I should have liked to have a sister."

"As I am sister to the King, so I am your sister now too."

She blushed red as a rose. "I forget these things, at times," she muttered. "There is so much to learn."

"All things seem confounding when first we learn them, Majesty, and as soon as we are familiar with them they become so easy we think on them not at all anymore. So the intricacies of your position will become to you, given time."

"You give me such comfort, sister." She slipped her hand into mine. I did not seek to remove it as on we walked.

That night there was another supper, and it was merry, all of us now more at ease than we had been before. The King put his arm about Catherine as we all walked from the table to the Presence Chamber so we could watch dancing again, and he smiled. "You are so happy in each other's company," I heard him say to her. "It makes me merry to see it."

"I am so pleased the Lady Anne is Your Majesty's sister, and mine," Catherine gushed. "She is a gracious, gentle lady and she pays many respects to me. I think I admire no woman more than she."

"I am pleased to hear you two are such good friends," he said, although in truth he looked somewhat confused.

"She is delighted for us, my love." Catherine squeezed his generously fleshy arm, resplendent with jewels which flashed as burning fire into my eyes. "And is happy to be your sister, for she respects and loves you above all other men in the world. All this makes me joyous."

The dancing that night went on late, and, as on the previous night, the King left early. He wanted it made clear there was no resentment between former queen and present queen. With him there, it could be supposed the reason we were so polite was for his benefit, but without him, we could be seen as the best of friends without any outside influence. This was part of his pageant, demonstrating I was not displeased in my new life and accepted the royal couple.

All the same, there was an expression of bafflement on his round face as he departed. The King was accustomed to women competing for him. Our friendship, no matter how useful it was, was unnerving to his pride.

It made me want to laugh.

"I shall leave you to your gossip," he said, kissing our hands before he went.

"Do you ever notice," I said, a naughty smile on my lips as the King vanished from the chamber in a blast of trumpets and a swirl of incense smoke, "how women *gossip* whilst men *discuss*... and yet the events they speak of are the same?"

The Queen chuckled, her laughter ringing like birdsong.

Catherine and I drank much wine together that night. Giggling like girls, we shared whispered experiences of the King. Nothing we said was disrespectful, but some of our words hinted at our shared unpleasant experiences in the bedchamber. Oh, we were careful, knowing how another queen laughing at the King's ineptitude in the bedchamber had cost her a head, but we shared much. Later, we took to the floor. We walked out for dance after dance, gallants of court twirling and lifting us around the floor as we drifted like two elegant swans.

Our pleasure was only interrupted when Culpepper entered with two little lapdogs on bejewelled leashes, wearing ornate diamond-studded collars.

He was also bearing a tiny wooden case containing a pretty golden ring. "Gifts from your husband, Your Majesty," he announced, bowing to Catherine then to me as the dogs yipped and barked, twisting about in excitement. One became entangled in his lead as he tried to leap at us and had to be rescued before he choked himself to death.

"A sign of the King's devotion, Majesty," I murmured in the Queen's ear as Culpepper freed the agitated hound. "And a public signal that you have achieved all he wanted during this visit."

The Queen gazed upon me with the warmest of eyes. "I have *you* to thank for that, my good sister," she said, and lifted her voice as she addressed Culpepper. "My husband is so generous to me. I would have you thank him for this gift, for it pleases me to know how he cares for me." She turned to me. "As my husband is so generous to me, I would be generous to our good sister, the Lady Anne, whose amiability and friendship I do cherish. So, I offer these gifts to you, dear sister, that they might cheer your days and you might look upon them and remember the friendship of your King and brother, and of your Queen and most devoted sister."

"Your Majesty is so generous and good." I swept into a deep curtsey. "I accept your gifts with a merry heart, knowing the Christian kindness in the heart of Your Majesty, and seeing the friendship you offer me."

A buzz of conversation erupted as Culpepper handed the leashes to one of my servants, a page, Florence de Diaceto, who had been with me ever since we left my homeland. I smiled gently at Diaceto's wry expression as he tried to handle the dogs as they yipped and pranced about his ankles.

Catherine opened the case and took out the ring, a little Tudor rose crafted from gold, glimmering with tiny diamonds and rubies. She placed it upon my finger. "You are my good friend," she said, clasping my hand in hers. "I wish you all the happiness in the world."

I was a little worried that the King might be displeased that Catherine had passed his gifts on to me, but when Katherine of Suffolk came to me the next morning, she was beaming. "The King is delighted with the show you two put on last night," she told me.

I glanced at the Tudor rose on my finger. "I think it was no show, my friend, but a moment of spontaneous generosity from the Queen. I worried that perhaps the King might be angered at the Queen giving away his presents, so this is good."

Katherine howled with laughter. "It was what the King *wanted* of his Queen, Anne! He knew her generous heart could not rest without offering a gift to you, so he sent one for her to present. It was set up, staged, and the Queen performed her part excellently, as did you."

Suddenly I felt sad. "Catherine knew it was a set-up?"

"No, she knew nothing. Actually, she was afraid, like you, that the King might be displeased."

I thought a moment. "It was a test," I said.

My friend inclined her head.

My heart ran cold. "The King wanted to test Catherine's abilities as Queen. If she had kept the gifts, there would have been no public disgrace, but the King would have known she was not quite suited yet for this role."

My friend spread her hands before her. "But she passed the test, so all is well."

I shook my head. "What worries me, my friend, is that the King feels he needs to test his Queen at all."

Chapter Four

Hampton Court Palace
January 1541

"It is good to see you at court, Highness, and to see you so close to the Queen." Jane Boleyn, Ambassador Wyatt at her side, had found me in the gardens early one crisp morning. I was watching my maids walk my new dogs, Bragge and Bold, as I had named them, for both were not wanting for confidence. I smiled at Jane. Always I had felt a sense of loneliness emitting from my Lady Rochford, like a scent always hovering about her, yet when she was with the Queen, or now with Wyatt, she seemed less alone. Certain people had the key to her heart, it seemed.

"It is good to be at court, Lady Rochford," I lied, then went on to truth. "And good to see old friends, and new alike." I smiled at Wyatt. "You are here briefly, Ambassador?"

"A fleeting visit indeed, Highness, to appraise the King of recent developments at the Imperial Court in person." He bowed to Olisleger who, as Vice-Chancellor of Cleves, he had met at other functions. Every now and then I lost my translator to my brother's court because of his duties there, though he had been back with me sometime by that point and was to become one of Cleves' ambassadors to England in due course.

I had, however, almost lost all of my servants the year before. The King had sent out a decree, an Act against strangers which stated all foreigners had to leave England by September of that year. This had caused panic in my household and evidently someone had eventually informed the King that he had accidentally ordered all my servants into exile. The King had modified his command so the exemptions to the Act included the servants of my household and his own, another body of people it turned out he had also overlooked when the Act was first proclaimed.

"And how is the Emperor, and how go his relations with my brother?" I asked. Sir Wymond Carew, the one I disliked, had been appointed to intercept and read my letters, outgoing and incoming, so some of the knowledge of my homeland contained in missives did not make it through to me. I had been horrified to understand this at first, that *all* my letters, personal or otherwise, were being intercepted before they reached me. I had agreed to hand over my letters from home to the King's men, then had found that this was not enough and the King had appointed someone to waylay them, read and translate them – since Carew spoke and read my language – before they even reached my hands or eyes. I had thought I would be trusted to hand them over, but I was not, apparently.

At first I had protested, but since had simply surrendered. Protest too much and the King would think I was conspiring against him or had something to hide, and that would hardly do. But still, I resented Carew and his wife who also had a place in my chambers, no doubt so she could watch to check if any letters had snuck through, direct through Ambassador Harst or Olisleger, and since I disliked the Carews I had treated them as lesser than the servants of my homeland. This was not only personal dislike, their titles and positions *were* lower by rank than others in my household, but Carew had complained to the King of this, and I had been forced to adapt my behaviour there too.

It was a little embarrassing at times, the fact I was being so watched, because in private communications from Sybylla, my sister insisted on still calling me the Queen of England. She did not recognise the King's marriage to Catherine and both she and her husband believed I had been treated abominably. Sybylla was not afraid to say this, often and vehemently. Rumours of my mistreatment by the King were still rife – despite the King's best efforts at Christmas – in Cleves and neighbouring countries. Johann Friedrich had even put a ban on admitting new members to the Schmalkaldic League, which could have applied to anyone but clearly, due to the timing, was intended as a way of excluding the King of England, who had been so recently interested in joining the League. Sybylla technically committed treason any time she referred to me as Queen, for in the Act which had dissolved my marriage it was said that if any referred to me as Queen they were guilty of high treason and execution was likely. It was fortunate Sybylla was not in England, or she would have been arrested by now.

"Ah, well there could have been a permanent and most advantageous resolution to all the problems between your brother and the Emperor over Guelders, but I fear, Highness, your brother will not accept it."

Wyatt's warm brown eyes rested on mine, and I wondered, as I looked into that handsome face, if the other Queen Anne might well have loved this man. There had been rumours the two had been close. He was handsome to be sure, but there was a kindly intelligence and charm within him too, which sung from him. Lines under his eyes spoke of the depth of his feelings, of all he had lost, but there was still a merry humour at life there, which was not a little enthralling.

"What resolution was this?" I asked.

"Your brother was offered, as a bride, Christina of Denmark, the young widow of the Duke of Milan," he told me. "If he accepted the Emperor's kinswoman as a bride he might have been named King of Denmark one day, when the present one expires, greatly increasing his holdings and the wealth of your country, Highness, but the offer of the bride was contingent on his surrendering Guelders to the Emperor, and this he seems unwilling to do, even for so handsome a settlement."

I wondered at Wilhelm. Guelders was certainly important, it was strategically strong and a land of brave men, but was it worth this argument with the Emperor, and worth sacrificing such a worthy bride, one I had heard was not only rich but vastly beautiful, as well as the chance to become a king?

"It would seem Guelders is more a point of pride to your brother, the Duke," Wyatt went on. "But the Emperor presses his claim to that land too, and without compromise it would seem, I fear, Highness, that there may be war betwixt the Emperor and your brother." Wyatt looked about a little, checking who was in the gardens. His voice dropped a little lower. "Your brother is also, it would seem, in talks with France. There are rumours they will aid him in a war against the Emperor and François offers his niece again, Jeanne d'Albret, to secure their union. This does not please our King."

I narrowed my eyes in thought. "Because he might be drawn into war against the Emperor too? But any agreements he had with my brother about mutual defence ended surely when our marriage did?"

I had been told by Olisleger that another reason, besides desire for a new wife, that the King had so swiftly left our marriage and begun one with

Catherine was that my brother had been making pacts with France and the King of England did not want to be drawn into war on the side of his old rival. I wondered the King had not known of this before we married, for talks about alliance had begun long ago, but perhaps he had not known, or had liked the idea of war with Spain then. Before he had met me, when I was his perfect woman, it might have seemed chivalrous for him to go to war with the enemy of my brother. But once he had met me and I had disappointed him, he had welcomed the idea of being drawn into war, even in an indirect sense less, for if he was allied to Wilhelm and Wilhelm was allied to France, then if France went to war with Spain the King would have found his side picked for him. It was not something he would welcome.

"Indeed, but it still pleases the King not, for he would like his kinsman – since you are the King's sister now this means the Duke, your brother, is still a kinsman of a kind – to listen to him and heed his advice, but the Duke will not."

"Let us hope the Emperor will listen to another then, and not make war on my brother over this land."

"Sadly, Highness, I think that would be impossible. To my mind the Emperor values Guelders more at this moment than he does Milan or even the whole of Italy."

"Because my brother has it in his possession?"

Wyatt grinned. "Because of that, for certain, Highness, for the Emperor has a covetous, resentful nature, but Guelders is vital to his plans at the moment, and to his mind if it is important now, it always will be."

"But why this land so much?"

Wyatt's eyes narrowed a little. Clearly there was something I was in ignorance of. "The Turks threaten Hungary, Highness, part of the Emperor's domains. If he is to move soldiers and ships there, Guelders is the obvious if not only route. If your brother blocks this route, the Emperor might lose against the Sultan of the Ottomans. He cannot have that."

"I see." I wondered how much of this might have been in letters which never had reached me due to Carew's thieving fingers. My brother seemed to be marching swift to war with the Emperor. I wondered if France would be enough to aid Cleves in such a conflict. "So you think my brother will wed into France?"

"Into Navarre, in truth, for Jeanne d'Albret is the niece of François, the daughter of his beloved sister, but the alliance would be the same."

"I hope it could become a happy marriage, as well as a good alliance."

Wyatt smiled. "Speaking of upset, Highness, the French King was most saddened when he learned that you were Queen no more."

I chuckled. "I heard he was more confused, and that he sighed for me. I suppose it is a compliment since he is so concerned for me yet never has met me."

"I think he was sad to lose the King of England as an ally through your brother, but it was more than that. He has admitted himself concerned about you, Highness. He thinks a lady of a noble house should have been treated better."

I arched my eyebrows. "I never knew I was so highly thought of by the King of France."

"He said our King must 'live with his own conscience' over repudiating you."

Possibly he meant over the way the King had treated all his wives.

I smoothed my gown. "Well, if my brother is to wed the French King's niece, I suppose François will be my kinsman of a kind, so it is good he cares for me. I find myself gaining brothers in royal courts all over the world."

Wyatt chuckled. "You are a much sought-after sister, Highness."

I laughed a little too. "You say my brother has turned down a kingdom for this match, but I heard a son of Jeanne would inherit Navarre should the present King die without a male heir. This too is a kingship, is it not?"

"You are right, Highness, although Denmark would have been the greater kingdom, the peace more valuable and in all honesty the bride more alluring," said Wyatt. "Christina of Denmark is a true beauty of the world, Highness, as well as being one of the most learned and cultivated women I have ever met. Jeanne d' Albret, although noble, is at present only eleven or twelve years and although she may grow into her looks, I do not think she will be as handsome, nor as bright as Christina. I also hear she is not keen on the match with your brother, which is another blight upon it."

"Perhaps she will grow to love him."

"We can hope, Highness, for this indeed. Love is a thing which should never be squandered."

Wyatt looked so haunted then. I felt as if I had seen his true face beyond this laughing, smiling, charming ambassador. The mask slipped, just for a moment, and in that moment I saw his griefs, not yet gone, perhaps never to be gone. The past whispered to me at times, but it was inside him, I could see it, could almost see Anne and the others staring out at me from behind his eyes. Some people walk with the past, with all they have lost, and in some, the past walks within them.

As I excused myself and walked away, I tried not to frown or shake my head. What was Wilhelm doing? It seemed war with the Emperor was more important to him than a compromise which might well have brought about a profitable peace. Was he infested with that urge young men have to display themselves in battle? To prove their manhood in war and that was why he was taking himself and our country, and all our people, down this route which led straight to conflict with one of the most powerful men in the world? Even if he had France on his side it might not be enough; the Emperor had, after all, beaten France in the past and had taken François captive. Did Wilhelm wish to prove himself at the cost of his country, liberty, his life even? And just how much blood of Cleves would he spill, trying to outdo the Emperor?

Chapter Five

Hampton Court
January 1541

"The whole court is talking of *nothing* but your triumph," Olisleger gushed, a sheen of pride in his eyes and a flush of joy on his cheeks as we started to ride away from the palace. His breath plumed, a white feather of mist leaping into the wind, vanishing as the frozen air stole it away. Light snow was falling on the evening road, the night air chilled, the ground lit and at once shadowed by blazing torches carried by my men. *That is the nature of shadow,* I thought, its darkness cannot be seen without light.

I shivered a little, the cold spreading sharp fingers formed of ice upon my skin, tickling me. Even though I was wrapped in furs and many layers, it was cold and night was coming fast. The road was long to Richmond, but not too long. An hour or two if all went well and we would be there, at home, away from the King's court and all its sniping tongues. It was a hydra, that place, a monster who grew only stronger the more heads that were chopped away from its many necks, who grew fiercer the more flesh of its followers it devoured. I came to think in fact that what had been hewn away over the years from this monster was any goodness, and that was another reason why this beast grew stronger. A creature of evil, it fed on intrigue and hate, on death and destruction, on the creation of love and then the delight of its obliteration.

"I cannot pretend I will miss a great deal here, besides the Queen," I said to Olisleger. "No matter if all chatter of me is good at the moment, I am sure it is not to last. That is the nature of this place and all places; all is change. What we have we will soon not have and what comes in its place, for good or ill, we cannot control. That is why we must master ourselves, my friend. Self-control is the only true power any of us will ever know."

"It is said all over court how you and the Queen are the best of friends, as close as sisters of blood, and how gracious you were to each other." Olisleger, evidently having decided to ignore my reply, shifted his reins in his hands, pulling his glove further down his wrist. Squirrel fur inside it peeked out, russet red against dark leather.

I breathed in slowly, let it out through my nose. "It should be a sad thing, friend, that acts of kindness are so rare here in England that they amaze people so."

"People thought the Queen would be overbearing and proud," he went on, as if he did not hear me. Clearly his mind was full of this triumph of mine, as he saw it. "But she surprised everyone. Many are saying she was most queen-like during this visit, and everyone can see how pleased the King is with her and her deportment. Many are saying she simply reflected you, of course, Highness. Some are saying all the grace was yours and Queen Catherine merely shone in the light reflected from you. Those people mention you should have remained Queen."

"The Queen has much inside her that may lead England to goodness, and she will surprise everyone, given the chance." I turned my horse for the gates at the end of the path leading from the palace. "If they will give her the chance, of course."

I glanced back at my train, winding its way out of the grounds along silver paths flanked by banks of glittering snow. Skies above us were slate, marked by trailing clouds of white. In the distance I could see the moon starting to appear. The air smelt of iron. Snow would come thick and heavy soon.

At a window I could see the Queen, Jane Rochford beside her, watching us go. Catherine lifted a hand and pressed it to the window. It was like watching a child plead with a parent not to leave them. Perhaps there was something of that in our relationship. She was so young, and she knew not how to play this game she had been thrown into. Catherine would learn or she would fall, those were her options, and neither was a good one. Learn to play this dangerous game and one had to enter it, setting people against one another and throwing enemies and former comrades alike into the midst of the fire where the flames were hottest. Fail, and Catherine would die or be disgraced. My visit had been a brief interlude, a moment she had taken outside of these troubles. My company had been a break where she did not have to think on all that assailed her. She would miss me, and I would miss her. I spoke only truth when I said I thought there was much in her that was good. If the people of court and this country gave this girl a chance, she could blossom into a woman in possession of wisdom and kindness, she could become a great Queen.

I put up a hand, a salute more than a wave, in response to the Queen's hand still resting on the glass of her window. Even though she was too far away to lock eyes with, I felt our gazes meet, our minds connect, our souls murmur last words of farewell to one another.

It was dusk. I had dined with the King and Queen whilst my chests were being packed and horses prepared, and after our meal, had bade them both a fond farewell. Richmond was only six miles away, some by horse, some by boat, and although I would reach it in the dark, I did not mind. "My men will light torches," I had said, bowing my head to Catherine, who was urging me to stay. "So we may find our way through the darkness."

It was a message, of course. I was repeating what I had said on our first night together. "You are brave to travel at night," Catherine said.

"I am privileged to be surrounded by guards," I laughed, "and besides, there is nothing present in darkness that is not there in light, Majesty," I said. "Remember that."

"I will." The Queen squeezed my fingers. "I will remember all you have said."

They had stood outside a while to wave farewell, the royal couple and their household, and had gone inside as our party had ridden away. The King could not have been happier. I had been kissed so often on the cheeks I thought I might end up with sores there from his scratchy beard. The visit had been a categorical success. My sweet temper and joy was spoken of widely, it had been made clear I accepted the royal marriage, and now the world could see it. Due to my gracious behaviour, the King now looked like the glorious, generous monarch who had chosen wisely, bringing happiness not only to himself but to me and his new wife. Court was fair buzzing with amazement. This situation was unprecedented. I was unique. Every former queen had made unremitting trouble for the King and his new wife, and had been treated with hatred and contempt in return. A former queen and the present Queen being the best of friends whilst the King looked on with benediction was astounding.

As we reached the river and climbed onto my barge, I watched the oars dip into the water lit by torchlight. Lamps at the head and end of the boat shone on the water, as did ones on the sides, fire dancing on darkness. People on my boat, members of my household, talked softly, their legs covered with blankets, more furs tucked about their ankles. Some had hand warmers, little cylinders with glowing embers inside which kept the fingertips from freezing. Some sipped hot ale and spiced warmed wine, prepared on a brazier on the deck. I watched as we glided past homes, squat and tucked up tight for the night, smoke puffing gently from their chimneys — if they had them, some had merely holes in the roof — the shutters closed and small light inside from rush light, or tallow lamp. Families there would be gathered about their fire, or perhaps in their beds already since it was always warmer to stay there, safe in the covers, a husband or wife or sibling close to keep warm with. I hoped the houses we drifted past in the falling twilight were happy homes. I was going back to my own happy home, but court was nothing of the kind.

People were amazed about me and Catherine because they were accustomed to loathing, cruelty and disdain. Compassion and friendship were revolutionary acts at court. It was a sad thing, a lonely, desperate and fearful way to live. People thought such actions were the way to power and perhaps they were right, but only power of one kind. There are other powers in this world so vast and varied. Money may be the god many worship, influence upon the King may be their idol, yet do riches make life richer?

If that were the way of it surely a time would come when, unable to rise further, a man would stop and remain where he was, utterly content? Yet they never were content, these people of court, they never were secure or happy, they knew little love. They were rats in a cast iron pot held over a fire, scrambling and clawing at each other's eyes and throats, and all for the chance to leap from the sides of the pot and fly into the flames. It was a desperate existence, devoid of goodness, and what was remarkable was that all these people, some of the most educated in England, certainly many who were cleverer than me, all of them had convinced themselves this wretched, clawing, barren, loveless existence was the only one worth living.

That was what I found astounding.

It was as when a madman is mad but knows it not. He believes all he sees and hears and thinks is sense, but those outside his seething brain can see he is lunatic. The King's court was such a brain enclosed, no eyes outside to show it that it was mad, no tongues that would dare to tell it so. It seethed in silent insanity, alone, no one to aid it.

"It will be good to be home," I said quietly, not wanting to disturb the cold beauty of the quiet world. "Richmond is such a warm box compared to the other palaces. I think the King was generous in ensuring we would always be warm."

"When the King is pleased with a person he cannot do enough for them," Olisleger said.

And when displeased, cannot go far enough to harm them, I thought.

The King's pleasure in me was deep, it seemed. Seen now as the generous, merry monarch because of me, the King had presented me with an annual payment of one thousand ducats before I left Hampton Court, and he meant to do more, as I learned a few days later.

"More lands," I sighed to Olisleger, rolling up the paper that had been sent by the King after reading the list of properties now mine. "The King wishes me to know that I am a good and loyal subject and my brother values me, so I am assigned more lands."

"Land is always a good thing, my lady, why do you not sound happy?"

"I am happy with the gift, but I needed no material reward. I offered friendship to the Queen because I wanted to cheer a lonely girl, one I had always liked. This offer now of a reward for kindness makes it cheaper somehow, soiled."

"That is the King's way of rewarding such, it has nothing to do with you or the spirit in which you offered friendship to the Queen."

"I suppose that is true enough, but still, it jangles ungainly notes in my soul. This is why no one does anything for kindness's sake at his court, Olisleger. The King's rewards are as feverish and strange as his flesh."

My friend frowned. "You thought he was ill, when you were there?"

I nodded thoughtfully. "I think he was, a few of the nights we danced, Catherine and I, I think he went away because his leg was causing fever in his blood again."

"That is worth noting."

"To my brother, you mean? Well, you had better send the missive through your contacts, Olisleger, for Carew will open any letter I send and the King would not want me commenting on his leg." I smiled a little. "I might lose these lands he wishes to hand to me."

"I will ensure Carew gets his hands on nothing, Highness, have faith in me."

"Always, my friend. When I lose faith in all others, I will have my faith in you left."

I had my lands by the seventeenth of January. On the same day I received paperwork confirming my new status as an Englishwoman. Actually, what it said was I was not permitted to leave England without licence, but I tried to think on this polite imprisonment as my *belonging* to England rather than being a captive here. But all is change, as I said, for on the same day I received the letter informing me of my new wealth, ill fortune came for another.

Sir Thomas Wyatt, the man who had once loved another Anne, was arrested for high treason, and taken to the Tower.

Chapter Six

Richmond Palace
Winter 1541

"For what crime has he been arrested?" I asked Carl Harst, still in post as one of my country's ambassadors to England, and advisor to me, on the day they carted Wyatt to the Tower. I had sent Harst to court to find out what was happening.

"Treason, officially," he replied, generous eyebrows dancing on his forehead as they pranced up and down. "But truly, Highness, it is for embarrassment."

"Embarrassment?"

Harst explained that Wyatt, so recently returned from the Spanish court, had caused shame to fall upon my new brother, an act which apparently was worthy of death. Wyatt had called the Emperor ungrateful in public, which, however true a comment, was hardly politic. Gardiner, irked by Wyatt's accusation against the Catholic ally he desired most as a friend for England, and of course knowing the poet was a former servant of Cromwell, had sent word to the King. Harst did not know the exact charges, but they were likely to be spurious, and Gardiner's accusations would have got nowhere had the King not been shamed by Wyatt's public insult against the Emperor.

Wyatt's house had been searched, one of his men had been arrested and the whole court was no more talking of me and the Queen and our unlikely, beautiful friendship, but of how another wave of arrests of reformers was to begin. Everyone knew arrests led to deaths.

"Conservatives are anxious too, thinking Wyatt's imprisonment will lead to reprisals," Harst went on.

I chewed my lip. I had seen this before Cromwell fell, this chaos which ensued as a fresh war at court began between the two sides of the faith. The King had balanced reformers and conservatives for years by arresting some of each side whenever trouble reared its head, so arrests on one side of the faith caused arrests on the other. Harst said the halls of court had turned vicious, people were closing ranks. Even at Richmond, far from the fetid, fiery crucible of court, the air felt charged, like summer skies before thunder breaks. This was why I kept my views on faith to myself. I wanted to join neither side. I worshipped as the King commanded and said little to any other about my beliefs.

"Can anything be done for Wyatt?" I asked my friend.

"I know not." He paused, those eyebrows knitting with concern on his face. "Would you think to speak for him, Highness? It could be risky, and you do not know the man well."

Not well at all, I thought, but I had liked him. I wondered how well we must know a person before we speak a word to save their life? Must we only try to save those we love the most, was the world that small? Harst had a point, however, what was I to do for Wyatt? True, the King had affection for me at the moment, the Queen too, but affection was a fragile thing in this world and suspicion was hearty and ever rife at the court of the King. He never seemed to believe someone could do something simply because it was the right thing to do, there must also be another motive. What could he suspect here?

I tried to think as the King or his court would. People might suppose I was interfering because my natural brother was an enemy of the Emperor and Wyatt had insulted that Emperor. Speaking for Wyatt might spark something further in the suspicious brain of my adopted brother, like a cascade of rocks falling from a cliff. He might think I was embroiled with Wyatt in some plot dreamed up in Cleves to keep Emperor and King from being friends. Perhaps Harst was right and it was too risky. If I spoke for the poet, I could well make the whole situation worse, for him and for me.

A day later it became clear that fears of reprisals were not unwarranted when Sir John Wallop, ambassador to the French Court and a member of the conservative faction, was arrested for suspected papal sympathies.

"Everyone is on edge," Katherine of Suffolk told me. "Whispering behind doors has grown loud. There is a feral feeling in the air. People are readying to attack before they are attacked. It is hideous, terrifying. That is why I have come away."

"Sometimes I think you hate the court as I do." I played with a piece of tempting marchpane and then set it back on the green-glazed platter. I had no appetite.

"Sometimes I do, yet it is the furnace in which I was forged." The Duchess sighed. "It may be the fire in which I will one day be destroyed, too."

All knew Katherine for a reformist. Although her faith at that time was in the youthful stages of transformation, she had a questioning nature, and she agreed with much that men like Luther had to say. My friend had escaped many a time like this unscathed because she was high in favour with the King, as was her husband, but it was always possible something might slip in the mind of the King. He had killed friends before, women he claimed to love too. No one was safe, especially those close to him.

I did not want my friend in danger. "You could leave, live as I do in the country, away from the city."

She laughed. "I was not made for a country life. Even though I treasure time with my children, there is nothing for my mind to do in such a life. My sons are fine boys both, mistake me not, but I am an impatient mother when left to be a mother too long with nothing else to divert me. Were I born a man, I would have been at the side of the King, taking decisions which would affect the country, the faith, the world if I could have my way. I have the mind for it. But I cannot have my way. As a woman, I have to influence men to influence the King for me."

I sat back in my chair. "I think you underestimate yourself."

"I do not. I estimate most accurately the lengths of my power and its limitations. I know my life, my world, well, my friend. I understand the Queen, for her marriage is much like mine."

I lifted an eyebrow. Katherine had always sworn hers a love match but perhaps she had only said that when first we met because she had not known me well. "You are surprised?" She shook her head. "Charles loves me, I think, as best he is able to, but he knows me barely at all. We married when I was so young, I idealised him in many ways, thought him in truth cleverer than he is, thought he had more heart than truly he does. Now I am older, I see the differences between us more plainly than I could when I was first wed. It is not a shock he and the King are such good friends. They are alike in many ways. Both of them took young wives as much to boost their own self-image as for any affection they had for us. The more I age, the more I wonder if I will find myself cast off one day, as in his dotage Charles seeks out a babe in a cradle as his next wife."

My heart skipped unsteadily in my chest at her brutal honesty. "You cannot fear he would annul his marriage to you?"

"Not really." She sounded weary, cynical. "Most of the time he is proud to have a wife like me, I still have beauty and I have a mind some admire, though if I had not given him sons I think he would consider it. After the King led the way with disposing of the first Queen Katherine, it became acceptable for men to discard their wives once they were old."

I put my hand on hers. "You are far from old, my friend, nor does the only virtue of woman lie in youth. Your husband is a fortunate man to have you." Katherine was a few years younger than me, only twenty-one or so years by that time.

"Men get used to their wives, and in familiarity come to despise them," she said, her voice hollow. "They cease to appreciate the things they once loved and instead find them irritating. Where they once praised our wit and fire, after a while they seek to dampen it and silence us. What they do not have, men want more than anything, and what they already possess they do not respect or value. That is the way of the King, as it is of my husband."

"You are having troubles in your marriage?"

"No more than usual." She threw her hands up in the air. "Oh, we pretend and we put on a show, Charles and I. In public we are united, before the children we are loving, but in private, he wants to hear nothing from me. In bed he has interest, but not in anything that comes before. I may as well be a whore on the streets of Southwark for all the conversation he wants of me. I was married so young to him, Anna. I was fourteen, he forty-nine. When we wed first, I thought him a god, thought myself so lucky, but now I wonder. I was a grand heiress, you know, my two brothers having died when they were infants and my father passing too when I was seven; Charles was my guardian then. My mother was having trouble protecting my inheritance from my uncle, who was claiming my father had left some of it to him, and Charles came in, protecting me as his ward, and my mother and I were so grateful for it." She sighed. "I was supposed to wed his son, and then he decided to marry me himself. Henry Brandon, who I was affianced to, who I grew up with from the age of nine, he died not long after, some said of a broken heart. I was told the Princess Mary had another boy, a miscarriage but formed enough to tell it was a boy child. Either of those boys I might have wed, had they lived, but Charles claimed me and I always thought it was for love that he did so, but now I wonder if it was not always about the money I had, and if it was not just a boon that he liked my looks, found me comely in bed."

"I am sure it was not money, or lust alone."

"Perhaps not, but was it love? I was nine when I entered his household. The Princess was as a second mother to me, and he was supposed to be like a father, but he never was that to me. I admired him so, and he seemed to flirt with me even when I was young, even when I was growing up with his daughters. I thought there was always affection between us, so when the Princess died when I was near fourteen and Charles asked me to marry him, I thought ours would be a different kind of marriage, one based on love. I did not know until later how desperate he was for money. The Princess's dowry from France was a huge part of their income and when she died, he had it no more. My fortune, left to me by my father, was considerable, but not as large as that which Charles's first wife brought to him. But my inheritance was enough to stem the bleed of debt he was dying from."

Katherine's eyes seemed far away. "The world seemed full of death to me when I was young, I had lost so many people, and Charles was so alive, so sturdy in form, as if he could never be set down by illness, by death, as so many in my life had been. I think I fell in love with the idea of life, with hope, rather than with a man."

I frowned, leaning in. "What has changed, he is cruel to you?"

"He is not cruel in any obvious way, he does not strike me, but there are other ways a man may be cruel. He ignores me and acts as if I am not there. He will kiss me, pay compliment to me a moment before he wants me to open my legs, but at no other time in the day does he note me. My opinions matter not. About court I am something to put on his sleeve, a jewel, to make him shine a little brighter. I think one day I will have been so long ignored I will vanish, become a soft pad of slippers on a stair, a sound of a quill scratching paper, an imprint in a bed. There will be nothing of me left; a ghost haunting my own life."

I sat back, eying her with sympathy. If even what I had thought one of the happiest marriages of this country was a farce, what hope was there for the state of matrimony? Not for the first time I thought myself so fortunate to be a woman unmarried, a woman alone. "Is this why you come here so often?"

"Perhaps. It is good to be in company with one who is eager to hear me speak." She grinned.

"I am always eager for you to speak."

"Then let us continue. Why spend our lives talking of men when there are other matters, more important, to consider? What think you of the situation at court?"

I breathed in sharply and let it out slow. "Ridiculous and vile, and all too common. There is no need for any foreign prince to declare war against England. The people here turn on each other so readily they do the task for their enemies."

"Whilst the King remains in the middle, such situations as these will always go on," she said. "Men want more power, more riches, more influence. The best way to get ahead is to push another out of the way."

"This is more than a push." I stared at her. "I wish there was something I could do."

"For which, Wyatt or Wallop?"

"Both, although I admit I know Wallop not at all. Barely did I know of his existence until now, but though he is a stranger I do not want him to die."

"Wallop I know little too, but Wyatt is a good man," Katherine said, fingers playing with a girdle of coral at her waist. "But if you embroil yourself in this it could mean danger for you. Are you willing to risk so much for no reason other than sympathy for men you barely know?"

"I know," I said, and went on to explain my theory about making things worse.

Katherine pursed her lips in consideration. "I had not thought of such, but it is possible. When the King is riled up with suspicion, anything can push him over the edge, and he believes the most unlikely of scenarios."

"What are the actual charges?" I asked.

"The charge is treasonous talk, although I have heard spare evidence of it. The King himself seems dubious about both Wyatt and Wallop. In truth, I think Wyatt has been arrested because he was once Cromwell's man, and our odious Gardiner wants rid of all who would support the causes Cromwell upheld. Wallop is the revenge of the other side made manifest. I have heard little that would support the notion he is a papist, but since he has been away from court in France, I think he was an easy target for reformers to attack."

Katherine paused, looking troubled. She was interested in the cause of reform and although at that time she was not as ardent in the cause as she would one day become, she still considered herself on the side of reform rather than Catholicism. Since her Catholic mother had died some years ago, Katherine had felt more free to explore the questioning side of her nature and faith, the one which led her to reform, to Protestantism, and men like the former Bishop Latimer – recently released from the Tower after opposing the King's Six Articles, although he had been forced to resign over it too – were happy to answer many of her questions when she went to them. That did not mean, however, she approved of all that was done in the name of reform, such as this attack. Sometimes those we find ourselves allied to do things we never would have supported. "Surrey went to see the Queen," she told me. "It may be that the Queen might be persuaded to speak for Wyatt."

"Surrey is Wyatt's friend?" I asked. The Earl of Surry, Henry Howard, was the Queen's cousin. I had danced with him at Christmastide. I knew that the loss of the Duke of Richmond some years before, he who had been Surrey's boon companion, had made Surrey fierce in defence of friends, and he was also a courtier with more than a little experience. If another could be persuaded to take risks for him, such as the Queen, he would use them. I thought it possible, therefore, that Surrey might put the Queen in danger of the King's disapproval, in order to save his friend and keep himself out of trouble.

"Indeed, so perhaps the Queen will be charmed by her cousin into speaking for Wyatt and save you the trouble. She is fond of Wyatt, too. He once loved another of her cousins, you know, perhaps the affection springs from there."

I knew, of course, which cousin she spoke of. "That love of old might be reason enough for the King to take his life."

Katherine shook her head. "The King did not take Wyatt's head when the Boleyn faction were arrested, so why now? If he was ever to take revenge for the poet loving the same woman the King did, surely it would have been done when that Queen fell?"

"Wyatt was arrested then?"

"Aye, and spent time in the Tower. There was great fear for his life. Cromwell got him and another, Page, I think it was, out. They both worked for him afterwards, Cromwell I mean."

"I am surprised they were freed. The Queen who was then, she was accused of lying with so many men, I am surprised evidence was not found against those men too."

Katherine smiled a nasty smile; it did not touch her eyes and went nowhere near her heart.

"What is it?" I asked.

"The release of some prisoners made it look as if the others were guilty," she said. "It is important sometimes to have some who are investigated and excused, for it seems then that due process, that justice, has been served when some are released, and the others are kept prisoner. They were pieces to the puzzle, just as the others were."

I arched an eyebrow. "You make it sound so calculated."

Katherine's eyes glittered dangerously, and a distant look came to her face. "It was. You think any of what happened then was spontaneous? No. Fast it might well have happened, but speed was needed to take the Boleyns down. They were so powerful, even when not in true favour with the King they still had influence, and when they were high in favour nothing could touch them. It had to be a surprise attack, all of them felled at once. Some sent to death, some wounded, and their supporters gone so no one would petition for them. If anyone reminded the King how he had loved them, the scheme would have died. Rochester, Norris, Weston, they were all in the Queen's faction. Smeaton was too, although a minor role really had he in the household."

"What of the other, Brereton?"

"He was making Cromwell's life hard in Wales, was disputing him over legal matters and lands, and Brereton had the support of the Duke of Richmond until the scandal broke, so he always had someone to wield as a weapon over Cromwell."

"How long was he planning it?" She knew I meant Cromwell.

Katherine shrugged. "I know not, probably snippets of it had come to him over the years, he was a man to plan ahead. I would think the final plan was thrown fast together when needed, but that does not mean it was spontaneous. They knew what they were doing from start to end, all those in on it, they knew where the plot would take them. It is easy to suppose people are simply reacting at court, but sometimes, just sometimes they are not. They have planned what goes on, they have plotted the death and the destruction of another person, or a whole family, a long time. Try to remember that when events unfold, always, that someone here might not just be trying to react in order to survive but is instead trying to win. If you are in their way, they will have no compunction about removing you as easily as one might sweep a leaf from a path."

I shivered a little.

But in time it seemed Katherine was right about the King wondering on the guilt or innocence of these men. As court bared its fangs, ready to rip flesh from bone, the King paused, considering what to do. People said he was dubious about the arrests of both men. Perhaps he was finally tired of seeing his men rip each other apart, although I thought not. It was possible he did not believe there was anything in the charges, or did not want Gardiner to suppose that all his schemes would pay off. There was now no Cromwell to oppose Gardiner. Only Cranmer was left to keep the balance, so Gardiner could not be allowed to get too bold. He might start to think he ruled the King. But for whatever reason, the King was unsure and he hesitated. Wyatt was not safe, Wallop neither, but they were not under direct threat of death either.

"The Queen's jointure has been settled, finally," Harst told me, a look of disapproval on his face, a few days later.

Harst had never reconciled to the notion that Catherine was Queen instead of me. In fact, in the early days it had taken a great deal of persuasion for him to refer to her as anything but "the King's whore". And although that time had thankfully passed, and although I had told him I was satisfied with my place, he was one of those who thought they knew better than I did as to what was good or right for me. He continued to worry in other ways too, thinking immediately after the annulment that I would be poisoned, and since then had fallen into an occasional anxious thought that the King would take me as a mistress, since I was here in England without the protection of a father or brother. Harst thought it his duty to be that father or brother, so was always worried about me in some manner. His anxiety was touching in a way, although the ludicrous leaps of fantasy his brain could sometimes take in imagining disasters coming for me were breathtaking at times. I wondered how he slept, imagining all the many and various ways I might be disgraced, or come to death. He thought worrying prepared him for all that might come, but it did nothing in truth. What would come would come, and worrying about it did neither make it appear nor make it easier to cope with. It might be said, in fact, that exhausting himself in the present made him less useful in the future, when any of these disasters decided to come for me.

"All the lands the Queen was promised are now formally settled upon her, Highness. She owns estates in Essex, Cambridgeshire, Norfolk, Suffolk, Gloucestershire and Northamptonshire. The castles of Fotheringhay and Baynard's are now hers, along with forests, chases, parks, and all goods and chattels of all men and tenants on her properties. She is to have income from fines, writs, waifs and strays, treasure trove and forfeitures."

I tapped my lips, thinking. "Should the Queen outlive her husband, she will be wealthy, and the generosity of this settlement shows how greatly the King esteems her, because this is protection for her future."

Harst paled a little. "My lady, do not speak of the demise of the King, it is classed as treason."

"I spoke of it in reference to the Queen's jointure, there to provide for her in the event of... such a situation," I protested.

"All the same, it is safer to avoid such words, aloud."

Like the Boleyns, I thought. I sometimes wondered that my own Christian name was still allowed to be uttered here in England. How one could tie mouths and souls and seal obedience, by forbidding words. In our silence does the abuser trust so he might continue to abuse. The King plucked words from the mouths of people here, stealing them from their very tongues, so the only truth they told was his.

And yet for all that, he could not control the thoughts of people. He had tried, hard he had striven to do so, even passing laws to make treasonous thought punishable by death, but he could not stop people thinking what they would, for he could not become the one thing he thought he had the right to become: God.

"The Queen has spoken for Wallop and Wyatt," Katherine said, arriving later the same day on the Suffolk's barge. "But in such a way, Highness, that few guessed what she was up to. It was so subtle; you would be most impressed had you been there. In truth I barely thought it a petition until I considered her words later in full, but now I am sure it was."

She told the tale. Catherine had waited until one night after dinner, which was clever in itself as the King was always in a better mood with a full belly. She talked of her distress over the imprisonment of both men, making it appear her concern was pity, not politics. Pity was a suitable position for a queen to occupy. Politics was not. Our predecessors' final fates had demonstrated that.

"I know nothing of the charges," the Queen had said to her husband. "But I pity them both. All I wish for is harmony at your court, my lord. I heard they had both given good service in the past, and I sorrow to think of them now tortured by the removal of your love, which is the greatest blessing any man or woman can know."

"For your sake, sweetheart, I promise to think on the matter carefully," the King had promised.

"Clever," I said, nodding. "Clever Catherine."

The Duchess sat forward, her eyes enlivened. "You think as I do, then? She was appealing for the men, not simply expressing a thought?"

I chuckled. "Her other women, they think this? That the Queen is that innocent?"

"Plenty think it of her, but I think it was not just a thought wafting across her mind she expressed to the King, I think she planned this, took care with what she said so she could intervene for them but not put herself in danger at the same time."

I sat back and shook my head in wonder. "As do I, my friend. These women who underestimate her should take more care. It is a dangerous thing to suppose people to be below you in intellect or understanding. Those who suppose people to be below them are often the ones who take a fall themselves."

Chapter Seven

Richmond Palace
Winter 1541

"I wish I could take them down," I said, staring up at the ceiling with a baleful eye.

"The King would not welcome that, though this be your palace, Highness. He set them there for a reason." Carew looked frankly scandalised I would think of changing the palace the King had given me.

"Indeed." *He set them here to strike terror into those who are supposed to love him*, I thought.

Little figures upon the eaves stood out on the wood, spying on people walking to and fro below. With their leering faces and bulging eyes, they were not a pretty sight. People called them *eaves droppers*, and they were set there by royal command to remind people that even if they could not see their King, he always had eyes and ears trained upon them.

"Foul little things." I swept on along the corridor. "We are done for the day, Carew. My letters are all on the table in my study for you to copy and translate for the Council."

I left him behind. I still detested the man. Time and further company kept with him had not improved him in my eyes or estimation. It was not so much that he was set here to spy on me, that I could almost understand. It was that he always seemed to be hoping to find something on me, something he could take to the King to get me in trouble.

I suppose it was his job to discover anything untoward, perhaps he had even been offered a reward if he did well or had been threatened with punishment if he found nothing, but the pleasure, an actual *physical* pleasure, he clearly took in the idea of reporting me was distasteful.

Anytime he approached my letters it was with the shudder of some kind of lust, that in those pages he might find some dark secret which might have me arrested or send me to the block. He gave the impression that he liked the idea that he might be responsible for my fall. Perhaps he simply welcomed the idea of women in pain and fear, there were plenty of men who warmed to that, or perhaps he wanted to feel the silken cord of power in his hands, to be the one to slip it about my throat and pull tight, to hear me choke, or maybe he just wanted to be part of the game of court and watch another Queen fall. Who knew? But the man was no friend to me, that was certain. If I ever was in trouble, hanging from a clifftop by one hand, you can be sure he would step on my fingers and grind them into the rock, and he would only be upset if he got blood on his boot.

Hopefully my comments on the eaves droppers would satisfy his lust for something to report me for this week; God alone knows I would not otherwise have made such a comment in his presence, other than to satisfy his hunger for something to blacken my name with. This misdemeanour was slight, and would not get me in trouble. He was not intelligent enough to understand I had intended to say such in front of him. I knew that by the cunning smirk on his sallow face as he slunk off to translate my letters, and no doubt pen one of his own to his master at court. I still did not know who that was.

I walked on with my ladies, shaking the feeling of Carew from me. It was like bouncing fleas from a tapestry.

Richmond was toasty even on this bitter winter's day. I had always thought Cleves cold in the winter, but there was a different cold here in England; wetter and more clinging, damper too. A dryer cold possessed the breath of winter in the country of my birth. A cleaner cold. England had not this benefit. That week there had been days of snow, and the air was heavy with ice and moisture, yet you would not know this inside Richmond Palace. It was warm and snug, cosy as the holt of any ice fox. At the end of a corridor, I found Harst, who evidently had been looking for me by the expression on his face as I approached.

"Your Highness," he said with a bow.

"Lord Ambassador," I noted.

"I am come to tell you the King is in London, meeting with the Council," Harst told me, falling into step with me as we wandered along.

"Is he planning on coming to Richmond?"

"I doubt it, my lady. He is loath to leave his new wife for very long, and I think this is the longest he has left her alone. Three days parted."

"Three days is hardly a long time, my friend." I stopped to look at a portrait of the King's grandmother. Everyone always told me how stringent, proper and strict Margaret Beaufort had been, but she never looked so to me. Of course, she was always depicted in portraits in a headdress which looked like a wimple, always at prayer, and certainly I could see a light of resolution in her eyes, but to me she might well have been as much the rebel as a woman could be. I often wondered if she had, rather than been forced by nature, chosen never to bear another child after her first. Whether she had decided no more to risk her life for husbands, but to offer all her life to her son.

I had read many a book which had recipes for sallats for *"bringing on the courses"* or *"bringing down the flowers"* which was a politic way of saying they prevented conception or ended a pregnancy in the early months when it was still safe to do so. Many women chose to eat such a sallat each day when they had already numerous children and might risk their lives to bring more into the world, or who wanted a gap of several years between the birth of one child and another, again so as not to risk their lives by having children too close together. Was it impossible that a girl, such as Margaret had been when she gave birth to the King's father – barely thirteen had she turned, so I had been told – might have laboured so hard and long in her first pregnancy that she decided that to try again would bring death upon her? Might she have decided her one son needed her here, in this life, and so never allowed another child to root in her belly? And if this was so, she had been right, for I had heard it was she who had worked much behind the scenes to make allies for her exiled son, to bring about his kingship. Even the Battle of Bosworth, his famed victory, might not have been won if not for her convincing her third husband, Lord Stanley, to switch sides, which he dramatically did in the battle itself, charging into the field not for Richard, his King, but for Henry, his stepson. If not for Margaret, would these men of the house of Tudor have made it to the throne?

"And yet to passionate hearts, three days separation is a lifetime." Harst's voice called me back to the present and I smiled, for he could not quite contain the sarcasm tumbling from his mind. "There is news, too, about the Lady Mary, your good friend."

"I wish she was my good friend. I have little seen her for some time." I clicked my tongue in mild exasperation, turning from Mary's great-grandmother. "What of the Lady Mary?"

"Sadly, it is not good news, Highness. The King has ordered two of her maids taken from her," he said, "as punishment for being rude to the Queen."

The slight reconciliation Catherine and Lady Mary had effected around New Year had broken down as Mary slipped into her old ways. I had heard of some of the slights she had directed at the Queen, and now the King had evidently noted her lack of respect for the Queen and decided to punish her.

"The King did this before," Harst went on. "When Lady Mary was rude to… former Queens."

He meant the Boleyn Queen, of course. Whenever there was that awkward pause in a conversation as someone tried to find a way to speak of Anne Boleyn without saying her name, we knew who the person spoke of. I wondered what she might think, of becoming this awkward pause. It had a kind of power, almost made her name more memorable, her presence more physical. Something in me told me she might well have found amusement in it. Her humour had run to the dark.

I was saddened to hear this news of my friend. Lady Mary had not struggled with Jane Seymour as Queen, from all reports the pair had been quite close, but with Anne Boleyn, with Catherine Howard and with me, Lady Mary had struggled with each of us. She and I had reconciled, of course, but Mary and Anne Boleyn had only repaired relations just before Anne's demise, when the fallen Queen sent a messenger to Mary begging for forgiveness on the eve of her death.

I thought Mary was finding the idea of Catherine as Queen hard because Catherine's rise to the throne reminded her of Anne Boleyn's. Anne and Catherine were cousins so there might be a physical resemblance there, although I thought them very different in appearance from my limited experience of seeing a hidden portrait of the Boleyn Queen, but it was more the sequence of events, that a serving woman had replaced a Queen who had come to England from another land. Catherine's rise was too much an echo of Anne Boleyn's and the events too much a reminder of the worst time of Mary's life for her to ignore.

Catherine had become Anne Boleyn somewhere in Mary's mind and I, unlikely as it might seem, had become Katherine of Aragon. Mary saw me as the lady cast off, as her mother had been, and was outraged on my behalf. I had tried to explain to people who thought thus, because Mary was far from alone, that I was happy in my present state, but they did not listen and thought I should be incensed. Since I was not lost in anger, they tried to become lost for me. Mary was charging ahead with a war of revenge against Catherine on my behalf, which I had not wanted nor ever asked for.

"Lady Mary will blame the Queen for the King taking her maids away," I said, "though I doubt Catherine asked for this punishment to fall on Mary."

After a few days we heard that it was not only Mary who held the Queen accountable for this, but all Mary's supporters. There was something about the King. No matter what he did, people never blamed him. He had murdered wives and friends, wounded his people, destroyed their places of worship, made nuns and monks beggars on the roads, and yet people never blamed him. It was always someone else. When I said this to Katherine of Suffolk, she shook her head. "Of course, it would not be prudent to be heard saying aught against the King," she whispered. "But it is for another reason."

"What reason?"

"When women are struck by husbands, do they blame them? When children are abused by parents, do they hold their parents accountable?"

"Often they blame themselves."

She nodded. "Exactly, or another person. We cannot blame the one in control of us, for if the one in ultimate control of us is guided by evil, we are lost. All is rendered helpless, do you see? Blaming others, even ourselves, allows us to feel safe. If someone else is accountable for all the ills of England, the people can think the King is still a good man, but blame the King for all horrors that have happened in his time and the people are bereft of hope. That is why there is always someone else to blame, like his Queens, like Cromwell or Gardiner." She seemed lost in her thoughts for a moment then grimaced. "The Queen has thanked the King for chastising Lady Mary on her behalf," she went on.

"Did she have any other choice? To not thank him would incur his anger, surely."

"Of course."

I exhaled as I sat on a stool. "I like not this punishment. Taking away Mary's friends is spiteful."

"The King *is* spiteful," Katherine said quietly, walking to the hearth. "He always has been. Never does he forget a slight. He hates that his daughter stood against him in the past and now. She reminds him of her mother and his public, most mortifying shame when Katherine stood in open opposition against him. At Blackfriars, at the trial, Katherine made him look weak and cowardly before all his people. She held up all his carefully prepared, virtuous arguments to the light of day and demonstrated each one was false, each one was a lie. Katherine made it clear, and in *public* no less, that the King was governed by lust and self-interest rather than conscience and God. Mary defies him now, and he is reminded of all the wounds Katherine inflicted, and they all open, raw and salted in the wind."

"But everyone knew he wanted the annulment so he might be with... his second Queen."

"The King cannot admit who he is or what he wants," she went on. "He wanted another wife, yes, but that could not be his reason, nothing so base, carnal and savage a reason as lust. Even love was not righteous enough a reason. Love might look feeble in a king. So, he hid behind tales of God and his conscience, and Katherine knew it. And it was more than that. The King felt a fool when Katherine stood against him, for in those last few years when she was fighting against him with passion and intelligence, Katherine showed us all what a fine game of deception she had played before, what a long game too. Oh, he had been taken for a fool for decades. She had been *playing* the dutiful wife, humouring his fantasies and pretending love. She had been guiding him to rule as she thought England should be ruled. He was a puppet and never knew it. He had been duped by a woman with brains stronger and wilier than his and not just once but many, so many times. My mother and Katherine were great friends, and my mother knew Katherine's mind. Katherine showed her husband up as a fool, not only when he cast her off, but a fool to be tricked by her through all the long years of their marriage. That is why he came to hate her. The King's greatest fear is that people will see the man beyond the crown and not think that man enough."

"And that was what Katherine saw?"

"Katherine not only saw that man, my friend, she bested him, and the King will crush Lady Mary into the ground before he allows a woman to do that to him again, no matter if she shares his blood." Katherine twirled a bracelet of gold and garnet on her wrist, so it was the right way up.

"It sounds as if he is feeling more spiteful than usual, however. His leg pains him?"

Katherine chuckled. "You are remarkably good at seeing things though you are so far from court. Yes, his leg is infested again, the pus builds and so does his temper. He limps about court, sometimes with a stick which he hates for he thinks it makes him look old, and his spirits are dark. The Queen keeps trying to be bright and bonny, but I can see in her eyes she is terrified. He has not been coming to her at night, you see. When first they were wed he could barely be roused out of her bed, but now he does not come, and people see this, and they talk."

"Of what?"

She pursed her lips. "They say he has tired of her, that he will put her away. Many think it was a mistake that he married her at all. Only a child in the belly will cause people to think better of her, and if the King is not visiting that will not happen, will it?"

I felt my heart beat faster. "You think the Queen is in danger?"

Katherine lifted her eyebrows. "I think an English Queen of this King will always be in danger, no matter who she is."

Chapter Eight

Richmond Palace
Winter 1541

"She has not seen the King for ten days and is going quite out of her mind with worry." The Duchess of Suffolk handed her riding gloves to my maid, Madge, and smiled at her. Madge looked shy as a lad who spies a pretty girl for the first time and thinks he has seen the North Star. Katherine of Suffolk could do that to people, render them quite speechless with her charm, with her smile. It was not even that she was the most beautiful woman I had ever seen, Sybylla far outstripped my friend in looks, but Katherine had something else, something indefinable which shone from her very skin and eyes. She was a creature of gold and sunlight, of water and storm, something wild and charming and passionate, something enthralling.

"The Queen is afeared for not seeing the King?"

Katherine lifted her eyebrows almost into her French hood. "Afeared does not go far enough. She is careering back into her old ways of snapping and snarling, acting haughty and then fawning on people. She has become most erratic. I know not which woman I will meet when I enter her rooms. It is quite exhausting, and I think it unwarranted. Few people have seen the King, he truly is ill this time, but the Queen is turning lunatic in her terrors. I had to come away, if only for a few hours. If I can recover my spirits, I may be able to attend to hers better."

"Wine?" I asked when the Duchess paused to take breath. It was not only the Queen who had plunged into anxiety, it seemed. It is odd how emotions may become catching, as if they are a sickness.

"Please, Your Highness," she said in relief and after a brief pause added, "and does your cook have more of those violet and honey biscuits you had last time? I cannot get the taste out of my mind. A hunger for them has been haunting my belly and tongue since my last visit."

I chuckled. "I can ask the kitchens to make some, for I think I have already eaten the last of the previous batch this morning." I set a hand on my tummy, which was in truth flatter than it had been since I came to England even though I ate more now than I ever had. I was trimmer due to more time spent riding, hunting and dancing. In Cleves we had spent much of our time indoors, at sewing. "People will start rumour again that I am with child, if my cook comes up with one more delicious recipe."

"A little fat on a woman is good, it keeps us from looking aged and tired," Katherine said with a smile, and I knew she was right. It was quite fashionable in England to be a woman of many and most generous curves. "And the Queen, though she is far behind my age, looks weary now. She is not eating properly, and I hear from the maids who sleep with her that she is up all night too. It is showing on her face and in her behaviour. She is a bag of nerves. I believe she thinks the King will seek to get rid of her."

"But surely this is not the case?" I was concerned, however, since this was the second rumour in as many weeks of the King seeking to rid himself of the Queen.

"I do not know, no one does in truth. That he will not see her is not a good sign, it is true. You were not the only Queen who found herself sent away, my friend, when the King was up to something with his marital arrangements. One was arrested, another was sent into the country, you were dispatched to Richmond. The Queen fears, and not without justification, that when the King does not want a wife anymore, he makes sure he cannot see her before he moves to rid himself of her. She thinks this is that time. Queen Catherine is so close to hysterics she might burst at any moment, and I do not know that she is wrong. I would hate to tell her all will be well if it will not be. Poor child."

I wondered how many of us were thinking of Catherine thus. "But the King has not sent her away, he merely keeps away *from her* and if you say he truly is ill I would suspect it is because of that. He probably likes not the idea of his new, young, vibrant wife seeing him at a time when he is infirm and vulnerable. He thinks she is still fooled by the illusion he has cast over his own mind of his youth and beauty."

"We have, many of us, all said words akin to this to the Queen, the part about him being ill in any case, but she cannot hear us. Her ears are stuffed with something impenetrable."

"What?" I was confused; the Queen was ill?

"Abject terror," said Katherine.

I smiled, though it was not delivered with a great deal of humour. "It is his leg, not her, he is weary of," I said. "It is weariness with himself, his age, infirmity, he loathes not the Queen."

"That is true, but the longer this goes on the more she fears she has been set aside or will be soon. The King is ill with a fever, we tell her, but all the same, she sleeps not. The King's leg is stuffed full of inflammation, we say, but she fills her mind with terrors of abandonment and arrest."

"I cannot blame her. I thought the same when I was first sent to Richmond. When I could sleep, I had dreams of mounting the scaffold, a crowd braying for my head, my blood before my eyes as a river."

My friend shuddered, and I was sure it was because such thoughts had come to her too, the not-so-hidden reformer Duchess of court. "I blame her not either, we have lost many a Queen since our King started finding ways to get quicker to the 'until death us do part' section of his vows, but the trouble is that if he is not thinking anything of the kind, she is running herself down in her energy and destroying her looks for nothing, and let us face a stark truth when we say he married her for her looks and her vim, did he not? It was not for her mind or conversation, for he ignores her when she chatters most of the time. She is damaging the things he liked about her, so if he calls for her now he will see a woman tired, ragged and beaten low with weariness and fear. He may like her less like this, never understanding he is the one who caused her to look this way. He may find her nerves annoying, not realising he is the one who strained them."

"He will get better and return to her, and when he does, she will get better."

"It may be a while before he returns. The fever and his low mood are both more serious this time. His musicians sit idle in their chambers with no master calling for them. It is more than his leg. His spirits are decidedly low, so Charles says."

I frowned, that was not promising, it was true. Rare was the time the King would not call for music, happy or sad. This was strange indeed.

"The Queen is presiding over court with a fixed grin on her face as if she is some laughing doll made for a child," Katherine went on, shuddering a little. "She looks like a cornered animal."

At first, Katherine told me, the Queen had been allowed into the King's chambers to play the devoted wife, but as fever had settled in his mind it seemed he started to react to her presence with displeasure. I understood. I knew it was not the Queen in truth that displeased him, it was her *being there*, seeing him, witnessing him sick and old and tired and worn. He liked not the reflection of himself he saw in her eyes, nor the pity that no doubt shone there. He had called for Catherine but did not want her there, so she had gone away. She had tried to come back, once with a potion she had made for his leg, but she had been sent away again.

"The King wanted no medicine from Catherine." I could see his mind. "He did not want her to act as his nursemaid. He wanted her to see him as young, virile and fit, not old, haggard and ill."

The Duchess sampled a biscuit, brought up just that moment from the kitchens by Dorothy Wingfield, and still warm from the oven. Katherine closed her eyes as the delectable perfume of dried violet, lavender, honey and rose sugar rolled on her tongue. "I think that very true, my friend. He is ill in other ways though too; the weight he lost in the first months of his new marriage he has gained again after this Christmas. And what he has put back on has outstripped even the weight he was before he wed the Howard Queen. He has begun wheezing when he walks and limping heavily. He will use a stick only when forced to by the pain for he thinks it makes him look aged, although he makes good use of it for hitting his men and councillors with when they annoy him. He snaps and snarls at them all. The Queen tried to go to him again this morning and he would not see her. She keeps turning out for court functions and Mass, but she is on edge, and she is well aware people are calling her unnatural."

"For her fear?"

"For not tending to her husband."

My brow furrowed deep. "But she cannot tend to her husband if he will not let her into his chamber."

"And yet some still blame her for that and not him. They say she should be a more sober wife." Katherine made an expression of frustration with the world and resignation for its ways.

I shook my head, wondering at the propensity of the world to always find a way to blame a woman. It mattered not what for, they would find a way. "They mean an *older* wife, not a more sober one, and Queen Catherine cannot make years appear on her any more than the rest of mankind can prevent them from falling on us. He married her for her youth and vitality. Had he wanted a sober wife he would have stayed with me."

"People are saying once again that he should have," Katherine said, a note of warning in her voice. "Once more they praise you about court and condemn the Queen. You are now the ideal Queen and Catherine the unsuitable one. It filters through to London too, this talk. Plenty speak in your favour and say the King should take you back, for you would be a better companion for him, and a more mature, seasoned Queen for the country."

I almost laughed. "And when I was Queen, they condemned me for everything I was and loathed me for all I was not. If I became Queen again, they would want me no more and love me not at all. If every other soul in England has a short memory, I do not. The moment they have a woman they want her not, and the moment they do not have her, suddenly she is more desirable. This romance England thinks it plays with me is as false as the games of courtly love, and I have no desire for it."

All the same, not attending to the King was seen as abnormal, Katherine explained. If the Queen sent nothing and said nothing of his malady, then to the eyes of the world she was a callous wife, blind to the suffering of her husband, but Catherine was in a quandary for if she tried to send anything or see him it would be going against his commands, and he would hate her for it. On balance, it was probably safer to have the world hate her than the King.

Council and court were continuing on as though nothing was happening, but everyone knew something was wrong. Because the King was ill, suspicions were high and everyone was anxious. Petitioners coming to the palace gates were being questioned in case they were spies, or assassins dispatched to murder the King in his weakened, vulnerable state. Guards about the walls had doubled. People everywhere were talking of defence and attack.

And there were other problems.

"One of the maids taken from Lady Mary has suddenly died. People are saying grief at being separated from her mistress carried her into the arms of Death." Katherine took another biscuit from the plate and broke it gently, a scent of sweetness and flowers floating into the air, as if summer had come to us.

"That is ridiculous. People do not die over grief such as that. If her mistress had died and they had been truly close I might believe it, but not this."

Katherine dusted her hands on a napkin Kitty Bassett handed her. "However ludicrous this idea is, it is being whispered about court. People are calling the Queen cruel, and the fact her maid has died is hardly going to improve Lady Mary's feelings about her stepmother."

"And yet the Queen did not ask for the maids to be taken from Lady Mary."

Katherine pulled a face of amused exasperation. "My friend, if people are credulous enough to believe that a maid has died of grief for being temporarily separated from her mistress, do you not think they will also easily believe Queen Catherine asked for the maid to be removed in order to punish Lady Mary? That tale is more believable than the other, and when a person looks for things to dislike about someone they already dislike, plenty will be found, true or false." Katherine paused. "I have also found out about something else which may have brought this lowness of spirit upon the King."

"Oh?"

"Just as the King became ill, he had heard that defences he had built one or two years ago about the coast were already in need of repair. Ramparts in Dover, Portsmouth and Southampton have collapsed, and other walls and fortifications have been damaged by the sea."

"This has upset him?" I knew my face looked sceptical. I couldn't believe something so minor, to my mind, would trouble the King so.

"It is possible. The King loves his castles and prides himself on his defences, you see, but he is also highly paranoid about invasion, so the disruption of these defences might have led to him feeling unsafe, which led to lowness, which led to illness, but he has only himself to blame, I'm afraid. Perhaps the trouble that actually vexes him is guilt."

"Why so?"

"Because those defences were erected fast and therefore not well. I have seen some of them, the work was haphazard and shoddy. It is like the work on his palaces. It is swiftly done and looks impressive to the passing eye, but because care has not been taken and many corners have been cut, it does not last. It did not used to be this way. He used to have his men work hard, for certain, but they always took care. They do not anymore. The King wants things done fast but cares not about quality. He desires an impressive show, but there is nothing of substance underneath."

It sounded like the way the King approached marriage, and love.

"You may be right that invasion is on his mind," I said. "I heard there has also been news from Scotland that troubled the King. Harst told me that the King's nephew, King James, is preparing to pass legislation that would confirm Scotland's loyalty to Rome and Catholicism. The King has been sending letters north since before our marriage ended, trying to convince his nephew that breaking with Rome, as he has done, is the only godly thing to do. He fears James's friendship with Rome might lead to invasion.

Certainly, if there was a papal invasion which had a base in Scotland, England would be in a great deal of trouble."

"The King of Scots is passing bills confirming a Catholic view of the Sacraments," Katherine agreed. "And more laws, confirming no man may question the Pope's authority, so these fears are not without merit."

There were other bills too, ones which upheld the worship of the Virgin, and outlawed the destruction of holy icons. Scotland, being situated above the north of England, was right next to lands where the Pilgrimage of Grace had been born, and there was word that those of Catholic faith in the north might join with Scots to raise rebellion in England. The King's own people might turn on him again, this time with backing from Scotland. It was not long before Norfolk was swiftly sent to inspect border defences. The King was said to have raged for days about his ungrateful, "witless" nephew who blindly followed the Bishop of Rome rather than listening to his godly, wise uncle.

After Katherine left, I sent for Harst. "I need to know of the King's illness, and how serious it may be," I told him.

He inclined his head, his gaze careful. After warning me not to speak of the death of the King, he knew that was what I was hinting at.

I needed to think traitorous thoughts.

What if the King should die? I was not sure what position I would be in, truth be told. I was popular in England, this was true, but would there be a place for me if the King's leg walked him to the arms of death? There would be a regency council set in place for Edward, but the lad was still a child, and it would be years before he could rule alone. It was possible there would be war. There was a male heir, it was true, but many in the country supported Mary, and she was a woman grown. Was that why the King did not marry her off, in case she, if she had a husband and perhaps a child, became a more serious threat to his son?

"Physicians have pierced the ulcer, and it is draining," Harst said later that afternoon as I was still thinking on the possible outcomes if the King were to die. "This always happens. Usually, the wound is left open to drain, but sometimes it closes. When the leg becomes full of frightful things the King becomes unwell, and when they are taken away, he recovers. It will all be as it was when he is well."

But within a few days, this prediction was proved untrue. The King had still not sent for the Queen and was raging at his men.

"I hear that Thomas Culpepper has been whispering at court. He told the Queen's ladies that the King accused some of his men of throwing false charges of treason at Cromwell," Harst told me that night. "The King said Cromwell was the most faithful servant he had ever had, and traitors had made him kill him."

"He switches from one side to another so easily." My voice was strained and thin. "Norfolk was behind Cromwell's fall. If the King blames him, he may blame the Queen, too."

The next day we were told the King could be heard bellowing from clear across court, shouting that his people were ungrateful. He screamed that the English were an unhappy people to govern, never satisfied and never appreciative. "Soon I shall make them so poor that they will have not the boldness or power to oppose me!" he shrieked.

People were carefully whispering about what would happen when he died. I was not the only one thinking treason. Some days the death of the King felt imminent. On other days, we feared the rest of us might die, for the King's temper was so terrifying it seemed anyone might be arrested. The Council were trying to keep the King's condition quiet, but the King himself was loud and wrathful. Some whispered he was out of his mind. Harst muttered to me one afternoon that parties were already forming for Prince Edward and Lady Mary.

"They say there may be war," he said.

I knew not which side I should join, if any, and how was I to join them in any case? If I was heard talking of the King's demise, I would surely sign my own death warrant. Anne Boleyn had jested about it once and lost her head for it. I had a spy in my house who could inform on me. Yet if I prepared nothing, had no plan, what would happen to me? It would be hard to not take a side at all, and whatever side won would not appreciate those who had stayed in the middle as the fight went on.

I owned various properties in England, Richmond being the largest, which might offer protection, but it was just as possible they might be commandeered by one side or the other. I could be captured by a faction, held for ransom from my true brother. I could be forced to marry some lord to offer that man and his faction power or land or money. I could attempt to flee England but with my brother and the Emperor in conflict it was unlikely I would be granted safe conduct home and more likely I would be captured by the Emperor and used against Wilhelm.

Ironically, I was safer if the King lived.

And what if he did not die? In that case I had to stay clear of all this plotting, or at least not be overheard talking of it. That might be hard with men like Carew sneaking about my house.

"The King has *expressly* ordered that the Queen is not to visit him." Harst looked quite shocked by his own news.

"This separation may be a sign he does not wish to do her harm," I said, grasping to find something positive to light my way. "The King is furious with everyone he sees. Perhaps he has enough awareness to understand he might rage against his wife if he sees her and think of all we have heard. He screams about everyone *but* her. I think with this separation, he tries to protect her from himself. I would take that as a good sign."

I need a plan, I thought, *a plan in place so when the King dies I will not become kidnapped, or murdered, or married off to someone I want not. I must know what to do, who to trust.*

Considering the questions and fears in my mind, I could not imagine how terrified the Queen must have been at that moment.

Chapter Nine

Richmond Palace
Winter 1541

By Shrove Tuesday everyone was on edge. Through London panic spread from those surrounding the King, as if it had seeped into the waters of the Thames and bled all over the city, a sickness, a festering wound.

There were supposed to be celebrations at court, but not that year. They were all cancelled by order of the King. It was said his leg was better but his temper worse. Harst told me that had I heard the shrieks and bellows booming through the palace I might have thought a madman was loose in the halls.

Courtiers were told to go home, mark traditional celebrations with their families before Lent began, and the country fasted for forty days. Anyone left at court was not celebrating, but I held all the traditions at Richmond. I had, of course, to be told what some of those were. England marked events a little differently to Cleves.

"There will be pancakes and little dainties called Norfolk cakes made both for your household and to hand out as alms at the gates," I had been told by Harst. "They are traditional, and there are many diversions, games and tricks and suchlike, for the young."

"And the not so young," I said with a smile. "I wish to join in."

Harst huffed just a little, making me want to giggle. "Highness, you are not yet six and twenty. To an old man such as me, you are little more than an infant, therefore calling yourself not *so* young is inappropriate. Please desist, it makes the rest of us feel only older."

"Tell my people they may go ahead with the games of racing pancakes, I certainly wish to watch that, and the dinner at midday will be the main meal as we discussed, but I must retract my permission for the holding of the game of football at Richmond. I have since been told the King does not approve of the sport anymore and I do not want to have him hear I allowed a game he thinks poorly of whilst he is in this mood."

Harst rubbed his long nose. "A wise thought, Highness, I shall let the men know. In all honesty, the game frequently ends in a mêlée anyway, so we may as well keep to sparring with sword, the wrestling matches and the archery competition. Those at least are fights of an organised kind, and not likely to get out of hand."

"No one has quite managed to explain football to me. There are two teams, but they can be whatever size is desired, and numbers are frequently uneven, and they have to get a ball made of a pig's bladder past one another and into a net at the end, but no time is set for the end of the match?"

"Indeed, Highness, and then whatever happens, at the end the two teams and any spectators have a fight."

"I cannot think that is part of the game but rather a consequence, Lord Ambassador."

"That may well be, Highness, but that is what happens."

I tried to repress a smile. "Better we don't go ahead, then. Let everyone know, would you?"

The men were disappointed about the football match, but their wives were singing my praises. They little wanted to be attending to bruised eyes and broken limbs after the match. The day went off well in the end, this last, wild day of abandon before we marked Lent with sombre thought, abstemious diet and careful prayer. The day was merry, with popular plays performed by mummers and music played in the gardens. I handed out the prizes for the sword, wrestling and archery and the pancake race was most amusing. The men ran with pans in hand and had to flip the pancake as they raced. Many fell over, slipping on the fallen pancakes of others. I laughed so hard I thought I might do myself an injury.

"I am told it started in Buckinghamshire, perhaps a hundred years ago," Olisleger told me as I recovered from my laughter. "The story goes a housewife was making pancakes when the church bells rang for Mass. She was in such a flurry to get to the service that she ran all the way, her pan and pancake in hand, flipping it as she went."

I laughed again, wiping my eyes. It was a sweet tradition, I thought, and better than another traditional event people had mentioned to me where a cock was tethered and people threw things at it until it died. I had said we might skip that one this year. I never had liked entertainments such as that, and bull baiting turned my stomach too. I preferred something merry. Enough blood and fear was flowing in England without us adding to it.

As midnight came the entertainments dwindled and people become still and sober, as veils were pulled over statues in the church, over altars, lecterns and all things, casting the world in shadows. It was now time for celebrations to end and a time of reflection and fasting to begin. There would be no meat or cheese, eggs or milk on our dishes. Fish and grains and vegetables would be our companions now until Easter came.

Lent was a time to think about how to improve one's soul, a time of gravitas, consideration and prayer. I imagine the Queen was having a hard time thinking much on her soul, however, for she was distracted by being scared for her life.

Whispers about court and London once again said the King was tired of Catherine. That was why he had not sent for her in his illness, or after as he recovered, people said. He needed no silly, flighty girl in the autumn of his life, they went on, ignoring the fact that this time was surely the King's winter if it was any season. The King needed an older woman, people muttered, a nursemaid, someone who would prolong his life.

No matter that she had made him hale and healthy only months ago. That was all forgotten. Now Catherine was part of the problem. People muttered she was a drain on his strength.

Some were kinder about Catherine. The King was in company with a *mal d'esprit,* said some, and could not cast it off. It was not to do with his wife, but because she was bright and cheery he did not want to be near her whilst he felt dark and down.

I had my own thoughts. He had been feeling young, married to his new wife, riding and hunting as he had in youth. This illness had shown him the truth; he was old and could easily fall ill. It was not sickness that was troubling him. The veil of his fantasy of youth had been drawn back for a moment and he had seen reality.

There come times in life when we cannot ignore the truth, times when the pageant before us slips, the costumes fall away, masks tumble to the floor and we see what is real. Many people do not like it, a little fantasy is how most people get through this ridiculous parade we call life, and the King most especially had never welcomed it.

This sullenness followed by violent outbursts was born of the same womb as the anger he had felt when I had turned out not to be his perfect woman. Then, he had hastily replaced me with Catherine, and all had been well, the fantasy had continued with him as the young, god-like prince who all women adored and all men wanted to be. But this time there was a different problem.

A wife he could replace, he had done it often, but there was no younger model he could substitute for himself. This illness had forced him to be aware of his mortality. He felt his age upon him. It scared him, and in terror he was furious, and dangerous.

Chapter Ten

Richmond Palace
Spring 1541

"God be praised," I breathed, and I meant it, truly.

The King was well enough again that he had sent for the Queen, and they had dined together. This was welcome news, but it was not all good, as I was told.

"The King is most unsteady of mind and happiness," Katherine of Suffolk told me. "He is unstable and not easy to predict. In truth, it is a little terrifying, my friend, to be near him. I have known him a long time, through times good and bad, but never have I seen him like this, so changeable."

"In what ways is he changeable?"

"He rages suddenly," she said, her hands twitching nervously at her sides, "then he weeps without cause... laughs for no reason, chatters brightly then lapses into sorrow deep. Each moment with him may portray a different man entirely."

I blinked. "What are you saying? Is the King in his right mind?" My voice was the barest whisper, yet still I feared to say such a thing. It sounded as if my former husband was fast losing his wits. One of his ancestors had suffered madness, had he not? Another Henry, in the civil war. I thought it was the sixth Henry, but I was not sure, and whilst people would deny it was so, like Charles the Mad of France it *was* possible a ruler could go insane. If I remembered rightly the sixth Henry to rule England had gone more catatonic than frantically lunatic, but all the same a mad ruler was hardly a happy thought.

"The King is not... entirely in his right mind," my friend whispered. "We are to move to Westminster Palace in March and the whole court is on edge. The King is scaring everyone."

The King was no more infested with fever, but he was as unpredictable and savage as a man lost in a raging sickness. No one knew what he would do from one moment to the next. People told me one moment the King was mired in self-pity, moaning that his leg pained him and he could not sleep. The next he was brightly insisting on hunting the following morn or taking part in a joust. He would weep hot and vehement tears, lamenting wives and friends who had hurt him, then an hour later would be screaming about traitors who had deservedly gone to their bloody deaths. His unpredictable behaviour was causing others to act accordingly too.

"One moment the Queen will be smiling at a jest the King has made and the next she is cringing, flinching from a blow he looks set to rain upon her. Then she has to pretend she ducked for some other reason, for the fearful anger that appears on his face demonstrates he is affronted that she recoiled." Katherine pinched the bridge of her nose.

"He makes as if he will hit her?"

"Yes, and no," said my friend. "He gesticulates wildly and because it comes often with screaming and yelling, it does seem as if he is about to strike her. I see why she flinches. If Charles came at me in the same way I would think he meant to beat me. The trouble is, the King cannot seem to see what he is like, he apparently thinks his behaviour is entirely normal so understands not why she recoils from him. We all have entered a constant state of terror and unease. Placating one man in fever would be one thing, but at court now we are keeping company with a whole host of men stuffed inside the skin of one man, my friend; some are pitiable, some wild. There is no telling which man he will become next."

His men bore the brunt of his wrath since they were with him the most. When they tried to dissuade him from something ludicrous, like hunting or riding, which obviously he could not do since he could barely walk, he screamed at them, his face flushing deep with blood, turning shades of mottled black and purple. When they simply said yes, sire and no, sire, he glowered like a thwarted child, well aware they were humouring him.

To sit beside such a changeable creature was not a welcome fate for anyone, especially not when one word could send a man to prison or have a woman's head sail from her neck.

I gazed out onto the fields surrounding Richmond, the deer parks, and breathed in long and deep, flooding my body with pleasure and awe. My horse let out a sound as if he too was content. Guards not far away, following the path I made through the park stopped as I did, pulling up their horses so they would not disturb me, just as I had asked.

A pretty morning it was, mist rising slow and seductive in the distance, deer plodding as dark silhouettes against a rising sun of gold and silver. Bright light bathed the grass and the trees, the winding, glittering streams. A touch of frost was on the ground, shimmering like pearls. The Thames, to the other side of the park, was a blazing snake formed of liquid metal that morn, twisting her way about London. In the distance I could see hares racing on hillocks, long ears stiff in the golden light, long legs bounding, strong and free and wild. Red squirrels hopped through my gardens, filling arms and mouths with what they could gather. Far below me in a courtyard that morn I had watched a cat with fur as blue as smoke emerge from a woodpile, a fat mouse in her mouth. She trotted proudly to the kitchen, no doubt she had a brood of kittens in a warm corner somewhere waiting for food. The kitchens always encouraged queens to litter nearby. More cats meant fewer rats and mice near the food. And I thought more queens a good thing, for kitchen and for country.

It was early March. The court would be already on the move, piling into boats to head for Westminster Palace at last. Katherine had sent word saying the King had been in good spirits for more than a day. More than a day! How remarkable it was that keeping one's temper for a day was noteworthy.

My friend had sounded grateful about the King treating people well. *A person should not have to feel gratitude for being treated with respect,* I thought.

But this was a good day for the Queen. The court was to go to Westminster for an important reason. They would go to what was left of the old palace, damaged by fire decades ago and rebuilt in part, and there the Queen was to have her ceremonial entrance to the city. I had only an hour in the park then I would have to go too, but one of the many advantages of being a princess of the realm is having people to pack your bags for you.

This sudden announcement of the honour being done to the Queen had surprised everyone, even though everything the King had said and done for weeks had been surprising. But there was another reason this decision was curious. Whilst the King was ill, one of the rumours about his changeable spirits had of course been that he was displeased with Catherine and meant to cast her off. This abrupt turn-about flew in the face of such gossip. Perhaps this event to honour her was being done *because* the King had heard this gossip and wanted to reassure her and his people that she and he were to remain married. I hoped that was the case.

It was not a coronation, and it was true I had had the same ceremony and had still been cast off, but it was something.

For Catherine's ceremonial entry to the city, she had to cross London's boundaries. Delayed many times because of plague and winter storms this tradition had been, but now it was to happen. The court were to stay at Westminster a week or so, then when the court went to Greenwich on St James's Day, guilds, aldermen and the mayor of London would meet Catherine, welcoming her to their city as Queen.

There was a silver light upon the world, that fresh glaze the last breath of winter washes upon us. Smoke puffed from chimneys into a sky of fervent blue. Noble houses far away glimmered in pale sunlight. There was a hint of gold in the heavens, promising warmth when spring blew in. I could almost feel her waiting behind the cloak of winter. Soon she would be free of Hades and would step into the light, restoring life to the world.

I thought of Catherine as I turned my horse back to the palace, and thought how much truth the old tales had for us, for how much had changed when bright young girls of spring could still be forced to wed old, terrifying men of winter?

Chapter Eleven

Westminster Palace and
Greenwich Palace
March 19th 1541

I smoothed my gown as I left my chamber at Westminster Palace. My ladies in tow at my back, I walked down the stairs, heading for the grounds and water steps. There my barge would be waiting and my journey into London to be received as Queen would begin.

Ah, no.

My mind was wandering to a year ago. I was on the way to watch *another* woman be received as Queen.

I smiled a little. I wondered how often others got confused. Still some mornings I would wake and have to remind myself of all that had occurred, all that had altered in my life. Some mornings still I woke with dread in my heart, thinking I would have to spend the day trying to amuse the King, only to have the truth dawn on me and a sigh of joy to wash over my heart as I remembered I had only to amuse myself. That was all, and that was more than enough for me.

I cast my eyes back at the palace. Catherine would be coming down soon, her own ladies in a flock behind her. I could see her royal barge waiting just off the jetty, in the water, ribbons fluttering from the masts and oars, Catherine's arms and those of the King on banners flying from one of the masts. It was important the rest of us were in place before she appeared, then our barges would glide alongside hers and in front, accompanying her to her triumphant entry.

I wondered how many people would remember my ceremony. It had been most similar to this. Even the barges appeared to be wearing the same decorations. It was probably too expensive to replace them all completely. The badges and heraldic devices had to be altered of course, and here and there I could see a little fleck of black under the white lion of the Howards which had been painted over my black one of Julich. Of the streaming ribbons and banners however, I was sure many were the same.

I cast my eyes upon the grey-blue river, waiting for my barge to land. It had been an odd week but not without a little amusement. A scandal had broken out. Luckily it had distracted us all. A little diversion in the face of the King's vicious and frenetic oddness had been welcome.

A London goldsmith named Emlar had been hauled before the Privy Council. Silverware belonging to Eton College had been found for going for sale in the markets of London, and theft was suspected. Emlar declared he had bought the goods from a Master Hoorde, a former Eton student. Hoorde was brought in, along with a friend of his, Master Cheney, who was still at the College. Cheney admitted he had stolen the goods and implied that Nicholas Udall, the provost, had known of the scheme. Udall was also seized.

Udall was a man well-known at court, as not only had he written verse for Anne Boleyn's coronation, but Norfolk had supported him. He had acted as headmaster for seven years and was known as one of the best teachers in England. He had a brutal reputation, a tutor who inspired intense attention in students through their fear of his 'flogging days'. It was therefore surprising he should be implicated, but when he stood before the Council, rather than admit theft, Udall had instead abruptly announced that he had engaged in buggery with Cheney many times, the last occasion being only eight days before that meeting.

"Why would he announce that?" I had asked, laughing, to Katherine Willoughby when I had arrived at Westminster for the Queen's ceremony.

There was no good reason for Udall to declare such a thing. It had no bearing on the theft. Sodomy was a crime, of course, although no more a sin than adultery, and that was common enough. Before the split with Rome, I heard that in England sodomy had been dealt with by Church courts, but the King had made it a state crime, not because of any moral objection, but so it could be used against the Church, as everyone knew sodomy was rife in the cloisters. When it was brought against a man, sodomy was not usually a primary offence but was rather one of a cluster of crimes, often a final embellishment to secure a man's reputation as wicked in all ways. It had been used against Lord Hungerford who had died on the same day as Cromwell but had not been the major charge. Treason and witchcraft were taken more seriously.

"Well, it must be the truth," Katherine said. "Why else would he admit such a thing without anyone asking about it? Udall is trying to say that Cheney is setting him up. Mayhap the man has been blackmailing him, using their secret relationship?"

Udall was sent to the Marshalsea in Southwark, a comparatively comfortable prison. It was a sign of the Council's sympathy, and a mark of his social status that he ended up there. Far worse prisons there were in London. Cheney and Hoorde were brought before the Council, and it was established that whilst Cheney had been entertaining Udall on some of these occasions of intimacy, Hoorde had filched the silverware. Udall was found not party to the robbery, but was found to be in debt, which made some believe, as my friend had astutely suspected, that Cheney was blackmailing him. People suspected Udall might have known about the theft and kept quiet so Cheney would not expose their relationship. Others thought it equally possible he knew nothing.

"But then his confession makes no sense," I said to my friend. "To me, this looks as if Udall was being blackmailed, as you said, and saw this examination over the stolen goods as a way out. He had to accept the risk of being condemned for sodomy, but by confessing he escaped being under Cheney's power. Who knows? The man might have forced him to do much else which he would not have wanted, all for fear of being exposed."

"It does make sense that way," Katherine replied. "Living under the power of another, it cannot be a good way to live."

"We all are under the power of someone, my friend."

"Even the King?"

"Even the King, though it might seem not so at times, but he answers to other powers too." *Or he will someday,* I thought.

Everyone involved in the scandal escaped with their lives, which made me happy. It was, after all, unusual that such a thing happened in England, in my limited experience of the country. Hoorde went home to Shropshire, and Cheney to Bedfordshire. Udall spent a month in prison but was released and swiftly was back in favour at court. One of the things to cheer me was that Lady Mary spoke for Udall and was talking of inviting him to aid her in her translation of a Biblical commentary she was working on. It was a way to demonstrate her faith in him, and that no matter his imprisonment, he had not diminished in her eyes. Such a gesture from a woman who many still considered a princess of the realm and one who was known for her piety, meant a great deal in the restoration of his reputation.

"She is capable of such goodness, when she has a will to do it," I said.

Mercy had been on many a mind after this incident. Lady Mary had not been the only one speaking out for someone in need. The Queen had done the same, but the target of her charity was different.

"She sent warm clothing to Margaret, Countess of Salisbury, still a prisoner in the Tower." Kitty Basset had had an odd expression on her face as she told me this, for it was clear she admired the Queen for this and because of another she had helped, but Kitty was always disposed to try to think the worst of Cathrine for replacing me. It was also clear she thought the Queen's actions were dangerous.

My maid was not alone in this. People were amazed Catherine had dared speak for Margaret Pole, but she must have approached the King about this gift, and he must have allowed it. He had thought the Countess guilty of supporting a possible foreign invasion with Reginald, her son, leading the way for the Pope and Emperor, but nothing had come of those rumours. Despite this the old lady was still locked away in her prison chambers in the Tower of London. The Countess was popular with the people of England, she was all there was left of the old blood, the ancient royalty of England. "That is also why the King does not like her, of course," whispered Kitty Bassett.

"You should take care who you say such things to, Kitty," I had said, tapping her hand.

"I say them to you alone, Highness."

"Then take care who overhears you." I pointed to the eaves droppers, and she shivered a little. "I hear the King used to like Margaret Pole as a friend, when he was married to Katherine of Spain," I went on.

"That was long ago, Highness. Once he liked Katherine of Spain too, and others, but that changed."

"But the Queen managed to send the Countess these items, comforts?"

"A warm cloak, I hear, as well as two nightgowns, one trimmed with fur for warmth and a woollen kirtle. She also sent a bonnet, four pairs of hose and the same of shoes and one of slippers. My stepfather Lord Lisle had a delivery too."

I thought on this act of kindness with great approval. I knew the Countess not at all, but Lisle had been good to me. That he was still in the Tower after all this time and even after the fall of Cromwell who likely had been the one to falsely accuse him, it was unconscionable. Part of the reason I had agreed to take on his stepdaughter Katherine Bassett, whom I named Kitty out of affection, was because of this, and also because her sister, Anne, had served me well. Anne served Catherine now, transferred to the new Queen's household when I had stepped away from the throne, but I liked to reward those who had been kind to me, as the Lisles had, so had agreed to take Kitty in her place.

Kitty was a little more incautious than her sister, of course she had not been at court as long and she was not really at court now since I tried to stay away, but still, she had not learned to hold her tongue. It was something I kept trying to correct in her, but people will be as they will be. We cannot change them, we can only suggest. In many ways, Kitty reminded me of Amalia, my little sister. There was the same rush of impulsive chatter or love which came so easily to my youngest sister's mouth and heart, the same courage, the same determination. As Katherine of Suffolk reminded me of Sybylla, so Kitty did of Amalia. I was fortunate to have found sisters of spirit in England, even if I had been forced to separate from those of blood.

"It was brave of the Queen to beg for prisoners of the Tower," I said. They had been risks, these things she had asked, and the King was still not stable of temper. He could well have lashed out at her, but still Catherine had asked for favours and not for her, but out of compassion for others. She was a courageous young woman.

My thoughts of the past few days ended as I heard the slap of water on the steps. I paused, the scent of burning herbs and spices on the wind as the barge pulled up, long oars rising into the air as if in salute. Its decks were strewn with rosemary and rushes, another attempt to mask the stench of the river, and ribbons flew from its mast and sails, dancing upon the wind.

We were merry on our boat and when eventually the royal couple emerged and climbed on their barge, sitting on golden thrones as twenty-six oarsmen set paddles into the water, we all applauded.

Most people on my barge cheered with great enthusiasm for they were already deep in their cups and it was not past noon yet.

"Good news from the Continent, Highness," Olisleger said to me, joining me at the prow of the ship.

"Indeed?"

"It seems the Sultan of Turkey will not be attempting to invade Hungary, this year at least."

"That is good news," I lied loud enough for any to hear. I knew what he was really telling me was that if the Sultan was not invading Hungary, then Charles V might not be so distracted by war on other fronts and might turn on my brother, or indeed on my sister and her husband in the Schmalkaldic League. Olisleger could hardly present this news in such a way in public however, so had gone for a tactical way of expressing the information. In one way it might be good, however, for if it stopped the possession of Guelders being such an urgent topic the Emperor might leave my brother alone on that front. But Olisleger was not done.

"There is however trouble on other fronts. It is said the King of Scots is gathering an army, and one of significance; people are mentioning 60,000 men. It is thought he would only do so if he had promises from France, and France itself looks set for war for it is said François has sent men to Turin, which might begin hostilities with the Emperor there."

I could not stop myself grimacing. The Sultan pulling out of war with the Emperor was nothing but a bad thing, in that case.

"There is a rumour building that your brother may well marry one of the daughters of King François," Olisleger went on.

"But he is betrothed, surely, to the niece of the King of France?"

"They may seek a closer alliance."

As we sailed past the Tower, cannon shot rang out, marking the Queen's entrance to London. Brightly coloured barges bearing the Lord Mayor and his men met the royal party at the Tower. Dignitaries were rowed to the Queen's barge so they could welcome her to London as if she had never been there in her life.

From the banks, people cheered. Some, I had no doubt, did so for true happiness to see one of their own, an Englishwoman of an ancient Catholic family, set beside the King. Others, I was equally sure, cheered because they had been commanded to. To all, the Queen lifted a hand and waved. Screaming from the slippery banks of the Thames grew in volume. Children leapt up and down beside beds of rushes. Men swept dark caps from their heads, bowing low to their tiny Queen, and women took their skirts in hands and curtseyed. I was pleased to see that whilst rumours of hatred from the English people towards the Queen were rife, this did not seem to be so. It is easy to think, when we hear something ill, that everyone is thinking it, but the world has a mind most diverse. Even if some of those people had been commanded to cheer Catherine, there were many, I was sure, who welcomed her as their Queen.

We sailed on to Greenwich where we disembarked at the royal wharf. It was here that Catherine's first true triumph as Queen took place.

"My lord and King," the Queen said when we all had gathered. She took to her knees upon a platform constructed for this purpose. "I take this moment to beg for the lives of prisoners in your custody. For Sir Thomas Wyatt, I ask forgiveness and freedom. This man has wronged you, but I ask that you show Christian mercy."

The King pretended to look grave, although this moment must have been talked of between them for some days before this. It was all too staged. Even Catherine, brave girl though she was, would not dare bring up Wyatt at a time like this, before so many people, unless it was prearranged.

"It is traditional for a queen to ask a favour of her husband on such an occasion, and it is just as traditional for her husband to know of it in advance, Your Highness," Jane Boleyn whispered to me, evidently understanding I had seen through the pageant. I started a little at her voice so close. I had not seen her in the crowd. Some of the Queen's women were near her, but Jane had taken a step into the mass, perhaps just to talk to me. She always did have a knack of appearing like that, sudden and silent. At times I was reminded of a vixen.

"The Queen asked some time ago for mercy for these men?" I whispered, thinking to myself that when I had undertaken this ceremony no one had told me of this tradition, but then, the King had not been open to granting favours to me when I was his wife.

Jane nodded. "She wanted to ever since Wyatt was arrested, Highness, but she feared, so she waited for the best moment, and the King granted her this favour now as he was pleased with her."

Clever Catherine.

It looked spontaneous yet was anything but. Catherine was taking on the part of the Virgin who interceded with God. The King, like God, was the embodiment of justice, whilst the Queen, like the Virgin, was that of mercy. This pageant also appealed to the King's love of old tales of romance. Queens begging their husbands to show clemency was as old as creation.

The crowds heard, and there was muttering. I heard notes of surprise. Pleading for Wallop would have been considered normal. He was, after all, a Catholic, therefore a supporter of Norfolk, but the Queen had pleaded for Wyatt, potentially an enemy to the faction which supported her.

"For my gentle Queen, I have decided to pardon Sir Thomas Wyatt," my former husband announced.

"My gracious husband and King is kind and merciful," Catherine said as the applause died down. "And I, his grateful Queen, would humbly ask for the life of one more man, if my lord will hear me, not thinking me too bold."

"Speak, my Queen," said the King.

His face… God's eyebrows, he looked so pleased with himself, he was almost gloating. It was a little repulsive. How he enjoyed the Queen supplicating herself before him, it made him feel powerful.

She looked up at him, her face so childlike, like a little girl asking a boon for her playmates. "I plead for the life of Sir John Wallop," she said. "Another prisoner of Your Majesty, and another who hath done you wrong, but one whom, in your infinite mercy, should you think it fitting, might be spared to think on his sins and put his faults to mending."

"At the request of my gentle Queen, whose heart is so large and generous, I have decided to free both men," the King announced, after what I felt was a rather over-long dramatic pause where he appeared to be considering her request.

There was loud applause, and I saw many approving faces as the Queen rose from her knees. It was usual for queens to intercede for the sake of compassionate causes, and the fact that both men, on opposing sides in terms of politics and religion, were to be freed spoke plain of the fact that Catherine had supported neither faction because of politics but had spoken for the men out of pity. Pity was approved of, was suited to a woman, suited to a queen, but it left many wondering where her loyalties lay. I could see brows furrowing. All past queens had dabbled in politics, even quiet Jane. Catherine appeared to be pleading for people out of mere kindness, without a view to power. That was highly unusual but might be a refreshing change.

That was, if people trusted she *was* so disinterested. Many would not trust, would think this a show to hide her political ambitions.

I struck my hands together smartly and smiled at my Queen. "She draws from her true nature," I whispered to Jane Boleyn, "from kindness and compassion, and see how it makes her shine. If she does this more, listens to her heart and not the gossip of those who wish her harm, she will do well."

"I think so too, Your Highness." Jane smiled, bobbed a curtsey and slipped away to attend to her mistress again.

The Queen's plea, as I was well aware, was a handy tool for my former husband. Reversing a decision could make a king appear weak or inconstant, but should he change his mind to please his wife, it was viewed as chivalrous. This way, it would appear the King had been correct to imprison Wyatt and Wallop, and he would not have to endure the potential shame of putting these men on trial. There was scant evidence against them, so I heard, and Wyatt had a sharp, witty tongue that might cause harm to the King's feeble pride.

This was a public victory for Catherine. She had asked for something, and it had been granted. She had also neatly demonstrated, to most at least, that she was neutral in terms of politics.

There were conditions put on the freedom of Wyatt and Wallop. Both had to admit wrongdoing against the King and abandon their protestations of innocence. Wyatt was told he would have to return to his wife, from whom he had separated many years ago, and set aside the mistress he had kept since, along with his bastard children. Although Wyatt's personal life had nothing to do with his public behaviour, the King had been insistent.

My former husband wanted so much to appear a virtuous man, wanted the world to think he always considered the souls of his people as well as their actions. I thought it a poor idea to force a man and woman back together who clearly had no wish to be. Rumour was, Wyatt's wife loathed him. This was no merry event for her either.

My former husband would not like to hear what people thought of his own marital affairs *or* affairs outside of marriage, but those who pass judgement often fear to be judged. That is indeed why they pass judgement so swift and hard; they repel shame and blame from themselves by casting others down. Attack first, that is their motto, before they are attacked.

Wallop had to beg pardon for his crimes and abandon claims of innocence too. Neither man took their pardon lightly. Should they be accused of something at a later date, their admittance of wrongdoing at this time would stand against them and they would be even more likely to be executed.

"My Queen hath moved my heart with her gentle requests for mercy," the King said, clearly thinking himself a most merciful prince and indulgent husband. "And I have listened to her plea, for as Mary, Mother of God, showed mercy and forgiveness to those who killed her son, so the Queen, my good and faithful wife, shows mercy to those who would act against their King and country."

The crowds applauded Catherine, and she dipped her head, humble and submissive, but as she dropped her gaze, I could see a small smile of triumph on her lips. I welcomed it.

As I looked about that day, I saw hope. The Queen had demonstrated she was capable of impartiality and that the King favoured her. Many were still uncertain about her, but they were pleased by her actions. The King was unpredictable, frequently savage, yet at his side was a queen whose heart was not moved by gain, politics or religious fervour, but by the suffering of innocent men.

"We have a good Queen," I said loudly. "A good woman, and a fine sovereign lady watches over us. Let us give thanks to the Lord God for His benevolence in offering us a great King, and a Queen well worthy of him."

All about me people bowed their heads in prayer, and I saw Catherine glance my way, gratitude shining in her warm brown eyes.

*

"The Queen had a note from Sir Thomas Wyatt," Katherine of Suffolk told me.

I was due to depart court for my house again. Much as I had enjoyed seeing the Queen do so well, I wanted to be away from court. This pit was not for me; I was no snake.

It was the end of March and Wyatt was free. Leaving his cell in the Tower he was to go to Dover, where the King was heading, so Wyatt might beg forgiveness and admit guilt as ordered, Wyatt had stopped for a moment, so my friend explained, to write a brief note which despite its spare words, brimmed with gratitude for the Queen's intercession. Wyatt had thanked Catherine in the humblest terms and promised to be her servant in all days that followed.

"The Queen wishes she could have seen him pardoned, but only the King is to be there." Katherine picked up a small box of myrrh and grease from a table and sniffed the unguent inside, then smiled apologetically to my lady Dorothy Wingfield who was packing them away and handed it to her so she could put it in the case with the others. I had amassed quite a number of useful medicines and took them with me wherever I went so if any of my household fell ill, I could tend to them.

"Why?" I asked.

"There was some official excuse put about, I forget what lies were spun, but the truth is, the King wants Wyatt to know his power, to feel it in every fibre of his being." Katherine widened her eyes in mockery of the King. "If the Queen were there, the King might feel some of his power was draining into her, and Wyatt's gratitude might all be for her."

"Perhaps the King fears his Queen might ask that Wyatt might not be carted off back to the wife he dislikes, and who I hear dislikes him," I said.

"Perhaps, but I think the motive more personal." Katherine toyed with another box then brushed her hands and came to me. "The King has never forgotten or forgiven that the Queen's cousin was wooed by Wyatt once. For a while the King thought himself inferior to Wyatt, which was why he had to prove he had won that bowling match."

I inclined my head. I knew the story. When the King was courting Anne Boleyn, the two men had been playing bowls against each other. They had thrown their balls at the Jack. The King had pointed at his ball using a finger on which sat a ring Anne Boleyn had granted him and brayed, "It is mine, Wyatt!"

Not to be outdone in this little pageant of which man possessed this woman, Wyatt had stepped forwards. Although Wyatt's ball had been farther away, he had taken out a trinket attached to a ribbon which Anne had given to him, apparently in friendship. Wyatt had used it to measure the distance between the balls and told the King he hoped it might still be his, the "it" being Anne Boleyn, of course. The King had stalked off, furious. A few days later, no doubt warned or censured by Anne, Wyatt had departed from court.

"If the King had been secure, there would have been nothing to prove," Katherine went on.

"And now he will punish Wyatt for this, a thing which went on so long ago. The King has a temper most resentful, so it seems to me."

"That is why most fear when an arrest seems it might happen," said my friend. "Because the King stores all that has been said or done against him in his mind. If a person falls, they face not only crimes of the moment, but all they have done to upset the King in the past."

"Or indeed all a family member has done," I said. "Margaret Pole appears to be paying for the supposed crimes of her son."

"And for her blood." Katherine's voice dropped to less than a whisper. "It is too royal for the King's liking. In truth, her sons could voice a claim to the throne, and some might think it a better claim than the King's."

"Let this dangerous talk alone. Play cards with me."

We tried to talk of other things, but it was clear both of us were thinking the same, that the King would never allow Margaret Pole freedom. In truth I wondered how long he had desired an excuse to arise so he might lock her away in the first place.

Chapter Twelve

Hever Castle
Kent
April 1541

"I wish her well, if it be true," I said to Katherine of Suffolk as we strolled in the gardens at Hever.

The world was coming to life now the harsh face of winter had turned from us. Flowers were showing tiny, shy faces to the sun, which although cool that day was still bright. I had great hopes for the rose gardens this year, though they were not in bloom yet of course, but they were looking healthier. I had employed two more gardeners to aid the ones already in existence with the rose bushes in particular. I wanted all of the pretty park looking smart, naturally, but the sad state of the roses had given me sorrow when first I took on the house and I had been told they had not had the men needed to tend them. Roses, as one of the gardeners explained to me, do better with attention, with clipping and cutting back at the right times, with consideration paid to their soil. They were "not easy mistresses" as he told me with a grin, "but demanding ones, yet worth all the devotion shown to them." I wanted them to have the attention they needed now, and I hoped I would reap the benefits that summer.

I had vacated my beloved Richmond in favour of Hever, allowing the King and court to visit there. Although I could have stayed and played hostess to the King in one of his own palaces, I had chosen to retire to the country for a spell, claiming business of my estates in Kent drew me away. It was true I needed to catch up a little but in truth my last brief visit to court had been enough for a while. Court was exciting, that was true, but it was exciting in a dangerous way, a febrile, unsteady way I liked not. I preferred my pleasures to come with joy rather than trepidation, to remain steady rather than undulate like the waves of the sea, one minute high and the next crashing upon rock and shore.

Katherine of Suffolk had come visiting me at Hever and had told me that the Queen appeared to have missed one of her monthly courses. Normally Catherine would have ordered pads from the laundry by this time, and she had not. There was no blood on her sheets or her undergarments, which were checked by the laundry women. Those laundry women then passed on such information to courtiers who paid them well. The King, apparently, sent his men to enquire often on the state of his wife's undergarments. I blushed to think this might have been done with mine although it would not have been the King checking, since he knew he had left me a maid as good as he found me. But still, the thought others from court had been inspecting my most private items was rather revolting. I knew queens had no privacy, but all the same, this was a step even further than I had thought in the art of invasion. A husband I could understand had reasons to need to know about pregnancy but the idea the whole court was there, quizzing women about other women's most private garments, yes, it was a foul thought.

In this case at least it seemed it might be a good thing all knew of the Queen's possible condition, for although it was early, everyone was gossiping already that Catherine Howard *was* with child, which meant everyone was fawning on her in case she was. I hoped she was happy about her state if it was so. Of course, most women would be, yet in truth I shied from the idea of bearing children or raising them. I had always thought I would change my mind, as anyone I had dared tell had told me I would, later in life, and yet I had no more interest in the state of motherhood or pregnancy than I had years ago.

I sometimes wondered at my lack of interest in bearing a child, whether it was abnormal, as most people claimed, or if it was simply something many women felt and said nothing about, fearing that if they spoke the truth then the censure of the world would fall on their heads, all for not being normal. Were we all pretending to be this thing called normal which people told us we should be? This particular set of virtues and parameters which defined us as women, as we were supposed to be?

Perhaps more numerous than anyone would believe were the women thinking thoughts like mine about not wanting children, or other matters, and no one would ever know because we would, like as not, be arrested or locked away in a madhouse if we dared share the truths inside our souls. It was said that God gave women the ability to carry and bear children and therefore women should do so, but what of those of us who had no desire to?

Could that lack of desire not be a message from God?

Perhaps some of us were fated to become aunts and godmothers, but not mothers, and that was the way it should be. I loved my stepchildren, now my nieces and nephew of course, I had met and admired my friend Katherine's two fine sons, Henry and Charles, but I wanted to bear none of my own offspring. I had no desire to offer any more of my life to another person, since I had already lived so much of it for others, for my family, my brother, father, my country, short-lived husband and his people too. I had given them the power to command this one life I had once, and now I was free of that obligation. What was left of my life I wanted to be dedicated to me.

I suppose it was the same reason I did not want to marry again; I should like the rest of my years however short or long to be mine. Some might name me selfish for such a thought, but I had surrendered my own will and wants once, when I was sent here to wed the King, and I saw no reason to do so again. Should it be that all others were catered to in my life, *by* my life, but not me? Did I not deserve a turn now that all others had had theirs, to be important in my own existence?

Perhaps it was an odd thing for a woman to want. We are taught from birth to be good to others, to serve, to obey, to submit, and therefore there is nothing left of us, or for us. All that is there is there to serve others, all we have is given up to others. I had played my part, and now I had done this, I did not want to do it again. Perhaps I was abnormal, but I was happier unnatural than I had ever been natural.

Of course, had I expressed these thoughts about not wanting children, or having a life of my own, to certain people they would have told me that it was the Devil who was telling me I did not want children, but I doubted that was true. If anyone needed more people in the world, it was the Devil. Whom else was he going to tempt away from the goodness of the world and into the evil?

I always wondered about the Devil. If God was omnipotent, as the priests and Church claimed, how was it that the Devil had any power? Could God not just have waved a hand and been done with evil influence upon the world? Did the existence of the Devil mean that God *wanted* his dark former angel in the world, to test and try people to see if they prevailed against wickedness? In which case, did that not mean the Devil and God were not enemies, but partners of a kind?

And so, if the Devil were whispering in my ear not to have children, perhaps it was a test from God to see if I would, but in all truth and honesty I had tried my best when married. I would have borne a child if I had been given one and no doubt I would have loved it. But given the choice, I did not want to bear a daughter to have her face a marriage such as I had, or a son who might well grow up to be a man like the King.

If I had a place in this world, a task when it came to children, I would rather try to guide those already here, and the children I still was close to of my annulled marriage needed me. Their father was frequently not with them, and when he was they were in fear of him as much, if not more, than they were in love. Those children had been brought into this world and all had lost their mothers, mostly because of the actions of their shared father. Then I had been sent to England. I liked to think if I had not been sent to wed the King by God, perhaps I had instead been sent to befriend three lonely children. I could not replace their mothers, but I could offer my companionship where I was able, my support and friendship. I was not permitted to see them often, yet Elizabeth wrote to me, Mary too and I saw Mary when I could. Edward was more distant, but I hoped he remembered me kindly.

But it was different for Catherine; the Queen needed a child. A child, preferably a son of course, would secure her place as Queen. I also hoped, however, that she was of a different mind to me and would welcome a babe in her belly and arms. Catherine was full of love, and I hoped she would have someone close to her, this child if rumour was correct, to offer that devotion to.

"Of course, she is young," I went on as we strolled, trailing a hand along a creeping tendril of jasmine running along a wall kept warm by the sun. "I hope the King will have talented women about her when the time comes to guide her through the process of birth. In Cleves we are famed for our midwives, you know. My mother had us attending births from a young age, so we knew all the stages of labour and what to do. I think I respect no women more than midwives; they are as generals in a battle only women fight, commanding here, guiding there."

"Sadly, my friend, I think if the Queen is with child the King will insist she have doctors, as Jane Seymour did." Katherine stopped to admire some honeysuckle, its leaves dark green, shimmering in the sunlight.

I was most concerned to hear this. Many people talked about the death of the Seymour Queen, saying that had she been attended by midwives she would have been in better hands. The doctors the King had insisted on did not know the skills of birthing as women did. Many male physicians were lacking experience and had little idea what they were doing, yet they were suffused with arrogance because they had been to a school which taught them that they knew everything and women nothing. I had even heard of a scandal in London of late where one doctor insisted, after attending a birth, he was removing the afterbirth when he in fact hauled out the poor woman's innards. She, of course, died. He, of course, charged the family for his service.

"Seventeen is not so young," said Katherine. "I am sure she is hale enough to give birth no matter the attendants. I had my first son at fifteen and I seem to remember doing most of the work."

I thought it a little sad, in a way, too, Catherine's potential pregnancy. Much as I hoped this child would bring Catherine joy it might well deliver her sorrow instead. If Catherine had a son, he would be surrounded by a household who were more like guards, as Prince Edward was. She would rarely see him and would not be granted permission to educate him. He would be a stranger to her.

Perhaps a daughter might be better for her happiness but even a princess would not be safe, no woman was. When a daughter married, her husband could do as he wished with her. He could force himself upon her, beat her, humiliate her, parade mistresses before her and she would be able to do nothing. The only weapons she would have would be dignity, self-belief and her womb.

Of course, I reminded myself, *you have done fine and well for yourself using dignity, Anna. So, there is hope.*

There is an exception to every rule, said the sardonic voice of the lost Queen in my mind. *That you are fortunate does not mean that others are decidedly not.*

That was true enough. It is always a mistake to go about thinking that your experience of the world is the same as everyone else's, or that you all start or indeed go through life with the same advantages. It should be clear this is never the case, but it is always an easy trap to fall into.

Yet even with such possible destinies, a daughter might be better for Catherine, in one way, but the King wanted no more daughters. He had Edward, his heir, and now what he wanted was a spare.

"Is she merry?" I asked.

Katherine stopped on the path. When I looked at her, she had bunched her mouth, not so much with contempt as pity. "She is not," confessed my friend. "It may just be the moods that fall upon women at such times, but in truth I have not seen her lower of spirits or as despondent. I think she fears or dreads the idea of a child."

"If she thinks she could have not much to do with her child when born, I understand her dread," I said. "I considered the same when with the King, that I might give birth to a child and then barely see it. To have a baby but have little to do with its upbringing, if you want to have much to do with that upbringing, such a thing is hard." I shrugged. "Perhaps there are other matters she fears. Mayhap she believes the King might stray if she is with child and fears that. Perhaps she fears childbirth. Perhaps it simply is the moods, fluctuating and consuming, which fall upon us from time to time."

"It could be all those things, or none," said Katherine.

When Katherine returned to court she sent word. The Queen had told the King she thought she *might* be with child. Catherine was not sure, but she suspected.

"It is clever to tell him now, even if she is not sure," wrote my friend. *"If the Queen bears a son, she will have no enemies of worth. She will be secure in the King's love and will know power, but if she bears a girl her*

position might become weakened. Queen Catherine knows the time of pregnancy is powerful because it is the time of possibility. The King will keep her safe, grant all she wishes, and if she uses this time to rouse his fear of losing her, he may not care in the end if she bears boy or girl. She will use all the time she has whilst with child, and during that time his hope will grant her much favour."

I understood what she was saying. I had heard that when Queen Anne was with child, and had been very ill, the King had been so panicked about losing her that he had even said he wished she would miscarry the child rather than she die and leave him. Only a few years later he had her head cut off, so clearly he was not a man to stick by his word, but all the same if the King was still as deep in love with Catherine as he had been at the start of their marriage then the thought that he might lose her now would be unbearable. Katherine of Suffolk was right, this time was powerful, and the Queen had decided to use it from the very start.

I thought about how people often underestimated Catherine, and I wondered at it. There was plenty of proof she had a strong mind when she chose to use it. Yes, she was young, could be flighty and carefree, or she had been in the past. She was not classically educated, but there was a mind beneath all that, sharpened and growing sharper still as she traversed the court of the King.

People claimed she was foolish for her schooling had been basic, and that was true enough in one way, but there is more than one way of being intelligent. I remembered a man at my father's court, a great scholar, whose mind had been filled with so much thought and wisdom that all men went to him to drink in his words, yet he did not know how to work the lacings on his shirt. Most nobles did not dress themselves, it was true, but this went beyond that. Some people who are most talented of mind in some ways are entirely lacking in others. And some who are thought to be ignorant because they have a lack of education turn out to be vastly precocious in other ways.

I had a feeling there was much in the mind of Catherine, Queen of England, which would amaze people, given the chance.

Chapter Thirteen

Richmond Palace
April 1541

"Do you think it will finally be settled between them?"

Olisleger shrugged, an eloquent gesture for all its simplicity. "Who can say, Highness, but I somewhat doubt it. Your brother tells me he is unlikely to attend."

Olisleger was returned that morn from Cleves, where he had briefly been. My brother and the Emperor were due to meet at the Colloquy of Regensburg that month, and the Emperor had told my brother to bring with him proofs that Guelders was his territory so the matter could be settled, but if Wilhelm did not appear, this would not be settled.

Wilhelm was, instead, to head for France and he could not be in two places at the same time, so clearly he was not even going to put in an appearance at the meeting the Emperor had commanded him to attend. Before he had left, Olisleger told me there had been a brief panic when it was found there were four thousand mercenaries in Cleves, and men thought they had been sent by the Emperor. Wilhelm had gathered his soldiers in case of attack but when he sent a command for the force to leave, they did so without fuss or quarrel. It was said that, in the end, they truly were mercenaries, and they were merely passing through Cleves, seeking employment. It was also said their numbers had been exaggerated.

What was for certain was, however, that the Emperor was turning up to this Diet to speak to Wilhelm and my brother would not be there for he was off to secure alliance with France, and to become formally betrothed, then married to Jeanne. There were rumours the Emperor was heading to the Diet with an army at his back, and should Wilhelm not turn up it was likely that army might be set on my people or be used to prevent my brother getting back home.

"Can the Elector, my sister's husband, calm the Emperor, if Wilhelm does not appear?" I asked, and became worried by Olisleger's expression, which became pained. "What is it?" I said.

"I do hear the Elector, too, might not turn up to the meeting."

"Does every man on this Earth wish to goad the Emperor into war?" I exclaimed. "Has the King been told of this yet?"

"I believe he will be written to when your brother reaches France and the betrothal is secured," Olisleger paused. "I should also tell you, Highness, your mother is unwell. I am told she is on the mend, but for some time she was quite low in health and vigour."

Fear leapt on my back and stuck his sharp fingers in my chest. "Is anyone with her?"

"Your sister, Amalia, is tending to her as well as the women of the Frauenzimmer, and I am told your brother visited her before riding for France."

"Tell me of anything you hear, and I will write to her now, so she will know I am thinking of her."

I went to my desk, my swan feather quill in hand. For a long time, I just stared at the paper. I knew not what to write, what to say.

Mother had been asking that I come home ever since the King and I separated, and although I had explained many times that I could be taken prisoner by the Emperor, or that the King did not want me to leave, she still continued to ask. I think she knew that I wanted to stay here, no matter the danger, for going home would be to return in shame and spend the rest of my life under the power of my brother, who might marry me off anywhere, if another man would even have me after all this. Here, I could be with friends, be as free as I was likely to ever be, be content and run my own household, but not in Cleves.

The trouble was, I was sure a part of her knew that I didn't want to come home. That made me feel guilty.

And it was a guilt I would bear, for although I loved her and wanted to see her, that desire was weaker within me than the passion I had for freedom. I sighed, took up my pen and wrote to her, telling her I loved her and I missed her. That at least was true.

Chapter Fourteen

Richmond Palace
April 1541

"More merchants on their way to Chapuys, Highness," Kitty Bassett said, gazing from the window. "That makes three large merchant vessels this morning already, and I think one small." I had asked her to keep count.

"There will be even more, further upriver." I joined her to stare out of the window at the graceful ship sailing towards the city. Richmond was downriver from London's centre, to its west. Greenwich, where these men and their boats were heading, was further to the east. All the merchants of London would be on the water today, taking their petitions to the King or to Chapuys.

Mary of Hungary, kinswoman of the Emperor Charles, had forbidden English imports to the Low Countries and Spain. It was part, I had been informed by an agitated Harst, of a plot dreamed up by the Emperor to force the King into making an alliance with him. Some merchants were off to beg the King to make terms, and some were heading to Chapuys to converse on the matter.

Were the Emperor himself to enforce trade restrictions there would be talk of war, but Mary, Governess of the Low Countries, could do it on his behalf, causing at least a temporary problem and later the Emperor could blame her for all this uproar, attribute it to a feminine weakness of mind or lack of understanding about politics, or perhaps to her emotions which men seemed to think were always ungoverned and wild in women. Being a woman, the Governess of the Low Countries could bear the Emperor's sins, that was what she was there for.

It was said all this plotting had been done at the request of Chapuys, who had felt his influence wane at court and wished to impress the power of the Emperor upon the King again. Already there had been retaliations in England. A Dutch ship had been seized and Spanish merchants had been boarded and threatened by the King's men. Goods coming to dock had been apprehended and merchants from Spain and other Imperial countries were heading to Chapuys each day, asking him to recover their confiscated merchandise and ships and get the restrictions dropped before they lost all their business with the English. It was chaos, so we heard.

"I hear, Highness, that the King means not to deal with Chapuys at all," Kitty went on, still staring at the water. "He is sending men directly to Mary of Hungary, my sister wrote me from court of it. The King was bragging of it to his men when they were visiting the Queen."

I said nothing. I was not sure what to say. If these talks failed and the King was forced to ally with the Emperor that would put me, daughter of a state opposed to the Emperor, in a difficult position. It would be unlikely I would be invited much to court anymore, and I did not mind that, but it also put me in potential danger in other ways.

Kitty turned, sensing my distraction. "The King is talking daily of the Queen's coronation, so I hear."

"I hope he will crown her; the Queen is a good woman."

Kitty made a disgruntled face she barely attempted to hide. "None of that," I said, a hard edge to my voice, but it was not too hard. Kitty Bassett was my fervent friend. This was sweet to my heart but it also unnerved me a little. As she was my best maid and companion I was close to her, but she had taken on my friendship, especially of late, with a kind of zeal bordering on the obsessive. It was clear I had won her respect, affection and heart, and she was of course one of those who believed I should still be Queen in Catherine's place. She had spoken of it, with a breathtakingly perilous lack of regard for her own safety, on more than one occasion before others and although I stopped her now before anything of criticism of the Queen or even worse, the King, should pop out of her unguarded mouth, I knew she still harboured thoughts of the kind.

She was protective, my Kitty, of me, yet this came out in ways contrary to my best interests, for if her wishes came true they would, ironically enough, force me into a life I had no desire for whatsoever, simply because she thought it was the best life for me, the one I deserved. We can be destroyed by love in so many ways, it is a dangerous thing in truth.

People could not seem to see that I was happy with my lot. Here and now, I was more content than ever I had been. Yet such people, in a quest to give me all they thought I deserved, would make me unhappy, forcing me back into a marriage I had never wanted in the first place. Odd it is to understand that to love someone is not always to want the best for them. If people think they know what is best for you, this is a frightening thing, a controlling creature who will latch about your throat and squeeze. They think you do not know your own mind, such people, and they think they should be in control of your life. They will make you miserable, just so they can be proved right.

The King had announced nothing regarding the potential pregnancy of the Queen, but everyone knew it was a possibility. Catherine's ladies in waiting watched her every move, they knew she had not bled that month and even if her ladies did not talk of it, men of court were now paying high prices to washerwomen and laundry folk who served the court, a few handsome coins for their information and the Queen's most intimate, private matters were splayed out on a table for the world to gawp at.

I wondered anew who had inspected my wedding sheets, sniffing them perhaps, their nose up against the fabric trying to tell if there was King's seed upon the linen or not. There had been no blood, of course, since the King had failed to rise to our occasions, but I wondered with revulsion how keenly anything else on the sheets had been examined. Did some stranger know the scent of me, perhaps better than I did?

"Is the Queen happier?" I asked, watching a ship bearing the banners and sail style of the Low Countries float past, elegant as a dancer it moved on the water. Swans were flocked along the riverside, a collar of white on the grey-blue water. In the distance I could hear them honking and calling, thousands of them.

"My sister says she is bright when with the King, Highness, but low at other times, perhaps she misses him when he is not there."

I doubted that was so. Catherine probably missed his men; they were lively company, and one in particular had always had her attention.

"It is said the Queen will be crowned at Whitsun." Kitty paused, biting her lip. I knew she wanted to say I should have been crowned.

"Let us hope that will be so," I rushed over whatever Kitty was about to blurt out.

Catherine was my friend, that much I knew. I wanted her crowned for her own sake but I had to admit, it would be good to have a friend so high in the court. If trouble came with these sanctions of the Emperor or if greater trouble came if the King and Emperor made peace, I might need some friends.

*

"He sent his sorrows and said the Scots' line was unfortunate," Harst told me. "But it was clear to all the King was all but skipping with glee. As he spoke of sorrow, he had a great smirk on his face."

I tried not to shudder at the insensitivity of the King. Marie de Guise, Queen of Scotland, had given birth to a boy, named Robert Arthur, who had died at eight days old. A day later, his one-year-old brother James, Duke of Rothesay, heir to Scotland's throne, had also died. Two heirs, two babies lost, so close to one another. I did not know how their mother was still standing. There was a whole nation grieving and a mother and father deep in sorrow, and all the King could do was gloat and offer hollow words of comfort.

I could imagine my brother might be as pleased as the King, however. The sons of Marie of Guise and James of Scots had possessed a claim to the duchy of Guelders through their mother. They were no more now, and unless the royal couple had another son there would be no Scottish claimant throwing his hat into the ring for consideration as lord of Guelders.

The King had been angered at James of Scotland, his nephew, for refusing to break with Rome, and for suspected involvement with unrest in the north of England as well as in Ireland. No doubt my former husband thought these tragic deaths of infants just punishment, doled out by God, for a nephew refusing to cede to the will of his *wise* uncle. Sour loathing rose in my gullet. I swallowed hard, reminding myself I was no longer wed to this man, and though he might be my King and brother I was not responsible for him.

Still, to have such a man as this representing one and one's adopted country, it was a vile thing.

"Afterwards he became maudlin," said Harst.

"For the sake of his nephew's children?" A spark of hope which ignited within me that the King might have a speck of decency within him was soon extinguished.

"No, for himself and his own child. Edward. He started to talk of the fragility of fate, and it was clear he was talking of the possibility of losing his son." Harst adjusted one of the three golden chains he was wearing over his black doublet, and golden fire flashed in the light from the window.

"I had hoped you were to tell me the King sorrowed for his kinsman, and his kinsman's wife," I said. "To lose one child is bad enough, but two children, two heirs, this close together? Were I a suspicious person I would think poison was at the heart of this."

"You think these deaths assassinations, my lady?"

"I know not, but if I did and I heard the King of England was merry about the deaths of these boys, I would be suspicious." I folded my arms and tapped a finger on my opposite sleeve of velvet. "The King should consider that more, that men might suspect him and his behaviour must therefore be above reproach."

"Like yours, my lady."

"I am a woman, my Lord Ambassador. Most of us learn early and learn harsh that we must always be above reproach for if not then we will be blamed for everything." I sighed. "Did the King emerge from his melancholy mood?"

"The Queen managed to unpick it from his brow."

"You make it sound as a tick to be dislodged."

Harst smiled. "There are similarities. She is quite skilled with him, you know. I have watched on more than one occasion as she handles him. It is quite proficient manipulation."

"Manipulation?"

My friend spread his hands. "I say it not as a bad thing, Highness. With a man like the King straightforwardness and honesty are like as not to have one land firmly in trouble. He is more accustomed to flattery and falsehoods; therefore they are what must be used. He started out in dire doom about the fragility of fate but by the end of the afternoon he was sat contentedly on his throne, his hand on his wife's belly, grinning, as she sat to one side of him."

"Has anything been said about the Queen meeting the King's children?" I asked.

"No, and many think that is odd, but now she is with child perhaps it will go ahead. Eight months she has been Queen and still the Lord Edward and Lady Elizabeth are strangers to her."

Chapter Fifteen

Richmond Palace
Holy Week 1541

Holy Week came, and despite the elevated hopes of reformers like my friend of Suffolk, it came in and went out as Catholic as ever it had been before the break with Rome. During Lent that year, people had even been arrested for eating meat, something reformers were prone to do as they said there was no reason to fast as people did in Rome. Reformers had hoped the King would remove the tradition of fasting. He did not.

It seemed the King was entirely done with pretending to make alterations to his Church that might please reformists. He adored the mystery and magnetism of the Catholic Mass, that was plain enough. He liked being Head of the Church in England, of course, that was not about to alter, but most of the ceremony and pomp from the Catholic Mass he wanted to retain. In many ways that pomp was so akin to his own power, the display and show of monarchy, that I think he might have believed it sacrilegious in more than one way to disband all the ancient traditions. Some of them, indeed, conferred power to the Crown, so God's power become synonymous with that of the King. The King welcomed that.

I was on display from time to time but not as much as the Queen was. Easter was a high holiday of course and normally I, as sister to the King, would be called to court, but perhaps the ongoing problems with the Emperor and Mary of Hungary had made the King chary. I had to attend church with all my court, be seen to be celebrating in the way the King's Church ordered at Richmond, but was not to court called.

It was not as bad for me, however, as for the Queen. She was being watched not only to check her behaviour now, but so everyone could ascertain what was going on in her belly. Everywhere she went, eyes followed, watching for signs she was indeed with child. Most people were now sure she was. It had been reported all over London, and England no doubt, that Catherine felt sick of the morning, had complained her breasts were tender and no blood had come. Her condition would not be formally announced until the fourth month when the child quickened, for that was when a soul was set within the babe by God, but everyone wanted to know now if this was for certain, so they might work out their next moves.

If the little Queen was with child, she would need to be wooed, or it would displease the King. If she should bear a son, she might become powerful, so it would be good to be her friend. If she died, another candidate for Queen would need to be produced, and the highest houses were already busily inspecting daughters to see which might please the King if Catherine went the way of Jane Seymour. Death and advancement were on everyone's mind, and I am certain Catherine, who was talented at sensing the emotions of others, could feel every thought, friendly or vile, floating her way from the hungry ravens of court surrounding her.

This seemed to be affecting her, for the more the Queen was on display the more she seemed to retreat inside herself. Women whose feet she washed on Maundy Thursday, seventeen of them to match the years the Queen had lived, said she looked dazed, as if she was not really there.

"I think she needs some exercise," said my friend the Duchess. "The King barely allows her to walk anywhere, even to church she is carried in a litter. She needs to walk and get some air, but hardly will he let her out."

"You may be right, but he thinks of her now as a pouch which carries a precious jewel."

"There has been some odd behaviour from the Queen again too. I am sure restlessness is at the heart of it."

"Such as?"

Katherine told me a tale. Queen Catherine had given a gift to Culpepper. It was not unusual, presents often were exchanged at Easter, but she had given it personally, which was uncommon. It was a fine black cap with a jewel stud on the front. "Then she told him to hide it, or say it was a gift from his family if anyone asked."

"But she did this, gave the present, in front of people?"

"Her servants, Jane and Kat, were the only ones with her, but at court someone is always watching, and when she gave it, he replied, 'Alas, madam,' in a jesting tone, 'why did you not do this when you were a maid? Now I am lost to you but may only offer you my love from afar'."

"It sounds as if he is trying to act the part of a courtly lover."

Katherine gave a swift nod of agreement. "It does, and yet though his response was conventional and perhaps expected, the Queen was oddly offended and said if that was all the thanks she was to have she would not have given it to him. What was odder was, even though this slight incident seemed to offend her, she was lively after, happier."

"Strange indeed," I said, though I thought it not strange at all.

Catherine had great affection, perhaps love for Culpepper. She could not stop herself giving him a gift, then feared to be found doing so in case anyone saw her heart, and she was affronted when he responded to her honest affection with a false, courtly game. Yet she was happier afterwards because she had seen him and spoken to him. I could see it plain as day.

I only hoped others could not.

*

That night I watched the altar being stripped of its coverings and ornaments. Wine and water were poured over it and it was wiped, to show how Christ had wiped clean the sins of man. I felt my heart lift, as though I, too, might have been redeemed. In such moments as this, where something of grace seemed to touch my heart, that was when I believed most keenly in God, and believed God loved us, all of us, no matter how we chose to worship.

It is the moments we are overwhelmed by emotion and upheld by it at the same time which make life worth living. Without the restless, violent surge of awe within our hearts, how do we know we are truly alive?

On Good Friday, the King and Queen crept to the altar on their knees, a vastly uncomfortable process which was much harder for the Queen in a gown than for the King in hose and stockings. I heard the Queen had taken extra care to ensure layers of lace were upon her chest, so as she crept forwards she did not pull down the front of her gown, exposing her breasts to God or to the priest waiting at the altar holding a crucifix for the royal couple to kiss.

Reformers were scandalised enough by the ceremony even without the Queen of England's paps bursting from her gown. Creeping to the cross was antiquated, seen by many, even Catholics, as superstitious, but the King wished to honour the tradition. He said it was because he honoured God. It was not. He was afraid of other monarchs calling him ungodly for the reforms brought about in England, and for the many marriages he had made. The creeping was an act supposed to show humility, but since only royalty did it, it was nothing of the kind.

I saw this for what it was. The King was retreating from reform even as he pretended to stand at the fore of change. I wish I could tell you that made me less afraid of him, but it did not. Cowards in positions of power are most dangerous.

After the adoration of the cross, the King went to a smaller altar nearby to pray over a dish of rings. By ancient custom, the prayers of the King would infuse these trinkets with the power of God, and he would hand them out as signs of favour. A few would be granted to the Queen to distribute too. They were cramp rings, protection not only against many medical afflictions, but also against the powers of Satan. Some were sent to me, a favour.

I turned over the two cramp rings I had been sent in my hand. This was an English custom, not one of Cleves or the Empire. The legend went that the first cramp ring had been given to Edward the Confessor by a pilgrim who was returned from Jerusalem. That ring was given to the King as a cure for cramp, hence the name, and for the falling sickness, and upon the King's death his ring passed into the keeping of the Abbot of Westminster. It became known, not betraying a great deal of imagination, as Saint Edward's ring. After this time arose a common belief that descendants of Edward the Confessor had taken into themselves the power to make more rings like this first one which could work cures. And so, each monarch of England ever since had blessed rings on Good Friday and sent them to people they favoured.

They were not pretty rings, just a mere band of silver or gold combined with iron, with markings upon the band or a motto written about them. They were quite bland compared to most of the rings that I wore upon my fingers and I did not truly believe that the King had any godly power to cure me of any ailments, but I wore the ring all the same for it was a mark of favour to be given one by him. To ignore marks of favour from the King would lead to one falling into disfavour most perilous for certain.

He thinks he may bless items like this, I thought, *as Jesus and the saints did, and bring the touch of God upon a person. He thinks he may command the power of the Almighty.*

There was little of God in my new brother. Christ had instructed mankind to treat others with kindness, but the King dealt in contempt, cruelty. God was all-powerful; my brother feared other men. Christ had been a rebel, leading a revolution against the traditional ways of the world for the betterment of all people. My former husband had rebelled against the Church for his own desires and backtracked on those beliefs which had granted him power as soon as it suited him, without surrendering the power he had gained. Christ was unconventional, the King was as conventional and traditional as it was possible to be. It is odd how people frequently think they are doing acts which are so new and revolutionary and yet they do not see how conformist and conservative they truly are. It was also odd the King thought himself so pious and godly, when he had done so much ill, caused so much pain, and much of it for purely selfish reasons.

It seemed I was not the only one who thought thus of the King.

There came news. In the north, men had birthed a conspiracy to kidnap the Bishop of Llandaff, the King's northern deputy and president of the Northern Council. Relatives of Margaret Pole were found amongst the swiftly captured ringleaders.

This potential uprising was minor, and easily foiled, but the fact that rebellions kept arising was telling. The King thought his power absolute, had claimed dominion over the deeds and even thoughts of his subjects, but not all were subdued. The north had been stamped on time and time again, but men there rose time after time, refusing to be beaten.

I supposed it was a lesson for us all, the trials of resilience.

It should have been a lesson for the King, that men saw what he truly was, but some people never do learn.

Chapter Sixteen

Richmond Palace
April 1541

"The Queen's women have requested linen pads from the laundry." Harst stood at the window, looking out at the verdant deer park which surrounded Richmond.

"So, she is not with child," I said.

"It would appear not. People are saying because the Queen so ardently wished to have a child, her body tricked her into thinking she had one. It is a sad thought, is it not?"

I twirled the newly given cramp ring on my finger. Beside the Tudor rose in gold it sat, as if peasant had been seated beside prince at a feast. "A sad tale and an old one, friend, that a person wishes so hard for something that they think it has appeared in their lives, then find all they saw was a shadow."

I thought of the King, of his fantasies about me. He had dreamed up the perfect woman and then I had appeared, far from perfect and certainly leagues away from the King's ideal of perfection. Catherine had replaced me, she who was his rose without a thorn, even though that phrase was used to describe him more often than her. *Lunatic fantasy,* I thought, that the King had no thorns. He was covered in them, more blackthorn hedge than rose bush was he.

There is a problem not only with fantasy of this kind, but with perfection. Perfection does not exist in the realm of humanity. There is not a person who has not one flaw at least. In truth it is what makes us human, and interesting. What is interesting about perfection? It has to stay one way and never change, never alter. The wonder of life, to me, was that a person entered as an innocent and spent all their life learning, and one cannot learn, cannot grow, if one is already perfect. The King chased a fiction, a mirage hovering in the mists of autumn. He looked for something which could not be found.

And so, he was doomed to unhappiness for the King was always looking for his perfect woman, but the truth was she did not exist. His search for her had led to many women, remarkable women, being destroyed because they were not this idealised, flawless one. Catherine had more warning than the others, more knowledge of what might happen to her so she could put on a better show than Anne or Katherine of Aragon ever had, but to always present a fake face to the King, to always be trying to be this false person, this fantasy of the King, just so he would not put her away as he had others? It was a hard trial for a young heart. And now, in his eyes at least, his perfect rose had a blemish, she had failed him.

Court became quiet as news that the Queen's courses had come whispered through the walls. The King admitted to his court he was sad but fortunately he was so moved by the sorrow the Queen exhibited that he did not become angry with her. He told her he was eager to come back to her bed, and together they would make their child, the one she apparently so longed for.

"I see you have been crying, my sweet wife," he said to her.

"I weep for I know I brought hope to Your Majesty and then took it away," Catherine had said with tears in her eyes. "I wished so earnestly for a child. I knew how it would make Your Majesty happy and content to hold another son in your arms. Perhaps I wished too hard. It is said that when a woman yearns for a child, the body may play tricks upon her weak mind."

It was clever, her little speech, announcing that everything was her fault saved him any shame at not delivering a child into her belly. I doubted she believed anything she said, but it worked.

"You wanted only to please me, my Queen. It is not your fault. Women do not know their bodies well, and you are young." The King had smiled benevolently. "There is time."

But when not with his wife, the King was in a dark mood, and everyone felt it. I knew it for suddenly I had Katherine of Suffolk, the Countess of Rutland and others visiting whenever they could, bringing this dainty for me to try or this book for me to look at, or coming because I *had* to hear the latest news, and I knew what they were doing. They were trying to escape the atmosphere the King excreted all over court. I had never known a person who could affect an entire palace, or city even, with but the changing of his temper, but with the King, all things were possible.

It was not just the news the Queen was not with child that caused consternation in England. There was word of trouble. The conspiracy in the north, thought crushed, was not and became a small uprising, led by Sir John Neville, a fervent Catholic. Men had been found trying to meet under a banner of rebellion at the spring fairs that year, with the intention of denouncing the King's tyranny. It was said the purpose this time was to depose the King and bring back the true faith. Unfortunately for the rebels an informer was amongst them. The uprising was put down, executions occurred, but talk of security was on everyone's lips. People found a way to blame Catherine for this unrest, unbelievably. Had the Queen truly been with child, rather than being mistaken, it would have offered more security to England, it was said.

"There are whispers this may put Margaret Pole in danger again," Katherine of Suffolk told me.

"The Countess is in danger?" I asked. "But she had nothing to do with this uprising, how could she? She is still in the Tower."

"But the King suspects her still. Her son shamed him and is an ally of his enemies, and she is Catholic."

"So is he. That was made obvious this Easter. He might as well suspect himself."

My friend laughed. "He may, one day, when he runs out of others to blame." She became more serious with a sigh. "He likes not how common people talk of the Countess, the sympathy for her. Anger about her imprisonment was alleviated when the Queen sent clothes to her, but no matter what his people say, still he thinks the Countess a traitor. The King believes if she has not acted upon traitorous thoughts yet, soon she will, or her sons will."

"She would be punished for something she has not yet done? For something her family might do?"

I already knew, of course, this was law. Treason needed only to be thought. It was intent that mattered, not deed.

My friend nodded. "She might, if he thinks her a great enough threat."

Chapter Seventeen

Richmond Palace
May 1541

The wind howled outside my window, a lost, lone wolf looking for his pack. Rain splattered the diamond-shaped glass panes. It was dark outside, and the shutters were not yet up, at my insistence. I liked to watch the wildness of the world at times, marvel at storms and the feral power they held. Safe I was inside a room, inside a palace, I was a voyeur upon this outside world of rain and wind and darkness. I sat at the window, looking out into the screaming gloom. My face glowed in the glass like that of a phantom as it stared not at the world outside, but back, into the darkness inside my eyes.

It looked as if another Anne was staring back at me, the one who had eyes as dark as this night, the one who was as strong as this storm. The eyes I had seen in her portrait hidden away at Hever seemed to shine back at me from behind my own eyes. Was she here? A ghost sat just before me that I could not see, but who could see me?

I wondered if she had sat at this window, stared out on a night like this, watched her own eyes and wondered, as I did now, if they were hers indeed. There are times we watch our own reflections and wonder, who are these people we have become? Some have more to wonder on than others, the alteration more complete from who they should have become, to who they did become, from who they once were to what fate and their own choices made them into.

Perhaps I thought on this lost Queen this night for the present Queen was at last due to meet Anne's daughter, and Jane's son, in the morning. Catherine was at Baynard's Castle, her official residence in London. Once it had been mine. Catherine would go on to see her stepchildren when the dawn came. That castle had been Jane's before mine, Anne's before Jane's, Katherine's first of all, and now another Catherine owned it.

I stopped for a moment, wondering if the Queen who now was had been named for the Queen that the King had married first? It was common, a mark of respect, to name daughters of noble houses after the reigning Queen of a country, and when Catherine was born that would have been Katherine of Aragon. Something about the notion made my spine creep. Catherine Howard had been a baby when the King was wed to the woman she was named for, and now that baby was his wife.

Wife... my brother had become formally betrothed then married now too, not to the Emperor's choice nor to a daughter of the King of France but to Jeanne d'Albret of Navarre. Apparently, she had protested the match in the most violent terms but still the betrothal had gone ahead. What choice, in reality, did women have? We were supposed to be able to protest a match to a priest, the Church was supposed to protect us if our families would not, but we rarely were heard, even more rarely were we protected. If powerful men wanted a match to go ahead, it went ahead. The complicity of the Church was easily gained with coin.

Wilhelm spoke not Jeanne's language and she not his, and she was not enamoured of the idea of leaving her country for this common, barbaric land of Cleves, as she had apparently called my homeland. Since my brother had arrived in France, sickly Jeanne had announced at various times that she would rather enter a convent or throw herself down a well or commit suicide than marry the Duke of Cleves. My brother was almost twenty-five, she twelve, and yet it sounded as if she had a stronger will than many a grown man. At the wedding she had stood still and refused to move towards the altar, so her uncle King François ordered that someone pick her up and carry her there.

The consummation was symbolic only. The pair were put to bed in their nightclothes, but that was all. This was agreed because Jeanne was of a delicate constitution, and it was further agreed because of this that she would remain in Navarre for another year.

In truth, the niece of the King of France and daughter of the King of Navarre should have married someone higher than my brother. When the match had first been talked of, I had been betrothed to the King and then had married him. Like as not it was the fact that I had been Queen of England, and Sybylla, another sister of the Duke of Cleves, was Electress of Saxony which had swayed François to even consider such a high match for

Wilhelm. Without his sisters, would he have this bride or alliance? I doubted it. There was news, however, amongst the congratulations floating about Europe, that my now-married brother might not make it home again.

The Colloquy of Regensburg had concluded, with neither my brother nor the Elector of Saxony turning up. The Emperor was most annoyed, so we heard. There had been no resolution over Guelders, and there was now a great possibility my brother would be captured on the way home by the vexed and insulted Emperor. Sadly, Wilhelm did not seem to be taking this threat as seriously as he should, and had sent an insolent, goading letter to the Emperor after Maria of Austria had refused to offer Wilhelm safe conduct through the Low Countries, saying it was not her place to grant such but the Emperor's. Wilhelm's letter stated that as *so* many in his party, more than a *thousand* of his escort in fact, were French and since the Emperor had an agreement of peace and safe passage with their King, he hoped he would not be attacked by the Emperor. He had also mentioned the 800 horse my mother had mustered and sent to him for protection. Wilhelm was boasting of his allies and their strengths. I wondered if the Emperor might read these feeble numbers and laugh at my brother's boasts. What were 1,800 horse to the multitudes of soldiers and mercenaries the Emperor could command? What were my brother's boasts but a pathetic puff of air?

I was not sure why Wilhelm was acting so rashly as to not only insult the Emperor by not turning up for this Diet, but also to taunt him on the way home. Did he think it clever, or had he no experience, perhaps, of the cruelties men were capable of? Immediately after the Diet Charles V had gone to Italy with 7,000 mercenaries, and in retaliation François sent around 10,000 Swiss Guards to Piedmont, sparking rumours that war was imminent.

It would be some time before I was told my brother had made it home safe, and every day when I wondered on him, I felt a strike of terror, like a lance through my chest, at the thought I might lose him.

A movement behind me, shadows shifting in the window glass, stole my eyes. Women were bustling with purpose, ready to prepare me for bed. "I am not ready yet," I called without turning. "I wish to sit a while longer, watch the storm."

They retreated. Of course they wanted to be away to their own rooms, the ones who were not sleeping in my chamber that night. Some had husbands they would want to see, some children nearby and some probably just wanted to be alone, and all of that I could sympathize with, but I was the mistress here and I wanted to watch the storm. That was the way of it. Enough of my life I had spent obeying others, doing things because it would please them, making myself a good girl as everyone told me I should be, making myself small so others appeared greater when standing near me. I had spent all my short marriage trying to please the King, and nothing about me was ever destined to please him so I had set myself an impossible task there. Perhaps that was the final straw to break the proverbial camel's back. Poor camel, such a weight that beast always carried. Trying to please a man who was nothing but displeased with me showed me something; I could not work miracles, and more importantly, failing to please others was not going to kill me.

Of course, it could have, had the end of my marriage played out as the ends of others had. But I had been fortunate.

Eventually I gave the command to prepare my rooms for the night. Shutters would go up, plates would be cleared away, cushions plumped, ready for morning. My women brought hot water, lavender buds floating on the surface, whirling in spirals. I washed, thinking of the Queen and her meeting tomorrow with Lady Elizabeth.

I was glad the clever little daughter of the King was to meet Catherine. They were cousins, and it would be a good thing for Elizabeth to have a new mother. She longed for one, I had seen it in her eyes when I met her. Catherine was also young enough that the two could in truth be sisters, which might bring them closer. The King was in Essex with his son and the Queen was to join them after she had spent time with Elizabeth.

Elizabeth struck me as much alone in the world. Prince Edward had people about him all the time, watching him, caring for him, keeping the one precious son of the King safe. Lady Elizabeth was not exactly neglected, she would never want for food and servants, but she was not important in the eyes of many, although I had heard recently that it was possible she might become so, if the King chose.

At the time the Statute of the Six Articles had been passed in 1539, the King's statement on how religion was to be practised in his lands, another Act had gone quietly through. This one was in relation to marriages annulled during the "time of popery" and said that once a marriage had been consummated, no pre-contract nor degrees of kinship could be brought about to annul it. Marriages during times of popery could be said to include the marriage of the King and Anne Boleyn since the King pushed forth the Act of Supremacy and announced himself Head of the English Church in 1534, a year after they were wed. Henry's marriage to Anne had been annulled not on the basis of the charges of treason set against her, but on the basis that he had had a relationship with her sister, Mary, before he and Anne were married, which by Catholic law made Henry and Anne related. This Act, however, decreed that this had been an invalid reason to annul their marriage. He therefore had the power to recognise that he and Anne had been married until the moment of her death. He had the power to legitimize Elizabeth.

He had, however, thus far not chosen to do so. The King preferred areas of grey about his dealings, it seemed.

Elizabeth was probably unaware of this Act which might redeem her status as a princess, and she, unlike Lady Mary, was a child, a helpless child with few supporters. Her mother had made many enemies and Elizabeth's father had married three times since he had ordered Anne arrested and decapitated. What did this young girl know of the world but loss and pain? And, being as intelligent as she was, could she be unaware her father had brought the greatest loss upon her, not only depriving her of her mother, but of her place in the world? A sad thing it is to lose a mother, but to know your own father was her killer, that is a hard fact to wrap a heart and mind about.

I put my arms up as my women unpinned gorgeous hanging sleeves of velvet. Diamonds sewn into the folds glinted in the guttering candlelight. Amber shadows shifted upon tapestry on my walls, making embroidered men and women seem to scowl or smile as light passed over their faces. Swans and other birds were caught in the candlelight, their wings seeming to move as draughts billowed gently behind the cloth.

I wished the Queen luck as I washed for bed, prayed for her as I retired. She might well need luck and the intervention of God, for she was also to meet again with Lady Mary.

Mary had been to see me not long ago. It was odd, perhaps, that we had become such good friends after such a rocky start, but ships do sail on water so we may at times make a sturdy platform on a wavering substance.

We had begun our peace when I was Queen, but now I was not her stepmother, or perhaps now I was not trying to fill her beloved mother's place, it appeared I was even more welcome as an aunt or sister. I sometimes thought it strange, her deference and respect for me, for we were of an age with one another, but still I was always considered by her to apparently be in a role of maturity above her. When first we had met, I had thought I was a good year older than Mary, she being born the year after me, but my friend Katherine had informed me it was a matter of months which separated us, I was born in the summer of 1515, in June so I actually shared a birthday with my former husband, and Mary in the February of 1516. Our mother's pregnancies must have overlapped a little.

I had told Mary again I thought she should try to get along with the Queen, but I was not sure if she had listened to me. She was subdued, however. Her father was excluding her more and more from his presence the more Mary showed she did not like Catherine, and this lack of favour was not only something to fear, but it made her miserable too. No matter what he did to her, no matter what he had done to her mother, Mary loved her father. It was a desperate, horrible love, one I was not certain at all was returned, but it lived in her sure as sunlight danced upon the earth each day. When he turned his royal cold shoulder to her, she was plunged into misery, and when Mary knew misery she often became sickly, leading her to believe that God disapproved of her troubles with her father.

But at the same time she was enough her mother's daughter to think the King was wrong and needed saving from himself, and so Mary was stuck in this dual world, this twilight of existence where she loved and admired her father yet thought him easily corrupted, where she wanted to save him from his own sins and loathed his choices, where she loved him and desired his love but never found it returned as she wished, even when he seemed to approve of her. In truth, Mary could have been happy had God snapped His fingers and sent us back to a time when her father and mother were married, and she was their sole beloved and precious child. Once she had been that to both of them, but that was long ago. She still wanted it, always, however. It is a hard thing, to be loved once then to have that love fade for no reason, for nothing you did, yet to still have that person in your life. The thought is that they can learn to love you again, but it never works. Love is not something to be learned, it is there, or it is not. For the King that love had died, and Mary was fated to worship ever at the feet of its ghost.

"I think you would like the Queen, if you would allow yourself to," I had told my former stepdaughter, now friend. "She is kind, sweet and although she may be younger than you and perhaps not as clever in some ways, that is no reason to dislike her."

"There are many reasons to dislike her, she supplanted you." Mary straightened her shoulders as if preparing for war.

I kept my tone gentle. "You are well aware she had little choice in the matter. Catherine Howard did not come to court with some grand plan to become Queen, Highness. She came to court to do as other young ladies do, to dance and to serve and hopefully to fall in love with the one she was told to wed. That the King fell for her is nothing her fault." I stared at my friend. "Continue to treat the Queen badly and the King will treat you the same way," I said. "If you would make peace with the Queen you could win a true friend but nothing will you gain by continuing this war against her. It is pointless, the King loves her. End this circle of spite, Mary. Reach out as a Christian to her, as your mother would have wished."

"Chapuys says much the same, although not about kindness for kindness's sake," she said glumly, as if being nice to a person was the worst advice ever she had heard. "He says if I continue to make it obvious I do not approve, the King will cast me out, or arrest me."

"It is possible," I said.

She glanced at me sharply. "But I am his daughter, and he loves me, I know he does."

"He has loved many people who now are no longer here."

She shivered a little, the coldness of my words striking her. "You too think he would harm me, arrest me?"

"I do, if he thought you were against him, and he wants the Queen and wants her in his life. If you oppose his wishes, you are against him. If you are against him, you are his enemy. He kills his enemies. It is that simple."

"I am not his enemy; I only wish to show him the error of his ways!" Mary's pale face flushed.

"The King thinks his ways have no errors. And what do you want him to do? He is married to Catherine, they have been married for a time now. You want him to cast her off? She would be ruined. They are married in the eyes of God, and that is an end to it."

"You were not ruined when he ended your marriage and were he to leave her he could come back to you."

I tried not to roll my eyes in frustration. God was trying to teach me patience with this conversation, I needed to appreciate the lesson. "The King does not want me, he never did, and I am happier as his sister. Cease trying to control that over which you have no control, Highness. The King is deeply unhappy with you, and he will punish you. I do not want that."

Mary's jaw set hard. "I am his daughter; he would not harm me truly."

My voice dropped low. "You should not go about thinking that he will protect you. That you share blood matters not and that he once loved you matters not. The man you knew as a father when you were a child is gone, Mary. Nothing is going to bring him back. The man you are dealing with now is not that happy, sweet man from your memories. It is another man, one who has destroyed people who he loved and who loved him, one who has altered his country and the world to have what he wants, when he wants it. You keep hoping the father of your memories will turn up again, you are relying on it and that is why you keep flaunting his wishes, but it will not happen. Deal with the man who is here, not with the man you *wish* was here."

I paused a moment. "Once you believed he could kill you. I remember people telling me of it, in the year the Queen who replaced your mother died, you thought you would be invited back to court the instant she was gone but you were not. Until you capitulated to your father's will, you were in danger. Some said you would be arrested, taken to the Tower. You believed then your father could do such, or why else did you sign his papers saying you were a bastard and your mother's marriage never was? Why did you agree to your father's title of Head of the Church? You knew he could hurt you, that he would hurt you if you did not surrender, so you did."

"But he did not hurt me then, and he will not now."

"He did not hurt you because you surrendered. It was not love that stopped him, it was your obedience, given at a time most clever. Be clever now. Your life and freedom are his to decide, and if you go against him all that you have, all you think is yours by God given right, will be taken from you." My voice turned less harsh. "I do not think your mother ever wanted you to become a martyr, Mary. I think she wanted more than anything that you should live, that you should have a future. You cannot do that if you are here no more."

She was quiet for a long time after that. I knew not if my words had sunk in but perhaps they did. With Chapuys and me both talking to her, hopefully something had made her consider her position anew.

Chapuys no doubt had an eye on the preservation of her life, and, just as he had tried to aid her mother, he was now trying to keep Mary out of danger, despite her best efforts to become a martyr. In all honesty she could be in a better position now than she had been for years with the King and it was the time to try to be close to him if she wanted power.

When the King had married Catherine Howard, an Act had been put forth which stated that a non-consummated marriage was made void by a second marriage following, which was consummated. My marriage to the King, therefore, being unconsummated, was invalid because his marriage to Catherine, which came after had been consummated. All well and good, and you might think this concerned only me and the King and his new wife, but in truth it meant something significant to Lady Mary and her prospects because it meant that her mother's marriage to Arthur was invalid, and her mother's to the King was valid, as long as the King accepted that Katherine of Spain and Arthur of Wales had not lain together. But technically, this softened the stain of bastardry which lay on Mary's shoulders and meant that, much as with her sister Elizabeth, her father could choose to make her legitimate once again.

But that was the sticking point, he had to choose to do so. He could keep her a bastard too, if he so wanted. There had been talks of late about marrying Lady Mary to the Emperor, but the Emperor would not accept a bride who was a bastard. She could be restored to the succession, or her sons could if her father chose, she could become Empress of the Holy Roman Empire. Much was in her sights.

It was therefore the time to be making friends with her father, but instead Mary was pitting herself against his wife.

Perhaps Mary saw outright defiance as courageous, emulating her mother's stand against the King, but there are times when such a stance is more foolhardiness than courage. What use is it to race into battle, one soldier against many? Mary was not going to win against the King. Her own mother had proved that. This was also, out of all the things she could have stood for or lost her life over, rather a petty fight to take such a stand on.

Chapuys, I was sure, was thinking about the long game, pondering which battles to sacrifice along the way in this war. He had to keep his best soldier alive, see her married safely to a Catholic prince, keep her in line for the throne. That was how he and his master would restore England to the Catholic Church, and it was a plan with merit. No matter the King's decrees, many still considered Mary the true heir. Not only was she older than Edward and was a Catholic, but the Prince had been born when the King had broken from Rome and was an excommunicate, raising doubts about Edward's legitimacy amongst those of the old faith. Not everyone held with that view, but some did, which raised the possibility of civil war in the future, and many might simply support Mary because they knew she would restore England to Rome. It was not only me who had considered the King's death. Many were committing treason daily.

But there would be no future for Mary if her father found an excuse to throw her in the Tower or imprisoned her as he had her mother. Mary was his daughter and his subject, and he could do with her as he wished, which might well include executing her if she was found guilty of treason. Mary might wish to join her mother and become a martyr, but Chapuys wanted nothing of the kind. He saw her defiance for what it was; guilt. After she and her mother had fought so long, stood their ground with firm resolution, Mary felt guilty for agreeing her mother's marriage had never been and accepting her place as a bastard, so Mary's guilt had stuck a mask on its face and come back to her, disguised as defiance. Guilt was trying to trick her, trying to put her in danger so it might be satisfied when she was punished, or hurt, or if the King took her head and sent her to meet her mother.

Chapuys was there to save her from herself. As was I.

Everyone needs friends, particularly ones who see what we are up to better than we do. The ambassador had his own trials but took on Mary's with the patience of a good father. I wondered if she thought of his troubles. His master, the Emperor, had stopped paying the ambassador. I was told it had happened before, and it was not uncommon that kings, richest of all men, left dependants in trouble. That was why they were so rich; they kept others poor. They had plenty of money because they rarely parted with it.

The ambassador was struggling with finances and at court. The King had blamed him for the trade impediments with Mary of Hungary, probably not without cause if court gossip was to be believed, and as a consequence his audiences with my former husband had become strained.

As I climbed into bed with Kitty, my bedfellow that night, and the hangings were pulled about us, I felt my heart sigh with fear and excitement. I wanted Catherine and Mary to get along, I wanted Elizabeth to have a new mother. The duty of a wife and queen is to maintain harmony, so continued disharmony in the royal family was likely to reflect badly on Catherine more than anyone. But these things I wanted so to effect, I could not. This was up to them.

I listened to the wind howl in the darkness, and when I tumbled into sleep, I dreamed of my mother calling to me from far away, pleading with me to come home.

Chapter Eighteen

Richmond Palace
May 1541

"Oh, but I am disturbing your reading."

"Nothing about you could ever disturb any part of me, my friend," I said to the apologetic Katherine of Suffolk, come to see me.

She had indeed interrupted me reading a letter from Sybylla, writing to say the Emperor was ignoring the Schmalkaldic League again, too busy with the threat of the Ottoman Turks to do anything meaningful against the League or other Protestants in Saxony and other lands, other than command they were to hand back lands taken from the Church and Catholics, which no one in the League was going to do. The idea was to oust the Catholic religion from the League's countries, thereby excluding its power from their lands too. Catholicism could not continue to grow in those countries if all its roots had been dug up.

Sybylla also wrote however of less good news, the most sensitive parts in our code, of Moritz of Albertine Saxony who was due to become its Duke. The man had been brought up by her husband, but Johann Friedrich had purposefully neglected Moritz's education in the hope that this man would not pose a threat to his own sons. The two branches of Albertine and Ernestine Saxony each had sprung from the House of Wettin, and Moritz had shared claims to lands with Johann. Often the two branches squabbled over who had the rights to certain taxes in these shared lands, and after having been brought up by Johann, apparently Moritz loathed his former guardian, so his coming of age and ascending to the Albertine ducal throne was no good thing for my sister or her family. He was unlikely to join the League and quite likely to join with the Emperor instead.

My sister had written some of this in our code, as I said, but not all of it. Despite the fact that Olisleger had sent word when he was in Cleves to Saxony that my missives were being opened and read, it seemed Sybylla either had not believed this, or possibly thought that the idea that I should be kept abreast of events in the world was more important than the fact my former husband would read this too. In truth, I had become valuable to the King in this way, members of my family sending such news to me was an open source of information to him, one not requiring him having to pay an ambassador to gather.

"I hear the meetings went well, between the Queen and her new stepchildren," I said to Katherine of Suffolk as we sat down on bright embroidered cushions near the fire. Some of the cushions had honeysuckle and bulls on them, some had pomegranates and castles. Although no one would tell me for certain, I believed they had been decorated by the hands of former Queens.

The present Queen and Elizabeth had apparently got on handsomely and the Queen had given her stepdaughter some necklaces, which it was said the Lady Elizabeth was now wearing every day. Catherine had publicly admitted herself charmed by Elizabeth, which I knew was entirely possible because I too had met the girl. I had never previously found myself speechless before someone younger than me, but Elizabeth was a curious creature. She was not beautiful in a conventional way, but she was fascinating in many ethereal ones. If I could imagine meeting one of the old folk in the forest and being tempted away to their world, it would be a creature like Elizabeth I would imagine meeting. She had some ancient magic in her, I was sure.

From that meeting the Queen had gone on to congregate with her other stepchildren at the Waltham Holy Cross in Essex. I wondered what she had thought of Edward, if he was still as fat and unhealthy looking as when I had seen him. Then had come the meeting with Mary, but from what I heard Mary finally had listened to those who wanted to protect her.

"Lady Mary did well. The Queen complimented her dress – it had one of Lady Mary's unusual high collars which ladies are starting to ape about court," Katherine of Suffolk told me, her hands motioning to indicate a high-throated collar. "They each said the other looked well and complimented each other, asked after their journeys, that kind of thing. It was not conversation to set the world afire, but it was polite and in public, and that is a start." Katherine looked pleased. Although on different sides of the faith in the present, and Mary was not one to be great friends with those who questioned the Catholic Church, she and Katherine had been close when they were younger. On Katherine's side some of that old affection remained still in her heart.

Mary said nothing snide or cruel but kept a steady stream of compliments showering upon the Queen, and Catherine did the same. There was nothing of significance in their conversation, but nothing ill either, that was indeed a start. Bridges burned cannot be mended in a day. They require a little clearing first, before new wood can be set out.

"The King of course now thinks them the best of friends."

I smiled. "Men understand us so little."

"Why should they bother to try?" Katherine laughed. "By law, by convention and Church law we women are the ones who have to make ourselves pleasing to men, not the other way around. They do not have to make any effort with us, that is why when we find one who makes the slightest effort we think him marvellous. If he were a woman, we would see he was underachieving."

I laughed a little but wondered at the vinegar souring her tone. Were she and Charles not getting along again? Perhaps they never had and hers had seemed the perfect marriage because she was so very good at pretending it was.

The visit between Queen and stepdaughter had ended with Mary being invited to court, so ended well. Mary was delighted, and the Queen reportedly was not unhappy.

"I was pleased the Queen asked to see Prince Edward," Mary said to me when she came to Richmond not long after. "The King is so busy he has little time to see his son, and my brother yearns for his father. It was nice for him to have the Queen there, interested in him."

From the look on Mary's face, she yearned for her father too, but as I had thought before, not the one that was present. Perhaps in trying to bring the King and his son together more often she was trying to resurrect her father of the past, trying to find the lost place where his heart was buried.

So many of us try to avoid the past, Mary was trying to breathe life into its long-dead corpse.

"The Queen is a good woman," I said. "I am sure she will do your brother good."

"She got on well with Elizabeth too," said Mary.

"So I heard, but then, your little sister could charm a man who was blind, deaf and dumb."

Mary chuckled, "She could, it is true."

Sometimes I marvelled that Mary loved her sister so. I would always have supposed she would have hated her, had I not heard her speak of Elizabeth. Perhaps that came later, people said it did, but for my part I think there was always something in Mary that loved her sister. Mary's love and expression of love was often confused, I could not blame her, after her childhood. The way she had been taught to fashion love had become mixed and bemused, but always there was a part of her twisted heart that loved Elizabeth. Always there was something in Mary's soul shining for that little girl.

Chapter Nineteen

Richmond Palace
May 1541

"All court is praising how the Queen has brought about Lady Mary's full and merry restoration to her father's love," Olisleger told me.

Pleased though I was, I was not sure it was a full restoration. It might be temporary, but the moment she did something the King did not like, Mary would be in danger again.

Of course, I did not say that. "I am glad for the Queen, but Lady Mary too deserves praise, she did her part in this public peace."

The King had been delighted with the new concord between his wife and daughter and had buoyantly granted Mary permission to reside at court permanently, as long as Catherine agreed, which she had. People were saying this was the most important step in the relationship between father and daughter since Mary had submitted to her father's wishes over the annulment of her parents' marriage, and this most important step had been brought about by the King's wife.

Queen Jane had greeted Mary at court when Mary had submitted but had done nothing to bring about a *true* reconciliation between father and daughter. This time Catherine was being granted the credit of their reconciliation. She was, it was said, an even greater influence for good than Queen Jane, most clement and supportive of all the King's wives.

"It is as I always said," I mentioned to Harst a day later, a smug little smile on my lips. Who does not like to be right, after all? I was no saint, and I thought I was due a little smugness. "The Queen, when given a chance, surprises everyone."

"I admit I am surprised," he said as he smoothed his doublet, a shimmering black. "Though I have noted good qualities in her I thought her not mature enough to bring about something like this."

"Indeed, and look how she shines when her natural self comes out. She could have done as other Queens did and been spiteful, banished Lady Mary from court for good or ordered the reduction of her household, she could have thrust Mary into humiliating positions serving Elizabeth, or asked the King to confiscate her plate, jewels and books. But no, Catherine approached this with kindness, and look how pretty an outcome it has."

I understood from those who had witnessed their encounters that the two women were still being extremely careful about their budding friendship, sticking firmly to subjects on which there could be no possible friction. They complimented clothes, talked of the weather, that kind of thing, but it was the peace they had forged which was important. The two had been on a course for a clash and it was clear Catherine would have been the one to win, but at what cost to her or Mary? Cause trouble in the house of the King, even if not by her own fault, and the King might look on Catherine with eyes less loving than before, and what then? A slip here, a slip there, and soon enough she could find herself buried in a rockslide of loathing.

But then, as always when something went well, something went wrong. Out of nowhere, as far as I could tell, there came rumours.

"There is talk, Highness, that the King will set the Queen aside and take you as his wife again," Harst said, looking quite pleased with himself as if he had brought it about.

I threw my hands into the air. "What is wrong with the people of England? Whatever they have they do not want. When I was Queen no one wanted me there and now I am not my restoration is all they desire! I hope the King has put these rumours to bed?"

"The King knows not where they came from, but the Queen was most upset by them."

I exhaled through gritted teeth. "Indeed. I find it most irritating, my lord, that I go out of my way to make it plain to the world I am the Queen's friend and yet people try to set us against one another, using me to harm her! Do they think now she is friends with Lady Mary the Queen is in need of another enemy in the royal family, so they have chosen me to be that enemy?"

"The King said to her, 'If I had to marry again, I would not take the Lady Anne to wife'. This seemed to calm the Queen, although she was still low for a long time afterwards."

I shrugged. "Of course she was."

Harst looked puzzled. "I do not understand, Highness. Why should that not have comforted her?"

I shook my head at the blindness men seemed affected by at times. Why could they not see? "The King did not say he would never marry another, or she was the only one he loved, he said, 'if I *had* to marry again'. That would not reassure any woman, Harst. If he had to, he would marry again, that means at some point he has thought about a time without Catherine and assumed he would be fine. What might have happened to her in this scenario, however, is anyone's guess."

Chapter Twenty

Richmond Palace
May 1541

"It was said once of me too, and was not true," I said.

"When was such a wicked slander said of you, Highness?" Harst sounded both baffled and outraged, a curious combination. He looked like a shocked ape from the menagerie at the Tower.

I turned to him from my place at the window. "On the morning after my wedding night, do you not remember? The King felt my breasts and body then trotted off into court and implied to his men that I was not a virgin. That is as good as calling a woman a whore, it is not? And much as it was untrue of me, so I am sure it is untrue of the Queen."

Ugly rumours had come running to court from London, and not just ones saying that the King was to switch wives yet again. It was being said Catherine was a whore.

Such things are often said of women in power. The easiest way to discredit women in all ways is to hit them in the reputation. The moment a woman was thought loose of morals it meant, apparently, she was unworthy in other ways, her mind weak, will feeble, her word not to be believed. Accuse a woman of being a whore and any further accusation would stick too, and if proof was needed of this we just had to look to another Queen Anne. When she had been tried it had not been adultery which sent her to the executioner's block but treason, yet adultery was the charge everyone remembered. Adultery was not punishable by death when she was married to the King, but the *charge* of adultery levelled at her allowed the more serious one of treason to be readily believed. If a woman could betray her husband in bed, obviously she must have been also planning his death.

I found it particularly curious, for men could sleep with a million and one women and never have this accusation of all-encompassing immorality levelled at them. Why was their morality so different to ours? Why would they not be similarly afflicted when they bedded many partners? God had not told but one of the sexes to be chaste or to save themselves for marriage and the other not, and how was one sex to be chaste at all if the other was not? Some females had to be bedding all these men, unless they were bedding each other, and that meant these *men* were rendering the women immoral, did it not? And just why did men look down so on women who had had many partners, was it because they loathed a woman who would give herself to them? Did men hate themselves so greatly that they considered women who bedded them to be nothing *because* they had bedded them? Contradictions were many.

But this slander was being put about regarding Catherine at this point in time because she had been doing well. That was the truth of it. One of her enemies, probably on the Protestant side of the faith as she, however unwillingly, represented the Catholic, was setting this rumour about, I was sure. She had done well lately, had been getting on with her stepchildren, had been shown favour by the King, so someone had come to try to knock her down at least a little, or if it could be managed, a lot.

I often wondered about this kind of mentality, for it was not only court politics or faith that made people attack others, as desperate dogs in the baiting pit bare fangs, no. It was an urge born of jealousy, that if someone has what you do not, they should be punished for it. The odd thing is, perhaps you would not want that thing you think you so desire if it actually became yours. Few understood in truth the precariousness of the position of Queen, especially to this King. Even those who had watched one fall after another all these years could not quite grasp what it was to sit in that position and feel the world tremble under you. There was nothing quite like it, a deep-rooted, raw terror of being in a trap, waiting for something to claw its way through the bars and devour you, so those who envied Catherine's power, as they saw it, her riches or her influence did not see the troubles which came with her position, the frail, sharp line she walked of favour, the constant peril she was in, trying to appease a highly dangerous and changeable man. Had they been a day in her shoes, they would have taken those shoes off and thrown them as far from them as they could, and yet, for jealousy of her position, they spread rumours to try to punish her.

Human beings are capable of such greatness of spirit at times, such lowness of spite at others.

And the trouble was for me, yet again I was being used by these gossip mongers, these peddlers of hate, against the Queen.

The truth was, I was an easy story of woe to sell. I had become to some a tragic, romantic figure. More people than just Mary saw me as the second Katherine of Aragon, and therefore Catherine Howard became the successor to Anne Boleyn, especially to those looking for a reason to dislike her. These people did not see, or perhaps chose not to note, the stories of gay abandon and happiness, of endless card games and dancing into the night which went on at my house of Richmond. Instead, they told a tale of how I had been cast off and was humiliated.

I had in truth been more humiliated when I was married to the King. The King had seen to that.

But no matter, I was a character in a tale, not a real person to those who would spread such tales. I was good and saintly, therefore Catherine had to be wicked. Women were one or the other, we never could be anything balanced, anything in between, anything human.

In London it was being said the new Queen was of poor character, was a harlot, a whore. They had said the same of Anne Boleyn, of course, before and after she married the King. Anne was not alone, even Jane Seymour's reputation had been questioned for it had been said she was the King's mistress before she was his wife. I had been called a whore by the King himself and even saintly Katherine of Aragon had not escaped with her reputation unscathed, for the question as to whether she had had sex with Arthur and lied about it had dominated seven years of argument about the validity of the King's first marriage. Many after had named Katherine the King's jade, claiming she had known their marriage was invalid and lain with him in any case.

Fortunately, at court the Queen's reputation was immaculate. The mistakes of her first few months as Queen had been forgotten, and she was now spoken of with respect by many. Catherine had done the King good, it was said, and was performing as a natural woman should by bringing the torn royal family into harmony. Lady Mary was her friend, and she was kind to Lady Elizabeth. It was said Prince Edward loved his new stepmother and had laughed much in her company. Catherine had spoken for Wyatt and Wallop, and demonstrated she was above politics and religious squabbles. The King adored Catherine. She was doing all she should, and not interfering where she had no business. Not since Queen Jane had a queen done so well.

People did speak of how she loved fine clothes and jewels, and she did, but I did not see this made her so different from the queens who had come before her. I had been told, in fact, that in comparison to Anne Boleyn, who was not mentioned by name of course in my enquiries, Catherine's accounts contrasted most favourably.

The truth was people who wanted to would find something to fault in Catherine, and I think she came to understand that too, for soon I heard she was not morose, worried about what was being said of her, but had thrown herself into a round of gaiety. There was dancing in her chambers and music each day.

"Why should she not celebrate?" I asked Harst who had come with disproving words about the constant festival in the chambers of the Queen. "If she mopes about, morose and lost, people will say the rumours are true. If she goes to church more frequently, they will call her a hypocrite. If she is to be censured one way or another, why not be censured for being gay and merry? At least she is happy, even if her enemies are not." I tapped his arm with my finger. "And remember, friend, I have as many gatherings here, if not more."

"Well, perhaps, Highness, but..."

"There is no but. Either it is fine for a woman to throw entertainments or it is not. Which is it, Harst?"

"It is fine, Highness, of course," he said, surrendering since he knew to continue would get him into trouble.

"Wise man," I approved, and chuckled at his deflated expression.

Chapter Twenty-One

Richmond Palace
May 1541

"The Queen and me becoming friends has pleased my father, so he has called on me in my chambers many times." Mary's cheeks flushed a little, a spark of joy in her eyes. She looked pretty and content. It pained me in truth. Her happiness was so dependent on others, like her father, and so she would ever be let down for we cannot rely on anyone else to bring us happiness, and especially not a man as inconstant as her father. This happiness would fall from her, and she would be hurt again. *But she is happy now, Anna,* a voice reminded me. *The future will bring what it will bring, the past is done and all we ever have is the present.* That was true, so I stuck a smile on my face and tried to make merry with my friend.

"I was wrong about the Queen," Mary went on, almost gushing, which was a rare thing for her to do. "Though I still consider there could be a better Queen called to the throne, I think there is not a better companion for my father. Her lightness of spirit complements his sometimes darknesses of mood. She makes him bright of soul when he has spent time with her, and he takes more exercise in her company."

"If she is his ideal wife, then she is a good Queen," I mentioned.

"I only mean, I think it a good thing for a queen to be highly educated and Catherine is not, but she is not foolish as I once thought, and although I still think her young and untrained in the ways of royalty, she is learning fast. If a queen is educated, she can advise the King. Catherine cannot do this, but perhaps I underestimated the other ways in which she aids him."

The King would not listen to a wife trying to advise him these days, I thought. *Perhaps before, with the first Katherine, with the first Anne, but no more.*

"We are none of us perfect," I said with a smile. "When I start to think on the ill traits of a person, I remind myself that I have ill traits too. I do not mean that we should simply forgive every action a person takes without consideration – such as should we remain friends or confidants with them if they have, for instance, demonstrated they cannot be trusted? Probably not – but when my mind tries to draw me into the easy path of standing as judge over another, I try to recall that I too am imperfect, that I struggle to do well each day and that God made each of us thus, so there must be a purpose to our imperfections."

Mary narrowed her eyes. She had a curious gaze, for she was short of sight, and it made her eyes look penetrative when she concentrated. It was as if she could see into your soul. "What do you think that purpose is?"

I shrugged. "Perhaps it is as simple as character is built through experience and often through overcoming difficulty. If some difficulty is within us, it is harder to see, harder to overcome than the challenges which lie outside us. Perhaps it is a challenge from God; that if we can deal with these things within us, these challenges, and even if we do not learn to overcome them totally but only become aware of our failings and seek ways to contain and master them, we can be said to be greater of soul and more worthy of the love of Christ. Perhaps also, in love for us, God gave us imperfections so we might all, if this we understand about ourselves, come to know compassion all the more for our fellow man. Perhaps our imperfections are there to allow our hearts to expand, to love more deeply, to cherish more sweetly, because if we see our own failings and those of others, we know we are the same creatures at heart."

Mary was staring at me. "Where do you find such wisdom as this?"

"It was not from a book, if that is what you mean. I am not Norfolk, prone to pluck out the ideas of others and present them as my own, not on purpose in any case."

Mary chuckled. "I did not think that was what you were doing, I just wonder. Sometimes, Anna, when you talk it is as though you have lived a thousand lives."

"Some mornings, when I have played late at cards and drunk deep of the barrel, I feel like I have," I laughed. "Now, tell me more, your father and you are at peace, and you and your stepmother are becoming friends, all this is true?"

"Yes, I believe so. We still talk of nothing we could possibly argue about, the Queen and I, but I find I start to look forward to her visits now. I dreaded them at first for I made friends with her when I still did not like her, but I think she has found her way to my heart. She is quite sweet, in a simple, innocent way."

Mary was reserved about her heart, for reasons I could understand, of course. She did not expand her circle of friends often, so this admission, however hesitant, was significant.

She went on. "The Queen is steadfastly ignoring the recent slanders – which I am sure you have no doubt heard – about her, which I told her I approve of. I am not so sure about her continual dancing and merriment in her chambers, but after having been to one or two entertainments, I can tell you they are not as wild as the gossip makes out."

"And the King is there too."

"Yes, and actually I think the long nights have been good for him. He stays up with the Queen gambling and dancing and feasting and as a result he has been sleeping well and deep afterwards. In the morning, he is found oft in a merry mood which has brought about civil Council meetings and happy, settled courtiers. Seeing the Queen is, indeed, a good influence, people at court are warming to her. She said, Highness, that she was following your advice when I asked her about it."

"Oh?"

"The Queen said you were one of the wisest people ever she had met, and you had told her to do what was best for her, and in doing good for herself she would do it for others too."

I smiled. "She is good at the role she has taken on. In truth the Queen does not need to understand politics or foreign affairs in order to be a good Queen. She has to be peaceful, happy, merciful and bring about harmony, and she *is* bringing about harmony between you and your father as well as his other children. If she is not negotiating trade deals or fiddling with the faith, she is bringing merriment and peace to court. She does well."

Mary nodded slowly, her fingers playing with a cross of gold inlaid with pearl and emerald at her throat. "She seems to have more confidence. The Queen has started to attempt things she has not dared before. She listens now to petitions from courtiers and tries to take an interest in her estates. She orders jewellery for herself and has designed a partlet... that is an item of clothing worn over the top of the breasts."

"I know the word, my friend."

Mary inclined her head. "I should not doubt your English, you speak better than many raised or born here now. Well, the Queen's partlet carries sixteen diamonds set into a cipher of *H&C*, for the King and her, which has pleased the King greatly for all other items she owns with ciphers he has ordered for her, you see, but this one she made. She makes small bags which she carries too, little pouches of velvet drawn closed with golden cord, with buttons of diamond and hinges of wire gold. Other ladies are copying her, so they have become quite the rage at court. She has embroidered cushions and blankets and is starting to make her private quarters and gowns her own. They carry her mark, now."

Mary's eyes and mine strayed to a cushion bearing a pomegranate. I was sure she too suspected these things, carrying the badges of her own mother, had once graced Queen Katherine's apartments. We were surrounded by ghosts, always.

Mary rushed on to tell me that other places, too, carried the Queen's mark. Catherine's heraldic beasts were upon the palaces now, and some modelled in wood sat upon striped posts in the gardens. Catherine had even been honoured by being set into glass. At the King's College Chapel of Cambridge, a portrait of her had been used as the image of the Queen of Sheba in a stained-glass window.

"The King thought it fitting," said Mary. "The face of Solomon was based on my father's likeness, so it was thought apt the Queen be Sheba's Queen."

There was another window in the same chapel where their initials stood proud amongst emblems of the Tudor line. "To demonstrate my father's authority as Head of the Church," Mary said in a flat, hollow tone.

In truth, the window had been designed long before Catherine became Queen. It had been commissioned before she was even born. The King's man, Flower, had been granted the task of making eighteen windows and died when only four were done, delaying the project as another artist was found. The east window, where the Queen's likeness now stood, was one of the last to be completed, and although another Queen could just as easily have taken her place, the design had been modified when Catherine became the King's wife. These were little things, but carefully and quietly Catherine was entering the heart of England.

"My father has been distracted, for one of his men has been ill," Mary mentioned as Kitty set a plate of sliced marmalade and wafers at her side. The marmalade was from Spain, and I thought might remind her of her mother.

"Which one?"

"Culpepper. It has been a hard year for him. His mother and father passed to heaven within eight months of each other. He has seemed more morose this year, and no wonder for it is hard to lose one parent. I cannot imagine losing two."

Oh, but you can, can you not? my mind asked. *You lost your mother in truth and now you feel you have lost the man your father once was.*

"The lad has had many gifts of land and money from my father," mentioned Mary. "He will not inherit much from his father, I am told, but the King has helped. And Father freed Culpepper's man, Brice, when the man was caught brawling recently. The Queen has sent some food to Culpepper too, things known to be good for healing. The King asked her to make sure she was enquiring after the lad when he could not, when business of state called him away, so she has undertaken this duty of care too, and does well at it."

I wondered if I was the only one who understood how things were between the hearts of Culpepper and Catherine.

"She is not alone in her thoughts, you know," Mary said.

I felt I had missed something of the conversation. "Who is not?" I asked, wondering for a moment if Mary had read my mind and saw what I had thought of Culpepper and Catherine.

"The Queen, when she said she considered you the wisest woman she knew, she was not alone."

I smiled. "I do not think I am wise."

"Then you are alone in that, for the Queen is not the only one who thinks thus of you, I do. She said you had given her advice to follow which made her life better, and I will say the same. Thank you, my friend. You told me much I had no wish to hear, but I needed to hear it."

I blushed a little. "I am glad I helped, and often, Highness, the things we least wish to hear are the things most valuable, are they not? The things we fear to learn, the truths we are loath to face, they are the things we need to look square in the eye, for if we do not, they will sneak about our backs and stab us in the heart."

Chapter Twenty-Two

Richmond Palace
May 1541

Early one morning, guards went to the Countess of Salisbury in the Tower of London and informed her she was to die in a few hours' time.

Condemned by Act of Attainder during the time of the White Rose Affair which occurred some years before, Margaret Pole had always known that the King had the power to decide she was to die at any moment. For some reason he had decided the hour had come.

Yet all the same the Countess demanded to know the reason she was to die now, after all this time, and so suddenly. She asked what crime it was that she had committed. No one had an answer for her, but I knew.

Uprisings in the north, small though they were, had fed the wyrm of suspicion which crawled inside the heart of the King. The Countess would die to satisfy his lust for revenge upon her son, who he could not touch, and to lessen his fear of rebellion. He would strike at a ringleader of rebellion, before they became a leader, murder their intention before it became reality.

He would think it a lesson for his people too, what would happen if they betrayed him. To me it was a lesson indeed, in the evils the King was now capable of.

Margaret was trooped from her rooms early that morning to a green near the Tower called East Smithfield. She was not granted a private death within the confines of the Tower, something her royal blood should have dictated was hers by rights. Margaret would die outside, like a person of low consequence, under the eyes of the world. Anne Boleyn had died in private, within the Tower, for she had been a Queen, but for this Countess who could have been a Queen there was no such respect shown. This was not the last of the indignities she was to suffer. Death rarely has dignity in truth, but this was a rare death which came for the Countess, one intended to insult her, her sons and her house.

There was not even a scaffold, only a block set upon the damp grass, glistening with dew. Perhaps thankfully there were few witnesses, for the usual crowds that would have gathered had not learned she was to die. Only one hundred and fifty people were there.

A stupefied Margaret fell to her knees on the grass, prayed for her soul, for the Queen, and for all of the royal family aside from Lady Elizabeth, who she had never seen as legitimate. Her prayers for Lady Mary were the most fervent. Margaret had loved Katherine of Aragon as a sister. Guards rushed her through her final prayers and ordered her to place her head on the block.

Some said afterwards the old lady refused, declaring loudly she would do no such thing, for she was no traitor. Others claimed this was a fabrication, and that, confused as she was, Margaret bowed her grey head, praying for God to accept her soul. She was sixty-seven years old and might well have expected to die in her bed, not like this.

The boy chosen to kill her was inexperienced. The usual headsman was in the north, executing rebels there. When the first blow fell, it was clear death would not be clean, for his first clumsy strike cleaved into her back. He pulled it out and tried again, and again, as the Countess gasped, gurgled and screamed her way to death, blows raining on her back, shoulders and head, missing the neck time after time.

The Countess was hacked to death. Her end was bloody, long and agonising.

When finally dead, she was loaded on a cart, taken to the chapel of St Peter-ad-Vincula and there her brutalized body was interred. She was the niece of kings, daughter of a duke, wife of a knight, Countess of Salisbury in her own right, friend to a Queen and once one of the richest and most pious people in England. Some said her blood was more royal than that of the King. Some said that was why she died.

Within hours, the tale that the Countess had proclaimed before death that she was no traitor was everywhere, all of London talking of it. The story of her death became more gruesome with each retelling. Before the day was out, I heard of men chasing her, chopping at her with swords and axes as she screamed her innocence to all who would hear her.

"It would have been better for the King had he invited the whole of London to witness Margaret's end, for the stories grow wild," I said to Harst, who had come to inform me of her death only to find I already knew. "Gossips in the kitchens here are telling tales that butchers' boys have told them whilst delivering meat that she ran from the headsman, and he chopped her to bits whilst in flight. People are claiming she was not dead when her body was pulled from the block and that the pious old lady has been buried alive."

Harst dabbed his forehead with a cloth, red and sweaty after dashing to Richmond. "I know, Highness. I have heard them too. Some whisper the death is all a lie, and the Countess is alive, has escaped the Tower through one of the privy shoots, and is on her way to bring her son the Cardinal to England so he can seize the throne."

"Take some wine, or ale, to refresh you, friend." I indicted to my women to bring the ambassador a cup. "You look set to faint on your feet."

"I knew you would want to know of the Countess, Highness, so I hurried."

"You could not get ahead of the wind and the water of the Thames, Harst, and for the speed at which this tale is being told I have come to think river and sky have grown lips and tongues this day to whisper with."

As it became accepted the Countess was dead, a hostile air settled upon London, bitter as a winter ice-storm. Resentment and wrath hung heavy, a lingering foulness on the wind. No one supported what the King had done. The Countess had been conservative of faith and politics, but even reformers had respected her. There was no evidence she had been part of the White Rose Affair, and no evidence she had been embroiled with the late rebellion in the north. She was an old lady, one who had done much good in her lifetime in terms of alms, charity, friendship, loyalty and prayer. All knew her death was intended as a strike at her son, Reginald, and all knew the King feared the royal blood pulsing in the veins of the Poles. That was the reason she had died. Or perhaps there had been too long a gap between the executions of nobles. The King did not like it when his subjects became complacent. He preferred them on edge, uneasy.

And now they were decidedly not easy, for not a single soul was merry with what he had done.

All the King's recent attempts to rebuild his image in Europe as a paragon of princely virtue and munificence flew apart at the seams in the wake of the Countess's death. There was an explosion of outrage. Her execution and the manner of its doing was condemned by all, in every country as a grievous crime, and the King was defamed as a vicious tyrant. People in France compared him to Herod, and in Italy he was named Nero. Talk of the deaths of Cromwell, Anne Boleyn and her brother, as well as Sir Thomas More and Fisher, rose anew. Even those who had thought the Boleyn Queen a witch and a whore now used her death, along with others, as examples of how wretched a beast the King was. The royal houses were aghast. He had killed one of their own, you see, one with royal blood and he had possessed no evidence, truly, that she had been a traitor.

Four days after the Countess died, the court left Greenwich for Westminster. The spikes on London Bridge, usually bearing heads of traitors, had been cleared of skulls. Many said the King was making space and more deaths would come. Fear was rife in particular about Edward Courtenay, the King's young prisoner who was no more allowed to take fresh air in the confines of the Tower. He was little more than a child. Some said he would be publicly executed, others muttered he would die quietly, smothered in his bed like the brothers of Elizabeth of York.

The mood at court was savage, unhinged. I heard two guards were arrested for robbery and hanged the following day. The very next morning, Sir Edmund Knyvet found himself surrounded by the King's officers, ready to cut his hand off for brawling within the confines of court. The charge was not untrue, for he had punched Thomas Clere, a young poet in Surrey's household, but such crimes were common and had been swept aside before by the King. My former husband had pardoned and released a servant of Culpepper's not long ago, held on the same charge.

But now the King was angry. Wounded by rising talk of his evil, barbaric nature, he wanted to lash out. He did not see that to act without mercy would only prove all his critics right. He was becoming what they accused him of being. What a dangerous state self-pity is, self-destructive as well as destructive to others.

"I will stay here, and keep as far from court as possible," I said to Katherine of Suffolk.

"I am considering a trip to my estates," she admitted. "It has been long since I saw my children but at the same time, they are an excuse, I admit. This is not the moment to be at court. No one is safe."

"What happened to Knyvet?"

"Well, Surrey went straight to the Queen, his cousin, begging for her aid. The charge was minor in truth, but the King's surgeon had been ordered to cut his hand off."

"Over a fight?"

"It was hardly even that. It was a hasty spat over a game of tennis. Knyvet did not intend to hit Clerĕ as hard as he did. But this 'bloodshed' they accused him of causing was a nosebleed! Clere did not even want this punishment done, and Knyvet is a cousin to Surrey and the Queen, so it was a disgrace in many ways."

"Did the Queen intervene?"

Katherine nodded. "It was wily, the way she managed the King, masterful, I thought. She managed to persuade him to wait until after his dinner to pass sentence, saying it would upset his digestion to have to deal with something so grisly before eating."

"Wily indeed," I said. "He is always in a better mood after he has eaten. She did that before, did she not?"

"Ah, but wait, my friend, it ends not there. She waited until he had eaten much, then called for more food, and presented many dishes which are his favourites. She had ordered the kitchens to make them after Surrey went to her, so it was planned, you see?"

"As a battle might be."

"Indeed. Then, when the King was slowing in his eating, becoming sated, the Queen announced it was a shame that young men, like Knyvet, could not take such anger and strength as they possessed to war, as is natural for men, and unleash it there. She said men like the King did not lose their temper over simple matters such as tennis for they had been tested in battle so knew how to control their own anger and power, and it was a foolish thing Knyvet had done in case the King needed men who were eager to fight in war, or if rebellion came. The King agreed with her. 'It is true, young men today do not know how to master themselves,' he announced, to which the Queen said she agreed and added that Knyvet seemed to understand this for she had heard he was asking that the King's officers strike off his left hand so he could still be of use to the King and wield a sword in his master's service with his right. The King was most interested in that, for it sounded like a true Englishman, one of courage and loyalty, was Knyvet."

I smiled. "What else said the Queen?"

"That Knyvet regretted the punch he threw at Clere, although she added that Clere had by all accounts forgiven him and admitted he himself was somewhat to blame. She said it was a shame a young man had lost his head for but a moment and now would be punished. The King grew a little angry and demanded to know if she thought Knyvet should be pardoned, to which the Queen said she did not think to even have an opinion for *she* knew not how to control men as the King did, but that she simply thought it a shame that a man *so* obviously dedicated to the King, *so* keen to fight for his sovereign, should lose a hand over a moment of heat. She said no more, but later the King pardoned Knyvet and he kept both hands. It was proclaimed about court that if anyone else offended they would be shown no mercy, but the Queen won, my friend."

I smiled and put my head to the side.

"You are going to say I told you so, are you not? About the Queen's adroit ways?" Katherine asked with a grin.

"I have no need, friend, for you said it for me." I laughed.

Chapter Twenty-Three

Richmond Palace
June 1541

Mercy had won out for one man of court, and at the same time another was not so fortunate. Lord Dacre was arrested not long after the Knyvet affair, charged with killing a man by accident, although when details of the event were relayed to me it did not sound much like an accident.

Dacre and his men had been poaching and had been spotted doing so by two local men. Worried about this discovery, Dacre's gang had set upon the locals, eight against two, and one of the men they attacked died as a result. Evidently the one who survived told the tale to a magistrate, as Dacre was arrested and at his trial pleaded he had not meant to harm the young men. Few believed him. It probably would have been much to his advantage had both died. Dacre evidently understood no one believed him so changed his plea and declared he was guilty, throwing himself on the mercy of the King. Despite his obvious guilt it was expected he would escape with but small punishment. Nobles often did when they abused common people.

Yet Dacre was sentenced to death. People thought he might be pardoned later, the King would give him a little scare perhaps and then he would be released, but a day later one of his kinsmen and six of Dacre's companions hanged. The next day Dacre was dragged through the streets of London to a gibbet in an intended act of degradation before death. Usually, noble prisoners died clean, with dignity, by axe or sword. Yet in this case, rather like that of the Countess, everything was done to ensure Dacre had no dignity. At the last minute a messenger came telling them to delay the execution until after dinner. Everyone, including Dacre, thought he would be pardoned... until three of the clock, when he swung.

Dacre's estates were confiscated, and his title was forfeit to the Crown. His goods were rich and plentiful, and people said this was why he had died. Some whispered there was another, more personal reason, although what that was I never did find out. Perhaps the King had some private quarrel with him? That same week Leonard Grey, former Lord Deputy of

Ireland, was condemned to death for treason. He was beheaded three days later.

People looked at the parboiled heads gathering on the spikes of London Bridge and knew they had thought right to suspect the King had cleared the old to make way for new.

*

As summer washed upon England, bright light shining on the new heads atop London Bridge, all talk was of the progress the King and his court were to make. Everyone talked of that, resolutely of that, trying not to dwell on the fresh round of executions which had begun.

"There is talk the Queen will be crowned in York, on progress, when the King of Scots comes to meet with the King," Katherine of Suffolk told me.

Progress was to take the court north that year, ending in York, where it was rumoured the King of Scots would meet that of England for a summit meeting. The King, it was said, wanted to make his own League, like that of Schmalkaldic, for mutual defence. Scotland, as England's neighbour, would be a most useful admission to such a league, although not a likely one. For all the blood the two men had in common they shared little fellowship.

"Has the King said he might honour Catherine this way? The north too would be honoured, would it not? Has a Queen ever been crowned there?"

Katherine played with a pearl come a little loose on her gown. "Never, as far as I know."

"It would be a sign of his belief in the Queen, and of reconciliation with his northern subjects after the Pilgrimage of Grace."

Katherine nodded slowly, leaving her pearl alone. "The King has spoken of it. But I know not how serious he is about it. He certainly wants to make a show before the King of Scots, a display of power and might. You say it would be an honour for the north, but this act could be taken another way, that the King wants to stamp his authority upon the often-rebellious north, and upon his nephew of Scots. The Queen is doing well, mistake me not, but talk of a coronation in York is sadly not a sign of favour to her or the north, it would be a sign to the King's people and his enemies of his domination. The north tried to reject him as King, to his mind at least, for that was never what the leaders of the Pilgrimage of Grace proclaimed, but the King sees it still as a rejection. Any rebellion he sees thus."

"So, they tried to reject him, therefore crowning his Queen in York could be taken by the people there as him forcing his rule and power upon them anew," I said, nodding, talking slowly as my tongue grasped all my mind was pouring out into my mouth. "It is good you are here to explain these things to me, my friend. I fear I will never grasp hold of all there is to know of your country."

"It is your country too, now," Katherine said, putting her hand on mine. "You may not have been born here, but England has adopted you, as it did my mother. I am half not of this land, yet I consider it mine. And England is in your blood through your ancestry. You are related to Edward I, are you not? You are therefore not being introduced to this country, you are but *remembering* tales and politics of your lineage," she smiled with an affectionate twinkle in her eye. "Besides, I never saw one so diligent about learning all she can of a country. I think you put Katherine of Aragon to shame and though she, like you, never shed her accent entirely, she tried with all she had to learn much of England and Wales. I swear by God's eyebrows you already know more than she did."

I smiled. I had been trying to learn, indeed. Whilst I did not consider myself poorly educated, it was true that in comparison to many highborn women of England I was lacking in some areas. I had therefore set myself a task to compensate for the deficiencies of my youthful education. Histories of the country, kings, queens, battles, wars, had been sent to me at my request and although I struggled still with reading English – my speech being far better than my ability to read in this non-native tongue – I was trying. When I struggled too much, I had one of my ladies read the histories aloud to me.

"If we want to interpret the present, we must understand the past," I said to my friend.

Katherine laughed a little. "The trouble is, even with books of history you never can learn all there is of the past."

"What do you mean?" I was worried then, thinking the education I was giving myself was inadequate.

"Books of history, they are all written by men, and not one of those men was ever impartial," Katherine explained. "They all came from somewhere, therefore hated men from somewhere else. They all grew up in different ways, often resenting those who grew up in better style, and looking down on those who grew up poorer. Some of them may have been devoted to their people, some to the King, but every one of them carried his own opinions and the books of history are flush with those opinions, so a king here may be thought commanding and decisive, where others might be called tyrant for doing the same things. A Queen might be named improper by some and free thinking by others. We are always looking at one person's interpretation of the facts when we read history, and it is always the victors who have the opportunity to write the books we remember. Those who fell and those who failed, they have very different tales to tell."

"You think, then, there is no value in learning what I learn?" I felt dismayed.

"Oh, there is great value in it," she said. "The facts are there, many of them spelled out, but it is important not to abandon one's own critical self. Never believe without question someone who speaks through a page and never believe all that is written down is the truth. It is important to always question, but there is great worth in your studies, for in truth the pursuit of history is an opportunity to delve into the collective mind of mankind, to launch oneself into the mythology and stories of our people, to understand what motivates and moves us. Study deep enough, my friend, and you will find much that will make you admire, and revile, the human race."

"You talk of history as if it is mythology," I said.

Katherine grinned. "Myth, fable, history, story, it matters not what you call it. The history of our people is a collection of stories and as with any story there is much that one might take of it that is good, and much that is intended as a warning. We are all standing about a fireside, on the edge of the world, my friend, trying to see the light for the shadow. If we are wise, we come to understand they are but two sides of the same thing."

*

The King was talking of war with France again, although bragging might have been a more accurate way to put it. Sometimes his yaps reminded me of my dogs, Bragge and Bold. Tales of his glorious battles had flowed over court, through London, along the water to Richmond, and I had been admitting myself amazed with his prowess in war. But as I listened, I remembered the advice of the Duchess of Suffolk and took a peek between the lines, into the shadows.

When you dug into those tales, there was little of glory to find. At the Battle of the Spurs, the King's most notable victory, I learned the enemy had fled upon spying greater English numbers than were previously supposed, and very little fighting had actually taken place, just a small rout. Flodden, the best and most wondrous battle of the King's reign, had in fact been won for him in absentia by his Queen, Katherine and the present Queen's Howard kinsman the old Duke of Norfolk, father to the present one. People spoke of how the King was energised and ready to go to war now, but that also was a lie, or at least a half-truth.

Were the King to attempt to ride into battle it might well be the end of him. He was feeling hale again, this was true at the moment, but he had grown so corpulent after his last illness that he often had to sleep on the ground floor, for he could not heave himself up the stairs. He wheezed his way about his chambers and limped from room to room on his reeking leg. This was not a man who should be heading into war personally. One battle and his heart would surely surrender. I doubted his men, Norfolk chief amongst them, would allow him to ride into an actual battle, but entering into any kind of engagement would put a strain on him. Should the King go off to war, it might be the last time I saw him.

In consequence of all this talk of war, I had been thinking again of what would happen when the King died. If there was no war of succession, and Edward was made King, I had decided that Edward Seymour and Norfolk would do battle for the regent's chair. They were the men rumoured to be closest to the King at the moment, and each represented a different side of the faith. Cranmer was a possibility too, but I doubted a member of the clergy would be allowed to head the regency council. The King would not want the possibility of the Church gaining too much independent power. If the Queen had no child, her importance would cease when the King died. That might leave her unprotected, rather like me. I was likely to be seen as an inconvenience to a new ruler, my income, my houses, my household all expenses they would not welcome. I might find myself unwanted in England when the King was dead.

I was not the only one thinking of the future, of plans to be made. Before any trip to France could be undertaken, other matters needed to be secured first. This was why the court and King were going north on progress. The King needed to be sure that the north, birthplace of so many rebellions, was at rest before he left, and he wanted to make sure his nephew was not about to do what his father had the last time the King left for France. James IV had invaded, and Katherine of Aragon had seen to it James had regretted that decision, for a while anyway, as after he died on that battlefield I doubt he thought much of anything anymore.

The trouble was, Katherine of Spain was not Queen anymore, another Catherine was. Howard though Catherine was, so she had the military in her blood, little Howard was hardly a warrior-queen. Katherine of Aragon and Castile had been raised on campaign, had known what to do when enemies came calling, had known how to act. Catherine Howard was young, unexperienced and although I thought much of her I did think it likely that whilst she was capable of caring for the country, she might panic if placed in the position of defending England whilst the King was away.

But the King did not intend his country to be invaded or glories to be stolen this time. That meant making peace with the north and his nephew before going to make war on his rival.

Talk of crowning the Queen in the north was a move in this game for another reason, I had realised. Catherine was a Howard, daughter of the line of the Dukes of Norfolk, and a Catholic, officially at least, which was the form of faith the north favoured in general. Her great-grandfather had been a loyal supporter of the House of York, and popular in the north. The Queen was therefore a useful pawn in this game of placating the King's people. A Howard Queen on the throne might make rebels think the King was their man again. Catherine was to be brought out and shown off, another enticement to good behaviour.

I wondered what I could use to entice men to accept me, once the King was gone. I had a feeling that unless Seymour or Norfolk, whichever won the tussle to become Lord Regent, could be convinced I was needed in England for I was popular with the people, they might find me more liability than asset.

Chapter Twenty-Four

Richmond Palace
June 30th 1541

"The King is not about to take me back as his wife," I wearily said to Kitty who had brought this rumour to me. Why was it always the same rumour? "The last I heard he was to crown the Queen in York, and he is not even taking me to the north, so how he is meant to be crowning me there, I know not!"

Yet another rumour had arisen that the King was to set Catherine aside and take me back. This had come about because of these rumours of war with France. The French were of course allied with Cleves. Scotland was allied to France too and might invade England if François asked. Therefore, it was said the King would cast off Catherine and take me north as Queen to be crowned in order to keep peace.

It was ludicrous. The King was not worried by war with France, he was seeking it. It was true he wanted James of Scots to ally with him, to make a League, but I would sway nothing in that regard if made Queen.

"But if the King sees how valuable you could be to him, Highness..."

"Stop." I commanded, my tone unusually harsh. "Just stop. I have many times told you not to talk in such a way. If you cannot listen, Kitty, I shall have to take on a head maid who can and release you back to your mother in Calais. It would sadden me, but these days are dangerous, and I cannot have such talk in my house."

"Do not send me from you, Highness." She all but threw herself to my feet and grabbed the hem of my gown, kissing it. "I should die!"

I lifted her up. "You should not die. You would be sad and that is a different thing. Speak not so easily of death, Kitty, nor do things to bring yourself into danger of it. Speaking of me as Queen is treason. The King will not stand for such, and I shall not be able to protect you if he hears of this. You may well put me in danger as well as yourself for mentioning this. Keep all that in mind and have a care for your life."

"I will, Highness."

I did not believe her.

*

I was told the noise as court left Westminster was magnificent, deafening, more like an army marching out than a royal couple and their servants leaving for progress.

This progress, I had learned, had been planned when Jane Seymour was Queen, and had been postponed when she became pregnant. The northern coronation once dreamed up for the King's so-called favourite wife was now to take place for another Queen in preparation for both peace and war with other countries. Every man of England worth his name was on the move along with, so it seemed, every horse, carriage and ship.

"Not a horse spare in London, Sussex, Essex or Kent!" I had heard many a man exclaim over the past few weeks. It was, of course, an exaggeration. There were still spare horses, but despite the male habit of exaggeration – something they always claimed women were prone to do, remaining entirely blind and deaf to their own propensity to hyperbole – it was true there were far fewer beasts left in the city and southern counties than before. Fewer carts, carriages and ships too. They were all needed to carry the court and all the King's goods north.

The King wanted an opulence of finery waiting for him in York. On a normal progress a large amount of furniture and furnishings would be dismantled and taken along, so the King and Queen could have comfort everywhere they stayed, but on this occasion the King had another King to impress, so in addition to all that was being carted along with the King, a vast wealth of goods, portraits, tapestry, wall hangings, fresh herbs and floor rushes, plate, jewels and clothing, was being shipped to York by boat. When King James of Scots arrived, the idea was to convince him that all the King's palaces were this fine, that all this wealth was simply left there, in the north where the King rarely visited, just waiting for him. The King wanted to bowl his nephew over with his magnificence.

Looking at the masses of goods being stripped from all palaces – and at Richmond I had had to willingly 'offer' goods to the King on his request too – which were on their way, being shipped down the Thames and out to the sea, I could see that James might well be struck dumb by what the King had brought to display. Another option was the King of Scots might not have space to slide even sideways down the corridors of York Castle between all the ornaments, tapestry and goods.

By sea were horses, tents, courtiers, servants and artillery setting out to sail north. By road many thousands more were preparing to ride. Usually, perhaps one thousand horses escorted King and court on progress. This time there were five thousand.

In the busy days before they left, many a person had expressed awe at the numbers readying themselves to ride, saying it was as though the King were heading off to war. Which was, of course, what he was planning to do when he returned. "Of course, a summit meeting is often like a war," said my friend Katherine, lounging in a high-backed chair in my chamber but days before she left. "It is more polite of course, a summit, more dances than in war and yet what is war but showing off, one King to another, challenging the other to prove who is greater? A summit meeting is the same, but rather than do battle with swords we do it with conversation."

I laughed. "You should put that to the King about France, save England the expense and loss of life war will bring."

"He would not listen. He tried to take France once by conversation and it ended in him making friends with Spain instead."

I knew what she was speaking of. "My mother told me of the Field of the Cloth of Gold, and the wrestling match with François."

Katherine grinned a little wickedly. "So many tales I heard of that time when I was little. Mary Tudor, who was as my second mother for a long time, she used to tell me and her children tales of it. Of course she did not say the King was humiliated by François. All the English there present had to develop loss of memory of the event, but Eleanor, Frances, Henry and me, we all heard the tales from servants who went, who saw, who laughed when the King was not looking."

"So some talked of it."

"Aye, and the King never forgot it. Always he has wanted to take France, it belonged to his ancestors, so perhaps it is his right but in truth his ambition has much more to do with François throwing him in that wrestling match than any ancestral claim." She shrugged. "So, you see? It is a boast, war, it is showing off. If men stopped trying to outdo one another can you imagine how peaceful the world would be?"

I laughed. It was true that France had been the seat of the most memorable English victories in war, not for our present King but his ancestors. The King had always wanted to be known as the second Henry V, a reputation he had never managed to achieve. In youth he had tried, and failed. This plan of making war on France was a little like his marriage to Catherine Howard; a way of recapturing lost youth and unachieved dreams.

This dream of honour and glory, of chivalry and knighthood, had once been that of the idealistic young prince come to the throne on a wash of hope and faith. Where had that young man gone? I had never met him. Perhaps he had never really existed. The King had just turned fifty, so if he had any hope of achieving these lost dreams of youth, it had to be now.

This northern progress was the same, a big boast as Katherine called it. How cheered was I that I was not going.

The King was making a mighty show of force and strength, an imposing display of authority. He and his court would march north, infuse his subjects with loyalty and potential enemies with fear. That was the message he wanted to send, but it had the potential to go badly wrong, encouraging treason in place of trust. "Norfolk said so to the Queen," Katherine of Suffolk told me the next day, come to say goodbye before the court rode out. She was to go ahead, meet the court and King at her estates with her husband. It was a sign of great favour to play host to the King and his court. "Norfolk went to the Queen not a day ago and warned her if this goes not by hap, we may have more trouble than peace from it."

"Why so? I thought Norfolk would be in favour of this progress. I hear he has been trying to get the King to ride north for an age."

"There will be public ceremonies where the King forgives those who rose in rebellion against him," Katherine said, frowning a little. "He will also collect huge taxes from those who supported Neville in the late rebellion. The King thinks this will subdue the north, remind it of its loyalties, but he knows not the temper of his people. If they are humiliated, as I think and Norfolk obviously suspects the King intends, this could rile them up again. The north will never forget the Pilgrimage of Grace. They are unlikely to forget the ruthless treatment of rebels, or of the monasteries, either. If they think they are being insulted, again, this progress could have an opposite effect to the one the King desires. And this show of might could be taken another way. People might look upon this display and tremble not, but instead think this is a sign of how greatly *the King fears the north*. The same could be true of the King of Scots. All this pomp and show could be taken as a sign of the King's weakness, his insecurity."

"I see, so what did Norfolk want the Queen to do?"

"He thinks her a gentle, merciful influence on the King and asked her to continue to do that, try to oppose the wrath the King might express, mitigate it. The north might then see the Queen as their hope, for she is a Howard, one of them already in blood and if she can influence the King to compassion they will have a monarch to fear but his consort to love. That is how a populace is controlled, love and fear in equal measures. Fear, you see, is not all powerful on its own, for it offers a person nothing to lose but suffering. That is why rebellions start. When people have nothing to lose, they rise up. If the Queen offers love, there *is* something to lose. If she offers love, control is complete."

I grimaced.

"Like it or not," said my friend. "No one has a more effective way of controlling a population. What if all the disaffected people of the world should rise? We would be the first they would go for."

"I think the people have affection for you and me," I said.

"I mean us... the gentry of the world."

"I think the common people know some of us have kinder intentions than others." I paused a moment. "I take it the Queen said she would try?" Katherine nodded. "So that is her task on this progress. And I hear you are to entertain the King and court a few days? A high honour."

"I wish you would come," she said.

"I am happier here, and I will be not alone. There are a few left behind."

"A very few," Katherine chortled.

A small Council was to remain behind, made up of Cranmer, Audley and a few other nobles.

"Lady Mary is coming," she mentioned, hoping to tempt me. Mary was being taken on progress as another sign to the north. In that region many had supported Katherine, and one of the terms of the Pilgrimage of Grace had been the restoration of Mary to the succession. That had not happened, but the King was bringing her along to show how well his daughter was now treated. I had no doubt she was also on display so he could point out she was in her father's power. Should any conspire to use her as a figurehead against him, she was right at his elbow and would not escape his vengeful hand.

"I will do well here. Richmond is lovely in the summer, and besides I think the King did not want me there in case I upset the plan about the Scots' King when they meet. My brother's marriage into France might come up, reminding the Scots' King that it would be more profitable to remain friends with François than join the King in this League, and the King would not want that."

"That is *if* they meet. I hear James has sent no sure promise they will."

I blinked. "But, all this preparation, the volumes of people and all the ships going north with goods. I thought it for certain the two kings had agreed to meet?"

"Oh no," said my friend, waggling her finger. "Nothing firm has been promised at all on the Scottish side, but our King is certain, that is the trouble. In his mind they are to meet and if they do not his expectations will be crushed. That is never a good thing."

"Then I am glad again I am not going." I went to a cupboard in the chamber and brought out a pot. Handing it to Katherine, I said, "I want you to give this to the Queen, and tell her it is from you."

Katherine arched an eyebrow. "You are not trying to poison her, are you?"

"The opposite. I want her to have life in her womb, I hear this will aid that."

"Why should you want the Queen to have a child? Security for England?"

"It would be a thing good for England indeed, and it would make her more secure, and she is a good Queen, a calming influence on the King's frightening behaviour. I think it would be better to have her as our Queen than replaced, which might happen if no child comes."

There was another reason. If Catherine were to have a child, she would remain influential in the event of the King's death. I needed someone who was my friend and had power at court if the King died. I was hoping this could be Catherine. She had spoken warmly of me more than once. I believed we were friends and might be better ones were we allowed to meet more. I hoped she would help me.

"Why do you not give it to her?"

"I think it would be better coming from a woman with children. My mother always told me in cases of infertility belief is a beneficial virtue. If a woman believes she can have a child, she often will. If you tell her this aided you in the getting of your two fine sons, it might aid her."

I went to the window as Katherine left. Mist sailed over the treetops, thick and murky. Dark clouds floated overhead, and the earth was wet, glistening as diamonds. In the distance I could hear thrushes calling as they winged into the skies.

"Sign of a storm, Highness," said Kitty, joining me at a window as the thrushes flew past, a cloud of dark wings.

I inclined my head. This summer had been wet where the last had been dry, but for all the moisture falling upon the world at the moment, I did not think that was the storm the birds were warning us of.

Chapter Twenty-Five

Richmond Palace
July 1541

"The progress of the royal progress is slow."

I laughed, glancing up in surprise from my embroidery. "Harst... did you just make a *jest*?"

Harst inspected his fingernails, a little smirk hovering on his lips. "Fear not, Highness, it happens but rarely, once a decade or so."

"Then I am honoured to have been present for the occasion."

Harst smiled. "The King wants to stop at every town, I hear, so Queen Catherine and Lady Mary can be shown off to the people. Crowds are turning out in lashing rain and rising wind to greet them."

I imagined it was indeed poor on the road for it had not ceased to rain here at Richmond. When I went out, which was not often, I rode along wet tracks with my household, the scent of mud and water on the wind. Tiny, flowing rivers washed alongside roads, gold with glinting sunlight, the water burbling over tiny rocks, making the edge of the path gleam. Birds were in the skies, taking advantage of any moment it was not raining constantly. Bedraggled deer stood forlorn in the woods, hardly bothering to move as we rode past for they could see we were too weighted down with dampness to attempt a hunt. The fields were starting to flood in places; wide, grey mirrors of water reflecting the clouds and sky above.

The world in its wet cloak was pretty, mistake me not but it became unpleasant soon enough, the damp seeping into clothes, the saddle growing moist and slippery, stockings turning soggy, the scent of damp wool rising from cloaks filling the air with its sweet, cloying fug. I was often glad to get indoors, to my own chambers. Although the court would of course stay at a house each night, it would always be a different house, a new place to get used to and then leave again. It was never home, and home is what we want when we want comfort.

A new home was being made for a woman much promised and bargained for, with a man I once was connected to. Christina of Denmark, the much sought after widow of Milan, was to be finally married that month and her second husband was to be my old betrothed, Francis, the Duke of Lorraine. Odd how the twists of life may take us turning about one another. Christina had turned down my former husband as a suitor when she was widow of Milan, and Francis had been the means by which I was separated from that same man. Now they were a pair.

The King had not reacted with grace to this match. He refused to acknowledge it as a legitimate union and forbade his ambassadors from attending the service. I had found this most amusing, privately of course.

Despite this notable marriage, much of the talk that summer in England was of an affair at court. Lord William Parr had lately taken a mistress, one of the Queen's ladies, Dorothy Bray. Dorothy was unmarried and only seventeen, the same age as the Queen. Usually, a maid living with a married man would cause a scandal, but the King had turned a blind eye to this one, and for good reason, so Kitty informed me.

"The wife of William Parr, Anne Bourchier, caused a greater scandal, Highness. They married when she was ten, although the match was not consummated at that time. Anne was a grand heiress. Her father had been the Earl of Essex, the one who fell from his horse leading to his title going to Cromwell, for a short time. After Cromwell's death, it seemed likely that the husband of Anne would inherit the title, as she was by then the only surviving child of the Earl, and the King did not seem disposed to grant the earldom to Cromwell's son. Anne came with a substantial amount of jewels and other wealth, so seemed a fine match."

"So, what was the scandal?" I tucked my needle through the heavy cloth I was embroidering with lions, if it turned out well I thought I would send it to the King. It was important to send gifts from time to time, keep him appeased and thinking well of me.

Kitty smiled. "She is a rebel in character, my lady. Anne has lately run off with a penniless member of the clergy, a love match all claim, she has become great with child, and has told her husband that she never had loved him, and never would."

"I see so, after Anne throwing convention to the wind, William Parr taking a mistress must almost be a relief to the King."

Plenty of people were talking about it, some calling Dorothy Bray a whore, although I heard she was hardly the first mistress Parr had taken, so clearly he was no innocent either. Others talked of Lady Parr and her wild ways. Most could barely believe this Anne had abandoned all sense, as some put it, and run off with a man with no money. For my part I wondered if she was not happier than anyone could imagine. Perhaps she had not money, but money is often something which makes us sad rather than merry. With money, there is never enough, for a rich man always thinks himself poor, but with love, a little may satisfy us more greatly than anything coin can buy.

Within days of the court leaving London, the rains truly came. I had not been many years in England it was true, but I had seen nothing like the rain we had during that summer. Richmond sprung leaks in places and had to be patched. The wind wailed and every day we were lashed with rain, thick and hard.

"Is this normal?" I asked Kitty as I stared out into the darkness of relentless rain. I shivered; the chambers were cold as autumn.

"Only a few times have I seen it this bad, Highness," she said. "I pity those on the road, on progress."

"Call for a fire," I commanded, pulling my shawl of fur tighter about my shoulders.

"It is summer, Highness."

"Is it?" I asked, pointing at the window. "Someone needs must inform the sky of that, then."

Kitty laughed. "We would have to sweep the chimneys, the King orders such is done before they are lit again."

"Then have them swept. I shall not freeze to death or have my bones snap inside my flesh for want of some warmth."

Progress was indeed miserable in such weather. I heard ladies of court had to be bundled into litters and at each town they came to, every reception had to be held in draughty, sodden tents. The King still wanted to show off to the crowds who still, despite the weather, gathered, but they needed some protection. The weather was ghastly that summer.

At Richmond after a week of unrelenting rain, we had a day of sun, then three more of rain. Then a day of sun and four of rain. It was warm again, which was well enough but still I had to order fires lit in the hearths. The palace was starting to feel damp.

Then suddenly there was a rumour the King's artillery and soldiers had not been taken along as a mere display of might. "There is word the King fears assassins, or an actual rebellion whilst he and his court are in the north," Harst told me. "Some say he means not to meet with the King of Scots, but to attack him."

Little prepared was I for future rebellion or war when the King died, I was certainly not ready for one now. I had thought when the King fell ill that I needed a plan for the future, but all I had even now was half-formed thoughts. Months on, and I still had nothing.

And now all said the King might well be marching into war.

Chapter Twenty-Six

Richmond Palace
July 1541

By July, as the court reached houses like Dunstable and Grafton Place, the weather was so appalling there was talk of progress being cancelled. Tales filtered back to London about how the court crawled along roads mired in mud, carts and wagons getting stuck each time their wheels rolled. Stumbling horses struggled along waterlogged lanes and courtiers were getting soaked to the skin every day. At Richmond cruel and vengeful skies loomed low in shades of ominous cobalt and menacing grey. Rolling clouds, dark and angry, roamed the skies, hastened along by storm-winds curling in the heavens. The charged air smelt of malice and revenge.

Even wrapped in layers of wool and leather, I was drenched within moments of leaving the house if I ventured out hunting or walking, which was not often. Every now and then, however, I had to get out. Richmond was a large palace, but I needed the air of the world on my face from time to time. I came to often regret my excursions. Bitter coldness pinched my flesh and rain slapped my face. I returned not sated by exercise but rather feeling as if I had been assaulted.

Much time that summer was spent inside. Since much of autumn and winter were also spent indoors, this was a strain on many a temper. The idea of being cooped up for most of the year was not pleasing to anyone. The settling into the season of winter feels more comforting when one has spent plenty of time outside in summer, it is easier to reconcile to the warm indoors if the outdoors has been thoroughly explored not long ago, but this year we had already been long within the palace and now there would be a longer period still of being trapped. It made Richmond feel like a cage.

At night, sleep was stolen by wind battering windowpanes, spattering the glass with rain. In the background of my dreams the wind was a fearsome power of night and darkness, of air and water thrown loose and lost wild. A madness, glorious and fearful, of the night storm invaded my dreams. Wild and wicked the tempest screamed, its call at once daunting and exhilarating, liberating and free. I dreamed of Sybylla, in the forest, handing me a cloak made of feathers. "Where have you gone, sister?" she asked me.

"I wandered into a hidden world," I told my sister, "there I ate of the food and drank of the wine, and I joined the dance."

"Then you are caught in this dance everlasting," she said. "Take the cloak, it may yet help bring freedom."

I gave the cloak of feathers to Catherine, who had appeared in the forest, and she flew away. I woke just as an arrow shot into the sky winged her and I cried out, ending the scream as I woke, scaring all my maids.

Perhaps the Queen was on my mind because I heard she was suffering, the cold getting to her bones and making her feel unwell. Many people had fallen ill this progress and there was word the Queen was low in spirits, though trying stoutly to rouse herself in time for each appearance at every new town or city. Plenty of complaints were filtering back to London from those made miserable by this progress. The only one who attempted to pretend all was well on progress was the King. On days it was merely drizzling rather than pouring, he was insisting on hunting. Catherine, as his wife, was forced to go along too, wrapped in soggy, cold layers, riding at his side. I cannot imagine she took much pleasure or pride in his hunting. I heard men herded deer to the King, so he could shoot them as they ambled past him. Hardly a test of skill, to shoot something at point blank range.

"The Queen might be cheered by news they had at Dunstable," Harst told me, "for there Queen Catherine was told she is to become the first Queen Consort of Ireland. The Irish Parliament is to meet this month, and they are to change the King's title from Lord of Ireland to King of Ireland. There will be great celebration when this becomes known, for the King has ordered prisoners to be freed, wine to flow in the streets, a Mass at the cathedral in Dublin and bonfires to be lit."

Others told me the people of Ireland might not be so pleased by the King's new title. Ireland had been granted to England, I had read, by Rome in the reign of Henry II. Some men of Ireland thought that when the King broke from Rome, Ireland should have become her own land, governed by Irish lords.

But if Queen Catherine of Ireland was pleased by her new title, it was temporary, for we heard the Queen had been taken ill. "She walked into her chambers one day, gave an order for a hot bath and fell to the floor," Harst told me. "She has been put to bed. Many are saying she must be with child."

"Perhaps she is with child, but I think it likely the child herself is exhausted."

She lingered in fever that night and the next day. The King did not go to her. It was customary, if hurtful. He could not be near sickness in case he became sick himself.

The Queen's women gossiped she might be with child, but doctors announced it was weariness, brought on by riding in inclement weather. She was bled and told to stay in bed. No riding for at least a week.

"This could be a good thing," I said to Harst.

"How so?"

"No matter what the doctors say, if the King thinks the Queen is with child, a coronation in York is even more likely."

Chapter Twenty-Seven

Richmond Palace
July 1541

"The whole country is demanding news from progress on the Queen's condition. People are most upset. Some are saying the King is too hard on his wife, making her go here and there and everywhere with him, and some are on tenterhooks, certain she is with child." Olisleger, back from another trip to Cleves, looked scandalised himself.

The court were lingering at Grafton Place, waiting for the Queen to be well. "If I were her, I would stay in bed and avoid all the gossip about me," I said.

Excuses were sent ahead so people would know the court was delayed, but not why. The King did not want anyone, particularly his troublesome northern subjects or King James, to think there was anything wrong on progress. It was said the court were all merry and healthy, in an effort to convince everyone that delays were due to them enjoying themselves.

Eventually the Queen came from her chambers, and all said she looked blooming, which added to rumours she was with child.

They set out the next day for Northampton where they stayed for two days before heading for Pipewell, a former abbey owned by Lord Parr, still the much-talked-of gallant of court, who was a fine and generous host. I was told the King spent his days meeting with the Scots ambassador, who had arrived with a barrage of complaints for the King's attention. Catherine entertained the court in his absence.

They left Pipewell and went to Lyddington, a village in Rutland surrounded by sprawling countryside. Housed in a magnificent manor house, once the residence of the bishops of Lincoln, they stayed a week, hunting, walking and dancing inside when rain came, which was often.

"They are at Collyweston Palace," said Harst some days later, "once home of the King's grandmother, Lady Margaret Beaufort."

"Is the King happy to be there again?" I asked, leafing through missives come that morning. I spotted Sybylla's hand and seal and set it to one side, so I could savour it. Amalia was an infrequent writer, but Sybylla sent letters to me often. "He must be merry, heading to old, favoured haunts again."

"Perhaps, although, my lady, you should know he cannot be that affectionate towards the north in truth, for whilst he has been to some places he never has been to York."

"Never has been?" I asked, looking up. "But... England is such a small country. How can it be the King has not been to all of it?"

"He has ever thought the north full of savages, as far as I can tell, and nothing has altered that now. He prefers the south of his country."

"If he never has been north, how can he know which he prefers?"
Harst chuckled.

I knew a little of the house they were at. The King's bastard son, Henry Fitzroy, had lived there once. Collyweston was the seat of the Duchy of Richmond. Margaret Beaufort had been the Duchess, of course, which was why she had resided there. That house was full of ghosts.

"The King has been questioning the Queen about her illness. He wants her to publicly announce she is with child, but she is unsure," said Harst.

I cocked my head to one side. "She cannot announce it unless she knows for sure."

"I think the King would prefer, sure or not, she announce it."

Naturally the King wanted a child now, in his wife's belly. It would be another demonstration of his power, of his link to God. Riding north, possibly to meet his nephew, and at that auspicious time announcing his Queen was with child would be the ultimate triumph. Then a Queen carrying the Duke of York could be crowned in the Duke's own city. It would be perfect.

But Catherine remained unsure, and that was likely to frustrate the King.

Chapter Twenty-Eight

"Where are they now?"

"Grimsthorpe Castle, Highness, in Lincolnshire."

"Seat of the Suffolks?"

"Indeed."

I hoped the two Katherines, one a Queen and one a Duchess, would be merry together. I heard their husbands certainly were. Tales came to us of Suffolk and the King drinking and eating too much and guffawing about what sweet young things they had managed to marry. The servants had many tales to tell, they all flowed back down to London. Some of the comments the King and Suffolk had made whilst deep in their cups had hardly been ones I wanted to hear. Their wives' quinnies were not supposed to be matters discussed in public, yet they had talked of them. I hoped the two women did not know what had made it back to London about them. I had heard many a jape, riddle and tale thought humorous by the English by that time, and whilst the English humour always ran to the lewd, the stories I heard of what the King and Suffolk had said about their wives made me blush.

Perhaps the women were busy with each other, so did not hear aught of their husbands' foul mouths. They had much in common, Catherine and Katherine. Both of them had married men much older than themselves, and although Katherine of Suffolk was a reformist, her questioning nature taking her deeper every day into the path towards being a fervent supporter of the new faith, and Catherine Howard said little of religion, probably because it was safer, they were not dissimilar in spirit. They both had been set into positions of responsibility when young, had stepchildren who were older than them. It could be said Katherine of Suffolk had had a harder time in some ways since Brandon's children from his first annulled marriage were ten years her senior, and Katherine had all but grown up with his daughters from his second marriage to Mary Tudor. Frances Grey, née Brandon, was two years older than Katherine, and Eleanor was about the same age as my friend. If anyone was to understand how it felt to be a younger girl thrust into a position of authority over older ones, such as Catherine the Queen had been with Lady Mary, it was my friend Katherine of Suffolk.

I thought the Queen could learn from my good friend. Katherine of Suffolk had her own troubles but she found joy in life where she could, and she also managed her husband with consummate skill. Brandon was a fool and a dullard, I had ascertained this from many brief conversations, yet Katherine behaved as though he was still the handsome, young and charming man he had been long before she had become his wife. She flattered and charmed him, and generally this led to harmony between them, at least on the surface.

Troubles they might have in marriage, but on the whole she managed to exact a great deal of freedom whilst in the married state. More, perhaps, than the Queen. Part of that was because she had provided heirs. Two fine sons graced Suffolk's line of course, so Katherine was secure, which allowed her freedom, to an extent. Wombs are the ties that bind most women and our means of becoming free, if we are clever enough, and lucky enough. Fertility might grant freedom if a woman had the wit to use it well, or it might entrap a woman, bind her deeper in chains.

I hoped Katherine would find a moment to give my potion to our Queen. It was an unpalatable mixture, mugwort, the piss of a sheep, rabbit's blood and mare's milk, but I had heard it worked wonders if a spoon was taken each night before bed. I had the recipe from one of my mother's herbals, and Sybylla swore by it, writing to me that she had been dosed with it before the conception of each son.

In the meantime, I had worries of my estates. "What of the harvest?" I asked.

As dry as last summer had been was this summer wet. I could see despair on the faces of common people as I rode out, for they knew their crops, and therefore survival, was in danger. They lined up along waterlogged roads to cheer me, swirling puddles and tiny rivers flowing about their feet, but I could see fear, dark caves in their eyes. How would they feed families, animals, through winter if their wheat, barley and vegetables died, drowned in the mire? I gave alms as I rode past them, charity of food from my gate too, but it was not enough.

"The harvest is indeed in peril, Highness. It may be testing to collect your taxes and rents too, if people cannot make enough." Carew, come to give his report, looked troubled.

"What do we do in such times?"

"Give alms and food from your gate, charity where we can."

"Can I give relief to these people, are there other measures? Can I give respite from taxes?"

"We could release grain from our stores, Highness, but only if the King gives you leave to, and as for the taxes, that would only be possible if he relieves you of your burden to him from your estates. Your houses and lands are, in effect, still his in many ways."

We feasted that night on a fat stag the King had killed and sent to me as a gift. I stared at the blood oozing from the rare deer on my plate and I could not feel hunger. The King would send gifts of meat to those like me who needed it not, but what of his people, starving in the winter this year because they could not grow enough food to sustain them?

Chapter Twenty-Nine

Richmond Palace
July - August 1541

"The Queen has scolded Norfolk, before all her ladies," Olisleger told me, a barely concealed smirk on his face. Like many, he had no affection for the ever-groaning Duke whose digestive system always troubled him more than his conscience. "News of it is everywhere. He wanted her to promote him to the King, get him more sway and influence, and she refused, saying it was not her place to instruct the King."

Norfolk had caught up with progress after parting with his King in London, and had found his master in a rare mood when they reunited. The King was displeased with some decisions the Queen's uncle had made in his absence and had told him so. Norfolk thought his enemies, Suffolk in particular, had spoken against him and this was the cause of the King's displeasure, but it was not. Norfolk was to blame for Norfolk's actions. It is only the weak of mind and spirit who seek to blame everything they do on someone else.

Within days, it was all about court that Norfolk had spoken of Catherine's 'malice' towards him, but the King was pleased with her at least. The Queen had shown where her loyalty lay.

After three days the court reached Sleaford as dusk fell. There they were to rest until preparations were complete for their glorious entry to Lincoln, the first true test of progress. Sleaford had been chosen as one of the stops for good reason. The manor they stayed in had once belonged to Lord Hussey, the former chamberlain of the Lady Mary. He had been beheaded for supporting the Pilgrimage of Grace. The King was starting this stamping of authority, or insecurity, upon nobles of the north.

"At Lincoln, the King and Queen will be presented with gifts and the sword and mace of the city," Harst told me that night as we ate dinner with my household in the Great Hall. "There will be a Mass in the cathedral, and people will make humble submissions to the King, bringing gifts of money and taxes. It is vital that this first submission goes as planned and is recorded well. This will be the first but not last submission of this progress." He cut into his venison, another gift from the King, and rolled a slice in the frumentary served with it.

I picked up my wine and sat back, looking at Harst who was at my side. "So, if anything goes wrong there, news of it will be sent ahead to York and other cities. People will take it as an ill omen, and it will set the rest of progress and the King's suppression of his potential enemies at risk?"

"At great risk."

"Let us hope it goes well, then," I said, sipping my wine, a fine malmsey.

*

"More to the dance!" I announced, "there is too much chatter in this hall and not enough dancing!"

People laughed and fresh couples joined the next at my command. My musicians, two of them new, both Moorish and highly talented, struck up a lively refrain as the dancers arranged themselves. Incense poured into the air and swept in circles overhead as the dance began. Hands clapped as legs shifted and feet slid across the floor.

I had been somewhat surprised by the King arriving at Richmond not long ago. He had been on a hunting trip through his royal parks, a break from progress before they entered Lincoln, and was travelling fast without the drag of the court upon him. He had longed for Richmond, so he said, and had therefore combined a trip here with some work he needed to do in London. For a night only he stayed, asking after my health at dinner and praising my musicians.

"I hope you were not sad to be not taken on progress," he said.

"Majesty, I was not," I replied, taking up my wine. "I truly believe, especially for the Queen's first large progress and for the fact this is such an important one, that the people should see you and the Queen, Lady Mary too, but not have that confused by the appearance of more distant family. You and the north need to become close in love again, and all focus should be on that. Sadly, and never by my wish, when I am near the Queen everyone watches to check we are friends, which we are, but I think I might prove more distraction than diversion, and I would not want that."

"You are a wise woman, sister," he said approvingly, patting my hand as if I were a dog.

Not long after he left, I heard a rumour that the King had spent his one night at Richmond in my bed. "I hope the Queen does not hear such a thing," I said to Kitty.

"I would hope she did," Kitty muttered. "For then she might know that the King loves you still, Highness."

"The King does not love me, not as anything but a sister," I said, "and I would not have the Queen think thus, how sad and angry she would be, and you would have me be the cause of her suffering? I like better fates for myself than that." I shook my head. "Is there no better gossip than me?"

"I hear rumours the Lady Mary may be wed to the Duc d'Orléans?" Kitty said.

"A second son, I wonder if she would be happy with that. Of course, the first is married already."

"Being married is not always a permanent state, Highness."

"Enough, Kitty."

"Yes, Highness."

Chapter Thirty

Richmond Palace
August 1541

With the King restored to them after his bizarre short trip to the south, the court had now made for Temple Bruer, seven miles from Lincoln, where they dined with the Archdeacon of Lincoln, and the next day more members of the King's clergy rode out to meet the court, their hands weighted down with gifts. They were dressed in red, and I wondered if this was a none-too-subtle reference to the blood shed by the north.

Lines of men bowed as the royal couple rode towards a tent, erected so they might change into their most glorious and regal of gowns before entering the city. Line after line of men swept into bows, taking their caps from their heads to demonstrate deference.

The royal party stopped in an open space so the King, in his Tudor green, could be welcomed by officials in an outpouring of sycophantic adulation. Green was of course a Tudor colour, but also one long associated with Lincoln in the myths of Robin Hood. The King adored that myth, had dressed up as Robin of the Hood to trick a wife or two on several occasions. Did the King think himself Robin Hood? He was more likely to be thought bad King John.

They listened to an address in Latin, then the clergy rode off to prepare for the Mass court would sit through once they entered the city. That was also where many men would come to beg the King's pardon for taking part in, or supporting, the Pilgrimage of Grace and other rebellions that had arisen. The King was to pardon them graciously, demonstrating his mercy and magnificence.

At a signal from the King, they all rode on to the tents to change clothes, and Catherine emerged garbed in a gown of shimmering silver. The King was to wear cloth of gold and silver, matching his wife but also *outmatching* her. Catherine was precious, he only more so, that was the message. I heard jewels were heaped upon the Queen, rings on her little fingers, pearls in her ears, necklaces about her throat and golden chains wrapped about her waist. Back onto the horses they all climbed and rode for the city, trumpets blasting and heralds announcing the titles of the King. Cheering began, and apparently some men with malign faces had to be nudged to applaud their King, while others wore expressions of open humility.

Just before the gates, more representatives of the city emerged and prostrated themselves before the King. Addresses delivered in English by the city's recorder thundered over the crowd. Gifts for the King were handed to Norfolk, who was riding so close to the King that Harst claimed a fellow ambassador had declared the Duke might have been mistaken for the arse of the King's horse.

The Lord Mayor offered a speech, shouting, "Jesus save Your Majesty!" before he began, and kissing the mace, symbol of his office, before handing it to the King. My former husband kissed it, and handed it back, demonstrating he endorsed the mayor's authority, and bestowed upon the mayor the right to uphold the liberties and freedoms of the city in his name. What those liberties and freedoms entailed, however, depended upon the King.

Catherine's gifts were smaller, more domestic. She was given fresh fish for her table, handsome pike and carp, which she thanked them for as officials took their place at the head of the procession and led the royal party into the city.

"The King's coat of arms had been erected on the other side of Stonebow, and streets had been cleaned," Harst said.

As Harst read from a report of the entry to the city, I could see it as if I were there. Gone was the running mud and blood that usually would be seen, and instead were freshly gravelled roads, newly whitewashed houses, and passages cleared of dunghills, beggars and prostitutes. Bells rang from every church in welcome and salute. The cathedral was set upon a hill, reaching up to the heavens.

"The front of the cathedral was almost completely obscured by people, and as the King and Queen dismounted, the Bishop of Lincoln came forth to welcome them. Before the cathedral, they knelt on cushions of cloth of gold as the Bishop presented a jewelled crucifix for them to kiss. He blessed them and they walked into the cathedral with the clergy holding the canopy of the Blessed Sacrament over them, as though they too were divine." Harst was still reading from a letter sent by another ambassador.

The King, of course, supposedly was divine. Head of the Church, King of England, Ireland and France, he was the chosen of God. But it was just another story. The King had *made* himself Head of the Church, and he was no more King of France than I was Joan of Arc.

The King and Queen knelt again in prayer at the choir as choristers sang a *Te Deum*. "Of course, some of the King's ancestors are buried in Lincoln," mentioned Harst. "The Duchess of Lancaster and Queen Eleanor of Castile are interred there."

It was actually only part of Eleanor which had been laid to rest at Lincoln. Her body was in Westminster Abbey, but some of her organs had been buried at Lincoln. And her monument, like so many, had been damaged by none other than her descendant.

All religious houses had been stripped of wealth by the King, and even the tombs of royalty had not been spared. The shrine of Saint Hugh of Lincoln had been Lincoln's pride, but it had been dismantled just over a year ago when the cathedral had been sacked by the King's men. Jewels and offerings had been taken away, gold and silver melted down.

"The only shrine remaining is to one who has never really been named a saint," Kitty told me, "not by Rome or the King."

"Who is this?"

He was "Little Saint Hugh of Lincoln", she told me, in truth a child who had been found dead at the bottom of a well, most likely murdered. His death had been blamed on Jews, and many had died in retribution. His shrine was untouched, possibly because he was not a true saint, or because sacking the grave of a child was a little more than even the King's greedy men dared to do in a house of God.

But Queen Eleanor's monument was damaged. Even in death, a queen could not rest easy.

"I hear the ceremony went well," said Harst.

I inclined my head. "I am glad of it, and can only hope, old friend, the progress continues that way. I fear what will happen if it does not."

*

The King and Queen were at Bishop Longland's Palace. We heard their tables were groaning with fat oxen and mutton dripping with honey and herbs. At Richmond I was no less merry. Though I had concerns about the King's health, about possible war with Scotland or France, and what all this might mean for me, I did not allow the people of my halls to suffer for my worries. Happy rests the heart which does not pass on its pains.

Each night we made merry and played. The scent of wine was on the air and dinner had been fine. Servants had moved from table to table, refilling communal goblets and taking away empty platters swimming with swirling fat and juices, only to bring more. All the leavings from our tables were to be given to the poor who would come to my gates knowing there had been a feast that night. Because we had eaten well, so people nearby would too. It was another good reason to hold feasts. Anything left over from our tables of the everyday was given to the poor, but when I held feasts there was so much more to give out that evening and the next day.

The day had been long, we had been out hunting in the parks, the skies blessedly devoid of rain for once, and my people were tired but merry. Now the tables were cleared away, folded against the wall and the dancing had begun, I meant it to go on late into the night.

Later, as I was in my chambers, I sat at my desk, thinking on much. I was too enlivened to wish for sleep. My ladies were slumped in chairs, fallen to sleep waiting for me to be ready for bed. Only one candle was lit on the table. A long drip, like a soft spine, ran down its wasting length. It cast light and shadow on the room in equal measures.

I was committing treason again, thinking on the death of the King.

Would I go home, if it was offered to me? It might be forced upon me; I knew that well enough. I did not want to go home. Miss my family though I might, I wanted to remain in England, free as I was now.

I needed to have an escape route ready, not so much away from court or London, but from the possible dangers that would gather about the throne when the King died. I needed a powerful friend, more than one if possible, who could protect me and my interests. *A ward*, I thought with a wry smile. I needed to make myself a ward to someone.

I thought of the Queen. They were now at Lincoln Castle, where she had learned of a spinster named Helen Page, condemned for minor felonies, one being whoredom. The charges against her had been made by her employer, a man who claimed she had enticed him into her bed then got with child and had tried to run away from his house, stealing goods from him. He had cast her out.

I suspected that she, like so many girls, had in fact been raped or at least coerced into sex by her master and when he had found out about the child he had cast her out to prevent his name being tarnished. Catherine had most likely suspected the same since she had intervened for this woman, commanded her parish to support her and her baby and sent money to her too. This, amongst many of her actions, made me consider that the Queen was the one I should rely on when the King was gone.

But would she be enough?

It was true that as a widow she would be rich, if pregnant or with a child in the royal nursery she would have influence, but would her support be enough to uphold my claims to my property and to remain in England? The King's commands were supposed to support my claims, but I doubted they would be honoured if men like Edward Seymour or Norfolk became regent. The Queen herself might even be sold off to another husband after the traditional mourning period, used as a pawn in the high stakes game that would follow the death of the King. So, even if my strategy to appeal to her as a friend worked, even if my plan to have her conceive was successful, would it be enough?

I knew not.

Brandon might speak for me; it was possible for his wife loved me. If he were chosen as regent that might aid me. But I doubted he would be. This would be a tight, hard and clever game that was played when the King died, and Brandon had not the brains for it. Besides, Seymour and Norfolk were too strong on the opposite sides of faith for Suffolk to get a foot in. The struggle would be between them, I was sure.

I could marry. I was rich, a good prospect, still young. But I did not want to. The thought of being in a man's power again, of being commanded to open my legs out of duty, to have to obey where I was told to after all this freedom I had enjoyed, it was repulsive. The thought of a husband made me feel sick. The trouble was, if I did not choose a husband, one might well be chosen for me. Much as the Queen was in danger of being married off to a supporter of her uncle when the King died, so I was too. Would I find myself carried or dragged down an aisle? If such had happened to the daughter of the King of Navarre, why not to me?

Some said the Lady Mary would be set up as Queen, but I still thought the Prince would have the largest body of support. Edward Seymour was the Prince's uncle, and many knew him to be cleverer than Norfolk, so I thought him more likely to succeed in a struggle for power. Norfolk had much money, but few wits, and if I supported Norfolk, he would most likely marry me off where he decided, without reference to my wishes. He was that kind of man, not one to leave a woman free and happy in the world. Such an idea was an affront to his principles, which as far as I could see meant making everyone else as miserable as his troubled digestive system was.

Seymour might help me, though. If I offered support to him from the first, he might maintain me as the King's aunt. He would need members of the royal family to support him since he came of a house lower than that of Norfolk. The gratitude of Seymour might be enough to sustain my life, to be lived as I wish it to be. I might have to accept less money, fewer houses, but that I could do.

But what if another path should open, and Mary became Queen or Regent? Then, I would have no trouble, for Mary and I were friends now, and yet England would have trouble, would it not? Many might support her but plenty of others thought as the King always had, that a woman could not rule England.

I did not think that way. If Mary was put forth as Regent, I would support her. Seymour would be a second choice and Norfolk last. It was not a perfect plan, but it was something, and as for its execution I would simply have to watch and see what unfolded before I made a move.

Chapter Thirty-One

Richmond Palace
August 1541

As the court left Lincoln and rode for Gainsborough, staying at the hall of Baron Burgh, we heard rumours of odd happenings on progress. *"The Queen was out of her rooms at night, exploring the castle of Lincoln with the Lady Rochford,"* Katherine of Suffolk wrote to me. *"Many are scandalised, but I am less surprised. Some do not know there is less formality on progress, and many people get up to odd adventures."*

I supposed, though I had never been on one as Queen, that just as my friend said, on progress the rules of court, often restrictive and unvarying, were relaxed a little and that was what the Queen was taking advantage of.

If the Queen was enjoying freedom, the King was growing more restricted. I heard that at one of the palaces they stayed he again could not make it up the stairs, and a separate room was made for him on the ground floor. An excuse was put about that the King needed his room there so he could leave swiftly for the hunt with the dawn, but the real reason was he was too weighty to manage the stairs, and his leg was paining him. Constant riding, kneeling in church, and hunting whenever he could had taken a toll. The ulcer was angry, red and inflamed, Katherine of Suffolk wrote to me.

It was probably all to put on a show for James of Scotland that had caused the King to act this way, in any case. He wanted reports to run to James stating that the King was always on the hoof, was out hunting every day as if he was a young gallant, had ridden away from the north to London and back again, just on a whim. For the sake of boasting to a young man, the old King had once more ruined his health.

The court rode along the Great North Road to Scrooby Manor in Nottinghamshire and stayed a night, then crossed into Yorkshire. Just as they passed into this county, they were met by a delegation of six thousand men, come to welcome them and present themselves in submission to the King, as commanded. Those who had taken part in rebellion were fearful, understandably, but perhaps the fresh air had infused the King for he was bright and friendly with them all. Those who had rebelled came to him on their knees with one named Sir Robert Bowes speaking for them all. He made a long, apparently rather overdetailed, confession of their collective treason, and thanked the King humbly for granting them pardon.

Katherine wrote to me she thought it might have been wiser not to go into so much detail; it might remind the King of many wrongs he had forgotten. Bowes promised that if any "relics of indignation" remained, they would be dismissed, and he delivered a stack of submissions in writing, along with nine hundred pounds.

The King declared he forgave them but warned them never to test his mercy again. Remembering what I had been told of the brutal killings after the Pilgrimage of Grace where the King had promised mercy then delivered death, I wondered what these men thought the promise of a king, especially this King, was worth.

The court's first house in Yorkshire was Hatfield in East Riding. It was not large and most of the court stayed at a hunting lodge nearby. Others had to beg beds in the houses of local nobles, sleep under canvas, or take refuge in lofts and hay barns. The King's party and the Queen's were few in number, but it was said they were enjoying the intimacy.

I wondered how much intimacy they could be having, for the land was good for hunting, and rich in fish, so the King went out and shot as many defenceless, herded beasts as he could then took to the water in boats to swoop endless fish into nets and throw them flapping, gasping and helpless, to the banks. One day, the King shot two hundred stags and does. It was not hard, so I heard. They were paraded past him in a line.

Floods of people arrived as they tarried at Hatfield. The King wanted to linger a while, gluttonous for blood, which granted all left behind in London a chance to catch up. Marillac, the French ambassador, arrived and Katherine wrote to me that Norfolk had pounced on him, eager to pretend that war between France and England was not about to happen and the King was instead thinking of war with Spain. The ambassador was not fooled.

No matter how many battles he had won and fought in, Norfolk was not keen for more. He thought the King's plan to invade France yet again was lunacy and was sure his sovereign would die.

"They say Marillac is trying to convince Norfolk to support the idea of one of King François' sons marrying Lady Elizabeth," said Kitty, pinning a brooch of azure enamel decorated with six diamonds to my chest. "They think that because Lady Elizabeth is Norfolk's grandniece, he will support the idea, but he told them it would be dangerous for him to suggest it, since other men would suspect he was furthering his own interests."

"He means the *King* would suspect," I corrected. "And he would be right. The King becomes daily more unsure of Norfolk's intentions and loyalty, that much is clear."

"I hear from a friend at court that Norfolk has suggested that the French concentrate on marrying Lady Mary to the Duc d'Orléans," said Jane Rattsey.

"The King will not marry his daughters off whilst he lives."

Kitty stopped before me. "The King will not leave them unwed, surely, Highness."

"He would rather they remain alone for the rest of their lives than he should have to think of restoring them as legitimate," I examined my reflection in the silver mirror. "Princes will not surrender their heirs to the King unless Elizabeth and Mary are seen as legitimate and restored to the succession. They are not about to match their legitimate sons to bastards, and the King will not accept lesser sons for his children. But the King will not go back on all he has done. He will not make them legitimate. If he was going to do so he would have already done the deed. I believe he thinks reversing his decision would make him look weak, or cause people to question his acts."

"I hear, Highness, that the King has granted Norfolk permission to say Lady Mary might be restored to the succession as legitimate," Jane said, playing with a locket of gold I had given her which lay upon her breast.

I shook my head. "It is a trick, a distraction. The King will keep the French talking, then he will invade. He will not restore Mary, to my sadness and hers."

"He has said this, Highness?"

"You think the King confides in me?" I laughed. "We are friends, but not that good friends."

"Then how do you know?"

"Because I see much. I'll wager the King told Norfolk to say to Marillac that Mary's restoration was to be a secret, for a time?"

Jane nodded, her eyes widening. "That is what I heard."

"And it will remain that way. The King is fishing. He means to net the French with lies whilst he prepares to hit them over the head with a club. I doubt they are foolish enough to believe him, although Norfolk probably does. He is fool enough for anything."

Jane and Kitty laughed.

"Now that remains in this room," I said, turning to them.

They swore to keep my secrets.

Chapuys joined progress too, and we heard he and Marillac took to amusing court by inventing wilder and wilder lies about each other. I received each tale with laughter. I wondered if the ambassadors knew all people of England were tittering so hard at them, for they only seemed to redouble their efforts, as fools do when they hear the chuckling of a crowd. When not inventing outrageous falsehoods about his rival, Chapuys spent most of his time with Lady Mary.

At Richmond we were enjoying lighter days. The rain had ceased to fall every single hour and so I ordered my household out into the fresh air as often as possible. I did not have to tell them twice, it was hard to get people back in, in truth, after so long cooped up like chickens or rabbits in a captive warren that summer. Some nights we stayed out in the park in a forest of tents, when we were done with the hunt.

As I lay under canvas, hearing rain pelt the cloth over my head, I thought of the future, I made more plans but often I simply lay there and listened to the rain of the night, the calls of owls, the noise of things scurrying about the tent. I listened to the crackle of the brazier and smelt the scented wood and I told myself that when I was tempted to concentrate on the future and on worries, I should take that moment to enjoy the present, for never would I have this moment again, never would I be this young, never would I know this peace, and if I did not take time to linger in the present, it would pass me by and I would never appreciate it.

There might come a time when I would look back on my freedom as a sweet dream, which had lighted the hours of my nights, and now was passed.

*

On progress we heard the King had turned proud and arrogant, telling Marillac to inform his master how many fish, birds and beasts the King had killed.

"I hear the ambassador was less than impressed," tittered Jane as we stood at the edge of the woods. We had been riding, and were resting the horses as we wandered a while in the clearing. I was reminded of when Sybylla and Amalia and I had seen the sign of the hidden people, told tales of them in the forests of home. For a moment my heart ached, thinking of my sisters so far away.

Leaves dripped with dew, and ivy was wound about the trees. Lichen, gold and green flowed up bark, catching the light which streamed through the branches overhead. "I heard the same. The ambassador said King François was not likely to be overawed by the King's charnel house," I said. "The King of France hunts boar and stag in the old way, on horse and with sword, pike or arrow. He does not simply slaughter all he sees as his men herd it past him."

Charnel house was an apt description. *"Each day I pass stacks of dead birds and fish, more than any man could eat,"* Katherine wrote to me.

"Fish kettles simmer over glowing embers all day, broiling the King's catches in herb-flavoured broth. Some are being packed in salt, sent on ahead to feed court when we reach York, others are being prepared for feasts each night. Whole deer and haunches of meat are being sent out to local nobles, signs of the King's favour. Little is being granted to the needy, even though this summer has been poor and they will be hungry come winter. I keep telling Charles he should suggest alms to the King, but he will not."

No, I thought, that would involve thinking of someone else, and the King was not one for that anymore. His men in times past encouraged him to think of himself as a God, and now he believed in their lies. But he was not God of the Christian faith, he was one of old, who played with people as if they were toys.

Chapter Thirty-Two

Richmond Palace
August 1541

"The King is telling everyone that at last his good nephew has seen sense," Harst told me.

"I imagine he is."

The King and court were at Pontefract Castle, a place with an evil reputation. Richard II had died there, murdered, most said.

From my reading, these personal lessons I was giving myself, I knew Pontefract was one of the finest castles in England. It had recently been renovated for the royal stay of twelve days, one of the longest stops on progress. Its tiny chapel of Saint Clement was charming, I was told, but there was another available to court, as Saint Clement's was undergoing repairs.

"The castle stands on a rocky outcrop, nine towers rising dark and long, like bony, pointing fingers, into the skies," Katherine of Suffolk wrote to me. *"Each holds five or six storeys, which stare down upon many little courtyards arranged in a somewhat muddled manner, all added over the centuries. For it is old, this castle, men once called it the 'key to the north'. For many more years than men can remember, or care to, it has stood guarding the north for the King, but there are modern comforts, like bowling greens where stone benches are set into garden walls for spectators to watch from, though there is much that feels antique about it.*

"One of the oldest parts are the dungeons. I have not been in them, but I can feel them. Long, dark tunnels racing under the castle, leading to cells where men have in the past been shut away to die. It is not only this which offers the castle an ill reputation. Here, Richard II died, overthrown by Henry of Lancaster. Some say he was stabbed, others claim he was starved to death. The second fate would have been crueller, and some say

Richard's moans of hunger and despair can still be heard in the castle, echoing from the past. Some say he died in the King's tower, where our King sleeps, others claim the Gascoigne Tower as the place of his death. Whichever is the true one, I know not. We are with the Queen and she is the first resident of the Queen's Tower, it was built for the stepmother of Henry IV and never used."

The King's visit had likely done little to dispel this evil air. Men who had rebelled against the King had come again, more of them, as well as those merely suspected of conspiring. All were to beg forgiveness and offer money as tribute. They did so, adding long-winded speeches, flattering the King and thanking him for his unbounded mercy. All submissions were offered second, in writing.

The King, it seemed, had had some other good news too. Though he railed often enough on the duplicity of the Scots, it appeared he was lately convinced of the goodness of their King. "The Scots ambassador, Thomas Bellenden, joined the progress a few days ago," Harst had told me. "He suggested a meeting of kings as King James is worried by what the King is doing on the borders."

"What is he doing?"

"Various things which may well look suspicious," he replied. "Some of his men have secretly been encouraging raiding across the border, which has put the Scottish government understandably on edge. The King has also been refusing to extradite Scottish criminals who have fled to England, despite the fact that King James has promised to hand over any English traitors hiding in his lands, with the exception of clergymen. The King likes not that James shelters English clergy accused of papism. There have also been many inspections of late, led by Norfolk, on castles and fortifications along the border. Scots are troubled by the fact the King has carried out building work on many of these fortifications, and were only more alarmed when it was found his progress was this year accompanied by many soldiers, ships and artillery. The Scots think he is planning invasion rather than seeking pleasure."

"I see," I said. "And why do all this? Have the Scots been acting as if they might attack?"

"Not directly, though it is always a possibility." Harst sampled a honey cake. "The Scots' government has been sheltering and encouraging Irish rebels, some English as well, but there is nothing new in that. The King is most upset about James sheltering the clergy. He thinks it a sign that James will formally join with the Pope and Spain. That might bring about a papal-backed invasion."

I shrugged. "Many years has that been promised and never occurred."

"Indeed, but the possibility is always there, Highness. In truth, I think the King is annoyed that his nephew will not follow his lead and break with Rome. He has been urging him to do so for years, but James has always refused. I think the King is also irritated that despite many promises James has always found excuses not to meet with him."

"The King thinks of his nephew as a child." I narrowed my eyes. "And thinks, as his kinsman, James should obey him."

"Of course, the King thinks everyone should obey him, even those who hold the same title."

"The perils of conceit are many," I muttered. "But it seems now that James will meet him, at York?"

"The Scots must be truly nervous, with regards to what the King is up to," Harst said. "Perhaps this is why they agree."

"Clearly. So, the court is to ride for and tarry at York, waiting for King James? The King will think he has but to put an arm about James's shoulders and nephew will obey uncle. I wonder if that will happen."

Harst had a contemplative expression on his face, his eyes distant. "What is it?" I asked.

"I wonder if this is not a ploy, Highness," he said slowly. "The King fears Scotland may join with Spain and Rome, but perhaps he is looking the wrong way, ignoring the obvious ally in sight."

"What do you mean?"

"Well, Highness, Scotland's oldest ally is France of course. The Queen of Scots is French. Much as Marillac is in England to keep an eye on the King's intentions, I wonder if this offer of a meeting, the ever-hanging possibility of it, has not been set up between the *Auld Alliance*, Scotland and France, to delay the King, find out what he plans for France, and give King François time to prepare for war."

"If a feint, clearly it has worked," I said. "The King does not sound suspicious of James at all."

"Because the offer of a meeting plays to his vanity." Harst lifted his bushy eyebrows. "King François would know how to advise James, for he knows his English rival of old. He has always understood the King better than he understood himself."

"You know much of the King of France?"

"I have met him many times. He is intelligent enough to do something like this. The King of France is one of the ugliest men I ever saw and one of the most charming. He devastates women."

"How so?"

Harst chuckled. "By listening to them, Highness. It is a remarkable thing how many men of this world woo women but do not hear a word they say. To own the truth, François has the same effect on men, though what he wants of them is quite different. The King of France is an arch manipulator, mistake me not. I have met enough to know one when I see one, but he has a way of concentrating on a person so they feel special. For men this can be unusual, for women it is almost unique."

I smiled. "Some of us are lucky, my friend. You listen to me."

"Some women are lucky, Highness, that is true, but so many are not."

"I know this well; I am a fortunate woman in many ways."

We heard the King was jolly for days. He had long desired a meeting with the King of Scots, and now it was to happen. The King boasted endlessly of how he would convince his nephew, led astray in faith by the lies of the papacy, to break with Rome as he had. He announced that James had not seen truth, but, once led by his uncle, he would be freed of deceit and lies. The King of England was there to guide and lead his nephew to a new dawn.

I thought there was small chance of this. Harst told me that once the King of Scots had thrown one of his uncle's letters into a fire, he was so repulsed by what the King had to say on religion. King James had also responded to one of his uncle's lectures, sent by letter, about the perils of his people. James had said he had no need to fear his people, as he was loved, obeyed and respected in his kingdom.

The King had become enraged at this, probably because deep down, he knew he was not.

*

I scowled as I read Katherine of Suffolk's latest letter, for it was not comforting. Something was wrong, clearly, with the Queen.

"The Queen's temper has been strange for days. As in the first days of her marriage, where she veered between overconfidence and terror, she seems to have now gone back to the same wild behaviour, and none know why. She is well in public, the model Queen, but in private she is changeable. She seems tired and overwrought. Some say she is with child, but her courses are regular. She snaps at her maids, Joan and Margaret and Kat, and is rude to her grand ladies. Only Jane Boleyn escapes her lashing, cruel tongue.

The Queen's sister, Isabella, was sent out of the privy chamber yesterday after she entered, as is her privilege, without knocking. The Queen shouted at her in front of us all, although we were all at a loss to know why. Chamberers have been banished to the back stairs. The Queen seems paranoid, as if they are watching her. Something odd is going on, and there is a new addition to the household whom the Queen seems to want to promote to the King and appears to loathe at the same time. His name is Francis Dereham."

Chapter Thirty-Three

Richmond Palace
August 1541

"Why does the Queen keep him, then? She seems not fond of him."

Harst shrugged. "Some say she is doing a favour for her grandmother, since the lad was in the Dowager's household, I think at the same time the Queen was when she was a girl, before she came to court. There are rumours that before he returned to England, he was acting as a pirate in Ireland."

Dereham, this new servant of the Queen, was annoying everyone. He was proud and arrogant, acted as if he were the Queen's master or at least her favourite, and *"he is not as handsome as he thinks himself to be. Were he, he might be forgiven more as at least he would be pleasing to look upon, but conceit and contempt mar his features,"* as my friend wrote.

And yet the Queen had offered this old family retainer of the Howards a post at court and none knew why. He had no skills, no experience and no grace. It was said he had quarrelled with Catherine's grandmother, Agnes Tilney, Dowager Duchess of Norfolk and then had gone to court to ask Catherine for a post. Why it had been granted at all no one knew for the lad seemed to have few manners and fewer talents, although there was a bizarre rumour circling London that Dereham had been the lover of the Dowager Duchess of Norfolk, despite the wild disparity of age. That, according to gossip, was why he had got away with so much under her roof and why the Queen had welcomed him in now; he had threated to talk about his affair with the Dowager. The Queen had made him a gentleman usher.

"The man is boorish and brash, unwilling to listen to those who try to teach him, and brags constantly about nothing," Katherine of Suffolk wrote. *"Other young men, no strangers to bold behaviour in their sex, are divided about him. Some appear to want to worship him. Others, more secure in themselves, have seen him swiftly for what he is, and despise him. The Queen's ladies and many of my men loathe him. He is arrogant,*

and foolish. Swiftly he has started bragging about the favour he enjoys in the Queen's eyes, and about what close friends they were when they served the Dowager of Norfolk. He lingers at the table long after other servants have gone, as though he is King. When one of the Queen's men sent a page to order him away, asking if he thought he was of the Queen's Council, Dereham shouted at the page, 'Go to Master Johns and tell him I was of the Queen's 'council' before he knew her, and shall be when she hath forgotten him!'

There was an allusion of intimacy in what he said which no one missed. Katherine wrote that Dereham and Johns had a brawl about the matter, which only helped to ensure everyone heard about it. That afternoon the Queen called Dereham to her and scolded him, but nothing she said seemed to make an impact.

"None understand why she is tolerating him, and the rumour is he must have some hold over her. Some say it lies in affection, but she does not seem fond of him, so I can only think there is something of the past he knows either about her or her family which if it got out would be ruinous. The Queen is locking her doors at night. I think she is afraid of this man. In public she is the model Queen, but as progress goes on, in private she becomes odder and odder."

*

"They say there will be war between France and Spain now," Harst mentioned, looking from the window, out over the park. The morning's mist had retreated, leaving sunshine, and the grass glittered green.

I concurred; my former husband might soon have an ally to invade France with.

The Emperor and the King of France were close to conflict. Relations had broken down entirely, and everyone thought war was inevitable. Both kings had written, urging their ambassadors to sue for the King's support. Both wanted England as an ally, therefore the King once more thought his country the most powerful nation in the world, and he the most formidable King. Nothing made him happier than when people accepted his superiority in power or morality. It confirmed all his personal myths.

So, my former husband was reportedly in a fine mood, jovial and jesting, marching about court with all the spirit of a man half his age. In the meantime, Catherine was still having problems with this Dereham who now was starting fights with other men and had been twice caught brawling. Normally this would be enough for the King to banish him, but not so. *"Apparently the King thinks the lad charming, however, and so keeps forgiving him,"* wrote Katherine of Suffolk. *"The royal couple see something in this usher the rest of us fail to, apparently."*

There had been other odd occurrences, Katherine wrote. The Queen had her door locked one night and when one of her women, Mistress Luffkin, had tried to enter the Queen had been so angry that she had threatened to dismiss both her and Margaret Morton, who too had of late become inquisitive about why the Queen's doors were locked. Gentlemen coming with messages from the King had frequently found themselves confronted by locked doors during the daytime. No one knew why the Queen was taking these precautions.

"The Queen has become either afraid or highly secretive and no one knows why. She seems afeared that someone will come in the night to her and harm her, for she locks her doors so well and all the time. There have indeed been rumours of people sneaking about at night in the corridors, and perhaps this has alarmed her, but there are always a few courtiers who sneak off to moonlight adventures on progress. It is a time many become a little reckless. I know not why it has alarmed the Queen so greatly at this time, but this is her first progress, so perhaps she does not know of these escapades and how common they are. The truth is, she is acting strangely, and all are talking of it but the King. He is unaware much of court are talking of his wife."

"It sounds to me as if she became scared the moment she took this Dereham into her household," I said to myself. "Oh, Catherine, what does he know that scares you so much?"

Chapter Thirty-Four

Richmond Palace
September 1541

It was September, and fresh winds of autumn were blustering upon us. The days had turned clement, brighter and warmer than they had been all summer. Warmth and light entered our lives. That autumn seemed contrite, an apology for the soggy summer drifting in its sweet breeze littered with falling leaves and perfumed by bonfires burning brush and bracken. Autumn was determined to make up for the summer, so rolled in with sunny days, along with crisp evenings and mornings.

This season I loved well, in truth I did all the seasons for different reasons, I was not one to play favourites. Each had a place in my heart. Winter won my love for it was wild and cold and strong, summer for it was warm and the nights were long and smelt of jasmine and honeysuckle, autumn for it was crisp at either end of the day and sunny in between and I adored the trees changing colour and the skies turning gold and crimson of the morning. And spring, she was the time of hope when winter has lasted so long you forget what it is to have warm bones under the sunlight, but then the first flowers are sighted, the first babes of the trees and the forest, the first warm breeze flows by and there is expectation in the air. Spring is hope, the possibility of the year made manifest.

The King had left his northern progress for a few days to go to Hull and inspect defences. He had not intended this trip, but the opportunity had arisen because of a continued delay in heading to York. The King wanted to leave plenty of time, both so James could arrive, and so York had been worked on enough that it would stun the King of Scots when he set eyes on it. York would be the setting for a glorious meeting which history would remember, this was what the King thought. Scotland and England would become allies and the other leaders of the world, seeing the wisdom of Henry of England at last, would follow suit.

Many others, Norfolk amongst them, so Harst heard, thought James's promise to arrive a feint, and the longer there were delays in James heading for York, the more people thought this. But although various men had voiced doubts, the King would not hear any suggestion of duplicity. So York was still being prepared, and court was waiting for news that James had set out, therefore the King had time to spare. If war with France or alliance with Spain might happen soon, England had to be ready for counterattack. So, he went to Hull for a week.

That would have been fine but in his absence the court had apparently run to madness. Katherine wrote that Dereham was incapable of good behaviour and the Queen's household were out of control. Many resented Dereham, not understanding how a man with so few graces could be tolerated by the Queen. Others were resentful of Jane Boleyn, for she was the only one the Queen always wanted by her side. The Queen's recent threats to dismiss maids and ladies had not helped the general feeling of unrest and unsteadiness in the royal household.

Dereham had claimed to one man that when the King died, he would marry the Queen. It was treason to speak of the death of the King, and to suggest Catherine was his implied an intimacy most dangerous. The Queen warned Dereham again and sent him money, probably intended to silence him, and then appeared to promptly go into hiding. She retired to her closet with Jane Boleyn and would not come out.

Katherine wrote that ladies were arguing, gentlemen followed suit, and even chamberers were at each other's throats. When the King returned, he had tales of Hull, but all the court was talking of was the Queen's household. I heard of the King's plans to build new fortresses, for the present ones were old and, although formidable, needed repairs. But whilst he was pleased to see his wife again, he was not pleased to find the state her household was in.

"He told her she must keep order," said Harst, "and questioned why it should be like this now, when for the last year it has run smooth enough."

"It sounds like this Dereham is the problem," I mentioned, crossing my arms.

"The man must have a hold over the Queen's family, I see no other reason she retains him."

"Apparently the King finds him amusing."

Harst lifted his eyebrows. "I doubt he will find him amusing much longer if he finds out what Dereham said about marrying the Queen if... something should happen. Anne Boleyn said something of the kind to the King's friend Norris, and it was used in their trials when accusing them of adultery and treason."

I spread my hands before me. "She should cast him out. Whatever he has on her family it is not worth this risk."

There was silence a moment as both of us thought.

"Hull was but the start of cities the King will inspect, so I hear. Other sites will be fortified, so says the King," Harst went on, heading to safer topics, "Walmer, Deal, Partland, Camber, Sandgate, Pendennis and St Mawes. The south coast is important and must be defended."

The King was to build new forts and castles up and down the coast, so he boasted, armed with the latest in modern artillery. He had been reading of new tactics in formulating barrages of fire against enemy ships and landing parties, and was keen to put it all into action, or so he said.

I doubted he would truly welcome war if it came to England. Make it upon others, in their lands, he could I was sure, but if it came here, he would be afraid. I wondered if he would ride out to meet his foes if they landed here, or if, as when sickness arrived, we would find our King hiding in a castle as other men faced his enemies.

Chapter Thirty-Five

Richmond Palace
September 1541

"There will be great trouble if he does not appear." Harst sounded concerned.

"Is it for certain that he will not?"

Court had been a week in York, and there was no sign of James of Scots. He was hunting, apparently, and the King had announced with pride that his nephew was a fine and lusty young man, much given to his pleasures, but he would be there soon. The trouble was, it seemed he might not be.

If Sir Thomas Wharton was to be believed, James had shifted further away from the south of Scotland and was heading north to Falkland Palace with his French wife. When my former husband had enquired about this a vague reply, more concerning prisoners held by each side than a meeting, had come back. When the Scots ambassador had been all but assaulted on the matter, he had claimed the distance was not *so* far, and James had gone on a hunting trip. The King was putting this excuse about, making favourable comparisons between his nephew and himself. Their dedication to youth and pleasure was the same, so said the King, who apparently had deluded himself into the belief that he and James were around the same age.

I heard from Harst that the King had been offered another excuse, a secret one; James had gone north to set down a small rebellion. Harst said the King was privately praising his nephew for concealing dealing with a potential uprising as a pleasure jaunt.

The even more secret word amongst ambassadors, which no one would say to the King, was that James was not coming, and had never had any intention of doing so.

Perhaps this might come as a relief to the Queen, since her household was falling apart. It would have been the first meeting of heads of states since the King met with King François when Anne Boleyn was alive, before she became Queen. It would have put a great pressure on the new Queen at the best of times, and this was clearly not the best time for her.

But to the King, if James did not arrive, it would be nothing but an insult.

Money was being poured into York like water. All over York men had been working for weeks and were working still, hammering and building, shaving wood and chipping stone, making York more beautiful than it already was for this great meeting of Kings and nations.

York was a stunning city, I was told. "It is large and heavily fortified," Harst told me, "with two miles of wall wending about its houses. There are smaller versions of the King's political structures of the south there; a smaller Star Chamber, the King's Council of the North, and branches of religious offices, there to keep the Church under the King's control. Surrounded by marshes and farmland, rich with crops and animals, five heavy gates guard York, and cresting the rivers Ouse and Foss are bridges, shops and houses balanced atop them, rather like London Bridge. It is a centre of commerce and trade, but the formidable fortifications remind everyone how important York is in terms of defence."

I doubt the King forgot it. When the Pilgrimage of Grace rose, York had simply surrendered, despite those fortifications, opening its gates to the rebel Robert Aske's men with barely a whisper of protest. But then, the north, York in particular, naturally, had always been more loyal to the House of York than that of Lancaster. The King was the living combination of both houses, but his father had been the last heir of Lancaster, and this had not been forgotten. The north was more Catholic than the south, and loyalties to the Pope and Rome remained strong, if hidden.

York was not allowed to forget its rebellious past. Aske's body had swung above the castle long after the man himself had died slowly from lack of food and exposure to wind and rain and snow. Some said his ghost could still be heard moaning from the battlements, groaning over the betrayal of his King.

As the court had ridden through the streets upon arrival, we heard thousands had turned out, many on their knees, to beg the forgiveness of their sovereign. Before the city, on a field of grass, clergy had knelt before the King. Led by Edward Lee, the Archbishop of York, three hundred offending clergymen had sunk to their knees, begging pardon of their King and offering up money to appease him. Lee was one of the prime offenders of past rebellions, who had only escaped execution as he pleaded he had joined the rebels for fear of what they would do to the people if he resisted. It was doubtful the King really believed Lee, and certainly was not about to trust him without question again.

Into the cathedral the court had walked, a white and gold vaulted ceiling shimmering above them. Stained glass rained azure and emerald light upon them, along with gold and flickering purple. There they passed statues of Plantagenet kings, every king in fact since William the Conqueror. All were stone but one. Henry VI was made of wood.

"Cromwell had his statue destroyed, for it was venerated as that of a saint," Harst had told me when I asked why this was so. "But the King ordered it to be restored, as Henry VI was his great-uncle. They had not time to make a new one of marble."

Sometimes it seemed to me that my former husband was a man of the temporary. Work on his palaces, as Katherine had said, was hastily done and did not last. His fortifications were the same. His marriages failed and his wives were destroyed. His children were reduced from heirs to bastards. He sought to be remembered in greatness, but greatness requires permanence.

The royal party were in new lodgings, we were told, built beside the suppressed monastery of St Mary. What once had been the abbot's mansion now housed the Council of the North, and although many in York still called it St Mary's, the King had renamed it The King's Manor. The royal apartments were in a long, narrow building next to the river. More than one thousand five hundred workmen had toiled all summer to make it ready, and goods such as more beds and tapestry had been shipped from London. People said it was a sign of the Queen's coronation, but there had been no announcement.

Twelve hundred workmen were labouring day and night, working by candlelight in the gloom of dusk and into the black hours of night, crafting under the bright autumn sunlight by day, as the King prowled about, watching preparations and barking orders.

A sea of tents in glorious colours of red, blue, silver and gold stretched out about York, some in the castle parks and some outside the city walls. A steady stream of carts trundled to the gates, bearing tapestry, plate, portraits, clothing and furniture from the King's palaces in the south. When the King of Scotland got to York he would find it hard to fit inside his own chamber, for every inch of space was stuffed with finery. Items left behind, judged too costly to risk on progress, were now shipped to York with impressive speed, and every day more messengers went out, riding hard on fast horses for the south, to fetch more items.

It was a great deal of effort to go to for a King who many said had no intention of making an appearance.

Chapter Thirty-Six

Richmond Palace
September 1541

"Rumours abound. It is said Master Culpepper and Jane Boleyn are lovers."

I smiled at the letter from Katherine of Suffolk; how she loved to send gossip to me. In a way it was the lifeblood of court so it was important. And was gossip of this day, which was after all just another story, any less important than the gossip I read in the tomes of history I had requested?

"Jane Rochford declared, before all the ladies of the Queen, that Culpepper stole from her a cramp ring blessed by the King last Good Friday at Greenwich and has sent her a ring in return. She showed it to the Queen's ladies and the Queen, who was present, laughed too at the tale of mischief as all the ladies giggled. The Queen took a cramp ring from her finger and told Jane to send it to Culpepper and ask for her own ring back. 'And tell Master Culpepper that whilst an honest thief is the best kind, he is to stop stealing from my ladies,' said the Queen. It was a public intervention, demonstrating that the Queen is aware of the little game going on and is calling it to a halt, but in a good-natured way, before it runs out of control. It was perfectly in keeping with the duties of a queen and with that it seems the Queen has regained her sense of control over herself. Calm has been restored and although none really know why or how, it is most welcome."

Thomas Culpepper fell ill not long after this jaunt, Katherine told me. It was probably as well the boy was in his bed for soon enough most people were thinking to hide under theirs.

"Oh dear," I said when I was told, which was a gross understatement of the degree of my concern at the news.

The news was all over court and country. The King of Scots was not going to go to York and the King was furious. Rejection sat not well with him, and he had gone to great lengths to please and impress James. For a man who so resolutely neglected and abandoned so many people in his life, the King could not stand being ignored himself. This was the worst insult. James, a fellow King, was treating him as though he did not matter.

Ambassadors were racing out of York with swift speed. Not wanting to be near the King in his present foul temper, they were riding for the south. Soon, everyone in Europe would be laughing about this, every King in every court, all their lords and ladies. This was a gross, humiliating, public insult. I could imagine my kin in Cleves and beyond might well take a great deal of satisfaction in telling and retelling this tale, since they still did not like the King for the way he had treated me. Sybylla would crow over this, I was sure.

"The Scots King *must* have promises from France to do something as audacious as this." Harst sounded shocked, though he had heard plenty of rumours James would not turn up. "He must have promises of support if war comes. To just not turn up? To send word he will not be there? He might as well have thrown his piss-pot in the face of the King!"

I agreed. We heard the King was lost in wrath indeed. He was busy in his chambers, firing off furious letters to his nephew. Orders had already gone out, commanding that harsher measures were to be taken on the border, and Norfolk was occupied with answering floods of letters already pouring in from confused border officials who had been sent orders to expel Scots. They were asking about Scots women who had married English men. Were they to expel them? And what of the children? Were they to go or stay? Norfolk was apparently fielding a barrage of technical questions and the King would offer no help. The King just wanted revenge, of any kind.

At the same time there was trouble in other countries. The Emperor's younger brother, the Archduke Ferdinand, had suffered a terrible defeat at the hands of the heretic Ottomans. The eastern borders of the Hapsburg Empire stood against the infidels but there were rumours that soon Europe would be invaded, barbarians and their sultans savaging the lands, raping women and murdering children. I listened to such tales certainly with trepidation but also with some cynicism. It had been said before that all this would happen if England was invaded by Christians of other nations. One did not need to be not of our faith to become a monster in war. Any invading army was stuffed full of demons, no matter what faith they were. War consumed men, and turned out monsters, that was the way of it, and no tale of chivalry would convince me otherwise. War was a corruptor, even the best of men were despoiled by its power, its horrors.

Another problem was that men had been caught stealing from Windsor Castle, and had been dealt with lightly, much to the King's shock, by officials there. The King, hearing of this, was using it as an excuse as to why his court should leave York. Perhaps he was thankful the Ottomans had come, and robbers too. He was not leaving, tucking his humiliated tail between his legs and running away from the north because James had rejected him, of course not. He was *forced* to head south by duty, for the sake of honour, to keep an eye on his palaces, his capital and the future of Christianity. He was needed there.

It was probably a way to convince himself he still had relevance in this world, when James of Scots had just treated him as though he was unimportant.

"War is on the way," warned Harst, after explaining that Lord William Howard was due to come home from France where he had been acting as ambassador. It was said Howard was to be posted elsewhere, but many including Harst suspected the recall was a sign. It was common practice to bring ambassadors home when war was about to erupt, so he told me.

The King was certainly ready to wage war, against anyone, I believe. Lord William sent news that Queen Eleanor had been ill all summer, it was said because of the troubles between her brother the Emperor and husband King François. In her absence, the King's mistress, Anne the Duchess D'Étampes, and the mistress of the Dauphin, Diane de Poitiers, were vying to be known as Queen in name if not in truth. The Dauphin's wife, Catherine de Medici, who would truly be the first lady of France should Eleanor die, was barely mentioned in reports. She was a lady with small graces, in truth and smaller beauty. Aside from the procreation of children, the Dauphin showed little interest in his wife. I felt for her, since I too had been denigrated because of my looks. There was more to many of us women than beauty, if people had the intelligence to see it.

I looked up as there came a knock to my door and a page in the King's colours entered. "Highness, I am to tell you that the court is leaving York on the morrow. Urgent business calls the King back to London. His

Majesty sends his best wishes to you, his entirely beloved sister, and hopes you are well."

"Thank you," I said. "Please send my love to my brother. Tell him I will be delighted to see him in London once more. Only he, in his wisdom and grace, can truly keep order in our beloved city, and his people miss him dearly. It pains all the people of England to be separated from their august and benevolent King." I paused. "Be sure to relay that word for word."

"Of course, Highness," he said, stooping to bow.

"Will you go to court to welcome the King home, Highness?" Harst asked later that afternoon.

"I believe I will fall ill when the King returns and will recover as soon as it is said his temper is improved," I told him. "Only a fool would go to court now, if they have a choice. I pity the Queen. He will be unmanageable in this state."

At a window I sat that evening, watching twilight fall. The last light of day was a crimson fire reflected as pink and gold on banks of white cloud. An echo of power was sunset.

Was it not the same for court and King? Would James have done this in the past, when the King seemed all-powerful before his people? I doubted it. The glory days now were faded, the brilliance of court was waning, like the sun. The King and his court were on the edge of darkness, and I could feel night approaching.

Chapter Thirty-Seven

Richmond Palace
October 1541

The court crawled back to London. One legged cats moved faster. They were so slow I think I might have outmatched them in pace during my trip to England to be married. It was put about the reason for this sluggish speed was so the King might honour more loyal and loving subjects on the way, people who were keen to see him. A feeble excuse. My former husband was reluctant to return home, to hear the laughter of foreign kings, tittering about James ignoring him. He feared that scathing laughter echoing all about him in his palaces of the south.

A more flagrant insult could barely be imagined. To turn up and be cold would have been one thing, but to be treated with such nonchalant contempt was something the King could not bear. And someone would pay for this.

But not, apparently, the Queen.

"The King surprised her with a gift. In truth, everyone has been avoiding the King, and the Queen looked nervous as he entered her rooms today, yet he had not hard words for her, but a brooch. He said she had been an honour to England and to him on progress and for all that troubled him now, she was his greatest comfort," wrote Katherine.

The brooch held thirty-five diamonds and eighteen rubies and was set with a depiction of the story of Noah in enamel at the centre. I hoped Catherine was pleased. For the King to single her out for good treatment when everyone else was bearing the brunt of his rage and hurt was a compliment indeed.

Within a few days I hoped even more she was in a good mood, for she was like enough to be angry with me when she heard what I had heard. "I am with child, again?" I asked. "I *am* a fertile virgin."

Kitty had heard that there was a rumour that when the King stayed with me that one night in August, he had left a child in me. Nonsense it was, and I hoped that Catherine was in a happy enough state as the King praised her conduct on progress that she would not care about this rumour, but it was still a source of anxiety. There was always the chance she might believe one of these rumours and become sour towards me.

One of the sources of the rumour was that I had held the babe of one of my ladies, who lately had given birth, and people had seen me do so. I had been ill a little that month, not seen out a great deal and then when I was seen, it was with a babe in my arms. Apparently from this people had decided I had borne the child of the King, although if so, it could not have been conceived in August!

The study of mathematics does not matter to the art of gossip, I had deduced.

A few days later the court were at Hampton Court, not far from me. Just as I was formulating excuses not to go to court, I heard they had moved on to Chenies Manor, home to Lord Admiral Sir John Russell. It was as though the King did not want to give up on progress yet. Everywhere it was hailed as a magnificent success, and if the submission of the north was all it was judged by, perhaps that was true. But like a storyteller who cannot tell where to end his tale, the King kept on with progress, as though to extend its length would make people forget the insult of the King of Scots.

The King's leg must have been bad, for at Chenies the Queen had rooms in the upper storey, and he had a state room on the ground floor again. Progress had been hard on his leg, I was told. The wet weather had made his sores gammy and pungent.

The old excuse was put about court; that his bed of cloth of gold and silver hangings was put on the ground floor so the King could hunt with ease, rising early to head out into the park and hunt like the valiant young prince he was, but in truth he hunted little. Sometimes I heard he watched as deer were herded into pens and torn apart by his greyhounds, but more often he was sitting and thinking, so said his men. He was tired. James had made him feel aged and futile. I was certain war would come with France. The King needed to prove to himself that he was still relevant to this world.

The King kept himself occupied, catching up with news of Council. France was trying to stall England's war and prevent friendship with Spain by again offering the Duc of Orléans as a husband for Lady Mary. Chapuys was busily disrupting all negotiations he could.

"The Queen has been welcoming more old friends into her household," Katherine of Suffolk told me. She had ridden over to see me and after many weeks apart I had embraced her, not knowing until that moment how sore I had missed her. "She has many now, this Dereham of course, but others who served the Dowager when Catherine was a girl are there now too. This latest one is called Alice Wilkes, or Restwold, I forget which was her married name for the Queen has used both names since she arrived. She was living in Calais but has returned to beg a place in the Queen's household. The Queen was happy to see her and sent her gifts as well as giving her a post."

"The Queen is generous," I said, but something shivered down my spine.

"Someone wandered on your grave?" Katherine asked.

"What?" I must have looked shocked for she laughed.

"It is just a saying, when someone has a sudden shiver out of nowhere, we ask is there someone walking on your grave? My old nurse used to say a hare was hopping on the grave."

I was quiet a moment and she put her hand on my arm. "It is just a saying; I did not mean to frighten you."

I smiled but in truth I did not think it was my grave I had felt footsteps upon.

*

It was late October, and the court had gone to Windsor, so I did not need to come up with excuses as to why I hadn't gone to them for a while yet. Had they remained at Hampton Court I might have been forced to put in an appearance and I wanted to be nowhere near the King. I was enjoying the beauty of England too much to have my spirits dragged down by my brother.

Trees were blazing red and orange, the parks were green and wet. Leaf litter rotted, letting out a sweet smell of fresh decay. Mushrooms were starting to erupt from the ground, and on trees they grew as tiny fairy steps, winding up the trunk. The harvest had not been quite as poor as expected, although it varied from region to region. Mist rose in the mornings, dispelled by warm sunlight as afternoon fell. Birds were winging in grey skies, jackdaws cawing as they sought the last treats of trees and bushes. There was a speck of winter on autumn's cloak.

The King was in ill spirits. Visions of war had kept him alive and vibrant a while, anger surging in him, but there had been bad news. The King's elder sister, Princess Margaret, was dead. She had died at Methven Castle near Perth eight days ago of a palsy which had fallen upon her. If there was anything that could have made the King feel older, it was a member of his line, one of his siblings, passing from life. He was alone now, in the world. The King said that he mourned her, but I doubted he did. Her death only affected him because it brought thoughts of his own mortality closer. It was sorrow for himself, not for his sister, he suffered.

This was clear enough to me from the scandalous lack of ceremony which followed. Court did not even go into official mourning, for the King said he was busy with international affairs. His courtiers wore black bands for a week, and there was a Mass for her soul, but whilst the whole country had been forced to mourn the passing of the Emperor's wife, there were no such honours for Princess Margaret Tudor of England.

"The King did not approve of his much-married sister," Harst commented.

"She married fewer times than the King," I pointed out, "and all her children are considered legitimate. She protected them from the stain of bastardry, whilst the King did not shelter those of his own seed." I shrugged. "I think the King did not like that she was married a few times for it reminded him that he was too. I think he spoke harshly of her in truth because he saw his sins reflected in hers."

"It may also be that the lack of ceremony is an insult for her son," Olisleger pointed out. "A way of striking back at James."

That was entirely possible, for did we not already know that all family members were held accountable by the King when one did something wrong? Margaret Pole had taught us that lesson.

What did truly upset the King was another piece of news. Prince Edward was sick. The boy had a fever and was swiftly confined to bed by panic-stricken servants who were certain they would be held to account for allowing any wandering spirit of illness near the Prince and would soon find themselves without heads. From what we heard of the King's alarm and anger, they might have been correct.

The best doctors and physicians in England were sent to Edward, and they quickly agreed the Prince was in danger of death. The King, to no one's surprise, blamed his servants. He had been told they indulged the Prince, giving him whatever food he fancied, no matter if suited to a child or not. Raging that this same indulgence had killed Queen Jane, the King turned apoplectic with fury.

"What does the King expect?" Harst whispered. "The Prince *is* indulged. His household fear if they do not attend to and allow his every tiny whim they will be punished. Ceaseless indulgence ruins children. If the Prince is sick, it is his father's fault, for the Prince's servants fear the King so greatly they will not treat the Prince as a normal child!"

"The King needs someone to blame," I murmured. "He cannot blame himself. There must always be someone else."

"Perhaps it is a trait of kings," Harst said. "They grow up being handed all they want, told they are always right, so what else are they to think?"

"I think it a trait of men," I said. "Mistake me not, there is much to admire in some men, but the truth is that only the strongest of character depart childhood not believing that all they want should be theirs. Many think that they deserve the world. Only the strongest and most courageous work for what they want, treat others well for the sake of compassion and kindness. The rest fall for lies of their superiority because it is easier than accepting responsibility. The Prince is treated thus because he is royal, to be sure, but many an heir of a noble house, or of a hovel, is treated the same. Boys are cosseted often, far more so than girls, and this leads to them growing up into spoiled men, full of vices that no one has thought to correct."

Harst nodded. "It is true, indulged men become no true men." He sighed. "The Queen has prayed for hours every day for the Prince, everyone is talking of her devotion and piety. The King is thanking God for her at this time."

I folded my hands in front of me. "Although I doubt not that she cares for the Prince, I would think she tries to avoid the King, and that is why she lives in her chapel at this time."

"I, for one, would not blame her, Highness."

"I, for two, my friend, would not either."

Over the next few days vigils were kept for Prince Edward. I took part at Richmond as the Queen did at Windsor. The King did not go to his son. It was said his men had pleaded with him to stay, to remain away from the sickness for the sake of his country and people, but I doubt the King took much convincing. The King was petrified of sickness.

The next morning when I woke, the world was altered. All was well again. News came early. The Prince's fever had broken and he was out of danger. Churches were ordered to hold services of thanksgiving, praising God for saving the King's son. There was more. The King was going to hold a special ceremony, for the Queen.

"When the court reaches Hampton again, it will be held," Olisleger told me, reading from the letter just come to my door, delivered by Diaceto. "A special Mass, thanking God for sending Queen Catherine, the jewel of womanhood, to the King."

I beamed as he lowered the paper. "She has done well. I am glad the King is finally to make a public announcement of all she has done for him."

"What has she done?"

My smile fell and my voice dropped low, for I knew Carew was somewhere outside my chamber that morn. "She has kept company with a monster, my friend, kept an evil spirit appeased. And somewhere inside him the King knows that."

Chapter Thirty-Eight

Richmond Palace
October 31st 1541

The King's court made it to Hampton Court by the twenty-eighth of October, and all England could speak of was Catherine's ceremony. I suddenly wondered if this was a trick by the King, a way to make people talk of anything but his humiliation at the hands of King James. I hoped I was wrong. I hoped he was honouring his wife for good and true reasons, not to distract from his shame.

"The love of the King for his perfect Queen, his jewel of womanhood, is the word on all lips," Harst told me. "Flocks of people race to the Queen's chambers daily to congratulate her and beg for favours. Petitions are coming from far and wide for they know she has power and influence with the King so she may speak for them. Finally, she has been accepted as Queen by all, for all see how the King adores her." He smiled, "It is as you always said it would be, Highness."

"It is pleasing to be right." I wore a merry grin. "I am glad the rest of the country sees what I always saw in her. This is her moment. Troubles will inevitably come again, but I hope she will cherish this time."

The night before the Queen's service of thanksgiving was Hallows' Eve. Her ceremony would take place on All Saints' Day. Hallows' Eve was the first of three days at this time of year when it was said the lands of the dead and those of the living became linked. Souls trapped in purgatory wandered the earth, seeking a way to find rest.

"Is it the same as Midsummer?" I asked Kitty, for at that time it was said too that the realms of the other world and ours broke down.

"We do not play tricks as we do at Midsummer, Highness," she said. "But people take care. It is said there are places one should not wander as the witching hour begins, forests, circles upon the ground, humps in the earth, old passages and tunnels, these should be avoided."

"Well, I think we may safely say we will not be wandering about in the forest at night," I said.

"Some say this is the time of the dead, as we enter winter," she went on. "The reason we may play tricks and have japes at Midsummer is because it heralds the time of the living, but this time is different. We must honour those who have gone ahead, or they will be angry."

I put my hand on her shoulder. "Those who have gone before us, only are they angry if we dishonour them. If we have done all we can to be good people, if we have striven to do our best, they will never be angry with us. Only those who fear the past, or what it might whisper about them, have any reason to fear a ghost."

"We should still put the cakes out, on the doorsteps and at the gates, Highness," said Kitty, her brow and eyes nervous.

She spoke of soul cakes, an old tradition as I had been told. Some said they were to be left by tombs, to satisfy the dead if they woke and came wandering, but they were set out at doorsteps for soulers, people who walked out on the feast nights of All Hallowtide singing or saying prayers for the dead. Although I was unsure what the King and his men thought of this old custom, I told Kitty it might go ahead. If nothing else it was another morsel for poor people, who often were the ones to take on the ritual of wandering and praying for the dead.

That night it was not dark for the moon shone bright, and there was no wind. No tempest trailed the earth. I saw no ghosts wailing, the darkness swirling about them.

It was clean and cold and still, a large moon high in the skies. The brightness of white light shone from surfaces, statues in the grounds of the palace gleaming pearl and silver. Paths leading into the gardens were brilliant, luminous serpents wending about beds of flowers. Glistening white light bounced from walls that in daylight were red, warm brick. Everything was transformed. Everything was ethereal in the night's beauty.

I sat by the window that night watching this melding of shadow and shade, this pretty world I was a part of.

I did not know it was the last beauty I would see for a while, as ugliness fell.

*

On the day of the ceremony, we rose early. I was not to make my way to Hampton Court to be present at the Queen's own ceremony, but my chapel, like many others all over England, was to hold our own celebration of Catherine. I was determined to make much of it. By golden candlelight I dressed, the early hours grey and dark. Gold and silver were on my sleeves, about my throat and wrists, fingers and dangling from my ears. I wanted all to know I honoured the Queen.

My ladies in a line at my back, we came to the chapel and to the sound of my choir singing beautifully, rounds of voices bounding through the air in unity, we processed to the head of the church.

At court, the King stood before his people and thanked God for his wife. "I render thanks to thee, Oh Lord," he boomed. "That after so many strange accidents that have befallen my marriages, Thou hast been pleased to give me a wife so entirely conformed to my inclinations as her I now have."

All over England, congregations prayed and gave thanks for Queen Catherine. Lips muttered prayers to keep her safe, to keep her close to the King, to make her influence him into mercy and charity. Her life was sacred that day, her name uttered as that of a blessed saint in all the churches of England. It was the moment of her greatest triumph.

We feasted that night in honour of the Queen as well as the hallowed dead. Venison in broth and saffron yellow frumenty graced our tables, along with pottages of turnips and onions, herbs and sweet mutton. Carp with parsley and black pepper followed, along with mutton legs covered with crisped lemons and sugar, capons with almonds and sweet butter, and white pudding crafted of hog liver.

As fruit tarts and apples fritters, glowing gold with saffron, came in, I lifted my goblet to drink to saints who were no more honoured in England, and in my heart and with my words, I honoured the Queen.

The next morn, for All Souls' Day, I went to Mass again. All Souls' was not a holiday in the same manner as All Saints', but that year it was a public Mass in recognition of Queen Catherine, again. My ladies and I processed to the altar with lighted candles in our hands. Flickering light played on the whitewashed walls of my chapel, bouncing from gilt and gold on the walls, alighting on silver, making the church shine.

To find a way out of darkness you must have light, I had said to Catherine, I remembered that now, as I prayed for her. *When danger or sadness come, strike a flame. You are the source of your own light and darkness.*

But a darkness I could not imagine or see was coming for my friend.

The celebrated Queen of England was only to be lauded for so long.

Chapter Thirty-Nine

Richmond Palace
November 1541

No one knew what had happened at first.

Slight, odd things occurred at court. Nothing to make anyone panic, but just enough to be commented upon. Norfolk was asked to stay clear of court. One of his men had died of the plague, so Norfolk was sent away. The King was suddenly in meetings, unable to see anyone, even his wife whom the country and he had just honoured, but it was reasoned he had spent three days devoting all his time to special services for Catherine, and war with France was looming. It was not unreasonable he should be spending time with his Council.

The Queen took to her chambers to practise dancing with her women, so they were ready for Christmastide and as she did, messengers flew out of the castle gates on swift horses all that day, heading into London and beyond.

Then there was an arrest. Master Dereham was taken into custody. Charges of piracy had been brought against him and the King ordered him apprehended.

"Women are being questioned, women from the Queen's chambers," my friend Katherine told me. "They are being taken out one by one, and we have all been told not to tell the Queen, on pain of death."

"Why?"

"I know not, my friend, they have not yet called for me, they seem to want only women who the Queen knew of old, from the Dowager's house, but I tell you this feels like another time, long ago." Katherine shivered.

"Do you mean the Queen is in danger?" Something of dread was crawling inside my heart.

"I know not, perhaps it has something to do with Dereham? Perhaps she or some of her women knew what he had been up to in Ireland? He has been taken to the Tower, but why they would send a common pirate there, I know not. All I know is that something ill is going on."

"Should you warn her? Should I?"

My friend looked steadily at me. "On pain of death, said the King's men. Do not think for a moment they did not mean it."

*

On the sixth, Norfolk was commanded back to court. The King was holding meetings at the oddest hours, but most suspected it was because of the impending war. Then Charles Howard, the Queen's brother, was abruptly banished from court and no one knew why.

They came for her at night.

Catherine was in her chambers, dancing with her women. Dusk was falling; in these winter months the skies grew dark fast.

Servants had been lighting candles and fires burned bright with dark sea coal, warming the Queen's opulent rooms. Tapestry covered the walls; gold and silver threads winked in the yellow light making the room sparkle. All was as it should be, yet nothing was right. Shadows were everywhere, cast by candlelight. Catherine, the young Queen, danced in the shadows and the light.

She and her women had performed for less than a half hour when there was a knock at the chamber door. They stopped. The Queen's ladies were laughing, flushed and curious, for most nights they were simply left to their own devices.

Jane Boleyn smoothed her dress and her countenance and went to the door. The Queen signalled to her musicians to continue playing. Her ladies went on with their pretty dance.

And in they walked. The King's guards. A whole contingent marched into Catherine's chambers.

Her ladies came to a stop, nimble fingers of musicians faltered on strings. People stared.

"How now!" Catherine exclaimed. "What means this, gentlemen? Do you have some message from my husband? Is war upon us?"

The officer at the front stopped before her. He looked over at the still forms of her ladies; frozen, as beautiful statues.

"Queen Catherine," he announced. "By order of the King I am to dismiss your servants, all but Lady Rochford, and confine you to your quarters."

He paused and looked around grimly. "This is no more the time to dance."

Chapter Forty

"What has the Queen done?" I chewed my lip and tasted blood. I felt I should have found a way to warn her, although it was done so fast I doubted I would have got word to Catherine before the King's men came for her. One day had passed from the Duchess telling me something was going on to the Queen being confined to her rooms. Perhaps there had been no time for me to warn Catherine, but still, guilt gnawed at my heart. I could feel teeth there, chewing.

"None will say, but the King will not come from his rooms even as she is confined to hers." Harst looked pale, ill at ease. No one seemed to know why Catherine had been arrested, in all but name, only that she had.

Catherine was confined to her chambers. Only Jane Boleyn was with her. Chamberers went in to clean when the Queen and her woman were in the little chapel, we were told, so she had no contact with them. The King's guard were all around them. No one would tell me what was going on. I had demanded information, using the most imperious tone I could muster, from messengers who came to the palace, but they had no answers. All they knew was, the Queen was not allowed to leave. It was said the Queen was spending her time praying. In truth she had little else to do.

That was, until she tried to reach the King.

*

"They thought the Lady Rochford had lost her mind," Katherine of Suffolk told me, come early that morn with the news. "But it seemed it was all planned. Had it worked, the Queen might be free now."

The Queen had made a desperate attempt to leave her rooms and get to the King. It was clever. If she could get to the King, could plead with him over whatever crime this was she had done, she might stand a chance. Catherine clearly thought she was in grave danger, and she was not alone, everyone else thought it too. If the Queen could reach her King, she might convince his heart to remember the great love he had for her, a love he had only just celebrated before the entire country.

The King did not like confrontation, not with those he had loved. Perhaps he knew how easily he could be swayed by someone he had once had affection for. That was why he separated from each of his wives before he had cast them aside, and friends too, for he had done the same with men like Cardinal Wolsey, so I was told, and Thomas More, refusing to see them after he had decided to move against them. If Catherine could catch her husband, could see him in the flesh, she might be able to convince him not to abandon her.

Dereham and now another, a man called Manox, had been arrested and questioned. But why, no one knew. People thought there was something ill in the Queen's past for both these men were once of the household of the Dowager of Norfolk, just as Catherine had been before she came to court.

Still being held at Hampton Court, where the King also was, the Queen and Jane Rochford were in her rooms. My friend of Suffolk told me they had been quiet, model prisoners, until that morn when Jane let out an ear-splitting shriek, throwing herself hard into the tapestry on the wall. She flung her body around, yowling like a crazed hound, tearing cloth from walls. A woman gone suddenly and violently insane, apparently, she ripped her hood from her head and knocked over tables. Tapestry popped from the wall under her hands. Jane pulled it along, smashing and crashing into everything she could, wailing like a phantom lost to God, screaming at the top of her voice as though in mortal agony.

Guards inside the room ran to restrain her, as Catherine pulled the door open. "My Lady Rochester is overtaken with hysterical passions," she cried to the guards outside. They ran to Jane and Catherine slipped out of the door and flew down the staircase.

It was early morning. The King was a creature of habit, so he would be in the chapel. Catherine was young and fast, and by all accounts she ran as if her life depended on it.

Which perhaps it did.

She flew along the long gallery. Far behind her a shout went up. Cries of alarmed men echoed down the long corridors. The guards had taken a moment to look away from Jane, or perhaps her performance had come to an end and the guards knew Catherine had taken the chance to run. They knew what trouble they would be in for this. They had just as much to lose as Catherine did.

They charged after her.

She was almost at the chapel door when they caught her. Shrieking, she leapt forwards. Catherine screamed the King's name and beat her tiny fists on the door. Inside, the choir faltered. "Husband!" Catherine screamed. "Henry, my love, my King, my lord, please!"

There was no answer.

Hands grabbed her. She struggled. She tried to cling to the door. The men trying to tear her away were scared and angry, rough with their little Queen. They did not want their masters hearing she had reached the King.

But Catherine struggled too, dropping to the floor, clawing at the door. Blood ran from her fingers into the wood, staining it. One of her hands clung to the door latch, knuckles white as death. She struggled hard. She dropped to the rushes and grabbed on to the door, fingertips under its frame, between rush mat and wood, squashing flesh until bones creaked. She flattened herself against the door, crawling to it again and again as they tried to drag her away.

They lifted her. Catherine screamed as she knew she had lost the fight. She was still screaming as they carried her back to her rooms.

The choir started singing once more.

The service went on.

The King did not come out.

I wonder if he even lifted his head from his prayers as he heard the screaming of his wife.

Chapter Forty-One

Richmond Palace
November 6th 1541

"The Queen is alone now, Lady Rochford has been taken from her, some claim the Lady Rochford has truly lost her mind and others say it is an act to protect her from the King's anger, because she tried to help the Queen get to the King."

"But *why* is the Queen being kept from him? What are the charges she is being held for?"

My friend shook her head and spread her hands. None of us knew, not even Katherine of Suffolk who was close to the heart of court and whose husband was close to the King. Brandon apparently would not tell her anything.

They had taken things away from the Queen too that morning, in addition to her friend, little things, small comforts. Maids had gone in, taking up items such as combs, piles of handkerchiefs in chests, bottles of perfume, jewels. They took a little clock the Queen had loved, made in the shape of a book, decorated with turquoise and diamonds. They took another clock that had hung on her girdle inside a pomander. Books had been taken from her too, a brooch the King had given her of gold enamelled with white, about whose edges little boys danced about a king. It bore a personal inscription from her husband, etched in happier times. I supposed all this was meant as punishment, but for what we still did not know.

Rumours were flying, however. In the place of facts, we had multiple fictions. The Queen was pregnant with another man's child, some said. The Queen was already pre-contracted to another and the King had found out, others whispered. The Queen was actually related to the King for he had lain with her mother, and the Queen was in truth the King's bastard daughter, and he had not realised.

The more believable rumours were worse, in a way. The Queen had led a sinful life before she met the King, it was said. Her ladies had been questioned and many of them, who had known her as a child and a young woman – although a young woman she still was – had confessed much to the King's men. Then the King's men went to the Queen herself, Cranmer, Norfolk, Audley, Radcliffe, Gardiner, to question her.

"Where was the King?" I asked.

The King had gone, I was told. After the Mass where Catherine had been dragged away from the door, screaming, he had dined under a tent in the fields of the Chase, then left for Oatlands on a hunting trip.

"Gone hunting." I had to say it aloud again, I could hardly believe it.

Gone hunting? After hearing his wife scream for mercy, after emerging to find her blood staining the chapel door, perhaps seeing one of the fingernails it was rumoured Catherine had lost stuck in the wood, and calmly had her husband gone off to eat, then to hunt at Oatlands of all places, where they had been married.

The King had left, that was the truth. He wanted to hide. When all this, whatever it was, came out he wanted to be apart from it. He was not brave enough to confront Catherine himself, so he had others do it.

So many times, I wondered if this could have happened to me. If the King had thought to pursue the idea that I was "no maid" as he had told so many people when we were married, would he have come up with lies he would use against me? But what had been said of Catherine I still could not discover. All I knew was *something* had been said.

I remembered tales of when Anne Boleyn had been arrested. He had hidden then, and later feasted on his barge with gaggles of beauties about him as she languished near insanity inside the Tower. Would ladies of court be shipped to him now so he might select his next wife? Would he take his time, or would Catherine be sent to death quickly on false charges, so he might propose marriage to Anne Bassett perhaps, or Kat Tilney?

Were my friend of Suffolk not married, I would think she could be his next wife, for often had been the time I had seen the King's eyes soften to see her in a crowd, or heard his voice grow gruff with desire as he talked of her.

"Why did the Council go to her?" I asked Harst that evening.

"Again, we know not for sure, Highness, but there is word they questioned her about matters that occurred before her marriage."

I rubbed my temple, a headache there brewing. "*Before* her marriage, so they do not suspect anything of her during marriage?" Before her marriage was not a crime; a sin, certainly, but it was less dangerous.

"I would think they do suspect. If she played the whore before she was wed, as people are saying she must have, given the circumstances and the fact the King will not see her, men will assume she did after, too."

My jaw stiffened. "I hate that phrase, friend. You know as well as I do that not every woman accused of such *played* at anything, oftentimes it is forced upon them."

"You think her innocent, my lady?" Harst looked incredulous. He seemed eager to believe anything of Catherine, but then, he had not liked her a long time and his respect, when given, had come with grudges.

"I would like to believe she is, and even if not, my friend, if anything happened *before* she was married and not during, then she has still done nothing against the King."

"Other than lying to him, concealing a past he might like not."

"Which is not a crime, my friend, and if she has any sins in her past and they have been confessed and forgiven by God, then the King cannot complain."

"But perhaps if he wanted a virgin to his bed?"

"Still, it is not a crime if she was not one. He was not either."

Harst paused, obviously struggling with the ideas I was presenting, that it was not anything criminal to have concealed a past, *if that past existed*, from the King. Everyone was talking as if Catherine were already guilty, and I had not heard evidence that she was.

Harst sighed. "She has been granted licence to move about her chambers as she wishes."

I was astonished. "Had she not that before?"

"She was confined to one room for a while, after her flight from her chambers to the chapel."

"Well, let us hope that means the King is thinking to release her."

Harst looked uncomfortable. "What?" I asked.

"The Council were also sent to bring back the Queen's jewels, Highness, and to inventory them."

"*Inventory*?" I gasped in disbelief. "Is the Queen dead, then, my lord, that the King should wish to inventory her belongings?"

"They belong to the Crown," said Harst.

"Is she no longer Queen?"

Harst shook his head. "At present, that title is still hers."

"At present," I repeated. I liked not the sound of that.

*

That night there was more news. "We know what the accusations are," Katherine of Suffolk told me, breathless after hastening along the river and swift to my chambers. "I hurried back to tell you, for I knew you would want to know as soon as possible. There has been talk that the Queen may have been previously betrothed or married to none other than Francis Dereham when she lived in the Dowager of Norfolk's house. There is more, an accusation she may have had improper relations with both Dereham and another man named Manox, the other who has been arrested. The King wishes the truth of these matters to be discovered as if she were previously married to another man and it was a consummated match, her marriage to the King would not be valid, and if she had improper relations with either or both of these men, her moral capacity is not such that would allow her to hold the honoured office of wife to His Majesty, or as Queen of this realm."

I felt my heart fall. "And is this for certain?"

"It is said she has signed a confession admitting to it." Katherine looked sad. "It would seem our Queen had an active life before coming to court and in youth was not well watched by her grandmother. There are all kinds of tales about court now about how men at the houses of the Dowager used to sneak into the women's chambers and have feasts and parties there."

I stared at my friend. "This all happened before Catherine came to court?" I asked and she nodded. "Catherine was fourteen or fifteen when she first came to serve me. That means all this must have happened when she was very young, and supposedly under the protection of a relative."

Katherine of Suffolk nodded. "Even in the best houses there is not much protection for most young girls, Highness," she said in a tone as grave as death. "I think you and I both understand that."

Chapter Forty-Two

Richmond Palace
November 7th 1541

"I hear the Queen has said there was no formal marriage between Dereham and herself, yet they called each other man and wife." My friend's brow was troubled with a frown.

Apparently, the confession the Queen had signed was not enough for the King. He wanted to know more, to hear the tale of her youth from her rather than just from Dereham. It was something, I supposed, that she was allowed to put forth her side of the story. Cranmer had gone to extract this from her. I was glad of that. Sometimes he seemed strict, but I had always had the impression there was a gentle man hiding beneath Cranmer's severe eyes, one who would not be hard on a frightened girl.

Katherine had found out much of the evidence and charges against the Queen. The root of it had arisen from a man named John Lascelles, a former servant of Cromwell, who had gone to see his sister, Mary. He had said to his sister that she ought to seek out the Queen and ask for a position in her house as they used to know each other when serving at the house of the Dowager of Norfolk. Mary had said she had no wish to associate with the likes of Catherine. When her brother asked what she meant, this tale of the past had come out. In truth, though the Queen was the one accused, there were other motives for this to emerge.

Lascelles hated Norfolk and was part of the most zealous reformist circle of court. He was a man who had had a promising future until Cromwell's fall had ended or stunted it at least. After Cromwell died, the cause of reform had been set back. Only Cranmer was there to protect it, and the King had retreated, heading for the familiar arms of Catholicism. Lascelles had taken a post in the King's house, but not risen far. In his eyes, Norfolk was the cause of his career's stagnation and the cause of reform failing. Lascelles would have revenge.

That was all it was; revenge. For this, a young girl who had made a most promising Queen, one we had only just celebrated as a nation, was being attacked.

Lascelles had taken the story about Catherine to Cranmer, who had taken it to the King. I did not blame Cranmer; it was not as if he could keep such information to himself. He also was not likely to be one who took delight in punishing the Queen. Cranmer might want reform advanced, but it was not in his nature to harm innocents like the Queen.

The truth was, the Queen was caught in the middle of a struggle of faith and power. Catherine was simply the weapon used against Norfolk.

So, it was known now that Catherine had had relations with Dereham and Manox before marriage, that Dereham had confessed to sex and Manox to touching the Queen in intimate places. The King was horrified his wife was not the innocent maid he had thought her to be. Cranmer, fearing to say all this to his master's face, had left a note for the King in church, in his pew. The King was destroyed by his sorrow, it was said about court.

I doubted the Queen was very merry either, the world was calling her a whore and she was in peril of her life.

"Alas, my lord," Catherine had said to Cranmer, "that I am alive. The fear of death grieved me not so much before, as now the memory of the King's goodness to me is. When I remember how gracious and loving a Prince I had, I cannot but sorrow."

Cranmer had told her the King might well be merciful, for if no crime was done against him then there was a possibility of forgiveness.

"This sudden mercy, more than I could have looked for, shown unto me, so unworthy at this time, makes my offences appear before my eyes much more heinous than before," she said. "The more I consider the greatness of his mercy the more I do sorrow in my heart, that I should so misorder myself against His Majesty."

"Would he pardon her?" I asked Katherine.

"I know not, it is possible of course, but I doubt he would remain married to her. His perfect rose is blemished now."

There was more news. The Queen had protested that whilst it was true she had been touched by Manox and had relations with Dereham, she had been forced to do so by both men.

"She said Manox assaulted her, threatened her, and managed to get his touches from her in that way, and Dereham she says came to her bed when she was young and was deep in drink, at one of the parties in the Dowager's servants' chambers all are speaking of. The Queen said he scared her enough afterwards with his behaviour to take her whenever he pleased," Katherine told me.

"That sounds entirely believable to me."

Katherine wore a solemn expression on her face. "To me too. Other men will not believe it though, they will not understand for she does not say the men beat her into submission, she does not say she screamed out against it. If she told tales of strangers attacking her, leaping from bushes, all men would believe she had been raped. It is harder for men to believe that other men can be so callous, so cruel to a woman they actually know. That men could treat someone ill who is in their lives each day. Men know such crimes happen in war, they understand a soldier breaking into a house, forcing a woman on the floor. Most do not understand these things also happen every day, in houses next to theirs, to women they pass in the street. Honest men with decency in their hearts cannot understand. They think, they have the luxury of believing that because they would never do such a thing, other men could not do it. If they knew the secrets women keep, my friend, their hearts would break."

"Some of them," I said. "Some of them are more than aware of the secrets of women, for they are the ones who made those secrets."

"Most decent men, my friend, if they knew the masks some men wear, they would recoil in horror."

"I hope that is the truth." I stared at the wall in frustration, not seeing the tapestry there but the honest and eager face of Catherine when she had pleaded for prisoners, when she had welcomed me as a friend. I thought of her sending comforts to the Countess in the Tower, of all the good she had done which people had apparently now forgotten. "The trouble is, what proof does she have? If these men say one thing and she another, and all this happened so long ago? There are two men against her one woman, and we all know a woman is less believed in, in any case. She cannot show the wounds inflicted from fear or blackmail, as she claims this Manox used to get her to allow him to touch her, not the fright Dereham inflicted on her."

More people would want to believe the men. Believing Catherine was the liar was the easier option. The world remained good and true if she was lying, for it meant rapists and molesters were not walking amongst us, looking like ordinary men. If she was telling the truth, awful, dirty, nasty things were crawling under the surface of the good and honest world. If she was telling the truth, women and children were not safe.

"Cranmer appears to believe her, however," Katherine went on. "That is what his men say. The Archbishop appears to think that Dereham forced himself on Catherine once, then used that one time to force her into calling him husband and letting him do it again."

"So, this Dereham said perhaps that if she did not call him husband and did not allow him into her bed again, he would tell her uncle, mayhap?"

"That is the way of it. It may be that Dereham did this because he thought he could gain a Howard bride in such a way, that if Catherine were deflowered by him, and if she had called him husband which could be seen as a verbal commitment, a betrothal, if you like, then he would have promise of marriage *and* consummation, and so the Howards would be forced to give her to him. It could have been done this way on purpose so an untitled, unimportant young man could force his way into the nobility. It has been done oftentimes before, a man raping a woman to force marriage on her, thereby gaining her fortune."

I frowned. "Catherine had no fortune, though."

"To a man with even less money she would have seemed rich, and the Howards would have given him much to keep him quiet, plus she was vulnerable, obviously not well watched and so easy for him to gain access to. He might well have extracted a good house and a place at court from the Howards in return for silence about what had happened between him and the Queen."

Catherine's words on the matter of Dereham had been, "All that he did unto me was of his importune forcement, and, in a manner, violence, rather than of my free will and consent."

"You know the trouble is people will say she invents this, to excuse herself," I said.

Katherine rocked on her heels. "And yet it might very well be true that he did all this, and she was young and innocent enough to fall for it."

"But she says they never married, and she only lay with Dereham outside of marriage? So, she has not become a bigamist upon marrying the King."

"Indeed."

"And this Manox only touched her?"

"He was her music tutor, when she was even younger, perhaps ten or eleven? He presumed to touch her. The Queen says he kissed her once or twice, but no more. Her grandmother thought he was getting too familiar with Catherine and sent him away. But the Dowager apparently knew nothing of what he tried to do or what he had already achieved. Most of those questioned on the matter seem to agree Manox was a man Catherine did not like, but some women say Catherine was fair in love with Dereham. Mary Lascelles said the pair were wont to kiss and hug, hanging by the bills together, like sparrows."

"What is seen on the outside, my friend, is not always a true reflection of what goes on between two people. Besides, Mary's brother might have had her say that, to harm the Queen and Norfolk all the more."

"I know that well, but other evidence is mounting. Mary Lascelles said the Queen oftentimes stole the Dowager's keys to let Dereham into her rooms, but the Queen denies that as well. Again, this might be a fabrication to darken the Queen's name, but one trouble is that when Catherine first came to court Dereham came after her and they met. Then he left for Ireland. He says he went off to make money so they could marry, but she says she cut ties with him and told him to leave her alone. But then there is the trouble that she made him an officer in her household after her marriage, when he returned."

"If he had all this to hang over her, I am not surprised she did so," I said. "Surely he got the place through blackmail?"

"Indeed, I am sure he got the placement by threatening the Queen that he would tell the King of her past." Katherine exhaled loudly. "But other men look at this and think it strange, think that if she was afraid of him, why did she let him into her life again?"

"*Because* she was scared of him, that is why! He had power over her!"

"I understand, my friend, and you understand, but other men do not, or they will pretend they do not for it is of advantage to them to besmirch the Queen and in doing so remove her uncle, perhaps."

There was silence a moment.

"Cranmer is to write down all she has said, and the King is to examine it." My friend spread her hands and shrugged. "It may be that she might not be Queen after this, but as far as I can tell she has committed no great crime against the King. Nothing happened after her marriage, other than her granting posts in her household to Dereham. It may be she can retire to a convent, spend the rest of her days atoning for her past."

"A past which, if she is telling the truth, contains few serious sins of her own, but only ones inflicted upon her by other people."

I shook my head, feeling tears in my eyes. I could already feel the condemnation of the world falling on Catherine, so hard and fast and heavy, and yet I saw another story entire. I saw a child, innocent, unprotected, who had a large heart always willing to think the best of people and was in spirit a little too trusting and foolish, who had been used by men, and abused by them.

"I know," said my friend, watching my face. "But, consider, Anne, consider what another fate could be, and you and the Queen herself might well think a convent the best option."

I shivered, a skeletal hand seeming to pass down my spine.

Chapter Forty-Three

Harst came later that evening, carrying fresh news gleaned from court. Yet none of this produce did I like.

More men had gone to the Queen, asking the same questions, then new ones. "The trouble is, Highness, it is now known that the Queen has been lying about some particulars of her tale."

"Which are those?" I rubbed my head; there was an ache there growing, refusing to let me alone.

"It seems her grandmother, the Dowager of Norfolk, knew full well what Manox was up to and that was indeed why he was sent from her house. The Dowager caught the Queen and him in an embrace and seeing the danger, sent him away. The Queen has confessed this is the truth and claims she lied before because she was simply trying to save her grandmother from shame. This might be the truth, but altering her story has made her look guilty, as if she might have lied about Dereham too."

"So what do they ask her now?"

"The same questions, but perhaps in more detail."

"How do you know all this?"

"The men guarding her door hear much, especially when the questioners grow loud."

I swallowed. "They are shouting at her?"

"They are, Highness. I know not what else might be being said. In honesty, what is whispered might be worse than what is shouted to a prisoner."

I stared at him. "You mean they are threatening her?"

Harst nodded. "I think it possible. There are plenty of men of court who would love for Catherine to fall, for with her tumbles Norfolk, perhaps the entire Catholic faction. She is young, is a woman, has never been known for possessing sharp wits, so she may be easy to intimidate into saying something to incriminate herself. They will not be easy on her, those who want Norfolk out. Even his allies may turn on him and the Queen at this time." Harst looked sorrowed. Despite his general dislike of Catherine, I do not think he wanted her to face anything of this kind. "It may well be she has done some wrong in her life, but they will make it appear as bad as they can."

"We have all done some wrong in our lives, my friend."

We heard the King's men asked Catherine why she had offered Dereham presents when he was in her service, which might be thought a sign of intimacy. The Queen explained they were gifts granted at New Year's and no more than that. They asked her if she had said she loved him when in the Dowager's house, as he was apparently claiming, and Catherine said she remembered not using those words. They knew of a French fennel flower he had bought for her, and the Queen told them how she had owed him money for it but had paid Dereham back.

They wanted to know if she had made a band and sleeves given at New Year's. For a woman to make items personally for a man was a sign of affection. The Queen said she had not made them.

There were other things, gifts Dereham claimed he had given her, or she had given him. He had left money with her when he went to Ireland, a hundred pounds, which was a vast amount, and such an amount would seem to indicate they were at least engaged, but the Queen said he had left it to her as a trusted friend, nothing more.

"Yet the sticking point is that they called each other man and wife and then had lain with each other," Katherine told me. "Even though there was apparently no ceremony held before a priest, this promise, this act of calling each other husband and wife combined with consummation could be enough to make a secure contract and prove they are man and wife before the eyes of God. Talk of marriage followed by carnal copulation, is sufficient to prove a contract."

The Queen said it was no contract, for it was not of her free will and consent.

One thing in her favour was that she had not become pregnant. It was widely believed that conception required a woman to enjoy sex. That there had been no child despite many couplings suggested the Queen had not enjoyed sex and had indeed been raped.

But it was not what men commonly thought of as rape. It was not rape that was understood. It was not violence of fist, not bruising of skin, it was not a stranger happening upon a woman in a dark lane and beating her until she submitted, and if after all this they considered Dereham to indeed be her husband, it was not rape, for a man could not rape his wife. By law, no matter how a husband took his wife, how violent or hard or cruel, it was not rape.

It was a law I despised.

"I hear the Queen's confession has gone to the King, Cranmer helped her to write it in terms His Majesty would welcome, and the King is merry to hear the confession of his wife."

Merry? I thought. To hear that sex and men had been forced on Catherine, one after the other, since she was a child? My mind shuddered at this man, for the sake of appeasing his own pride he would prefer his wife had been forced into these acts than that she had entered willingly? He would prefer a child had been assaulted?

It was a masterful letter Catherine wrote; we gained a copy some time later.

I, Your Grace's most sorrowful subject and most vile wretch in the world, not worthy to make any recommendation unto Your most excellent Majesty, do only make my most humble submission and confession of my faults. And where no cause of mercy is given on my part, yet of your most accustomed mercy extend unto all other men underserved, most humbly on my hands and knees do desire one particle thereof to be extended unto me, although of all other creatures I am most unworthy either to be called your wife or subject.

My sorrow I can by no writing express, nevertheless I trust your most benign nature will have some respect unto my youth, my ignorance, my frailness, my humble confession of my faults, and plain declaration of the same, referring me wholly to Your Grace's pity and mercy. First, at the flattering and fair persuasions of Manox, being but a young girl, I suffered him a sundry times to handle and touch the secret parts of my body which neither became me with honesty to permit, nor him to require. Also, Francis Dereham by many persuasions procured me to his vicious purpose, and obtained first to lie upon my bed with his doublet and hose, and after within the bed, and finally he lay with me naked, and used me in such sort as a man doth his wife, many and sundry times, and our company ended almost a year before the King's Majesty was married to my Lady Anne of Cleves and continued not past one quarter of a year, or a little above.

Now the whole truth being declared unto Your Majesty, I most humbly beseech you to consider the subtle persuasions of young men and the ignorance and frailness of young women.

I was so desirous to be taken unto Your Grace's favour, and so blinded by the desire of worldly glory that I could not, nor had grace to consider how great a fault it was to conceal my former faults from Your Majesty, considering that I intended ever during my life to be faithful and true to Your Majesty ever after. Nevertheless, the sorrow of mine offences was ever before mine eyes, considering the infinite goodness of Your Majesty towards me from time to time ever increasing and not diminishing. Now, I refer the judgement of my offences with my life and death wholly unto your most benign and merciful Grace, to be considered by no justice of Your Majesty's laws, but only by your infinite goodness, pity, compassion and mercy, without which I acknowledge myself worthy of the most extreme punishment."

"Cranmer helped her, the good man," I murmured when I read it.

Catherine, clever though I thought her in many ways, was only possessed of the rudiments of language when it came to writing. I knew, for she had served me. This letter had been written by the Archbishop and I knew as I read it that he was trying to save the poor child.

Cranmer gained nothing by helping Catherine. It would be better for him if she ceased to be Queen. She represented the old ways and he the new. He understood she wanted no part in politics or faith, she had made that obvious, but she was still a symbol of power for conservatives. Take Catherine away, and the King could marry a new wife, one of Cranmer's choosing, who might speak for the cause of reform. And so the scales would tip again and policy and politics would change as the King's bedfellow did. But whilst it was to his advantage to remove her, Cranmer had no wish to see Catherine hurt. Taken from the throne, yes, but not harmed. He could have simply worked to destroy her, as Cromwell had Queen Anne, but Cranmer was not a violent man. If he could spare her what her cousin had suffered, he would.

"The King was cheered to know his wife was never unfaithful," said Harst. "He is to return to Hampton Court and there is word he is of a mind to forgive the Queen."

I crossed myself. I had not done so for a long time, I was never sure whether to do so or not in England so had thought it safer not to in case the King thought me popish, but that action of childhood came to me now, and I drew comfort from it. I could almost feel my mother at my side. "Would to God that is so."

"I should tell you, Highness, however, that the Archbishop thinks that the Queen was indeed pre-contracted to Dereham. He admits the evidence is tangled, but they called each other man and wife and lay together as such. But no one thinks the Queen is guilty of adultery, Highness, and there is no word of treason. There is no great crime, and no crime deserving of death. There is word that if the King does not take her back, she might retire to a convent, or she might have her marriage to Dereham formalized."

I baulked at that. "I am sure she would rather take the convent. It sounds as if she tried her best to get away from the man."

"At least there is hope for her, Highness. The King is of a mind to show mercy. This Queen at least might escape with her life, as you did, madam."

Chapter Forty-Four

Richmond Palace
November 8th 1541

If we had hoped in the evening, there was despair rising in the morning with the sun. The Queen's household was sent away. The few maids Catherine had were to stay with her, but her ladies were sent home. That was not a good sign.

"Her Grace the Dowager of Norfolk is now being questioned by men of the King." Harst looked weary from running back and forth to court for me all the time. "The King is angry so much ill happened to the Queen as a young girl in her grandmother's house. The Queen's youthful waywardness speaks of neglect, and the Dowager may be punished. The Dowager is worried for her son, Lord William, people say, for he is coming home from France unaware of the trouble at court. I understand she wanted to send word to him but was stopped by her people, for they said it would look bad, and they were right. But like the Queen, the Dowager is not in danger of her life. She was negligent in her duty and should have been aware of what was going on in her house, but there is no great crime."

That was what everyone said, all the time, no *great* crime. They meant no crime deserving of death done by Catherine, of course. Few people spoke of the crimes against Catherine. Even the most sympathetic seemed to think she was at least partially to blame.

I knew now death was unlikely for Catherine, I hoped it was, but it seemed she would not remain Queen. Less frightening was that thought than the other possibility that remained; the poor girl becoming wed to this Dereham. Married off to that angry, intemperate man who had caused nothing but trouble at court? The man who had upturned her life, her success, ruptured her position, her standing and reputation? To be given to him, handed over so she was unable to escape? Poor Catherine would be punished for the rest of her life by such a man, I was sure, beaten black and blue, raped each night. There was enough evidence from his brawling at court to tell me he was a man quick to solve matters with his fists and if he had shown scant respect when she was his Queen, just how far would his treatment of her sink when she became his wife? The Queen evidently saw this future unfolding in her mind too, for she had asked several times that if it came to a choice, she would rather enter a convent.

Catherine had never shown a great deal of interest in the faith and given her protestations of innocence I believed she did not think herself guilty of a crime she needed to atone for. Therefore, she was using a convent as a means to escape a man she was afraid of. If the King would not protect her, perhaps God would. This said to me that all she was saying was true.

"At least the dissolution of her household demonstrates that the King has no replacement for her in mind," I said to Kitty. "Perhaps she is indeed to be sent to a nunnery."

Perhaps there was indeed hope of mercy. What had she done, after all? She had lain with a man before marriage, and there was a supposition she was promised to him. I myself had been cast off, officially at least, because of a pre-contract. Perhaps Catherine would be treated as clemently as me, although I could hardly hope she would be rewarded with lands and money.

"She is to be sent to Syon Abbey," I was told that night by Harst. "There, the Queen will live, Highness, until affairs are settled, but I am told she will be treated with the state and dignity of a queen."

"I think it a sign the King may forgive," I said, my mind working fast. "He does not send her to the Tower, after all, not even far from his palaces. Syon was where Lady Margaret Douglas was sent when her affairs were discovered, was it not? She later returned to court." Hope fluttered in my heart, many feathers beating fast.

Was this a sign? Was the King thinking affairs before marriage were lamentable certainly, but perhaps forgivable? Might Catherine not be cast off, but remain Queen, and this time with no man holding secrets over her head? Was it possible?

I understood so much of her past behaviour now, her insecurity, her haughtiness, that false pride people had spoken of which I had never seen for myself. It had all been a front, a mask. She had been terrified this would come out and ruin her. If little Catherine could be Queen without the fear of discovery looming always over her, how different a soul she might be. If she was given the chance to grow into a woman, rather than remaining a scared child, what a woman she might become.

I had always thought there was something inside her, hidden, trying to get out. She had had to conceal so much that perhaps she barely knew who she was, and if she was capable of such kindness, balance and compassion whilst under terrible pressure, I wondered what she might be like without it. So much effort had gone into concealing who she was and what she had done. Without needing to feel constant shame and fear, what might Catherine blossom into? If she had a life free of her past, she could grow into a Queen capable of true greatness.

If men would allow her to, of course. That was the trouble.

If she remained Queen, she would still be playing a part in one way. Oh, she would have to return as the contrite wife, earning forgiveness from the King. She might have to be obedient and penitent all her days, seen to be painfully, obviously grateful to him, but she might remain Queen. It seemed possible. Perhaps the King believed her story, or perhaps he missed her enough that he was willing to forgive her, for what had been done *to* her.

It was also possible the King might annul his marriage and keep Catherine as a mistress if he could not do without her. I doubted the King would hand her to Dereham, even if Cranmer believed they were married. The King was too jealous a man for that. If he could not have Catherine, no man could. That was the way his mind worked. So, a convent at worst, and perhaps, if he really could not do without her, a crown at best?

It would not be easy, living at the side of the King after this, but death is harder. And what if a mistress? Was it possible? It might be a quiet post. The King would not want people to hear he had cast Catherine off for being of ill moral character then taken her to bed. But it might be possible. He was vastly hypocritical when it came to morals. If so, what would she have? A life in the country, a few years of warming his bed, then perhaps freedom when he died?

The Queen was ready to be taken to Syon, we heard, and she was to take four gentlewomen with her, one being her sister Isabella, as well as two chamberers. Aside from Isabella, Catherine was permitted to pick her women, another encouraging sign of favour. She was to have a modest amount of furniture and clothing, but was not stripped of everything, which offered a little more hope.

"Will Lady Rochford be one of her women?" I asked.

Harst shook his head. "The Boleyn woman is being questioned," he said. "But she is well, by all reports and has said only that she loves the Queen."

A day later we heard this was not true. Jane Boleyn had in fact been sent to the Tower. Fresh rumours had come about, tales of odd happenings on progress.

Cranmer, sympathetic to the Queen though he was, had to investigate. His first loyalty was to the King. Had he allowed those rumours to pass by uninvestigated, he might have ended up on the block himself.

Had Cranmer been able to save her, I think he would have. Catherine might have escaped had the tales ended with Dereham and Manox.

But that was not where the tales ended.

Chapter Forty-Five

Richmond Palace
November 11th 1541

"The poor child, just as she had hope she would escape." My heart was a rock inside me, my throat was fighting the urge to vomit.

"It seems that hope is done now, Highness." Harst exhaled, a long, slow breath. "It seemed she would be safe indeed, but now she is in peril of her life again."

Catherine's enemies, or rather foes of the Catholic faction, had been digging and they had found something else to accuse the Queen of. Her past had not been enough. The King was on the verge of forgiving her, so they had found, or perhaps fabricated, something else.

My nerves were frayed. "It is like torture on the girl. Seventeen, Harst, that is all she is. To face this fear then hope then fear again. Would any of us have stood up to this at that age, at any age? To be accused and arrested then questioned, then to spill the secrets of a past of pain and shame to others and the world, to be given the hope of forgiveness, then to have that ripped away again. This is torture."

They knew about Thomas Culpepper.

I had wondered if they would find out that she loved him, and, as I believed, that he might love her. As it transpired, they had, but they were confused for the Queen had been incautious in one way and cautious in another. The relationship between the two had gone further than the glances I had seen stolen between them, but not so far as to be dangerous, or so Catherine and Culpepper protested.

On progress she had snuck out at night to meet Culpepper, this was a grand risk of course, but Catherine had ensured she always had the Lady Rochford with her. A chaperone. The couple had met, they had talked, but there had always been another person in the chamber, one who could attest that nothing more had happened.

"That was why her doors were locked at odd times," I said to Harst, "do you not remember that, the tales from progress? And the stories of people sneaking about, it must have been the Queen and Culpepper and their servants. She locked her door so none would come in and find her not there. That is why she was so irritated with her women when they came in without warning."

Harst rubbed his eyebrow. "The trouble is, Highness, although I know you wish to think the best of her, that this fresh tale makes her look even more guilty. Even if she had a woman with her, the Queen was still sneaking out at all hours of the night to meet one of the King's own gentlemen. People will say Lady Rochford is lying when she says nothing happened or that she always was with them, and she has not the best reputation for honesty at court as it is. Some think she informed on her sister-in-law and her husband, and some say Cromwell as well, for you know she used to be his creature. It is said she gave information to Norfolk's men when they went looking for reasons to attack and arrest Cromwell."

"Jane Boleyn is no more guilty of that than I am," I said stoutly. "That I perfectly believe." I was unsure why I believed this so resolutely, but I did. Jane was certainly intelligent enough to have done all she was accused of by malicious tongues, but for some reason I believed her innocent. It was something I read in her nature, something I could not explain.

"There is talk of three nocturnal meetings which occurred during progress," Harst continued. "Dereham spoke first of it, said there was someone who had replaced him in the heart of the Queen, and the Queen's ladies filled in the rest when pressure was put upon them. There seems much detail, madam, however, much intimate detail about these meetings, so either Jane Boleyn has talked or Culpepper, who is now in custody, has."

"How sad, that it must be either of them whom Catherine trusted," I said.

"Some say she even met him in a privy." Harst sounded outraged.

"Does the location they met at make her more guilty or innocent?" I asked. "Should it not be what was done, or indeed, what was *not* done, there?"

"But she was sneaking out to meet a man, Highness."

"I admit that does not look good, but, my friend, if that was all it was then she still has committed no crime against the King."

"Except for loving another man."

"Love is a crime, when it comes in innocence? When there is no betrayal of body? Perhaps it is a betrayal still, but she risked nothing of her body with him, so endangered not the pride of the King nor his line of succession. Can the heart help where it loves and where it does not? And if she loved this man and yet did nothing with him, not even a kiss, does that not speak of her greater courage and will power? Of her commitment to remaining true to the King in body and not forsaking her vows to honour her husband?"

Harst breathed in, lifting his eyebrows. "You have a generous heart, Highness, but few others will see it as you do."

"Of that, my friend, I am well aware. That is why I fear for her."

I looked to the window and saw nothing of the view outside. I knew he and others thought me naïve, but I was not. I was simply willing to believe a woman, where others wished only to condemn her.

Chapter Forty-Six

Richmond Palace
November 1541

The Queen confessed, again, this time to the altered tale, and blamed much on her friend, Lady Rochford. I had no doubt all she confessed was said in fear. All the same, Catherine stuck to the important part. She had met with Culpepper, but nothing had happened, Catherine insisted.

Jane Boleyn had wanted Catherine to meet Culpepper, the Queen said. Jane had encouraged it, bringing Catherine the first note which passed between her and Culpepper, helping to arrange meetings. She had helped to exchange gifts, and Jane had encouraged Catherine to flirt with Culpepper. Jane had stolen keys, arranged places to meet. She had refused to sit too near to the Queen and Culpepper when they met at night and it was the Queen who had insisted she come close, so there was no scandal. Jane had hunted out back stairs and rooms for them to use on progress. She had told the Queen that Culpepper loved her, had told Catherine that Culpepper was hers alone. Jane had told her Queen not to say anything about Culpepper when the issue of Dereham had come up. She had told Catherine to be silent about what had happened on progress when first they were arrested.

Catherine, certain her friend had informed on her, informed on her friend.

"Like rats they turn on one another," said Harst.

"Were you in their situation, friend, you would turn into a rat too," I snapped, and sighed. "It is easy, Harst, to sit on the outside and condemn people. Too easy is it. Fear does many a horrific thing to people, and when they think their lives are in danger, they will do anything to keep that life. Anything."

But one thing gave me hope and that was that despite all pressure, Catherine maintained that the reason Jane had been present was indeed as a chaperone. Culpepper and the Queen had not had sex, there had been no intimate touching, no caresses. He had done no more than kiss her hand and Catherine had neither asked nor thought for more. Catherine declared it was a game of courtly love and no more. Jane Boleyn and Culpepper swore the same. Meetings and talk had been all it was, there was no sin and no betrayal of the King.

"I hear they are pressing the Queen, for some of the King's men think she had carnal knowledge of Culpepper," Harst told me. "But the Queen said it was not true and she would not even meet with Culpepper until he swore on the Bible he wanted no more than conversation."

"Do you think they have hurt Jane or Culpepper?" I asked. "To make them say things?"

Harst nodded. "It is possible. Technically it is illegal in England, but there are ways to torture a person without it being seen and the King sometimes allows it, in extreme cases."

"The Queen must feel most alone, to think that her friend and closest confidant could have spoken against her, confessed to this new part of this story of scandal."

Harst looked weary. "I think that the least of her problems. Madam, you must face something; the truth is no one is going to believe she snuck out of her chambers, that she risked so very much, only to *talk* to a man."

I nodded. I knew this, I was no dullard. Even if I believed Catherine, others would not, and some had a vested interest in not believing her, in proving her guilty. There must be more, so her accusers thought, between her and Culpepper than them merely talking. As Harst said, who gambled so much just to talk to a man? The Queen had lied about her meetings with him to begin with, or at least failed to say anything about it, so she *must* be lying about what went on during those nights spent on progress. Once guilty of one thing, Catherine must be guilty of all.

There was an echo of the past in that accusation. Her moral reputation was trounced. No matter how hard she protested she had not wanted the attentions of Manox or Dereham, there were many now who, because of this news about Culpepper, would not believe she had been forced as a child. Forced both times? By two different men? The odds made it unlikely, and now it transpired she had snuck out to meet a man in secret whilst she was married. Her behaviour on progress cast shadows on events of the past. If Catherine had done wrong in the present, she had done wrong then. That was how people thought.

Women were usually blamed even if men had forced them. Women must have brought the act upon themselves in some way, that was the way the world thought. Women had led men on with smiles and soft words, with their bodies and the smell of their skin, with existing, with being something men liked to look upon and touch. How were men to help themselves when women were so sweet and beautiful? Women were always blamed, that was the way of things. Since Eve, women had been tempting men, and so men were innocent even when guilty and women guilty even when innocent. Since the dawn of creation we had been held accountable, and we always would be, until men became creatures able and willing to accept responsibility for their own actions.

If Catherine was a whore as a young girl, she was one now, that was how the world thought. It was how England thought. This was no Christian nation. There was no forgiveness here, no fresh start, no redemption. This was not a religion of love we had under the King, but of judgement. Not a faith of forgiveness but of condemnation. Whores could not be believed. If the Queen was lying about the past, she had therefore lied about the present. She *had* betrayed the King.

That was how the minds of the world worked. And the thoughts of the world were enough to condemn this young girl, little more than a child, to death.

Chapter Forty-Seven

Richmond Palace
November 1541

"Cranmer tells the Queen this night that she must sign a document which says she was indeed pre-contracted to Dereham." Katherine of Suffolk had sailed to Richmond that night, to bring the news to me.

"Why?"

"Because it may save her, Anna. If pre-contracted to Master Dereham, she was never married to the King. Therefore, anything done with Master Dereham is not a sin, and anything done since her marriage was not adultery against the King."

We went to the fire where perfumed juniper wood was burning. "Will she sign? They would make her live with Dereham, would they not?"

"At least she would be alive." Katherine sat down heavily on a cushion by the hearth. Her eyes, usually so bright, were dull with strain, and heavy bags hung under them. She looked haunted and perhaps this was not far from the truth. This time, a Queen accused, factions in danger all over court, arrests made and secrets unveiled, it was too like the last time. No matter what side anyone had stood on, they had not felt safe as the battle raged. Katherine was haunted as many were, by the ghost of Anne Boleyn and the men who had fallen with her.

Some said that when great battles were fought, after they were done, for years after people passing those fields could hear the cries of ghostly soldiers, the thunder of horses, the eerie screams of the dying. This time was like that, as if an imprint of the past was being played out upon the present. Phantoms surrounded us, unseen yet felt keenly.

I sat beside my friend, touching her hand. She smiled at me and as she did so I felt warm. At times like this I remembered nights with Amalia and Sybylla the most, our days of relative peace in childhood, sharing stories at the fire of hidden folk and monsters. I had not known how many monsters there truly were in the world. "There are worse things than dying, in the eyes of many," I said to my friend in a gentle voice. "Catherine tried so hard to get away from this man, Dereham. Delivering her to him might be as heading into hell for her."

Katherine's expression was grim. "The Queen thinks like you and is refusing to sign. That was the last I heard before I left anyway. She says she never committed adultery with Culpepper and never consented to Dereham. Some think she is being too proud."

I pursed my lips. "I think she is trying to avoid living with a rapist, a vicious man who wielded great control over her for many a year, but more than that, my friend, it just might be that the reason she will not sign this confession is because it is not the truth."

"She has lied a great deal." Katherine took a goblet of wine from Kitty with a brief smile.

I cupped my own goblet in my hands, the warmed wine perfumed with spices, cinnamon and nutmeg. "Every lie she has told has been to protect others, but this truth is perhaps to protect herself. There must come a moment of accountability in any life, my friend, and I mean not when a person is judged, but when they stand and announce their truths to the world, the truth of their lives, who they are, what their thoughts are, and perhaps this time has come for Catherine. I think, finally, this refusal to sign is a signal of pride in herself. This document could save her if she signs it, but what if it should condemn a part of her at the same time? A part of her soul?"

Katherine frowned. "But if she had been contracted to Dereham before marriage to the King then the most she is guilty of is bigamy. If the Queen lay with Thomas Culpepper, her crime is adultery against Dereham, not the King. If she signs this, she is guilty of little against the King, only lying to him. Cranmer is offering her a way out."

I set my goblet down. "A way out of one cage and into another trap. If it is as she states, and everything Dereham did to her was not with her consent, then this document nullifies what he did, it excuses it. It would grant him absolution *and* give him control of her again. Think of what he could do then to her, for the rest of her life. People may think her foolish for refusing to sign this, but I think not. She sees far down the line; she knows what could happen."

"The Council are saying that if such was done before marriage, God alone knows what was done since."

"If she is guilty of one thing, she is of all crimes." I picked up the goblet again, agitated, and sipped my wine, feeling the heat burn my mouth. It was pleasing in a way, the pain. It reminded me I was alive. "Is that the way of it? Men are so quick to cast this angel of the King as a devil now she has one fault."

"All the King wants is an annulment now. It would be wise for her to grant him that."

"The King may find reasons to cast her off without her agreeing what Dereham did was legal and just," I said. "There are other reasons a man may separate from his wife. The King must know of many by now."

"What of the men? She could save them."

"If Culpepper has done nothing then there should be no punishment. Perhaps Dereham should pay for his crimes." I paused, narrowing my eyes. "Besides, friend, did not Anne Boleyn sign a document much like this, in which she admitted she and the King never were married? Did she sign perhaps on a promise that she and those accused with her would escape with their lives? It did not save her. Bowing to all the King wanted did not save one life then. Why should Catherine believe this time will be any different?"

Chapter Forty-Eight

Richmond Palace
November 14th 1541

"The Queen is at Syon Abbey," Kitty came to tell me. A messenger from court, from her sister, had sent the news.

"I hope she finds some peace there."

There was none for me. Another rumour again had arisen that the King was to set aside his wife and take me as his Queen, and no one knew where it had started. I was praying it was not with the King. Since the King had sent his wife away, this time this rumour was all the more dangerous.

"People are saying you, Highness, are dignified and Queen-like, and all know you are a maid, unlike the Howard Queen," Kitty Basset said to me. Her voice took on a tone I had heard many adopt of late when they used words associated with Catherine; outraged, scandalised, as if they spoke of something dirty which might despoil them. Sometimes their voices dropped to a whisper as if her name should not be said. Would Catherine become as Anne Boleyn, an awkward pause in conversation, a whispered word which once had been her name?

"I want no talk like that here in this house, Katherine," I warned, and she blinked as I used her given name rather than my pet one. "I know you are trying to compliment me, but until there is a trial or a pronouncement, we know nothing about the Queen or what she has done, only what gossip tells us."

Most people had already heard all they thought they needed to and condemned Catherine because of it. She was being called a whore in the streets, one who had betrayed the King in heart, body and soul, despite the fact that no one had found any evidence she had done a thing since marriage except meet with a man secretly. Jane Boleyn still maintained nothing had happened, as did Culpepper.

But then, Anne Boleyn had not been executed for adultery, she had gone to the block for treason for it was said she and her 'lovers' plotted the death of the King. The adultery charge was laid at her door to secure the one of treason. There had not been any mention of treason committed by Catherine, no whisper of her plotting against the King.

Yet times had changed since Anne died. Ever since Lady Margaret Douglas had dared to try to choose who to love it had been law that any man who defiled, or intended to defile, a royal woman was a traitor. By association that could make the royal woman a traitor too which set Catherine in danger of execution, but there was still no evidence that Catherine was guilty. There was, in fact, the testimony of several people who had long been in prison now, people who might well have been tortured, that nothing had happened.

But would that stop the King?

The trouble was if intention was enough, they could make a case for it, and most people were disposed to think the worst of Catherine because she had had a 'lover' before marriage. They called her a whore for that, though it meant that in total Catherine had taken two men into her bed in her lifetime, and one of them was her husband. Two men, and she was named a whore. The women who worked by night in the stews of Southwark would laugh at the notion, and the King had certainly taken more partners to bed than his wife ever had.

Catherine's household were gone. Gathered together by Sir Thomas Wriothesley, they had been told she had "misused" her body, forfeited honour and respect. She was to be proceeded against by law, and was no more to be called Queen, but just Mistress Catherine Howard.

Everyone was still calling her Queen, however, when they talked of her, as they didn't know what else to call her. She was, after all, still married to the King and what else was the wife of a king called?

It was not only her title that was lost. Most of her family had cast her off, with Norfolk denouncing her all over court, and her sister Isabella reportedly ashamed to be still in attendance on Catherine. Norfolk had even announced Catherine should be burnt at the stake.

Would that be her fate? I knew not. It was the most extreme punishment permitted for female adulterers, but they had not proved adultery.

Yet if they wanted to prove that, they had Culpepper and Jane Boleyn in the Tower. If pain had not been used upon them yet it could be. The King might well allow it, wanting to get to the "truth". Torture was not supposed to be used on the sons of nobility, or women, but even if they did not hurt them in body there were ways of making people talk. Perhaps they would stop them sleeping or withhold food and water. They could whisper words in their ears, repeated over and over, telling them what had happened, until they thought that *was* what had happened. Make a person unsure of what is real and what is not, and the mind turns traitor and starts to play along. Enough time, and they could get them to say anything, I was sure of it.

The Queen was sent by boat to Syon. Margaret Douglas had been at Syon too, but she was there no more. She was gone now, sent to Kenninghall, where she was to be watched over by Norfolk. Syon could only hold one rebellious woman in its walls at a time, apparently.

I heard Catherine's rooms at Syon were spare and bare. There was no cloth of estate over Catherine's chair, and the chests containing the six gowns and their adornments that she was permitted to take took up little room. There would be no entertainment. No books but the Bible. No music, no dance, spare conversation. It was not a cell in the Tower, but that does not mean it was not a prison.

The world had come to judge Catherine. Lined up they were, in a row, ready to caw their accusations at her as if she meant nothing.

Let he who is without sin cast the first rock at her, I thought.

The trouble was, they all thought they were that person.

Chapter Forty-Nine

Richmond Palace
November 1541

I was hiding at Richmond. I had it set about that I was ill. I was hiding in my bed.

Afraid that the King might decide to go along with rumour and bring a proposal to me, I was staying where I was. Of course, I had considered that it might be advantageous to my people if I were to take his hand again, to become Queen. I had been raised to think thus – that high marriage and the good of my nation were more important than life and liberty – and so the thought came to me, but terror came not long after. If he even wanted me back, how long would I last? He had never liked me when I was his wife. True, we had got on better of late but that was when he was not forced to lie with me. I was not his kind of woman in bed, that I knew.

No, even for my people I did not think this would do any good. Each Queen that came lasted less and less time. I, who had lasted six months, had had the slightest reign and yet I was still alive. I did not fancy what my chances might be if I tried again. The position of Queen had a time limit on it, it seemed. I had no wish to try again and find myself lasting a year or less before some charge was levelled at me. Would the world be screaming whore at me some day? Braying for me to be sent to the Tower? Would I find my friends sent to prison, tortured to inform against me? Would I face a block on which to die or a long, slow death as a prisoner shut away?

The Queen was at Syon, and the King, so it was rumoured, was courting Mistress Anne Basset, who once had served me and whose sister Kitty still did serve in my house. People were saying this Anne would be the next Queen and that she was already his mistress. Had he been in love with Anne a while, and this was why Catherine had to go so swift? Was all that had happened, all these accusations against the Queen, a plot contrived against Catherine to set Anne into her place? Anne had powerful relatives, her stepfather the Governor of Calais, at least until his arrest. There had been another Catherine who fell so an Anne could rise. Was this to happen again?

Apparently, there was a common bet going on in the streets of London and about court; which woman would be the next Queen? Anne of Cleves or Anne of Calais? It was revolting. The Queen was still alive, was not condemned for anything as yet, yet people were wagering money as if her life and ours were a game.

And why was the Queen still alive? I thought it a sign. Anne Boleyn had been condemned fast, sent to the block just as fast, but Catherine had not been moved to the Tower and had been at Syon for more than a week. Was Syon a sign she would live? Perhaps there was hope. Perhaps none. My mind could not decide.

"They are keeping knives from the Queen, even when she eats," Harst told me; brought to my door he kept a respectful distance since I was in my bed. I made sure my women were there, many of them. I would have no tales questioning my virtue spread about the world.

"Why?"

"They fear she will hurt herself, consign her soul to hell."

I sighed, playing with my bedcap. "If I can guess even a fraction of the fear in her mind, friend, I would say she lingers there already. I wonder sometimes if the King is toying with her, trying to make her suffer because she has hurt him."

*

"Ambassadors of other countries have been told about the Queen," said Harst. "The French King announced she was a naughty woman, and Chapuys says he hopes she will go to a nunnery, to atone for her sins."

"I still have heard no true evidence of adultery." I put my swan feather quill in its pot and folded my hands on the table. I had left my bed, deciding that to stay there indefinitely would draw more attention to me and at the moment I wanted the King to forget me entirely.

"No man likes to be a cuckold, Highness," Harst said. "The King is sore hurt, so I hear, for finally he was happy, and it was all a lie."

I was quiet a moment. Was this what it all was about, then? The King's pride? Was that more important than the life of a young girl?

"The Lady Jane Rochford is gone mad, they say," Harst went on. "She lost her mind within three days in the Beauchamp Tower, and the King, in his mercy, has sent her to the house of Admiral Lord Russell so the lady may find her lost wits. Many Howards are rumoured to be soon to be arrested too."

"Who?"

"No one yet, but there is word many will go to the Tower. The Dowager of Norfolk, poor old lady, is one. She is accused of not bringing the Queen up correctly, allowing her too much freedom. She is old, perhaps her mind is tangled and that was why she could not keep order in her house."

I rubbed an ink spot on my finger. "I have met her a few times, she never seemed confused to me."

Harst went to stand by the fire to warm himself. "They say the Dowager was hiding a chest, Highness, full of papers about the Queen and Master Dereham. The King's men found her hanging over it, a candle in her hand, when they came to question her. She has been taken to her bed, for she claims she is sick. The Queen's uncle, Lord William Howard, too will go to the Tower. They say he has stolen plate from the King and kept secrets about the Queen. But Norfolk will not go. That old fox threw himself at the King, weeping over the wildness of his two nieces. He says he knew nothing of the Queen's sins. Norfolk called her a prostitute."

"That man would throw his own children into the water if he thought he could walk upon them to escape a sinking ship." My voice was as scathing as my heart felt.

"It is said Master Dereham meant to kill the King, perhaps, for he spoke of marrying the Queen when the King was no more, and that is treason."

Ah, so here came treason. I had wondered when it would appear.

Harst held his hands to the fire. "The Queen is now accused of adultery with Dereham too."

"Why?"

"People say that since she employed him, she cannot have been afraid of him and intended to resume her affair of old with him. Those who knew the two of them at Chesworth and Norfolk House are being questioned again, as is Master Dereham."

I understood. The King wanted to hurt Dereham. Dereham had Catherine first, made her no more a virgin. The King wanted revenge.

"The Queen was told of this, and she began to laugh, then she wept." Harst turned from the fire to me again. "People say she may lose her mind, others think it a feint."

I remembered the tales of Anne Boleyn in the Tower when she was arrested, laughing hysterically at her own jest about having a small neck. "I think it no feint, my friend."

Harst regarded me with sorrowful eyes. "You must prepare yourself, my lady. I know you have striven to uphold her cause, but people say she intended to commit adultery even if she did not follow through with it, Highness."

"Should it be that we can be put to death for an intention? To die for a fleeting thought, or one considered? There are so many things we all think and yet never act upon, should we die for all those passing thoughts, Harst?"

"Here, all things are possible, good and bad."

I was not so sure of the good. On the twenty-second of November Catherine was officially told she was the Queen no more. There was a proclamation. It said she had forfeited her honour.

Two days later I was informed by a messenger sent by the King that the Council had announced Catherine had led the King to marry her, using word and gesture to make him love her whilst all the time concealing she was "a base, abominable, carnal, voluptuous harlot" maintaining the appearance of chastity and honesty whilst living a vicious life.

When I looked on the tale of this girl, for girl she was, I saw viciousness indeed, yet not of her making. This viciousness of her existence was inflicted on her by men, by men who all had sworn they loved her.

Chapter Fifty

Richmond Palace
December 1st 1541

Snow was blowing across the stone courtyard, the grass in the park a frozen contusion of silver spikes. Winter had come early. Perhaps the King had brought it upon England, an expression of his sorrow. I had thought him the Winter King before, white of hair and cold of heart, but now that heart was pained, for Catherine had hurt him, I heard.

No matter that she had done nothing whilst married to him besides talk to a man. No matter she had not wanted the things done to her in youth. No matter that she was the one in prison, afraid for herself and for her family, who also were in captivity. No matter that she had never wanted to marry the King in the first place but had done the best she could in her unwanted role to promote unity, peace and mercy. He was the one who was hurt. The King was the victim.

The King was delusional.

I wondered how he explained all these strange accidents of marriage to himself; all these unnatural women who had hurt him. Either the King was the most unfortunate man in the world, or he was lying to himself. Five accidents are a few too many to be chance. The King made his own ill luck with women, he set them up as angels, but even angels have fallen from grace. Sometimes I wondered if God was not trying to inflict on the King all the pain and misery he had inflicted on others. An eye for an eye?

I had been quiet that day. It was an important day. The day a girl's fate would be decided, but, like so many times in her life, it would be decided through, and by, men. She would not speak for herself.

Dereham and Culpepper were being taken to the Great Hall of London's Guildhall that day, to face trial.

I knew a few names of the men who would try them: Norfolk, Suffolk, Russell, Audley... familiar names, old favourites of the King. Men desperate to prove their loyalty. This would be the second trial of the lovers of a queen that some had sat on.

I watched the flurry billowing through the air, little dancing flakes blown by a raw, barren wind, scattering this whiteness of snow across the frozen grass. Some flakes melted as they met stone and some stuck, gathering other flakes to them, making mounds. The world might be covered soon, held fast in frozen beauty as if time had ceased to move along. I wished it would be so.

Catherine's deposition would be read, claiming Dereham had coerced her into a sexual relationship, but that she had not done anything with Culpepper. I doubted it was enough to save Culpepper. It was true he was popular at court, and the King had loved him, but the King had loved others, and that had not saved them.

It was easy for the King to cast aside wives and friends. They were objects to him. And the more he did it, the easier it became.

*

"They pleaded not guilty, both of them," Harst told me, dusting the snow from his shoulders as Kitty took his cape and hat. Little puddles were forming at his feet. Outside the snow was falling thick and fast now, the world covered in glittering light as dusk started to fall.

I was almost surprised at their pleas. It was not usual; I knew that by now. Most people threw themselves on the mercy of the King and pleaded guilty whether they were or not, hoping that by appeasing the King by admitting guilt they might gain their lives in return as reward. It was almost unheard of for men to plead innocent. Aside from Anne Boleyn, and the men accused with her.

What more I heard pleased me less, however. Culpepper maintained he and the Queen had not had sex, but he blamed Catherine for encouraging the affair. She had drawn him in, giving him presents and sending notes, he claimed. Catherine had instigated the meetings, had spoken endearments to him. She was the one who had tempted him, not the other way around. I supposed he was trying to save his own neck, but still it made me sad. Men here in England, they spoke of chivalry so much and practised it so little. What good was carrying a lady's colours in the joust if you would not stand by her when a true battle came?

He was not alone in defaming her, however. Everyone joined in. Catherine was described to court as a base whore, who, by "maintaining an appearance of chastity and honesty" had led the King to love her. He had believed she was pure, and despite being a "harlot" she had "arrogantly contracted and coupled" herself in marriage. To them, as to all men, a woman who had lain with a man was no longer capable of purity of mind, honesty of word, or any virtuous quality. The body was all that mattered, not her mind, not her soul, and it mattered not if what was done to that body was by her pleasure or not.

It also did not matter what Culpepper and Dereham pleaded. They were condemned.

There was no proof of adultery, however. That was made clear to all at the trial.

Catherine's careful planning had worked, as her accusers could prove nothing. Anne Boleyn had been charged with actual adultery, but they could not cast that charge on these men or Catherine now. Culpepper was accused of criminal intercourse with Catherine, but when it was said there had been another present, this confused the court, and the subject was dropped.

"It was not safe to pursue such a line of attack, that was obvious," Harst told me, hands wrapped about a goblet of steaming wine. "Safer, it was, to prove they had merely *intended* to commit adultery."

Slight evidence was brought out, hearsay and rumour. It had been said Catherine had jested about having a score of lovers behind each door, so if Culpepper did not come to her one night another could. Proof, there was little. And for good reason. I believed she was innocent.

So why had she risked so much to meet with him? Was it simply for love? I had had another thought.

It had occurred to me that Catherine might well have been meeting with him for another reason. We all knew the King was ill; what if she had been preparing, as I had, a means to keep herself safe when the King died? If left on her own she could be taken by Seymour or Norfolk, used for their own ends, made to marry one of their supporters, much as I could. If she married Culpepper, she would render herself politically unimportant. He was not high or rich enough to be a threat to any powerful man.

I thought that was what they had been planning in these meetings, a way to escape the tumult when the King was gone, a way to be free, together, a way to a new life where they could love their partner. Neither would have said a word of this to their accusers for it would condemn them; to consider the death of the King was treason, but it was possible, just possible that was why they were meeting, not to become lovers now, but to marry in the future.

That was why there was no proof they had been lovers, because they had not been. Sex had not been the motive for the meetings, survival had.

But what need for proof when a *thought* is all a man must present to condemn another? Treason did not need to occur in order to be a crime. It only needed to be thought. Dereham had spoken of the King's death once. That was enough to condemn him. They found Culpepper guilty of intent to defile the Queen.

Intent was what they were found guilty of. Something not done. A thought as it was, unproven though it was, it was enough. Intent to do something was the same as doing it.

Perhaps Culpepper knew that. He changed his plea to guilty when the jury came back saying there was "sufficient and probable evidence" of intent to commit adultery, and the death sentence would be applied. Seeing death coming for him no matter what, Culpepper altered his plea, hoping to gain a more merciful death if he did so. Hearing what he had done, Dereham followed suit. They submitted.

"So, they said they *were* guilty?" I was confused. "I thought you said they maintained they were not."

"It was an admission they had been *found* guilty, but not an admission they were. It is common practice for men to do so when found guilty of treason in England. The only exceptions I know of were the men who died with... the other Queen." Harst breathed in and let it out slowly. "Those men maintained innocence until the end, all besides that musician, Smeaton."

"So, that means that all men who die for treason, die guilty. The law is always just, never wrong, as is the King."

"Their only hope now to die clean and not in elongated agony is to throw themselves on the mercy of the King, and so they have, Highness."

Their new admission of guilt was the final proof their accusers needed.

Both were found guilty of intending to seduce the Queen. Dereham was also guilty of withholding knowledge of her past. "That is a crime?" I asked.

"It was not a crime until recently. The King has made it one."

"Since this began?"

Harst nodded. "Since this began, Highness. He wants to punish those who kept Catherine's past from him."

"So they committed a crime without knowing it, for when it was done it was not a crime and now the King decides it is," I wondered. "We all might die at any time, for anything, Harst. The King has just to decide it is treason."

The men were to be dragged on hurdles to Tyburn, and there to be hanged, drawn and quartered. They left the hall with the ceremonial axes of the King's guard pointing towards them, symbolising their sentence. Norfolk laughed as the sentence was handed down.

With their guilt, Catherine's was decided, by association.

Chapter Fifty-One

Richmond Palace
December 1541

"The former Queen's three brothers and her cousin, Surrey, are riding through London, to demonstrate they are free, accused of nothing." Katherine of Suffolk lifted her eyebrows almost into her hairline as she told me this.

"Men are strange creatures," I said.

The King was vastly unhappy, Katherine informed me. He was said to be depressed, not taking to running about with ladies of court as he had when Anne Boleyn was arrested, but sitting, staring from the window. Sometimes it was said his sanity was feared for.

"My husband says when first he heard of the former Queen's antics, the King lurched from his seat at the table and called for his sword so he might behead the Queen himself," Katherine said. "And then, told he could not, he said he would have her tortured to death, so she might feel as much pain in death as she had known delight in lust."

"Poor lady."

The Queen's own sanity was in question. By all reports she was one moment calm and another hysterical. Catherine would scream, tear her hair, faint to the ground. Sometimes she just sat, staring at nothing, like the King.

Catherine's grandmother and Lord William Howard had been taken to the Tower, accused of misprision of treason, which Harst had explained to me was knowledge that someone was about to commit treason. The treason was Catherine's failure to disclose her past, for if she had been pre-contracted to Dereham and was a bigamist, any children of the King she bore would have been bastards. She was thought guilty of this, along with intent to commit adultery.

The truth was Catherine was being punished not for actual crimes, but for not being the perfect woman. She had destroyed the King's fantasy. For that, she would die.

I thought again how lucky I had been. I had not been the King's perfect woman either, but I had escaped. The King had not been in love with me so he had not sought revenge, other than slandering my name and reputation, when our marriage ended. He would have hesitated, too, to send a woman with a title such as mine, a born Duchess of the Holy Roman Empire to death on the block as he could with women like Anne Boleyn and possibly now Catherine, who were English born subjects. I had more protection than they had possessed because of my status. Katherine of Aragon he had been forced to send to various ill kept houses to be rid of her. I had been luckier than all of them.

I was lucky he had not loved me.

It was not just death looming over her that would cause suffering, Catherine was being punished. I was sure that was why she was still alive, so she could understand that her family, whom she loved, were being disciplined, so she could have time to contemplate her fate, to think on death, the pain of the axe, or on the tortured, sweet possibility of freedom.

Many had been swept up in the King's purge. Norfolk and his children had remained safe, these other Howards riding through the streets too, but the Howards were a big family and almost all of the rest of their house were there, in the Tower, with their servants. I was told the Tower was so stuffed with Howards that even the Royal Apartments had been pressed into use to house them all.

I thought of Catherine's grandmother. She was old, her bones brittle and joints inflamed. She would suffer. There would be no one to send her clothes as Catherine had to Margaret Pole. Lord William Howard too was there, and another Katherine Howard, Catherine's aunt, and her children with her. Friends of Catherine from her chambers too, I had heard the names Kat, Joan, Alice, Master Ashby of Norfolk House, Margaret Benett, Malena Tilney, Ned Walgrave and Lord William's wife Margaret. They were all in the Tower. They might be executed, they might be imprisoned for life, no one knew.

Norfolk was one of their interrogators, this was probably how he had kept his freedom. He would do anything the King wanted. Of course he would, this was how he had survived the last time, was it not? He had been sent to the Dowager's house to question her servants and her before her arrest. People claimed when she was taken away he took the opportunity to search for silver he knew she had stashed away. He had wanted it a long time, apparently, and took his chance when he had it.

There was not magpie or carrion crow of the world with as little heart as Norfolk.

Even Jane Boleyn would not escape. It was said she had gone mad, therefore the King would not be permitted by law to send her to death. It was illegal to execute the insane. But I heard he had sent his doctors to her. No doubt they would find she was entirely sane. The King would make sure she was well and hale, so he could dispatch her into death.

Only Mary Lascelles and her brother, the original accusers, were left free, I heard. A reward for bringing Catherine's 'true nature' to the attention of the King. I hoped that would comfort this pair when they thought of what they had done. How many would die because they had spoken of the past of the Queen? They could have saved them all, so many lives, just by not saying a word. The King would have remained happy, Catherine might have lived past the time of his death, all if people had just kept the past quiet. Why did we have to dig up so many graves, only to fill them with new corpses? The person Catherine had been, the one she had tried to leave behind, that was not the person she was anymore. Forgiveness, redemption, rebirth, this is what Christ teaches, but there was none of that here. One slip, one sin, even if not their sin, and a person was lost.

I thought of my homeland. St Nikolas's day was coming, the day on which it was traditional to give gifts in Cleves. Were I back home, had I insisted on going back when the King had set me aside, I might be in a place where it was warm and merry, where the halls would be ringing with the laughter of people all trying to outdo each other in giving gifts. Competition was a part of the fun, a little sparring of generosity. But I was not there, I was here, in this England I had loved so well. Was I starting to fall out of love with my adopted country, at least a little?

But then, *no*, I thought. It was not the country I did not love. It was its King.

There was a knock to the door. "Come," I called and Diaceto, my page, entered.

"What is it?" I asked.

"There are men sent by the King here, Highness," he said. "They have come to take two of your women into custody. They say they must answer questions."

I rose from my chair. "What women? What questions?" The rush of blood which surged about my body almost felled me. I grasped the back of a chair, the wood hard and solid in my hand, the only reality I had, or so it felt for a moment.

"Mistress Bassett and Mistress Rattsey." His face was pale, frightened. "They are thought to have spoken treason."

I almost flew down the stairs to the Great Hall where Kitty and Jane already were, pallid of face, their eyes huge pools of terror. They were surrounded by the King's men.

"Lord St John, where are you taking my women?" I asked as I came down the last stair, fighting to keep my voice calm, controlled, "and for what purpose?"

"To the Tower, Highness," Lord St John, William Paulet, answered. He had held many posts for the King, served however he was needed but at that time he was Keeper of the King's Woods as well as Wards. I suspected many of the other officers of the King were being used elsewhere at this time. In truth, the thought made me feel a little less scared; a higher officer would have been sent if whatever my women had done was considered truly heinous.

In truth the man looked vastly uncomfortable with this role he had been given. "They have been reported as uttering treasonous words and are to be examined on the King's orders."

"What words of treason are they accused of saying, for I would tell you here and now both are the King's devoted, loyal subjects."

Paulet held up a hand, not a sign of dominance but one of warning, and came closer. He spoke low and with care. "Do not say too much in their defence, my lady, for your own sake. You do not want to become included in the King's wrath at this time. The charges against your women are slight. I will examine them myself and I swear to you, I will get them back to you if I can, swift and unharmed. We need no more embarrassment to touch the King at this time."

"But... they must go with you? Can you not question them here?"

"They must understand what they were saying was dangerous, for you and for them."

"What did they say?"

Paulet stared gravely at me. "That the King should take you as his wife again," he whispered. "And though there are many at court who have said the same, they say it more carefully than your women did."

I shot a look at Kitty and Jane. *Curse your tongue, Kitty,* I thought. How many times had I warned her? And who had heard her and reported them? I could only think it was Carew. Curse him too!

"Go with these men and answer with honesty," I said to my women, staring into their eyes, trying to will them to have strength and courage at this time. I looked at Paulet. "I have your word you will deal with *them* with honesty too?"

He inclined his head. "You have my word, Highness."

There were men I would not believe when they said such things, but Paulet was not one of them. True, I had heard he bent like a willow to whatever the King desired in faith or marriage, in state and country, so he could not be entirely trusted, but I believed him when he said the King needed no more shame cast upon him at this time. If there was another large scandal, coming from my house, it might start to look as if all the women about the King were immoral, and that would not reflect well upon him.

Dorothy Wingfield came to my side, tears falling from her eyes as she watched her friends bundled out of the door. She almost fell, and I took her hand. "Stand with me, Dorothy," I whispered. "Stand, do not let them see our pain."

I watched them taken from me. I could do nothing to stop the men, nothing. My guards would not move against those of the King, and what could I, one woman, do against all those men? Helpless and afraid, I watched them take my women to the Tower. I wondered if I would join them soon. If I would be taken there, where another Queen Anne had fallen.

Chapter Fifty-Two

Richmond Palace
December 1541

"They have been taken before the Council," I was told by Harst, "and they have been reprimanded for their disrespect unto His Majesty."

"What is it they are accused of saying?" I was pacing up and down my room. The rushes were wearing thin and ragged under my feet.

"Mistress Kitty Bassett admitted that she wondered aloud 'if God was working His own work to make the Lady Anne of Cleves Queen again,'" he said, "and in reply it is said Jane said, 'it was impossible that so sweet a Queen as the Lady Anne could be utterly put down.'"

"Is that all?" It was bad enough; they had both called me Queen which technically was treason. If the King decided so, they could die for those words.

"Sadly not, Highness, for Kitty Bassett continued on to exclaim, 'What a man the King is! How many wives will he have?'"

I took in a deep breath and let it out slowly, my hands clenching at my sides. If the King had heard that last comment of Kitty's I could well understand why the women had been arrested. It was hardly something he wanted to think of himself. In the King's mind he had been married but once to Jane Seymour before he had been joined to Catherine Howard, for all other matches including ours had been annulled. The fact that everybody else remembered he had been married five times was not something any of us should be speaking of, particularly not as it seemed the King might be considering a sixth wife and the lady in question was none other than Kitty's sister.

It was widely rumoured at court and beyond that Anne Bassett was now the certain mistress of my former husband. He was showering her with gifts and had kept her at court. Now that it seemed for sure Queen

Catherine Howard would never return to the post even if she kept her life, it was said there would be a third Queen Anne.

Although Kitty might well have unwittingly saved her sister from such a fate.

It was surely shameful to the King that the very moment he was thinking of another marriage, his potential future sister-in-law was wondering aloud just how many wives he would take and if he should not return to his fourth wife. It was the kind of thing that, coward that he was, the King might hear and fear what his people thought of it, leading him to retreat from the lady in question. He would also likely not welcome a sister-in-law with such a loose and disrespectful tongue.

I had no doubt it was because of Kitty's link to Anne that my women had found themselves under arrest. It was not the fact they had talked of the King's marriages. If he was to arrest people for doing that, he would have to arrest everyone in England. No. It was because he was connected to this woman, through Anne Bassett and through me, and Kitty had shamed him.

I only hoped she had not shamed him enough that he would kill her.

It was being said that Kitty had not only uttered these treasonous words but also had said that Catherine Howard's crimes and the possibility of her execution were the actions of God who was showing the King that his previous marriage to me was still valid. I could only pray this was not true, or if it was, she would have the sense to deny it. Try to tell the King that God was against him and a person would pay with blood for it.

"What can we do to have them released?" I asked my man Harst. "Should I petition the King?"

"I would advise you against it, Highness." He swallowed, his Adam's apple bobbing in his throat. "The simple truth of the matter is, is that the more you protest the more the King may well suspect you had something to do with the treasonous utterances that these women have admitted to. At the moment the crimes are slight and Lord St John has said to me that they are willing to release both women soon, for in truth the Crown does not need any more dishonour cast upon it at this time. As it is, what we have here is two women with unguarded tongues, and from what I hear they have been scared into apologising and saying that they only said such because they loved you and wanted the best for you. Paulet means to try to catch the King at a time when he is not furious, and he will put it to him that the women appreciate they have done wrong, will not do so again and only spoke such because they wanted to see both their King and the lady they serve happy."

"I do not like the advice that the best thing I can do is to do nothing," I said, wringing my hands, "I feel entirely helpless as it is."

"Sometimes, my lady, it is best to remain quiet until the danger passes. Speak now and you could damage both their chances and yours of getting out of this with but a warning."

I took his advice, however much I did not want to, and it was sage in the end. Within three days of that conversation both women were returned to my household. They returned scared shells of themselves. Kitty and Jane, once such bright, talkative women returned pale, scared and close-mouthed. They were unharmed in body but were so different to how they had been before that they were barely my women anymore.

I did not need to reprimand them; the King's men had done enough to scare them. As I watched each one of them scurry about their duties like frightened mice, eyes downcast, nerves frayed, and afraid of being seen, let alone talked to, I considered what a power it was these men wielded. The officers of the King and his Council could so fulsomely change the personality of two people over the span of but a few days. If this alteration they had fashioned upon my women in so brief a time, what could they do to men who were set inside prisons for months, their bodies given over for torture? What could they do to women once high, who suddenly found themselves fallen and friendless in an already hostile world?

They could do anything to them. They could make them say anything they wanted. I looked at Kitty and Jane and I knew this was a truth as solid and as constant as the sun in the sky. People once had told me the King was loved, by women, by his subjects, his nobles. If that ever had been true it was not now. The sway he held over them was not love, highest of all influences. It was fear, lowest, meanest and most cowardly of powers.

Chapter Fifty-Three

Richmond Palace
December 10th 1541

"They are dead. It is done."

"Not quite done, my friend, the Queen still lives."

Katherine gazed at me. "Queen no more, yet still married to the King she is, and she will not escape this, Anna, you know that."

"I know."

Culpepper and Dereham had died that day. The King commuted Culpepper's sentence, but not Dereham's. Culpepper died by beheading. Dereham was hanged, drawn and quartered. Culpepper was of the nobility, albeit a lesser son. It was usual that those of noble blood died better than those of lower, but this was not the true reason Culpepper was spared suffering and Dereham was not.

The King wanted Dereham to suffer because he had been the first to take Catherine, to taste her. He had been her original master, leaving the King with spoiled, inadequate goods. Dereham had committed the more atrocious crime, but not against the Queen. Think not this was done for the fact he had raped her, no. This was done because of the crime committed against the King. Dereham had spoiled his fantasy before the King had even met her.

They had died that morn. The two men came from the Tower dressed in mourning clothes. Their clothes would become the property of the man who executed them, so prisoners dressed fine, a bribe for those who would kill them. Sometimes it worked and mercy was given, a swift death rather than a lingering one.

Tied to wooden hurdles, they were pulled from the Tower by horses, dragged four miles through the city, past jeering crowds who threw rotten fruit and shouted names, as if death was not punishment enough, to the gallows of Tyburn.

At the gates of Saint Sepulchre-without-Newgate, they were handed nosegays; a tradition all kept though none remembered why. Church bells rang as men recited verse, calling on people to pray for the souls of the condemned. At Saint-Giles-in-the-Field, they were given ale, a last drink before death. At Tyburn they were taken from the hurdles and walked to the gallows.

They had spoken, but not a great deal. No one could remember anything memorable from their speeches to pass on to me. Their words had been conventional; pleas for their families to be spared, blessings for the King, their murderer. Dereham looked weak, they said. He had been tortured in the Tower. Perhaps it was surprising he had stuck to his story of love for Catherine and a pre-contract. He never admitted he had raped her, or intimidated her into sex, but why should he? No one likes to think themselves the villain.

Culpepper died first. He knelt, put his head to the block and the axe took his life. He was done quickly. No so sweet a fate for Dereham.

Oftentimes, the family of a condemned man would slip money to the executioner, so if their son was to be drawn and quartered the executioner would ensure he was already dead when the knife came to his belly, by hanging him until he was dead. If Dereham's family tried this, they failed, for Dereham was certainly alive when the worst of tortures was inflicted upon him. The screaming rang through London for days, some claimed.

"Such a death was devised for the last of the Welsh princes, Dafydd ap Gruffydd, by Edward I," Katherine told me. "He tried to imagine the worst death he could, and this was what he imagined."

"My ancestor," I said, staring from the window. "Blood of my blood."

"We are, none of us, our ancestors, for good or ill," my friend said, joining me at the window.

"And yet I profit still from the lands he conquered, the horrors he did, the wars he undertook," I said. "Do I not? My position, my birth, part of them came from him, this man who devised the worst death he could imagine to use on another man, one which my former husband still uses today."

"I thought you had no sympathy for Dereham."

"I struggle with that, indeed. In life I had no sympathy for this creature, but to feel no sympathy when I hear of such horror inflicted on a man? That is harder. If a man does evil should evil be done to him? I know not, my friend. It seems to me to become a cycle endless."

Dereham was put into the noose, rope grasping his throat. The stool was kicked away, and he dangled, pissing and shitting himself as he choked for air, his body bucking, thrashing helplessly. As he started to spasm, the rope was cut and he fell to the floor, crying out as his ankle ruptured. Hauled onto a table, he was stretched out and tied down. A sharp knife cut deep into his body, rough hands first cutting his shaft away, then his testicles, then into his belly it went, so intestines could emerge, long, purple and bloody pulled in a line from him. His belly gaping, his manhood trembling in a bowl, his innards quaking on the floor, his head was finally cut off, ending his agony.

Both heads were taken to London Bridge, impaled on spikes.

After death Dereham was hacked into bits. Quarters of his body were sent about the city of London, displayed as warnings. Even in death he was not allowed to rest, would be afforded no dignity. If all Catherine had said of him was true, I was not sure he deserved dignity in death in any case. Culpepper's body was sent to Lambeth, his home parish, for his family to bury quietly.

"I wonder what will happen now," I said.

"I know not," my friend of Suffolk replied. "There will be another Queen, I would suppose."

When she looked at me, there was fear in her eyes. I knew not if it was for me or for herself. I had heard the Duke of Suffolk had not been well.

Perhaps she thought as I did, that if she was free, the King might well choose her.

*

Catherine's family were tried on the twenty-second of December. Christmas was coming, but it was no season of peace and goodwill in England that year. Lord William, along with Katherine Howard the Queen's aunt and the women of the Dowager's household were tried for misprision of treason and found guilty. Their lands and goods were forfeit to the Crown, but they were sentenced to life imprisonment, not death.

I had been told Norfolk might too be tried, but he escaped, slippery eel that he was. The Dowager, too, escaped, but I was glad of that. It was said she was too old to stand trial.

Under questioning the Dowager had tried to defend Catherine, had said that since all that had happened occurred before marriage, she thought there was no crime. She did not paint her granddaughter a whore and abandon her, as Norfolk had. The Queen's aunt Katherine, too, did not cast the Queen down as a wicked woman who had damned all Howards. They could not save her, these kinswomen of Catherine, but they did not speak ill of her either.

It was something.

Agnes Tilney was censured for bringing Catherine up badly, for laxity and for forgetting her duty, but the Dowager was not to blame. The men who had harmed this young girl were, and men were not done hurting her yet.

Chapter Fifty-Four

Richmond Palace
December 1541

"I am with child, again?" I asked, my voice this time verging on the hysterical. "I am most fertile with imaginary children, is that three now?"

Another filthy rumour, that I had borne the King's child and now we would marry for it was a boy, had emerged.

This was the same child, I learned later, that had been spoken of in the summer. Some people said it was not the King's child and I was a jade, like Catherine. The feasts I held at my house ended with me taking my men to bed with me, people whispered. There was talk I might be arrested for immoral behaviour, but nothing further happened because apparently there was enough of naughty behaviour from the present Queen to be investigating. At least one royal lady had to be innocent and virtuous, otherwise it might cast shame on the kingdom.

Later it was found that this rumour I was pregnant, and the one I might be arrested, were but gossip put about to defame me and it came from my very own household. Two more of my servants were arrested, both men, both Lutherans who were displeased I was not more on their side in terms of faith. They went to the Tower, to join Catherine's kin.

"I thought all were happy under my governance here," I said to Harst and Olisleger. "What have I done wrong?" In truth I barely knew the men who had been taken. One served in my stables and another in the kitchens. Both had confessed immediately that they had put the gossip about, and explained why, calling me a traitor to their faith.

But their faith was not the King's faith, and so they would be punished for defaming me and for promoting Lutheranism.

"Highness, you have done nothing," said Olisleger. "Those men, they wanted you to champion something which would throw you into trouble, and that is unreasonable."

"I am also not a reformer, so it would be hypocritical." I paused. "Was it Carew? Did he do something here, just at this time, to try to unseat me as well as the Queen?"

"There is no evidence of that, madam."

I gulped in air, trying to steady my nerves. I was jumping at shadows. "All the same, I want him watched," I said, my hands twitching at my sides. "I do not trust the man, and I am sure it was he who reported my women. It would seem I should not trust all people in this house, in any case, seeing as two men I barely knew tried to have me arrested."

"I will keep an eye on his doings," offered Olisleger.

I nodded. "Any news on the Queen or her fate now that the men accused with her are dead?"

"There is no word of what the King means to do to the Queen," Harst told us.

"The King does not want a trial. If so, it would have been done by now," I said.

When Anne Boleyn's end came, she had gone to trial fast and she had embarrassed the King... her brother only more so. The King would not have that again. There were other problems. Were Catherine to be tried, set before the people, they might be reminded how young she was. Eighteen she was by then, just, but in face and form she appeared younger. She was also pretty and there was still a common belief that those who were strong in beauty were virtuous of character. It might go against the King to present her in public.

At the moment, shut away as she was, she could become this monster the King's men were painting her as to the people of England, but appear in the flesh before the masses and they might well pity her, and come to hate him. No, the King would not have that. No pity for Catherine. Better to hide her away until he could kill her quietly.

Besides, what would that poor girl, already condemned, say at a trial? Catherine was no Anne Boleyn brought up to master rhetoric and wit, her skills fine-tuned in the most glamorous, intellectual courts of the world in her youth. Catherine possessed many skills but speaking in public was not one. The one time she had done so it had clearly been carefully rehearsed.

And to bring up all that had happened to her, parade the horrors of her youth before a court, a jury and the people, only to have men say it was not so and she was indeed a whore who had invited all the abuse piled upon her? No, she would not want that.

What worse shame could there be than telling the truth, and having it used against her, just another weapon in a long and painful fight?

Chapter Fifty-Five

Richmond Palace and
Greenwich Palace
January 1542

January came, and the approach to New Year was as dull as the Christmas before it. We passed a quiet Christmas at Richmond. There was a feast on the day, some dancing, but no one's heart was in it, and I hardly wanted raucous celebrations in case the King heard of them and thought it an insult.

My brother's wife, Jeanne d'Albret, sent to me a book of hours, a glorious little work of art with *A&C*s on the cover, for Anna and Cleves, as well as my coat of arms. The note which came with it mentioned that since I would soon return to a *better state*, as so I deserved, I would need a new prayer book. I came to think gossip that I would be taken back as Queen was rife in France as well as England.

It terrified me.

And yet, there could be a reason to accept should the King offer me such a position.

I did not want to, for my own sake if not for that of Catherine, still at Syon, her fate still a mystery. How could I act as if I took the place of a woman dead, yet know she was alive, a living ghost? It was gruesome to think thus, ghoulish, dangerous too, for what if the King was not thinking of offering me anything and he heard I was eager? And I was *not* eager. I had no wish to give up my freedom, this present life I had found such joy in. I did not want to be wed to a man who had once cast me off and could do so again, could find a way to kill me should I fail to please him again. I did not want to live in terror.

And yet, as Olisleger told me, and as had come to my mind before, there were reasons to consider carefully what I would do if the King asked me to again be his Queen.

"There is word your brother is gathering an army, a large one, and François is moving too," Olisleger told me. "War is coming, Highness, against the Empire, and our country will be at the fore of it. If your brother is to succeed, he needs more allies. If the King should take you back as Queen, England would become one of those allies and a valuable one. Welsh bowmen are still feared in Europe, many men could be sent, many skilled generals, and the King has a fleet of great ships. There are reasons to consider carefully, should the King offer to take you back as his wife."

"The King has never shown any preference for me in such a way," I said, voice wavering and my guts squirming as if they meant to flee my body in fear. "The most I have had of him is friendly, brotherly affection."

"That is a better basis for marriage than many couples have."

"Olisleger, Catherine Howard is still alive, she is still married to the King. You would have me take her place now? Whilst she is still alive? And forget not we know what the King is capable of. Many times I have thought myself fortunate that I emerged the first time still with a head on my shoulders, but you would have me go back again?"

"If it was the way to save your country, would you do it?"

"Even if England entered the war on the side of François and Wilhelm, that does not guarantee they would win it, nor would it mean I would save any men of my country from dying." My voice was high, scared. My friend heard it and dropped his tone to a soothing one.

"But England's involvement could sway the war, could decide it."

I shook my head. "I sometimes wonder if all the people about me have become swept up in the fantasy the kings of England have spun all these years. England is not as important to the world as it thinks it is. It makes itself appear so, it thrusts itself into wars and conflicts, and mistake me not, its men fight fierce, but this little speck on the sea, it thinks itself a giant cresting on a wave. One day it will discover the truth, and so will every other country. Its lies about its greatness may be magnificent, but this country is small and weak for it is only as strong as its King." My voice dropped to a murmur. "And this King is a coward."

I suppose whispering such could be used to prove my own cowardice, but it could be equally named prudence.

"Whether or not you believe in the importance of England, Highness, the Emperor does, and he may well hesitate, bargain, rather than make war if England joins with Cleves and France."

I swallowed, my breathing coming hard. That was true enough, what Olisleger said, but I could not give an answer to him then. I could not.

Half my heart, the half brought up to only and ever do my duty, to bow and obey and duck my head and agree when I was spoken to, that part told me I had to accept the King should he make a new offer to me. For my people, my country, for honour and for duty, I had to accept, I had no other choice. But there was another voice in me now.

The part which had known freedom, the part which knew the King for a monster, the part which longed to free Catherine Howard and ride away into the wilds of England, that part told me I could not accept. And I was right, too, that I might well not survive this time. I had been so fortunate the last time it was possible to get complacent, think myself special, but I was not special. I had merely been the lucky one that day. I might well not be that lucky again.

I was forced to go to Greenwich on the New Year to give presents of crimson cloth to my 'good' brother, but I tried to keep the visit brief, complaining of a fever which was upon me. I left early in order not to trouble my brother or his court with my illness.

The King gave me flagons and glass pots for New Year, expensive gifts and ones chosen especially for me. That attention worried me and enthused all those about me who appeared to be running on madness and seemed to think I would become Queen and have my tale end happily ever after. "Often gifts given by the King are quite generic," Olisleger said. "This could be a sign of affection, Highness."

I hoped it was not.

After I announced I was ill, the King kept away from me, and yet there had been an appraising glance he threw at me as I presented my gift, which I liked not. I felt as if I was being considered, a horse at market, and I ascertained it was not only my men telling me we should match again. Others, men of court, were saying this to the King too.

But that glance he swept over me, it was cold, as if he was trying to remind himself of what I looked like, and he had never liked how I looked. It was true I was prettier since I came to England, and it was also true I was older now, and the King seemed in the past, before Catherine, to have a taste for more mature women, but still, I did not think he liked me and I doubted, even if he thought me prettier now, that he wished to marry me when he knew he would be drawn into war then on the side of France and Cleves. One reason to separate from me fast was to avoid such a fate when first we had married.

Court was quiet and dim, few celebrations and laughs to be heard. The King looked old, his skin quite as grey as his hair. His men were urging him to marry again, as soon as his wife's fate was decided, but he said he liked no ladies of court. People told me this as though I was supposed to feel bad for the King, feel sorry that he had not another wife lined up already as the last waited to die.

They were still married, too. Catherine was his wife, and yet many others thought that he should have another wife at his side.

"Why does everyone only think of me, are there no other women in the world?" I asked Olisleger, and he looked uncomfortable. He understood just how reluctant I was by that time, was well aware I was terrified of the King and had been faking fever to get away from court.

"Your brother, Duke Wilhelm, is opening talks, or trying to, in order to get the King to take you back, in light of recent events. He seems to think there is a good chance you will be named Queen again. The news has spread through court, you have many supporters, Highness."

Many people willing to throw me into the fire, I thought.

"The King is still married, and the lady is still alive, her fate not decided at all."

"And yet there may be a chance, madam. Would you not want a chance to be Queen again? Even if you are unsure of the King, the position would be a great one. And the King is fond of you now, he speaks well of your beauty, which was the only thing he felt was lacking in you before."

"As well as my scent, conversation, manners and virginity, apparently." My tone was waspish. "The King will not want me back and it is unseemly, to say the very least, to be talking of this when Catherine is still his wife." I shook my head, gritting my teeth. "You are being commanded to open talks, as ambassador?"

"Myself and others, Highness." Olisleger's shoulders slumped. "Madam, you know how I admire and esteem you, but the truth is that I am a servant of Cleves, and your brother is my lord and master. I must do as he commands."

"I know." It saddened me that after all this time even those who I considered closest to me could be driven to work against my wishes because my brother commanded them. Much as it had not mattered that Jeanne of Navarre had not wanted to marry Wilhelm and had to be carried to the altar to make her wed him, it did not matter in truth if I did not want to marry the King again. If my brother decided it and the King agreed, it would happen.

I had thought myself so free these past years, yet it could all be stripped from me in an instant.

That is what people never understand about the freedoms granted to women, or lesser people. They are fictions. Our rights are fictions. Our liberty is a false show. Those who had power over us, they could take it all away, in less time than it took to draw a breath.

I had lived in giddy abandon for a while, and yet that life I loved could be stripped from me if men about me decided it should be so. My happiness was unimportant to them, my safety equally so. I would be thrown back into a perilous trap of a marriage with this lunatic of England if my brother decided it was for the best, and I would have no say.

We can walk about one day thinking we are free and have rights, that our voice matters, then have that all ripped from us the next. No one understands that the state we live in never is permanent and when another has ultimate control over you, every state is unsteady. I had thought myself free, but I could be shown brutally and without compassion that I was nothing of the kind. They could take everything from me, and no one would object in my name, no one would stand for me.

I was not free, I was trapped. Katherine of Suffolk was right when she said I was in a cage.

"Madame," Olisleger said. "I know you do not wish to marry the King; I know you fear him, but if it was for the good of Cleves…"

"You think I should risk my life a second time, as a soldier would in battle for his country?"

"I have always thought you a warrior, my lady, just of a different kind. And you know, you would not be as defenceless as you think. You are related to the Valois now, as well as Cleves. They would be added protection."

Marillac the French ambassador had of late been singing my praises. Where once he had condemned me as ugly and said I looked older than my years, he now declared I was full of virtue, patience and beauty. Of course, since I was now related to the Valois by marriage it would be impolitic to name me ill-favoured. What a crime it is to be an ugly woman! No, the French ambassador could not insult his own royal house by calling me anything less than beautiful.

In addition to the ambassador heaping praise upon me I had gifts from France, and the Queen of Navarre, sister to François of France, had sent her best wishes for the New Year. It was true my family was wider, my brother's reach more powerful, but still, "Katherine of Spain was the aunt of the most powerful man in the world and the King still cast her off," I said.

"There will always be a risk, but will you consider it, Highness? For the sake of your people, whose lot you may improve?"

"For your sake too, Olisleger, so you might sell me off to this man I loathe and not feel bad about it since I agreed!" I snapped, and then my shoulders drooped as I saw his face. "As I was sent here to protect my people once, I shall *consider* doing so again, but there is no guarantee the King would take me back."

"But your brother will be pleased you are willing to try, Highness. He has asked me to approach Cranmer again."

"Again?"

Olisleger looked uncomfortable all over again. In time Katherine of Suffolk would tell me that he had already approached Cranmer, when first the accusations against Catherine Howard were known. My brother had set things in motion the very moment he heard of her arrest, and had had Olisleger not only go to Cranmer but to Southampton too, asking the Admiral to write a letter to the King in support of me.

I had not agreed, but already I had been thrust into the path of the King.

I was certainly not about to throw myself at the King or attempt to lure him to me. Even if I had known how to do such things, I would have baulked at them whilst Catherine was still hanging in limbo, waiting for her fate to be decided. If the King wanted me back, he could ask. I was not about to hang about him as a fly might, trying to feed upon a scrap of honey stuck in his beard.

I hid at Richmond, and anytime anyone asked after me I told my people to say the fever still troubled me.

I was even more worried when the King sent a plaster of herbs to me, his own concoction of myrrh, fenugreek, radicchio and chamomile, to "mollify and resolve, comfort and cease pain of cold and windy causes," saying he was troubled for my health. Many people chose to read love into this noxious concoction of herbs, the idea that this showed concern and love for me. I hoped that all it meant was the King was concerned about the reaction of my natural brother and other heads of state if I happened to die suddenly in England, under his protection.

I was not alone in feeling few sorrows for the King. I had heard servants talking when I was at court. Some said Catherine would be left alive, to give the King more options. Should he take another wife, he might want rid of that new wife in time and take Catherine back. Many seemed not to believe now in the tales of woe the King told. They supposed that he got rid of wives not for any crime or sin, but because another maid was more desirable. I wondered if other people did not believe in the Queen's guilt, as they had not in Anne Boleyn's. And if they wondered about Anne, she who had made so many clear enemies, I was sure they wondered about Catherine too.

Catherine had made few foes, tried to do good where she could. There were few who hated her as Anne had been hated. Even those who wanted the Howards destroyed must have seen by that time that it had not worked. Norfolk remained at court, Catholics and conservatives were still in power. Their plot had failed. The King would remain as he was, stuck in the middle of the faiths. The wife he took was no more an influence on that, as once she had been.

Catherine had done worst of all his wives, in the King's eyes, committed the most terrible crimes, for she had 'betrayed' the King whilst he was happy, and when he had no other woman in sight. Before he had always had another ready to replace the one he was tired of. Only when Jane Seymour died had he been thwarted.

Catherine hurt the King more than any other woman, because he had not been the one to cast her off. It was he who had not been loved by her.

Chapter Fifty-Six

Richmond Palace
January 1542

"I did not write it!"

My famous calm was a stranger to me in those days. I was struggling to maintain command over myself. The Queen's arrest, my servants being taken too, the prospect of replacing Catherine, of losing all that had become dear to me, it was too much. I always had thought myself in control of my emotions and thoughts, but I had never been tested so, even when the King had set me aside and I thought I might die. There had been but a few weeks of uncertainty at that time before my new fate was handed to me. Now, event came on event, and I was being asked to make decisions, ones which would see me being the author of stealing my own happiness, ones which would force me to replace a Queen I had admired. I felt watched and hunted even by men I had trusted, I knew not who in my household was a friend anymore, and now this.

I felt as panicked as I had when first I heard the King was investigating our marriage and I thought he might have my head cut off, the second Anne to the scaffold in five years. A tract had emerged, apparently written by me, bemoaning my fate at being cast away by the King. It was in the form of a letter, which I had apparently written, to the King, and had been published in a book. It was called "The Repudiation of Queen Maria of England, sister of the Duke of Cleves". Quite aside from the fact I would hardly call myself Maria, which was my mother's name, proving that whoever had written it wasn't overly familiar with me, the tract had, it seemed, emerged from France.

"The King knows you did not write it," Olisleger tried to soothe me. "Calm yourself, Highness. He sends this information to us not because he thinks you are guilty but simply to make you aware of it."

I swallowed hard. "Who wrote this?"

"Perhaps it was François, or someone acting for him. He would like to draw England into his conflict with Spain which looms, and if you were to wed the King again then the King would be allied once more to your brother, who is allied to France. The King would be forced to unite with the plans of France as they head into war with the Emperor."

"The King of France will not achieve much by getting me arrested and beheaded for treason!" I waved the paper in the air on which the copy of the letter was printed. "This goes against the Act which dissolved my marriage. If the King believes I have written this, that I have called myself Queen in *writing* no less, I could be arrested, my goods and estates forfeit to the Crown. I could be executed, Olisleger!"

"The King has asked François to stop it being printed. He will not arrest you, Highness, he knows you are innocent."

I almost laughed. That had hardly helped another Anne, or all the friends of the King, had it?

The letter also contained some none too pleasing comments on the King, saying that it was a thing hard to convince a King or Prince of another viewpoint – my marriage being valid in other words – because some princes *"think most of the time that everything they want is lawful and permitted to them"*, which certainly sounded like a criticism.

"Highness, he does not think you wrote it, but would simply have you put in writing that you did not."

I did so, as swift as I could.

It did occur to me that perhaps Wilhelm had been behind it. Although the paper had emerged in France, it was possible he had told someone to write it, not caring that it might put me in gross and raw danger.

He seemed to believe the King was itching to take me back, but men do tend to believe wholeheartedly in that which brings them the greatest reward. Possibly he had convinced himself that I would be happier married again to the King, possibly it was easier to think that than to understand that he, my own brother, was trying to shift me into a chair most dangerous, one I had no desire to sit in again, all to further his own ends.

*

"If she wants a trial, my lady, there could be one," said Harst.

He managed to look a little sorrowed. Harst had never been a great supporter of Catherine, of course, but the fate of the child was on all lips in England at that time, and few there were who had not a little pity for her. Even those who thought her a whore thought her one who had not been used well. She was so young, you see. Younger still when all these stories about her had been born. Women were well aware of the dangers for young girls in certain houses, and men, though they liked to pretend otherwise, were not ignorant of them either. Had she been executed when the accusations were fresh and everyone was busy howling with indignation about her behaviour it might have been better for the King, but the delay in a sentence for the former Queen had led people to consider other thoughts, such as her youth, her kindness to prisoners, how she had reunited the royal family. Sympathy was forming for her.

Cranmer had gone to Syon with Suffolk, Lord Southampton and the Bishop of Westminster. The King wanted to condemn Catherine by Act of Attainder, without trial, her fate decided by Parliament, but really by him. But there was dissent. The House of Lords had grumbled, for although Catherine was not to be known as Queen anymore, she was still married to the King and was, technically, at the very least a princess of the realm. This made condemning her by Act of Attainder an affront to the state. They wanted her to have a trial, to be judged by her peers, as her Boleyn cousins had been.

"But the word is she said she did not want a trial, and would submit to the King's pleasure," he went on.

I understood. Everyone had already drawn conclusions, made their own judgements. To have the intimate details of her life, all she probably felt shame and horror in, drawn out, examined and no doubt ridiculed, was the worst nightmare. Catherine would not be believed in any case, not by men sent by the King, so why humiliate herself more?

And there was a chance here. The King wanted to decide her fate. If Catherine offered him that power, that last power, the King might be merciful. Submission to the King had aided other women; me, Lady Mary, Margaret Douglas. It might aid Catherine. If he was going to kill her, he would anyway, trial or not.

Submit. That was what she did. I wondered if she thought of me as she did so. I think she knew she was to die, for before they left, these men of the Council, promising she might live, she told them, "My only wish now is to make a good death, so I might leave a good opinion in people's minds now, at the time of parting."

"They stared at her, white-faced in shock, for they had just been telling her she might live, and there she was, accepting death," Harst said.

"Ask the King that my death might be quiet," Catherine said. "Not under the eyes of the world."

When they left, there were reports she became gay with the thought of death, perhaps at the thought of release. She ate happily, savouring each mouthful and drinking deep of wine. It seemed to me she had made up her mind to enjoy what little life she had.

Chapter Fifty-Seven

Richmond Palace
February 1542

I think the King had his wife fooled for a long time; he almost fooled me. Nothing happened for more than a week after Catherine submitted to the King. Many thought she might escape with her life, and Catherine was one of them.

But it was not a reward, this time, this hope that rose in her, thinking she might not die. It was a punishment. What good would it be to kill Catherine when she had accepted death? What purpose would that serve? He wanted her to suffer when death came. This period of peace, where she was allowed to abandon thoughts of death and take up hope for life, was simply a way to set her up so her pain would be greater, so she would suffer, so he could punish her more.

He had said it, had he not? When he had wanted to kill her himself, he had said he wanted her tortured.

It worked. She was lulled into hope. Catherine ate well and slept peacefully. She started to order people about in her tiny household. She acted with confidence, as if she might be pardoned.

No one told Catherine that on the sixth of February Parliament passed the Act of Attainder against her and Jane Boleyn. An Act of Attainder could condemn a person to death without need for a trial, hearing, or defence, or them even being present. It held that if any woman dared marry the King without "plain declaration before of her unchaste life unto His Majesty" then this was treason. Never had this been law before.

Adultery with the Queen was treason now, and failure to inform the King was also. Even though neither of these acts had been treason when Catherine had married the King, and even though it had never been proved she had committed adultery, with these changes to the law, Jane and Catherine were now judged as guilty of high treason.

They were both sentenced to death. The King went to his Parliament on the same day, thanking them for accepting his sorrow as theirs.

Another Act was passed. It said that should a lunatic confess to high treason before insanity fell upon them, they could still be executed. This was for Jane, so she could not escape by being mad, or pretending insanity.

On the ninth, Norfolk went to Syon. He told Catherine she was to die.

"Calm your womanish fears. It will be done in private, as you asked," he said. "On Tower Green."

Is it womanish to fear death? To fear injustice? I wondered.

Catherine was confused enough to think this was a test of her love for the King. "I acknowledge the great crime of which I am guilty," she said boldly. "My lord is a great prince and has ever been a good and loving husband to me. I regret that I acted against him and against England. I accept his judgement but would only implore His Majesty not to impute my crime against my kindred and family. Please, Your Grace, ask His Majesty not to punish my family, to show his unbounded mercy and benevolence to my brothers, to my grandmother, so they may not suffer for my faults."

She asked that her maids be looked after financially when she was gone.

"*Is* it a test?" I asked myself that night. Anne Boleyn had died a day after her men. The gap seemed proof. Months had passed since Dereham and Culpepper had died. That meant Catherine would not die, did it not?

It did not. They came for her the next day.

"She collapsed, poor child." Harst picked somewhat nervously at a nail, loose on his finger. "When she saw them, Suffolk and Southampton, the Lord Privy Seal, when they told her they were taking her to the Tower, she refused to go, said she did not deserve to die for a *thought*. They tried to talk to her, and she backed into a corner, taking hold of a chair to hide behind. They cajoled and shouted, then they grabbed her."

Shrieking loud with terror, Catherine was dragged from her chamber. They hauled her out, her nails scratching wood and flesh as she screamed, pleading for mercy. Into the barge they threw her. She got up and ran at them, trying to get out. They pushed her back, told her to sit.

They sailed quickly, three boats in total, bobbing on the water to the Tower. The last boat held many guards. In Catherine's boat there were four ladies who held her still, sitting on a seat. Guards rowed, paddles dipping in and out of the grey, churning water.

At the Tower stairs, Catherine came from the boat, trembling, silenced by fear. The Constable of the Tower, Sir John Gage, tried to welcome her as a great lady of court and country, but fell silent as he saw her face, dumb with horror.

"They say she looked like a terrified child," said Harst.

"Because that is what she is," I murmured.

They had to carry her to her rooms. Catherine collapsed. She started to weep, then to wail, and when she got inside her rooms, she beat her breasts and screamed, loud and long.

I wondered if the King, hearing this, would smile.

Chapter Fifty-Eight

Richmond Palace
February 1542

"They have told her to make confession before death, to attain eternal life." Katherine of Suffolk looked pale.

John Longland, Bishop of Lincoln, was the man who went to Catherine, trying to get her to confess, but Catherine said again she was innocent.

"I do not seek to excuse the faults and follies of my youth," the former Queen said. "God will be my judge. He will see what was done, and if it was fault of mine or others. I ask only that you pray for divine mercy for me, that God may grant me the strength to cope with the ordeal I must face."

It made many uneasy, this second time a Queen was being sent to death. For what crime was Catherine dying? She had never confessed to adultery, and there was still no proof she had committed it. The only proof of treason was the Act of Attainder and laws drawn up after she had committed her supposed crimes. Everyone was aware most of her 'guilt' was based on retrospective laws the King had only just created.

But there was no one to save her. There was no knight riding to her rescue. Chivalry was a fantasy. Another way to make women reliant on men, to trust blindly men who would betray them.

The Church should have been where she was tried, if adultery was the charge, and it would have been had the old laws been in place. Adultery was always tried by Church courts in the past and the sentence never would have been death. Even had Catherine sinned, it is men who hates fallen women, not Christ. Christ showed how men were to treat women. As they should treat men, as all people should treat each other. Equally and without judgement. Kindly, without cruelty. But there are few who follow the ways of Christ.

"Mistress Howard called for the block to be brought to her rooms," Katherine went on.

"Why?"

"She said she had heard her cousin, Anne Boleyn, made a good death for herself and she wished to do the same, but she had not her cousin's natural grace. Catherine wanted the block brought to her so she could practise walking to it, placing her head."

Tears stung in my eyes, and I turned my face to the window.

"Sometimes it feels as if the world is falling apart, does it not?" Katherine asked, joining me at the window.

"For someone, somewhere, it always is," I said. "We must be grateful for the days when the world is solid under our own feet, not slipping away, beyond our control."

Katherine nodded. "I will leave you now."

"You are for court?"

She shook her head. "I am suddenly of a mind to visit my sons. I should like to look upon innocence a while, remind myself goodness is alive in this world. I want to hear their laughter." She smiled. "I will be back in a few days, when things are... more settled."

I kissed my friend and turned back to the window. I stood there a long time that evening.

In the Tower Catherine Howard walked to the block over and over that night, rehearsing her own death so she would not stumble before the crowds in the morning, and disgrace herself.

In my rooms at Richmond, I succumbed to guilt and fear.

I told Olisleger that if the King should ask, then I would place my country's safety above my own and agree to be his wife again.

Standing at my hearth, I was numb with fear and shock that night. My hand strayed to my throat where a jewelled cross set with diamonds and bearing the letters *IHS* for Jesus lay against my skin. Once it had belonged to the King's favourite wife, Jane, but he had handed it along to me, along with many other trinkets, cast offs of women of the past he claimed he had loved, yet for him such items held no sentiment. It felt cold that night, against my skin.

You escaped the fire, said the voice of the fallen Boleyn Queen in my mind, *yet you would go back?*

"I never escaped the fire," I whispered. "I merely ceased to feel the flames awhile."

Chapter Fifty-Nine

Richmond Palace
February 1542

The thirteenth of February 1542 was a bright, cold day.

Early in the morning, Catherine was escorted from her rooms to the Tower Green to stand on a scaffold. It was erected on the same site where her cousin, Anne Boleyn, had died six years earlier. The execution was not public, but not private, either. A crowd of nobles, but not commoners, attended. Her uncle of Norfolk was absent, not wanting to associate himself with her disgrace and death. Most of the rest of her family were locked away in the Tower. Some might have watched from windows.

She was not under the eyes of the world, as she had asked, but she was not alone, either.

Catherine was dressed in black, her gown picked out from the few the King had left her with after arrest. Unlike her cousin, Catherine was not allowed to select the dress she would die in. Anne Boleyn had worn a blazing crimson petticoat signalling she was dying a martyr, but young Catherine Howard went to her death in black, a colour chosen by the King.

"They said she appeared sick and weak. Some said she could hardly stand, but she walked to the scaffold. She did not stumble, but made steady progress to the top, where she stood near the headsman. Catherine was... a small figure on the scaffold." The Duchess bunched her lips in pity.

Not one nature had blessed with height, Catherine looked small and frail, by all reports.

Catherine made a speech, but her words were badly recorded, even hours after I only heard snippets of what she had said. She spoke of Christ and the redemption promised to those who believed in Him. She asked the crowd to learn from her example and praised the good government of the

King. She said she had deserved a hundred deaths and asked the people there to pray for the King. Catherine proclaimed the sentence upon her as just, in keeping with the laws of the land.

"We should not read too much into such words," Katherine told me. "Everyone, innocent or guilty, says the same before they die, hoping humility will save further humiliation or death for their families. Catherine did not protest she loved the King and said nothing of Thomas Culpepper."

"She did not say she wished she had been his wife?" This was one of the tales being told.

"She did not say a word about him."

What was unusual was that Catherine did not admit guilt. Most people said they were guilty before death. She did not. Like her cousin before her, Catherine Howard chose to leave out this section of the traditional speech. She had confessed and told her confessor she had not sinned against her husband.

About to meet her Maker, Catherine would not lie. It would condemn her soul.

A few women, one of them her sister Isabella, were there to attend her. They took her hood and gave her the traditional cap. Catherine handed a purse to the executioner. Inside was his fee for cutting off her head. When Anne Boleyn died, this courtesy had been taken care of for her. Not so for Catherine. She paid for her own death.

Catherine walked to the block, knelt on the straw, and put her head on the block with dignity. She was practised. She knew the block well, after rehearsing her death the night before.

"She died by the axe," said Katherine. "No sword for her, as for her cousin."

"The sword is a guaranteed swift death," I said quietly. "The King wanted Catherine to know she did not deserve that." It meant, to my mind, he had known Anne Boleyn was innocent, for he had granted her this favour, this last mercy. But Catherine he wanted to suffer.

Thankfully, he did not get his wish.

She said her prayers and when she was done, the headsman swung. Catherine Howard died with one stroke and died clean.

Her women threw a cloak over her small body, and the head and body were taken to one side of the scaffold as Jane Boleyn emerged from her rooms. Water was thrown over the platform, then fresh hay, so Jane would not slip in the blood of her friend and mistress as she walked to her own death.

"If Jane had gone mad, she was calm by the time she died," said Katherine.

The King had of course passed his special Act allowing Jane to be executed even if insane, so it did not matter what her state of mind was. He did not mean for her to escape. Jane Boleyn, Lady Rochford spoke well, telling the crowd she asked for mercy from God and wished to be in their prayers. She praised the King. Some claimed she admitted she had lied about Anne and George Boleyn, unjustly sending them to death, saying, "Good Christians, God hath permitted me to suffer this shameful doom as punishment for having contributed to my husband's death. I falsely accused him of loving in an incestuous manner, his sister, Queen Anne Boleyn. For this I deserve to die, but I am guilty of no other crime."

"Is it true?" I asked my friend.

Katherine shrugged. "Accounts differ, I have already heard three versions of her end and speech, so there is no way of knowing if this is true or not, but if it is, Jane Boleyn exonerated her husband and his sister as her last act before death. Something perhaps to be admired."

Jane, too, died with one stroke.

Their bodies were taken to the chapel of St Peter ad Vincula. Stones beneath the altar were prised up, revealing, amongst others, the resting places of Anne Boleyn, George Boleyn, Thomas More and Lady Salisbury. There the two women were laid to rest.

Cannons fired over London, to say the deed was done. Another Queen, the second one to die by execution in England, was gone. Both had been the wives of the same man. I wondered if any other King would ever kill his wife or if my former husband would retain that unique, if troubling, distinction.

The King was in the country at the time of her death, hunting. The following day he came back to Whitehall to start celebrating Shrovetide with three days of feasting. The day he returned was the feast of St Valentine. The King, now a widower since his marriage to Catherine had not been annulled when she died, held a feast. There was more feasting two weeks later when ladies of court were brought to the King to entertain him.

He was looking for a new wife.

I sat at my window on the night the Queen died. I would still call her that, even if others would not.

A cloak of feathers I had once wished for, to carry me away from here. I had found my freedom, however fragile it was, however long it might last. I hoped that Catherine had found hers, and hers might be eternal.

There was a book at my side. Setting my hand on it, a volume telling tales of history, I thought on the power of stories. They told us of the past and formed the future, informed us who ruled us and why, and now stories had sent a girl who never had a chance to live, to her death.

The next day I went into the deer park. Guards rode behind me, but I told them I wanted them not too close. I carried with me the feather I had brought from home, the one Sybylla had found in the mashes near Swan Castle and given to me as a gift when we were children, the one Catherine had admired. For a long time I had carried it, a treasured possession, a part of my past, but another needed it more than me.

At the base of a tree, I set it down.

"I wish upon you a cloak of feathers, sweet child," I whispered to the wind. "May it carry you far, into the arms of the Virgin. She will understand all that happened to you. She will know you were not safe in this world, but she will keep you safe, Catherine. Nothing wicked of this world can ever touch you again."

The feather caught in the wind, skittering along the ground at first, as if unsure, then into the wind it was gathered, gaining speed as it vanished into the woods.

"Farewell, sister," I said as the white feather flew into the brittle, pale skies, vanishing into a cloak of whiteness.

Here ends *A Cloak of Feathers*

In the next book, *Under the Eyes of the World*, Anna
will enter the next chapter of her life as the
King takes a new wife, as death comes to the
royal line and as kings and queens rise and fall.

Thank You

…to so many people for helping me make this book possible… to my proofreader, Julia Gibbs, who gave me her time, her wonderful guidance and also her encouragement. To my family for their ongoing love and support. To my friend Petra. To my friend Nessa for her support and affection, and to another friend, Anne, who has done so much for me. To Sue and Annette, more friends who read my books and cheer me on. To Terry for getting me into writing and indie publishing in the first place. To Katie and Jooles, Macer, Pip, Linda, Fe, Pete and Heather, people there in times of trial. And to all my wonderful readers, who took a chance on an unknown author, and have followed my career and books since.

To those who have left reviews or contacted me by email or on social media, I give great thanks, as you have shown support for my career as an author, and enabled me to continue writing. Thank you for allowing me to live my dream.

Thank you to all of you; you'll never know how much you've helped me, but I know what I owe to you.

Gemma Lawrence
Wales
2024

About The Author

I find people talking about themselves in the third person to be entirely unsettling, so, since this section is written by me, I will use my own voice rather than try to make you believe that another person is writing about me to make me sound terribly important.

I am an independent author, publishing my books by myself, with the help of my lovely proofreader. I left my day job in 2016 and am now a fully-fledged, full-time author, and proud to be so.

My passion for history began early in life. As a child I lived in Croydon, near London, and my schools were lucky enough to be close to such glorious places as Hampton Court and the Tower of London, allowing field trips to take us to those castles. I write historical fiction for the main part, but I also have a fascination with ghost stories and fantasy, and I hope this book was one you enjoyed. I want to divert you as readers, to please you with my writing and to have you join me on these adventures.

A book is nothing without a reader.

As to the rest of me, I am in my forties and live in Wales with a rescued cat (who often sits on my lap when I write, which can make typing more of a challenge). I studied Literature at University after I fell in love with books as a small child. When I was little, I could often be found nestled halfway up the stairs with a pile of books in my lap and my head lost in another world. There is nothing more satisfying to me than finding a new book I adore, to place next to the multitudes I own and love… and nothing more disappointing to me to find a book I am willing to never open again. I do hope that this book was not a disappointment to you. I loved writing it and I hope that showed through the pages.

If you would like to contact me, please do so. I can be found in quite a few places!

On Twitter, (I am not calling it X) I am @TudorTweep.

You can also find me on Instagram as tudorgram1500. I am new to Mastodon as G. Lawrence Tudor Tooter, @TudorTweep@mastodonapp.uk, and Counter Social as TudorSocial1500.

On Facebook my page is just simply G. Lawrence, and on TikTok and Threads I am tudorgram1500, the same as Instagram. I've just joined Bluesky as G. Lawrence too. Often, I have a picture of the young Elizabeth I as my avatar, or there's me leaning up against a wall in Pembroke Castle.

I am also now writing on Substack, where my account is called G. Lawrence in the Book Nook. On there I publish articles, reviews, advice for other writers and I'm publishing a book there chapter by chapter each week. Join me there!

Via email, I am tudortweep@gmail.com a dedicated email account for my readers to reach me on. I'll try and reply within a few days.

Thank you for taking a risk with an unknown author and reading my book. I do hope now that you've read one, you'll want to read more. If you'd like to leave me a review, that would be very much appreciated also!

Gemma Lawrence
Wales
2024

Printed in Great Britain
by Amazon

54900740R00185